Motor

City

Motor City

ALFRED A.
KNOPF

NEW YORK
1992

Bill Morris

THIS IS A BORZOI BOOK
PUBLISHED BY
ALFRED A. KNOPF, INC.

Portions of this novel were published,
in slightly different form, in Granta.

Grateful acknowledgment is made to
Hudson Bay Music Inc. for permis-
sion to reprint an excerpt from
"Good Rockin' Tonight" by Roy
Brown. Copyright 1948 by Blue
Ridge Publishing Corporation. Copy-
right renewed and assigned to Fort
Knox Music Inc. and Trio Music Co.,
Inc. Used by permission. All rights
reserved.

ISBN 0-679-40834-7
LC 91-58561

Manufactured in the United States
of America
First Edition

FOR MY FATHER,

RICHARD MORRIS

ACKNOWLEDGMENTS

I would like to extend heartfelt
thanks to the owners and operators of Duke University for giving
me free run of their magnificent li-
braries while I was researching
and writing this book. Working
with Gary Fisketjon and Garth
Battista on the manuscript was a
dream. Also, thanks to the many
people who continued to believe
in me when there was no apparent reason for doing so: Rick and
Kat, Bob and Gretchen, John and
Lisa, Matt McDade, David New-
ton, Will Lashley, William Hall-
berg and Barney Karpfinger. And,
of course, Nicole.

The Thrill of the Month Club

One

*I*t was precisely at sundown on New Year's Day, 1954, that Claire Hathaway began to feel embarrassed by her new television set.

The Rose Bowl Parade was on the screen, but she couldn't take her eyes off the set itself. It was a twenty-one-inch RCA console with a gumwood cabinet and nubby brown fabric over the speakers, and it dwarfed the other furniture in her living room. She had gone downtown yesterday to buy a party dress and instead had come home with this thing. She had no idea what had gotten into her.

But her guests seemed to be in awe of her new RCA. No one spoke as the camera zoomed in on the last car in the Rose Bowl Parade, a mammoth, glittering Cadillac convertible with gobs of chrome on the outside and little American flags fluttering on the fenders and President Dwight Eisenhower and his wife, Mamie, alone in the back seat. The President and First Lady were sitting as far apart as they possibly could, smiling and waving to the crowd. The Cadillac was beige. The Eisenhowers' clothes were beige. Even their faces looked beige.

Norm Slenski started for the kitchen with his empty beer glass. He belched into his fist and said, "Hey, what gives? I thought this was supposed to be one of them new *color* TVs."

Everyone laughed except his wife. Wanda was the only person in the room who didn't design Buicks for a living and drink heavily on holidays. She hadn't moved from her spot at the end of the sofa or uncrossed her legs for over an hour. "Norm," she said, "that next beer's your limit."

"Righty-o," he called over his shoulder.

From her seat on the sofa Claire could see him in the kitchen. He put ice cubes in a tall glass, filled it nearly to the brim with scotch, then darkened it with a splash of Coca-Cola. He returned to the sofa and patted his wife on the knee. "Might as well go ahead and switch to Cokes now," he said.

Claire wished Norm and Wanda and everyone else would go home. But that was out of the question, she knew, because she'd invited them to watch the Rose Bowl two weeks earlier, the day they learned the commercial for the new Buick Century would air during halftime. Now her apartment was full of half-drunk car stylists who were mesmerized by this washed-out image of Ike and Mamie, and all Claire could think about was last night.

There was something she needed to remember, but toward midnight her memory had grown blurry. She had no idea how she got home; she awoke at noon on this sofa with a dry mouth and a throbbing headache, still wearing her green dress and high heels and pearls. That had never happened to her before.

She got invited to the party the day after Christmas. Harvey Pearl, the head of General Motors styling, had strolled up to her drawing table and casually asked if she would like to accompany him to the party thrown every New Year's Eve by Ted Mackey, the general manager of the Buick Division. Claire was stunned. It was the first time in her four years with the company that Harvey Pearl had said a word to her.

After she'd returned from her shopping spree yesterday—the sudden owner of an RCA color television set—she spent an hour doing her makeup and fixing her hair. She never wore makeup to work and wasn't very good with it, especially the mascara. When she was a girl her hair had been the color of fire; and though adolescence had cooled the flame, it still seemed to be lit from within, shiny, almost ablaze. On workdays she usually pulled it carelessly into her fist, gathered it with a tortoiseshell comb or barrette or ribbon or rubber band, anything to keep it out of her eyes as she bent over her drawing board, anything to keep men from noticing it. But this party was different. She felt like a high-school girl readying herself for the prom, and as she worked on her hair she sipped bourbon to steady her nerves. At the last minute she decided to wear her grandmother's string of pearls. She was so nervous when Harvey Pearl ushered her into the foyer of the massive white house that she went straight to the bar and downed three Old-Fashioneds.

At twenty-three she was by far the youngest person at the party and, besides Harvey, the only single person. But the drinks helped her relax, and she was grateful when Jack Winters, a neighbor of the Mackeys who said he'd made "a nice little bundle in ball bearings," cornered her by the fireplace and insisted on telling her about his recent trip abroad.

"Those Japs are doing some amazing things," he said, unable to take his eyes off the long arc of her neck or her bare shoulders. She didn't even mind the old goat's leering. "I keep telling Ted and Harvey that those Japs are up to something. But nobody at GM ever listens. They already know everything."

Well before midnight, Claire noticed a Negro maid helping Mrs. Mackey up the stairs. Claire hadn't said three words to her hostess all night. Watching her stagger up to bed reminded Claire of her vow not to wind up like that, a crumbling beauty, a casualty of life in the suburbs, too drunk to make it through her own party.

That was the last thing Claire remembered clearly. Now, watching the beige Eisenhowers wave at the crowd in Pasadena, she began to retrieve scraps from the end of the evening. On her way to the bathroom she had bumped into Harvey Pearl. He'd been telling a group of blue-haired women that Claire was the top designer in the entire Buick studio, a certified rising star. He was practically shouting and he kept spilling his drink. Several of the women patted their mouths.

Then there was an explosion—someone had thrown a glass into the fireplace. Everyone roared. Claire made her getaway and locked the bathroom door behind her. She spent a long time touching up her hair and makeup and admiring the brass fixtures, the black marble sink, the bright, fluffy towels. The wallpaper was rough, sort of like straw, or grass. She had never been inside such a house before, such a warm cocoon of thick carpets, dark paneling, marble, brass, twinkling whisky decanters, a view of a lake, a roaring fire fed by four-foot logs. She liked the living room best, especially the Persian rug and the Franz Kline painting, ancient geometries set against bold black slashes on a blinding white sky. When Ted Mackey saw her admiring it, he'd walked up and said, "So give me an artist's opinion. Is it worth a damn?"

"It's . . . it's gorgeous." She felt herself blushing. "Is it an original?"

He chuckled. "I sure as hell hope so. We bought it at an auction in New York last summer—my wife did, that is. You could buy a couple of fully loaded Cadillacs with what I paid for it." He cocked his head and studied the painting. She couldn't read his expression.

Then the thing she'd spent the day trying to remember came back to her. After the encounter with Harvey Pearl and the yawning old ladies, Claire had stepped out of the bathroom and walked straight into Ted Mackey's chest. He was wearing a herringbone blazer, a white shirt, a red tie. He smelled of wood smoke. Without a word he took her shoulders in his hands—she noticed instantly that his hands were strong and sure—and he kissed her firmly on the lips.

"It's midnight," he said. "Happy New Year. I'm delighted you could come."

Then he released her shoulders and walked down the hall to the living room, where everyone was standing in front of the TV set, yelling at the ball falling out of the sky onto the throng in Times Square.

Even now, watching the Rose Bowl Parade in her own apartment, Claire could smell Ted Mackey, could taste his whisky-and-nicotine kiss, could feel his hands on her bare shoulders. She forced herself to concentrate on the parade. Ike and Mamie were still waving and smiling, and they still looked beige.

"Hey," Norm said, "I'da thought Ike'd have a great golf tan. He looks like he just crawled out from under a rock." Claire saw Wanda kick his shin under the coffee table.

"Norm's right," said Amos Fuller, the only Negro in the room, probably the only Negro within three miles of the Huntington Arms apartments. "The man looks ill."

"Get with it, you guys," Rory Gallagher said. "The color's perfect. The reason Ike looks beige is because Ike *is* beige."

Through the laughter Wanda Slenski cried, "Look! Baton twirlers in *red* suits!"

Everyone cheered. So this was, indeed, color TV. The snow may have been whistling horizontally off the Great Lakes, and Detroit may have been sinking into another frigid mid-winter dusk, but thousands of miles away in Pasadena the sun was buttery and gold and girls in bright red suits tossed batons into the sky and the President and First Lady rode through the sunshine in a purring General Motors product, waving and smiling, waving and smiling. It was a paid holiday. There was plenty of beer in the refrigerator, plenty of snacks and dips on the coffee table. There was color TV. And Claire Hathaway had, at last, remembered the taste of Ted Mackey's kiss.

Two

*S*ix miles to the north, in a solid white house on the edge of Mirror Lake, Ted Mackey watched a football come tumbling out of the blue sky. Normally the Rose Bowl kickoff made him tingle, especially when Michigan was playing, but today he watched it dully. Betsy had stayed late cleaning up, and there was no evidence that the house had been full of roaring drunks just a few hours earlier—not a single glass with a lipstick print, no dirty ashtrays, not even a stray earring or cuff link.

Like everyone who has ever thrown a party, Ted had spent much of the day reliving the night before. The usual roster of business associates, neighbors, golf and gin-rummy buddies and their wives had showed up and filled the house with their smoke and chatter, growing louder and more amusing as the evening wore on. Jack Winters had tossed a highball glass into the fireplace. Don Cloesy, the biggest Buick dealer in Detroit, had shouted at his wife and stormed out of the house, leaving her in tears to find a ride home with friends. Walter Koether, who'd sold this house to Ted and built an even bigger one across the lake, passed out briefly on the sofa but rallied for the big moment at midnight. Since Ted had seen these things many times before, he knew the party had been a success and the thank-you notes and payback invitations to similar parties would begin arriving in a few days.

What stayed in his mind about last night was Claire Hathaway.

He had no idea Harvey was bringing her. Ted had seen her many times in the design studio at the Tech Center without giving her a second thought. At work she always looked severe, almost tomboyish, dressed in loose sweaters and blouses, pleated skirts, scuffed loafers, never any makeup. When he'd greeted her in the foyer last night he was astonished by her high color, her electric-green dress, the halo of reddish hair, her milky shoulders and throat. She was wearing pearls. And he noticed that she wobbled, suddenly several inches taller, on high heels. He found himself sharing Harvey's obvious delight at the way the arrival of such a hot property had inspired so much sudden ardor in the men and so much automatic suspicion in their wives.

He'd been unable to take his eyes off her all night as one, then another of his guests took her aside to size her up. It was amazing. She was a younger, unspoiled version of his wife. She was an artist and a knockout—just like Milmary in her prime. Since all desire is specific, he kept wondering what, exactly, made it impossible for him to take his eyes off her. As he listened to Jack Winters drone on about the assembly plant he'd visited in Japan—"You should see how hard those little fuckers work!" —Ted realized what it was. It was her ankles. She was standing in front of the fireplace admiring that sloppy abstract painting that hung over the sofa. He studied her ankles, astonishing fire-lit machines laced with pale blue veins, miraculously able to make the calf muscles surge, strong enough to support all that height and weight. He thought of buttermilk. He thought of a thoroughbred racehorse. She had nicked herself shaving, just above the left ankle. The sight of her standing in front of the fireplace made the blood hum in his veins, and he was thrilled by the way she'd blushed and fidgeted when he asked her what she thought of that stupid painting.

When he made a point of bumping into her at midnight, of course he planned to kiss her—he kissed all the ladies at the start of every new year—but he found his hands locked on her shoulders in a strange way, and when he kissed her it was not on the cheek, it was squarely on the lips, and it lasted an instant too long. He recalled now that she hadn't resisted and that his heart was racing as he'd walked away. In that instant, he realized, he had been out of control.

As he watched the football tumble out of the sky he felt a desperate need to keep that instant, that sensation of floating, from returning. It was one of the few things in life he could not afford. From where he stood he could see his sons playing hockey down on the lake and he could hear his wife and Harvey talking in the dining room. He fixed a weak scotch-and-water. He told himself his world made perfect sense, and he forced himself to concentrate on the television set as the football settled into the Stanford player's arms at his own goal line.

"Kill him!" Ted roared. "Take his head off!"

The bloodthirsty sound of his own voice brought him back to himself. For the first time he noticed how sharp the colors were on this new TV set. It was Milmary's Christmas present to him, and he figured it cost him at least five hundred dollars. The Michigan defenders in the familiar blue jerseys and yellow pants stormed downfield. When the Stanford ball carrier reached the fifteen-yard line, six of them hit him at once, an ugly, audible crunch. The football squirted into the air, and a startled Michigan player snatched it and ran untouched into the end zone.

"Touchdown! Michigan touchdown!" Ted yelled, jumping up and down, spilling scotch on the Persian rug. "Harvey, you sure you don't want to back out of that bet?"

But Harvey Pearl didn't answer. Ted didn't expect him to. He knew Harvey was looking over some old snapshots of the war that Milmary had dug out of the attic. He also knew Harvey hated football along with most things Detroit car people worshiped, from violent sports and cocktail parties to stag trips in northern Michigan, where the guys got good and drunk and shot up lots of ducks and deer. Harvey didn't even like guns; he preferred gardening.

At halftime Ted hollered into the dining room that their commercial was about to come on. When Milmary and Harvey joined him in the living room, Ted said, "You birds are missing a great game. It's 22–zip, Michigan."

"What period is it?" Harvey said.

"The second *quarter* just ended," Ted said. "It's halftime."

Milmary laughed. She was drinking a Bloody Mary. Ted thought she'd rebounded remarkably well from last night's performance.

Suddenly the television screen filled with a picture of a country road. There was a low roar—a powerful engine of some sort— and in the distance an unidentifiable dot. Soon the dot became a car—their car, the car Harvey had lovingly nursed through the byzantine design process, the car that would be Ted's biggest triumph or his biggest disaster. It was moving straight at the camera, moving fast, getting bigger and louder as a narrator began: "We at the Buick Division of General Motors are proud to bring back a piece of our illustrious past."

Now it was possible to see that the front of the car was a dazzling confection of chrome: headlight sockets that looked like sad, droopy eyes; a grille that looked like a frowning mouth with exposed metal teeth; and a front bumper that looked like it could scoop dead cows off the road, a silver slab punctuated by two sharply tipped, mammiferous bulbs.

"After a twelve-year absence, the Buick Century is back."

The engine was a roar now and the car looked like it was about to flatten the camera. The chrome winked in the sunlight. The car was hot pink.

"It's destined to be the car of the year, a sports car the whole family will enjoy, and it's at a Buick dealer near you."

Just then the camera cut to a side view of the car and the picture froze. Ted and Harvey had seen this car many times over the past three years, first as crude sketches, then as finer sketches, then as clay models and a full-blown, motorized prototype, and finally as mass-produced wonders clicking off the Flint assembly line. But not until that instant—when they saw the car frozen on the TV screen with the three ventiports shining on the front fender, saw the long swooping arc of chrome trim jumping off the pink and black steel—was the car actually born for them. Now their child was alive. It was on its own. It was for sale.

"And it's available right now. But hurry. Because the all-new Buick Century will go very, very fast."

Then, seen from behind, the car shrank toward the sunset. Suddenly the driver stomped on the gas and the car shot out of sight.

As the picture faded, Ted whooped with joy. He put his drink down and gave Harvey a bear hug, nearly crushing the breath out of him. They danced an impromptu jig right there on the Persian rug.

"I gather you liked it," Harvey said when Ted released him. He smoothed his jacket and straightened his bow tie.

"I *loved* it! Come on, you gotta admit, wasn't she sexy?"

"Oh yes, she was sexy all right."

"And didn't she look just a little bit dangerous?"

"Oh yes."

Milmary picked up her Bloody Mary. "While you fellows pat each other on the back, I'm going to go get the champagne. We'll toast your new car—and in case you've forgotten, Teddy, today is our eleventh anniversary."

Ted ignored the little dig. He was beside himself. He'd been waiting for this moment for three years, and for once in his life an event had lived up to his gargantuan expectations.

He switched channels to the Cotton Bowl. After a commercial for Altes beer, the screen filled with capital letters: PLYMOUTH. Ted turned up the volume. This was their prime competition, the number-three seller in 1953 behind Chevy and Ford—the car Buick, largely on the strength of the new Century, intended to overtake in 1954. As a narrator talked about "elegant appointments" and "Turbo-torque power," the camera circled a big dumpy blue Plymouth four-door sedan parked on a suburban street.

"No energy," Harvey said. "Zero sex."

When the camera got around to the front of the car, it froze. Ted and Harvey saw it at the same instant: the Plymouth's front bumper was a virtual replica of the Buick's, right down to the two pointed bulbs. Neither man said a word. They were both thinking the same horrible thought: Plymouth had somehow pirated Buick's design work.

When Milmary swept into the room with a bottle of champagne and three long-stemmed glasses, she looked at the men, then at the TV screen. She saw a blue car.

"What's the matter with you two?" she said. "You see a ghost or something?"

Three

*M*orey Caan lived alone with a gelded yellow cat named Fat Boy on P Street in Georgetown—"safely upwind from the seat of American power," as he liked to say—and while he generally enjoyed the feeling that he was the last bachelor in America, holidays were sometimes rough. He had avoided a trip home to Memphis this year, because he knew everyone in the family would take turns steering him into a corner to gaze into his big, wet eyes and ask the one question every bachelor dreads most: "So when are you going to settle down with a nice girl and get married?" His family no longer bothered to say "nice *Jewish* girl." They were that desperate.

Morey especially disliked New Year's Day, because he always felt fine and the rest of the world was busy recuperating from what he called Amateur Night. It wasn't that he condemned people for wearing stupid hats and getting knee-walking drunk and vomiting in all the wrong places. It was just that he had never developed much of a taste for alcohol—quite an achievement in itself for someone who grew up in the South, spent four years at that training ground for problem drinkers, the University of Virginia, and had worked for the past eight years on the fringe of that massive army of boozers and misfits known as the Washington press corps.

Morey had spent most of the day on the phone and his ears felt like cauliflower, but he didn't feel any less alone than he had when he made himself get out of bed. Now, after talking to his father, his sister, his brother-in-law, his niece, his nephew, after shouting a few pleasantries to his stone-deaf grandmother, it was time to call his best friend, Will Lomax, in Detroit.

This call would probably be the worst. Until four years ago Will had been Morey's roommate and one of the stars of the Washington press corps, the hardest worker, the hardest drinker, the most tireless skirt-chaser. Nothing seemed beyond his reach. After graduating with Morey from the University of Virginia, it took him less than two years to rise from a lowly bureau job with the *Atlanta Constitution* to a highly visible job with the *Washington Post*, and it took him less than a year at the *Post* to put together a series of articles on the local numbers rackets that nearly won him a Pulitzer Prize. Will Lomax suddenly found himself roaming the corridors of the Capitol, where doors had a way of opening magically before him.

When Morey landed a job covering cops for the *Post*, the two became inseparable. They showed up together at the Press Club bar, at cocktail parties, press conferences, Senators ball games. They came to be known around town as the Siamese Twins. Will always led the way, fluid and lanky, his hair as black and shiny as patent leather; he had a soft Southern drawl and lock-up-your-daughters looks. Morey always tagged along a few steps behind, the nebbish-kid-brother type with the rumpled clothes and exploding hair and eyeglasses that were beyond dirty, almost greasy, as though they'd just been fished out of day-old dishwater.

Then, one raw January day in 1950, Will walked into the Press Club bar and announced he was getting married and changing jobs and leaving town. To top it off, he was passing over the Social Register lovelies and marrying a social worker named Margaret Mason from "West-by-God Virginia," as he put it, and he was taking a flack job with General Motors and moving to Detroit. Hearing this was like taking a punch in the stomach. Morey actually had trouble breathing for a few minutes. The going-away party at the Press Club was more like a wake, and Morey got so drunk he vomited on the geraniums by the elevator. While he was patting his mouth with his necktie, Drew Pearson strode out of the elevator. Morey burped at him and said, "You're the biggest asshole in this town, you know that?"

But Will had stayed in close touch over the past four years. He visited whenever he was in Washington on business, which was more often than either of them had expected, thanks to the 1952 election, and they spoke regularly on the phone, usually on GM's nickel. Will had spent months trying to persuade Morey to write a magazine article about the completely redesigned line of 1954 Buicks, especially the new Century, but so far nothing had come of it. Morey pinched the bridge of his nose and dialed the number in Detroit.

"Hullo?" came a woman's voice straight from the fuzzy dells of West-by-God Virginia.

"Margaret, it's Morey calling from Washington. Happy New Year!"

"Well, happy New Year to you too, Morey. Hold on—Will's right here." Just like that the phone clattered on the table and she was gone.

As is so often the case with abandoned bachelors, Morey could

not comprehend his best friend's choice of a wife. He could see
her now in their bright linoleum kitchen: she would be standing
by the sink wearing a flowery apron; maybe it would be snowing
outside; and a roast with potatoes and carrots and onions would
be in the oven. She had brittle brown hair and a high, smooth
forehead whose blankness led Morey to conclude she had never
had a troubling thought, a worry, a doubt. But beneath that
innocent apron, Morey knew, there were firm, full breasts—
"free-standers," as the roommates had once dubbed them.
Granted, the woman had a tremendous body. But why had Will
Lomax gone and married it? Morey knew the official answer.
"I'm sick of this shit," Will had said that day at the Press Club
bar after breaking the news about his plans to marry a sleepy-
eyed girl from some West Virginia coal town.

"What shit?" Morey had asked.

Will waved his arm at the reporters lining the Press Club bar.
"I'm sick of hanging around in hallways waiting for some rich
bastard to come out of a locked room and lie to me, so I can
run and file a fifteen-inch story and then come in here and drink
with these guys."

Morey had to admit he had a point.

Suddenly Will's voice boomed over the telephone line. "What
you up to, boy?"

"Not too much, old man," Morey said. "Just wanted to wish
everyone a happy New Year."

"Same to ya. I suppose you reversed the charges again, you
cheap bastard."

"Wait a damn minute. This is my nickel—and my father happens to be the only honest pawnbroker in all of Memphis,
_Tenn_essee."

"Riiiight. And General Motors is in the business of providing
safe, cheap transportation."

They both laughed. It was the first time Morey had laughed
all day. He could hear babies squalling in the background.

Though on holidays he sometimes yearned for a family of his own, that racket made him realize how grateful he was to be the last bachelor in America. "So what are you doing today besides changing diapers?"

"Nursing a hangover and watching Michigan win another Rose Bowl, just like everyone else in *Dee*-troit."

"How's the book coming along?"

Morey never failed to ask about the book—The Book, the insider's story of the Buick Division he'd been urging Will to write for the past four years. As envisioned by Morey, it would chronicle the behind-the-scenes machinations of one of the larger divisions of the largest industrial empire in the world; it would expose sales hustles and the callousness of management toward labor and customers alike; it would blow the lid off the myth that GM was as tightly run as the nineteenth-century German army; and, not entirely incidentally, it would make Will Lomax a bundle of money and buy his one-way ticket out of what he called "the frozen hellhole," the great, brawling city of Detroit.

"I ain't done diddly on The Book," Will said.

"Why the hell not? You promised me."

"I know, I know. But the holidays—"

"Don't give me that bullshit."

"All right then. The sumbitches kicked my ass upstairs again."

"They what?"

"I just got another promotion."

"And another raise?"

"Naturally. Starting Monday I'll be working directly for Ted Mackey. His very own PR drone."

"The Great White Shark himself! Will, that'll be perfect for The Book!"

"Yeah, that was my first thought, too."

Morey expected more, but all that came was the low grumble of static. Finally he said, "What's wrong, old man?"

"Christ, I wish I knew. This is everything I've been working toward for the past four years, but now that it's here . . ." Morey knew from years of interviewing reluctant subjects that there was a time to go for the jugular and a time to hold back. This was a time to hold back. He waited. Then he waited some more. Finally the voice came again. "To tell you the truth, pardner, I'm scared shitless. I haven't had a good night's sleep since I got the news."

"What the hell are you worried about? You've got twice as much brains as Ted Mackey. You told me yourself he's nothing but a glorified salesman. Think about it. You'll be right there in the inner sanctum."

"I know that. But you've got no idea what Mackey's like. He's a maniac. He eats people alive. He—aw, forget it. I'll be fine. How's *your* book coming along?"

Now Morey remembered why he'd dreaded this phone call more than all the others. Unlike Will Lomax, Morey had never wavered from their shared undergraduate dream of becoming a writer—a "real" writer as opposed to a newspaper reporter or a freelance journalist or, God forbid, a corporate flack. And so, the night after the 1952 election, Morey had started writing a book. The working title was *Straight from the Horse's Mouth*. It was to be a series of direct quotations from Ike himself, verbatim gobbledygook, double-talk and gibberish, an encyclopedia of Ike-speak. While Morey did not believe that buffoonery in high places was something new under the sun, he did believe he had a responsibility to alert a dozing populace to its contemporary brand, Ike's brand, and in so doing expose the President of the United States for exactly what Morey believed him to be: a four-star moron.

Morey eyed the untouched stack of periodicals and newspapers beside his typewriter. He had promised himself that today would be the day he read, clipped and sorted them. Now, in addition to feeling sad and lonely, he felt guilty.

"I've been pretty busy myself lately," he said. "Been to Baraboo, Wisconsin, working on a piece for the *Saturday Review* about the 'Joe Must Go' movement, a bunch of guys who hate McCarthy's guts—" He heard a loud crash, followed by the bawling of two babies and Margaret's yelling.

"Listen," Will said, "I gotta jump. An H-bomb just landed in the kitchen sink. You keep in touch now, y'hear?"

"Will do." Morey hung up. He couldn't wait for Monday, when the holidays would end and official Washington would resume shuffling papers and telling lies and he could lose himself in his work. He sat at his desk and forced himself to ignore the coffee cups and the sandwich rinds with their blooms of blue mold. He didn't even shoo Fat Boy when he started slurping a glass of sour milk. He read in the new issue of *Time* that James Hagerty, Ike's press secretary, was going to allow reporters to quote the President directly at some press conferences for the first time. Morey's spirits rose. This was a major breakthrough for the press in general and for his book in particular. The Sunday *New York Times* had an editorial about the new policy: "The widest dissemination of the news is all to the good. But there is the danger that the participants will become mere actors in a gigantic show, and that goes both for the newspapermen who ask the questions and the presidents who answer them."

Morey hurled the newspaper across the room. Fat Boy scampered into the kitchen and hid under the sink. There's a new bomb that can blow a hole in the ocean floor, and the Russians are sure to have one of their own soon, but the President's two biggest worries are his golf swing and balancing the federal budget. Who cares? Inflation's low, employment's high, everyone loves the Republican in the White House, and they're so busy buying cars and making money and making babies they might as well be embalmed—even guys like Will Lomax, the original cowboy. And the best the *New York Times* can do is fret that reporters and presidents are in danger of becoming actors in some sort of big-top freak show.

Morey sat at his desk as darkness seeped into the apartment. He didn't bother to turn on a light. When it was dark he went into the kitchen and poured himself a stiff drink from a half-empty bottle of bourbon he'd bought for a New Year's Eve party two years ago. He sat at his desk, alone and in the dark, drinking silently, smoldering. An hour later Fat Boy came out from under the kitchen sink and curled up on Morey's lap.

Four

The carpet in Ted Mackey's office was the color of brushed steel, and it was so plush it swallowed Will Lomax's footsteps, gave him the strange sensation he was walking on air. As he crossed the room he noticed that the lace on his brightly polished right shoe was about to come untied. Then he noticed that the only things on Ted's desk were a black telephone, a glass ashtray and the latest issue of *Photoplay*. Ted was reading Hedda Hopper's prediction that Joe DiMaggio and Marilyn Monroe would marry by the end of January. What a happy coincidence. Will's wife had brought the magazine home from the beauty salon on New Year's Eve, and Will had groggily read it at the breakfast table this morning while giving the baby her bottle. The only thing he could remember was one sterling Heddaism: "If Joe and Marilyn tie the knot, they'll become Mr. and Mrs. America. If they split, who would get custody of the Wheaties?"

Ted was smoking a Chesterfield. It was not yet eight o'clock, but already there were three butts in the ashtray. "Morning," he said without looking up. "Have a seat. Harvey and John are on their way."

Will sat in a green leather chair in the corner and crossed his legs, trying to hide his unraveled right shoelace. Snow whipped past the big windows, blotting out the view of downtown, the distant smokestacks downriver, the hot frenzy of the first workday of the year; it looked as though someone had pulled a gauze curtain over the world. Maybe, Will thought, my windowless cubicle at the end of the hall won't be so bad after all.

Ted's lips moved as he read. Will knew his new boss fantasized ardently about Marilyn Monroe, knew he dreamed of hiring her either as the "Buick Girl" for a glittery ad campaign late in the year, when the sales war with Plymouth would get bare-knuckled vicious, or as the "Wildcat Girl," emblem of the two-seat sports car he was so eager to develop. Hiring Marilyn Monroe was, depending on who you believed, the greatest idea since ball bearings or else a guaranteed one-way ticket to the funny farm. Will wasn't sure what he thought about it, but he knew from numerous late-night discussions over numerous drinks that it was an obsession with Ted Mackey.

"Think about it," Ted would say, yanking his necktie loose and pounding the table after the scotch had gotten hold of him. "She's perfect. She's everything we want these new Buicks to be—she's gorgeous, she's sexy, she's just a little bit dangerous, but not *too* dangerous. That's what makes a new car sell. You don't believe me, ask Harvey. Hell, ask any dealer. Those guys understand. But don't try to tell those fucking accountants on the Finance Committee, especially that ding-dong Ned Schroeder. They'll tell you Marilyn Monroe's just another one of my hunches and they need to study it. Jesus! We've got a chance to sign the hottest piece of ass in Hollywood for the hottest car of the year—and those assholes want to *study* it!"

And then there was the calendar. Pinned to the door inside Ted's private office bathroom was Marilyn Monroe's famous nude calendar shot, the one of her stretched out on her left side, swaddled in red velvet, looking over her shoulder with her mouth slightly open. Whenever a first-time visitor—a union boss, an executive, a reporter, a politician, one of Ted's sports cronies—emerged from that bathroom, Ted would regale him with the astonishing economics of that calendar: six million copies were printed; the distributor made $750,000; Tom Kelley, the photographer, made $900; and Marilyn Monroe made $50. Every time Will heard that story he wondered if the guy who was hearing it for the first time had just finished jacking off in that bathroom, alone with the unclothed Marilyn Monroe. It wouldn't have surprised him. This town had few smooth edges, and very little about it surprised Will anymore. He certainly was not surprised that Ted Mackey told this story with great relish and not a trace of outrage or pity. If the woman's value exceeded her cost, Will understood, that made her all the more attractive to the general manager of the Buick Division.

Judging by the way Ted's brow was crumpled as he read Hedda Hopper's poolside prose, Will figured the proposition had just gotten a lot trickier. As a married woman Marilyn might lose some of the zing that was making her the hottest blonde in Hollywood; then again, as the wife of a reigning sports god she might be more palatable to jittery wives and thus even more saleable. Maybe a wedding wouldn't mean Ted Mackey was losing his Buick Girl; maybe it would mean he was gaining a center fielder.

Just as Ted slipped the *Photoplay* into his bottom desk drawer, Harvey Pearl and John Nickles strode into the office. As he rose to shake their hands, Will wondered how it was possible that these two men worked for the same corporation. Harvey was a dandy, a cocky little tyrant who'd had a hand in the design of more than thirty million GM cars over the past quarter-century, the visionary who had given Detroit its greatest money-maker since mass production, the annual model change. He wore his hair in a brush cut, and he favored bow ties and suspenders and suits that strayed a long way from the corporate uniform of dark blue. Will thought of him as a proletarian Napoleon. Today he was wearing a bottle-green suit, a pale blue shirt and a scarlet bow tie.

John Nickles, on the other hand, was textbook General Motors. The head of Buick styling had begun his career with the company nineteen years ago, and no one doubted that he would work there until he turned sixty-five or dropped dead, whichever came first. His claim to fame was the ventiports, the notched chrome holes in the front quarter panels that served no purpose but had become a Buick trademark over the years. Three ventiports made the car a "three-holer," the smaller Special and Century models, while the Roadmaster was a "four-holer," the big body, the biggest engine, the true status boat. John Nickles understood status better than anyone else Will had ever met. Yet he had a lumpy, bald head, and he always wore drab suits, white shirts, black shoes. Will had never seen him laugh. He thought of him as an executive serf.

When they were seated, Ted stood up, clamped his hands behind his back and started pacing in front of the windows. Will expected him to say something about Joe DiMaggio and Marilyn Monroe. But he said, "I trust everyone saw our commercial during the Rose Bowl."

Will twisted in his chair. The tone of Ted's voice reminded him why he'd dreaded this moment. Suddenly he felt clammy and tired. He nodded along with Harvey and John.

"And I trust everyone saw the Plymouth commercial during the Cotton Bowl," Ted said.

Harvey and John nodded. Will said, "Umm, afraid I missed it. The baby was sick all weekend."

Ted glanced at him, then looked back down at the brushed-steel carpet, continued pacing. "Well, for your information, the fucking Plymouth's front bumper is a spittin' image of ours. That means one thing: we've got a design leak somewhere. And that means for the next four years we're going to sit around with our thumbs up our asses wondering how much Plymouth knows about our new designs. We just spent forty-two million redesigning our line this year"—he looked straight at Will— "and now we're *fucked*!"

"Now hold on one second, Ted," John Nickles said.

"I'm not finished." Ted continued pacing. "You'll recall that the company canceled a quarter of a million dollars of advertising with the *Wall Street Journal* last year when they ran pictures of the '53 Pontiacs before the official unveiling date. And I don't have to tell you that Hugh Lund is no longer g.m. at Pontiac. He's at Studebaker studying upholstery combinations or some such shit. Why? Because if you can't keep your new models a secret, you've flushed your biggest selling point straight down the toilet. Am I right, Harvey?"

"I like to think so." He was grinning.

"Well, for your information, gentlemen, I do not intend to wind up studying upholstery combinations at Studebaker or anywhere else. So I intend to find out why the Plymouth's bumper looks exactly like ours—and everything else they know about our designs. Harvey, you got any theories on how this could've happened?"

"It's pretty simple, really." The grin was gone. "We had it happen with the '38 Pontiacs, only then it was so bad and we caught it so early we redesigned the whole car. It was a crash program, but we got the job done. Turned out Ford had paid off somebody at the tool and die shop where we took our blueprints. Needless to say, we switched tool and die shops after that."

"Get to the point," Ted snapped.

"I'm getting to the point, Theodore."

Theodore! Will had never heard anyone call him Theodore. The balls!

"The point," Harvey said, "is that I wouldn't be surprised if someone at Plymouth greased someone's palms at Kelsey-Hayes, which is where we had our front bumpers tooled."

"Okay," Ted said, "that's one theory. I've got another. Suppose someone in our own Styling Section—someone who wasn't happy, say, or someone who was on the take from Plymouth, or someone who was screwing someone at Plymouth, or had debts—for whatever reason, this person slips our drawings directly to Plymouth. They bypass the tool and die shop, and bingo, we're fucked."

"No way!" John Nickles yelped. He rose halfway to his feet, then sank back into his chair. "I had my very best people working on those front bumper drawings. I know for a fact that they're absolutely loyal—every last one of them."

"Easy, John," Ted said. "We're just thinking out loud right now. It has happened before, hasn't it, Harvey?"

"Oh, sure. You all remember the Battle of the Overpass, I trust."

This time Will nodded along with the others. Though he was not a son of Detroit, though he prided himself on having ink rather than gasoline in his veins, he knew all about the Battle of the Overpass. It was one of the nuggets of Detroit lore that first awoke him to the rococo brutality of the place. One fine spring day in 1937, when the UAW was trying to unionize Ford's assembly-line workers, old man Henry sent some of his goons down to greet Walter Reuther and three other organizers as they crossed the Miller Road overpass and approached gate 4 of the River Rouge plant. The union men had leaflets with them; Ford's goons had blackjacks and brass knuckles. They did their work well, beating one man until his spine was broken and he bled from the mouth, nose and ears. The goons even went after newspaper reporters and photographers, ripping up their notes and smashing their cameras. But one photographer from the *Detroit News* escaped and had to drive eighty miles per hour through city streets to elude Ford's men. The next day three of his pictures blazed on the front page. The first showed the union men smiling in greeting; the second and third showed the Ford men moving in, then beating and stomping them. The way Will heard it, old man Henry didn't give a damn about the bad publicity. All he cared about was keeping the union out of his plants.

"Well," Harvey was saying, "it just so happened that those Pontiac design leaks I just mentioned were discovered shortly after the Battle of the Overpass. When Mr. Sloan learned which stylists had betrayed the company, he was displeased, to say the least. I don't believe I've ever seen him so furious. After a Red Wings hockey game one night, those three stylists got jumped by some very rough guys in a parking lot near Olympia Stadium. Got their hands broken pretty badly, among other things. Of course Mr. Sloan has a heart, and when he heard that three of Pontiac's top stylists would never be able to draw again, he made sure they got jobs elsewhere in the company—night watchmen at the Buick plant in Flint, I believe it was. One of them committed suicide that very winter. But those design leaks at Pontiac sure stopped in a hurry."

This was news to Will. He prided himself on being unshockable, but this time he had underestimated the automobile industry's capacity for savagery. Beating union organizers was one thing; crippling your own employees was another. He felt disappointed with himself. He liked to think he had seen and heard it all. He'd spent hours in the men's grills in the posh country clubs of Grosse Pointe and Bloomfield Hills, listening to the rantings of retired auto executives. He had studied the liver spots freckling their hands and faces, had looked into their red-rimmed eyes, had listened to them rattle their tall glasses of gin and applaud old Henry Ford. "Those socialist bastards deserved to have their skulls cracked!" they would thunder. "That's the only language they understand!"

Now John Nickles leaned forward in his chair. "I really don't think this kind of talk is necessary. If we start looking anywhere, I think it should be at Kelsey-Hayes."

"Why?" Ted said.

"Two reasons. I have total faith in my people; and the only real similarity between the Buick and the Plymouth is that front bumper. If someone had slipped them our drawings, don't you think they would've used more of our stuff—the wraparound windshield, the moon hubcaps, the tapered beltline, something? I mean, that Plymouth could use some help. She's a dog."

"They might not have gotten the drawings in time to make major changes this year," Ted said. "That's the whole fucking problem. We don't know how much they know."

"Ted's got a point," Harvey said.

Finally Ted sat in his desk chair and folded his hands. Suddenly he sounded very calm, and Will recognized it as the calm that comes with iron resolve. "Okay, John, I want the names of everyone who had anything to do with the design of the '54 Century. Windshield, ventiports, bumpers, the fucking ashtrays."

"Yessir."

"And Will, I want you to talk to Red Van Hooven in manufacturing and have him find out everything he can about who had access to our design work at Kelsey-Hayes. I want to know who sharpens their pencils."

"Yessir. Mind if I ask why?"

The fine head of silver hair jerked upward. "Why? Sure, I'll tell you why. Because I just might see to it that one of our people gets on the payroll over there. And if I find out they've been selling our blueprints to Plymouth, I'll run their asses out of business if I have to burn the goddamn place down myself. That's why. You understand?"

"Yessir."

"And John, if it does turn out that someone in styling sold us out, you can bet that person won't be doing any more drawing—for us or anyone else. They probably won't be doing a whole lot of walking, either."

Will shivered. He knew this was not an empty threat. In that instant he remembered how it felt to sit in Washington with a notebook open on his knee listening to Joe McCarthy or Lyndon Johnson or Richard Nixon explain what was wrong with the world and how he intended to fix it, forever and ever.

Ted clapped his hands. "All right, hop to it. Harvey, I need you for a minute."

Will and John Nickles made for the door. "Oh, Will," Ted called. "One more thing."

"Sir?"

"Try lacing both of your shoes in the morning. And welcome aboard."

Five

The first thing Marilyn Monroe did on her wedding day was peroxide her pubic hair with a toothbrush. Though she had once told reporters she liked feeling blond "all over," she neglected to mention that "all over" included the wedge of troublesome dark curls between her legs. On her wedding day she dunked a toothbrush into a bottle of hydrogen peroxide, then dabbed and stroked the thatch until it was a uniform, fluffy blond. Marilyn Monroe was determined to be blond all over when she was carried across the threshold that night by her second husband, the famed Yankee Clipper, Joe DiMaggio.

The second thing Marilyn did on her wedding day was phone Harry Brand in Los Angeles. She told Brand, the publicity boss at 20th Century–Fox, that after a two-year run in the gossip sheets she was finally going to make all the rumors come true. She would be marrying Joe DiMaggio that afternoon at one o'clock in San Francisco City Hall. She asked Brand to tell all her friends. He promptly called every gossip columnist he could think of, then the Associated Press, United Press, the International News Syndicate and the major television and radio networks.

The bride and groom showed up at City Hall in San Francisco a few minutes before one p.m. He wore an impeccably tailored dark blue suit. She wore a simple brown suit and a black satin coat with an ermine collar. He was accompanied by Reno Barsochinni, his best man and manager of his restaurant at Fisherman's Wharf, and by Frank "Lefty" O'Doul, an old baseball crony. Marilyn was alone. Well, not exactly alone. There was, as she'd hoped, a mob of reporters and photographers and fans waiting in the third-floor corridor, and they peppered the couple with questions about their honeymoon destination, the number of children they intended to have, and with requests that they kiss, again and again, for the cameras. When the ceremony was delayed while a clerk typed the marriage license, Marilyn slipped into a phone booth.

She called her favorite gossip columnist, Sidney Skolsky, but got no answer. Finally she got through to Kendis Rochlen, a Los Angeles freelancer. They chatted for a while; then Rochlen asked the one question that mattered to her: "So tell me, Marilyn, how do you *feel?*"

"Oh, Kendis," she whispered, "I'm so happy. I have sucked my last cock!"

When Marilyn returned from the phone booth, DiMaggio, not yet married and already exasperated, snapped: "Okay, let's get this marriage going."

Judge Charles Peery appealed for quiet, and a hush fell over the newsmen and the crowd. The ceremony lasted three minutes. When it was over, the photographers asked the newlyweds to kiss again. They did. Then again. And again. Finally, his patience wearing thin and his lips wearing out, DiMaggio grabbed his wife by the arm. "I've had enough. Let's go." With Reno Barsochinni and Lefty O'Doul running interference, the newlyweds shoved their way to a waiting blue Cadillac and promptly sped south.

Joe DiMaggio, the son of a fisherman who now owned his own restaurant at Fisherman's Wharf, was suddenly the husband of . . . Marilyn Monroe, a product of orphanages and foster homes who married for the first time at sixteen, then went on a string of modeling and acting jobs, playing a cannery worker, a disturbed babysitter, a sexy secretary, a hooker, a borderline hysteric and, finally, an airheaded blonde in *Gentlemen Prefer Blondes* and *How to Marry a Millionaire*, the movies that sent her over the top. In an age of institutionalized cool—when a man and his wife, let alone two adulterers or an unwed couple or a prostitute and her client, could not be shown on-screen in the same bed—Marilyn Monroe was the solo volcano. This was the source of her soaring popularity. Speeding south in the dark blue Cadillac, she was too happy to realize it had already begun to become her prison.

After driving almost two hundred miles, they stopped in Paso Robles and ate steak by candlelight. A brave waiter asked for their autographs and they obliged, telling him they were headed for Hollywood. But they doubled back to the Clifton Motel. After making sure the rooms were equipped with TV, DiMaggio paid the four-dollar nightly fee and carried his blond bride across the threshold. They hung out a Do Not Disturb sign and re- mained in the room for fifteen hours.

Within a few hours of their departure the next morning for a remote cabin in the mountains above Palm Springs, the pro- prietor of the Clifton Motel, a savvy Greek immigrant named Jake Panapoulos, installed a plaque above the bed in room 33 that stated simply: "Joe and Marilyn Slept Here." The Clifton Motel was about to become a major tourist attraction.

Six

*W*hen Will Lomax floated across the carpets of Ted Mackey's office the next morning, he was delighted to see his boss reading the *New York Daily Mirror*. As soon as Will had heard about the wedding yesterday on the radio, he'd rushed out and bought every tabloid and gossip sheet he could find. He stayed up watching the eleven o'clock news, then got up early to read the morning papers. He had never felt more ready for a day of work in his life.

"Have a seat," Ted said without looking up. "Guess you heard they went ahead and got hitched."

"Saw it on the late news last night. DiMagg must've kissed her fifty times for the cameras. Poor guy." Ted kept reading. "Have you gotten to the part yet about the Clifton Motel?"

"That's what I'm reading now. Jesus."

"I know. Fifteen hours."

"Sounds like she wore him out."

"Or vice versa. I guess DiMagg swings a pretty big bat in the bedroom, too." Will had rehearsed this line all morning, and he was terribly proud of it. It was tailored to his boss's sense of humor, and Will was sure it would win an approving chuckle. But Ted simply grunted and swept the tabloids and newspapers into a drawer. He held out his hand. "Let's have that report."

Until he heard that curt command, Will had considered the report a miraculous achievement. He'd spent two days closeted with Red Van Hooven, Buick's manufacturing manager, a nuts-and-bolts Dutchman with a much better grasp of compression ratios than of the English language—the kind of guy whose idea of a relaxing weekend, Will supposed, was changing the transmission in the family Roadmaster. Will had listened for two days as Red tried to explain the setup at the Kelsey-Hayes Tool & Die Company. After a while it occurred to Will he might as well have been trying to get Red to explain what happens when a hydrogen bomb goes off. Red kept saying things like: "And the guy who renders the specs for the twist-drill operator doesn't have to know much about the car, necessarily, but he's gotta know the steel gauge on that drawing down to the thousandth of an inch, see?"

Will didn't see. He didn't know a camshaft from a carburetor. In his spare time he read the *Saturday Review* and John Cheever short stories and William Faulkner novels, not transmission repair manuals. But he kept peppering the Dutchman with questions until he saw one thing, then another, then two more. He spent most of the second day distilling what Red had told him into a neatly typed three-page report on the inner workings of Kelsey-Hayes, along with a short list of possible courses of action. The ordeal made interviewing a politician and writing a newspaper article seem about as difficult as getting drunk on payday.

It took Ted two minutes to read two days' worth of work. Then he said, "Sounds like Red doesn't think our problem's at Kelsey-Hayes."

"Kelsey-Hayes got the blueprints for our front bumper, front fenders and rear deck just over a year ago. They also got a lot of business from Plymouth and Nash. Red doesn't think a year is enough time to redo a bumper, let alone make wholesale changes. Harvey agrees with him."

"So Red's not ruling out that Plymouth could've gotten our bumper design from someone at Kelsey-Hayes?"

"No, he's not."

"And he thinks he can get someone on their payroll?"

Not since he interviewed Joe McCarthy had Will encountered

someone so convinced there was a conspiracy afoot. "Yessir," he said. "He thinks he can have a secretary working there by next Friday."

"Okay, tell him to go ahead and do it." Will started to stand up, but Ted motioned for him to remain seated. "We got our first two-week sales figures this morning."

"How do they look?"

"Good. Better than good. We moved well over ten thousand units in each of the first two weeks of the year. You know what that means, don't you?"

"Ummm . . ."

"Come on, come on. What's our sales goal for '54?"

"Half a million."

"Ten thousand units a week for fifty-two weeks equals?"

"Let's see. Five hundred and twenty thousand?"

"Bravo." The dark eyes focused hard on Will, made him feel hot and small. Ted leaned forward. "We can do it, Will. We can beat Plymouth! People are already talking about how much iron we're moving. The power's in those numbers now, and if we beat Plymouth I promise you some people around here will be going places. That includes you." Will had no idea what to say. Ted clapped his hands. "So quit sitting there. Get to work on Van Hooven."

"Um . . . there's one more thing, Ted. I just got off the phone with that freelance writer I know in Washington. He's meeting with a story editor from *Life* magazine tomorrow, and he thinks he might be able to sell them on a major article about the new Century, maybe a profile of you or one of the stylists."

Miriam's voice squawked over the box: "Ned Schroeder on line 3. He says it's important."

"I'd better take that," Ted said. "It could be about Marilyn. Let me know what happens with that writer. I like the sound of it."

Seven

*O*n his way to the White House to watch the President and First Lady board the helicopter that would take them to Camp David for the weekend, Morey Caan kept thinking about Will Lomax's phone call. It reminded him of their conversation on New Year's Day. Though a trip to Detroit at this time of year was about as appealing as a weekend of ice fishing in Siberia, he had to admit there was something intriguing about interviewing a guy like Ted Mackey. Will called him the Great White Shark, and Morey pictured him as the classic American industrialist, big and loud and utterly sure of himself, power-mad, puffed up with booze and red meat and hot air—a perfect target for a Morey Caan hatchet job.

When he reached the White House press gate, Morey could see the usual clot of reporters and photographers waiting by the helicopter, roped off like cattle. Hurrying up the driveway, he noticed a man with close-cropped hair sitting alone on the South Lawn. The man was wearing a trench coat the color of a mushroom, and he appeared to be studying the trees. Morey stopped and stared. "Holy shit," he whispered. It was Pete Hoover, a classmate and fellow history major at the University of Virginia, now a CIA agent, the star of last year's coup that brought the Shah of Iran back to power—and one of Morey's most prized sources. What the hell was Pete Hoover doing sitting on the South Lawn in a trench coat, staring at the trees?

Morey was about to call out to him when he heard the familiar braying of the reporters. He sprinted up the driveway and arrived, huffing, just as Mamie ducked into the helicopter. Ike stood on the grass smiling as cameras clicked and reporters bombarded him with their disjointed questions, babble so familiar to Morey he barely heard it anymore: ". . . planning to speak out against Senator McCarthy?" . . . "chinchilla coat" . . . "chance to play golf" . . .Then the President raised his hand and there was a sudden silence, as though the air had been sucked out of the reporters. No one breathed as Ike cleared his throat and called out, "Mamie and I both think they make a lovely couple and wish them all the best." Then he stepped into the helicopter and rose into the sky.

After scribbling the quote in his notebook, Morey turned to the nearest reporter, lanky Russell Baker of the *New York Times*, and said, "Who was he talking about? I got here late."

"Julius and Ethel Rosenberg," Baker said with a straight face.

"Very funny, Russ."

"He was talking about DiMaggio and Monroe, dummy," said mustachioed Mary Messina, 225 pounds' worth of Associated Press correspondent. "Come on, Morey. You of all people ought to know that Joe and Marilyn are a hell of a lot more important to Ike than our silly-assed questions about McCarthy."

There was much grumbling as the reporters and photographers shuffled down the driveway.

"I wonder if Ike invited Nixon up to play golf with him this weekend," Mary Messina said. Everyone chuckled knowingly.

"That'll be the day," Baker said. "I'll bet a grand Ike didn't spend four hours with Dick all last year."

"Don't believe I want to touch that bet," she said, and everyone chuckled some more. Morey hated it when he had to travel with this pack. Mary Messina was everyone's darling because her cynicism never slept and she cursed like a sailor and could drink all the men under the table.

There was more grumbling, but it lacked its customary edge.

Morey understood why. Ike's departure had generated no news, and that meant there would be no stories to file, no photographs to process. And that meant it was time to start drinking.

"The first round's on me," Mary announced.

This was greeted with cheers. When Morey looked up, the helicopter was already just a dark dot on the sky. He'd rushed all the way down here for one lousy quote that wasn't even good enough to use in *Straight from the Horse's Mouth*. Well, at least he'd spotted Pete Hoover out on the South Lawn. He'd been meaning to call Pete for the past week, ever since he'd overheard an intriguing conversation at the Press Club bar. It was one of those dreary wet Washington winter afternoons, and Morey was bent over a ginger ale, lost in thought. Mary Messina's broad back was to his right. She was talking to her boss, the new AP bureau chief. When the guy mentioned Eisenhower, Morey's ears pricked up. "So let me get this straight," Mary Messina said. "Walter claims Eisenhower singlehandedly starved a *million* Germans to death during the occupation in '45?"

"That's what he's hearing," the bureau chief said. "Apparently some of the POWs got so hungry they started making soup out of water and grass."

"Jesus. That's a huge fucking story."

"You're telling me? Walter says the CIA's looking into it right now."

Morey was paralyzed by the thought of Ike starving a million German soldiers to death after the war. A post-Holocaust holocaust. It would be the story of a lifetime, and Pete Hoover might know something about it. But now, as Morey reached the end of the White House driveway, he saw that Pete was gone. There was nothing out there but birds and trees and squirrels and a putting green.

Eight

*W*ill Lomax and Ted Mackey settled into the plush back seat of the silver Roadmaster. "Tech Center," Ted told the driver. This seat was like a sofa, Will thought, and he supposed more than a few Americans had been conceived on such vast, velvety, wine-colored terrains, parked on darkened city streets, on country roads, at drive-in movie theaters, under dripping trees and fat moons. Hadn't he read somewhere that Marilyn Monroe loved to fuck in cars? The back seat of Will's company car, a four-door Century, wasn't quite this big, but there would be plenty of room if he sat in the middle and got Margaret to straddle him. . . .

". . . writer coming to town," Ted was saying.

"I'm sorry?"

"I said I like the idea of that *Life* writer coming to town."

They were slanting through Hamtramck, past Polish bakeries and butcher shops, past taverns and Catholic churches and gambling clubs. It had stormed overnight, but now the clouds were gone and the sky was a hard shiny blue. The snow was still white. Hamtramck looked almost charming to Will, like some working-class quarter of Warsaw. The third shift at the Dodge plant was letting out, and men with lunch pails crowded the sidewalks, shouting merrily. Steam shot from their mouths. Barely eight o'clock in the morning, time for certain Detroiters to hit the taverns. What a life, Will thought, what a glorious life.

"Of course we need to handle this thing very carefully," Ted said. "We don't want it to backfire."

"How could it possibly backfire?"

"A million different ways. The more I think about it, the more I think it'd be unwise for him to do a profile of me. I happen to think I'd make good copy—I *am* the guy who got the whole Buick line revamped this year—but this is no time for hogging the spotlight. Better to let him talk to the stylists, or to Harvey . . . maybe even some marketing people or dealers."

"But he wants to write about you, Ted."

"Let me explain something. Showboats don't last in this company. There's a guy named DeLorean over at Pontiac. Believe me, he's one very hot shit. I played golf with him at Bloomfield Hills last summer and the guy wore a fucking lemon-yellow outfit. Even his shoes were yellow. He's making a lot of noise and selling a lot of cars, and I don't doubt that he'll be Pontiac's g.m. someday. But he won't last. He's too flashy and he's already making too many enemies. And there's another thing."

"What's that?"

"I talked to Ned Schroeder this morning. He tells me the Finance Committee is *very* impressed with our sales figures so far. He says they're leaning toward giving me the green light to go after Marilyn. They're even warming up to the idea of letting me develop the Wildcat prototype."

"Ted, that's fabulous."

"Yeah. So this is no time to start making a lot of racket."

"I see."

As the Roadmaster sailed past the Kaiser factory, Ted craned his neck. A truck was pulling out of the gate loaded with two-seater Kaiser Darrin convertibles, sporty little jelly-bean jobs with sliding doors. Ted grunted, "That poor bastard."

"Who?" Will said.

"Dutch Darrin. The man's a genius—look at those fucking ragtops. They're gorgeous. They even make Harvey drool. But Kaiser's so under-financed they'll never be able to make enough of them to recoup their investment. That's one mistake I'm not going to make with the Wildcat. It's not going to be some cute collector's item. It's going to be mass appeal all the way, bigger than the Corvette. That's another reason I've *got* to have Marilyn for the ad campaign."

The finality of his voice told Will not only that Ted would get to develop the Wildcat, but that he would somehow persuade Marilyn Monroe to do the ad campaign. Yes, Will thought, Ted Mackey was a car guy right down to the roots of his glossy silver hair. His instincts for what would sell were unerring, and his confidence was so infectious that Will found himself believing the Wildcat was, indeed, destined to go into production and become a monster success. No way it could miss.

The Roadmaster turned off Mound Road and stopped at the Tech Center security gate. Though it was still under construction, Will loved this place, loved the way the architects, Eliel and Eero Saarinen, had made it feel as though you were leaving the past behind when you paused here under the high, flat roof that floated over the security gate. Everything was sharp and clean and right. Even the snow looked better out here, like sparkling blue carpets. The uniformed guard waved the Buick through, into a world of orderly engineering and design studios, research laboratories, ponds and fountains, and the auditorium with its shimmering silver-domed roof that gave it the look of a flying saucer poised for takeoff. In a city where repetition and monotony had been elevated to an art form, a city of lunch pails and time clocks and production quotas, this place was the oasis. This was where people were paid to dream and experiment and create, and Will couldn't wait to get inside.

As soon as he followed Ted into the Buick Styling building he could feel it—the juice and creative voltage that flowed through the offices and corridors and bright studios, through the brainstorming sessions that sometimes grew heated, even passionate. Yes, it was the passion of the place Will liked, the way the designers cared about their ideas and their drawings and their clay models. It reminded him of a newspaper city room at deadline, and it was the exact opposite of the icy efficiency of the upper floors at corporate headquarters, where closing a factory and putting a few thousand people out of work caused about as much anxiety as deciding where to peg the quarterly stock dividend. This was Harvey Pearl's fiefdom, and he called it, with equal parts irony and pride, "the Beauty Parlor." Will had to admit that Ted Mackey, unlike most of the bluesuits, possessed a sure sense of style and understood the value of appearances, how much a car's look and feel had to do with its sales. But Ted hadn't gotten where he was by allowing his intuition or his appreciation of good styling to get the upper hand. The hard nose came first, always, and that was a fact of corporate life no one could afford to forget. That was what had brought them here this morning.

As usual, word that the general manager was in the building traveled swiftly. Everyone Will saw seemed to be buried in work, hunched over drawing boards, smoothing clay models, arguing over color charts. He breathed the perfume of ink and charcoal and clay and sawdust, and he marveled that Ted Mackey had the power to make an entire building's pulse quicken.

Harvey Pearl's office was behind an unmarked door. He painted his windows black, had no telephone, and kept all of his files and drawings under double locks. He changed secretaries about once a month because shortly after the war he became attached to one particularly efficient secretary and kept her for two years, only to learn she'd been making a small fortune selling photostats of his sketches to Crosley's designers.

"You watch," Ted said. "Five to one says he's got a new secretary."

Will followed him through the unmarked door. Sure enough, the secretary was a stranger to both men. She was snapping gum. She had yellow hair, and black smudges had been painted on her forehead where eyebrows used to be. She yawned and said, "May I help you?"

"Yes, we're here to see Harvey," Ted said.

"Your names?"

She wasn't kidding. Will found this hugely amusing.

"My name's Ted Mackey and this is Will Lomax."

"And which department are you gentlemen with?"

Suddenly the door flew open and Harvey Pearl and John Nickles stumbled into the office. They were cackling, tripping over each other. At first Will thought they were drunk, but it was barely eight-thirty in the morning.

"Donna," Harvey sputtered, "have you introduced yourself to the general manager of the Buick Division yet?"

Her jaw dropped. "I—you—how come nobody told me?"

Harvey and John roared with laughter. "Let's go to my office," John said. Out in the corridor, he and Harvey had to hold each other up. Ted gave Will a quizzical look and pointed at his ear and made a circular motion with his finger.

John Nickles's office was more conventional than Harvey's. There was a rakish Swedish desk/sofa/coffee-table ensemble, two phones, a dozen miniature car models, family snapshots, a window that afforded a view of the employee parking lot, a reassuring landscape of hundreds of shiny new GM cars. Ted sank into the Eames chair and put his feet up on John's desk. "You guys mind letting us in on what's so hilarious?"

"Listen to this," Harvey said. His eyes were red and wet. He rewound a reel-to-reel tape recorder. "You'll be hearing the voices of my new secretary, Donna, and a gentleman known to us only as Dick."

"Big Dick, apparently," John said, and he and Harvey howled again. Harvey started the tape.

"So you liked that, huh?" Donna's voice said.

"Damn right I did," a man said. "I especially liked it when you shoved your finger up my ass right before I came."

"Mmmm. Me, too. You shoulda seen the expression on your face when—shit, someone's coming, I'll call you right back."

The phone was hung up. A door opened and closed. "May I help you?"

"Yes," Ted's voice said, "we're here to see Harvey."

"Your names?"

"My name's Ted Mackey and this is Will Lomax."

"And which department are you gentlemen with?"

Harvey shut off the tape. He was grinning. "Well, Theodore, what do you think?"

"Pretty incredible. You mean you tapped the phone *and* bugged the room?"

"Nothing to it," John said. "I've also gone ahead and gotten together a list of everyone who worked on the '54's front bumper for you. I'm ready to wire the whole building if that's what it takes to prove they're loyal."

Ted took the list of names and started studying it. "What do you think, Harvey?"

"I think I'd like to have Donna shove a finger up *my* ass just before I came." They all laughed. "Seriously, I think if Plymouth got hold of some of our design work—and I'm still saying if— then my guess is that it had to come from the tool and die shop. I'm with John on this one."

"I'm working on that angle, but I've got to cover all the bases. You guys can understand that." When he got to the end of the list he said, "Oh, shit."

"What's wrong?" Will said.

"The last name on the list. It's Amos Fuller."

"Who's he?"

"Amos Fuller," Ted said, pinching the bridge of his nose and closing his eyes, "is one of my little projects."

"He's the first Negro ever hired as a stylist by General Motors," Harvey said. He seemed to sense how painful this was for Ted. "His father is Luther Fuller, the guy Ted knocked out cold at Olympia to win the Golden Gloves title."

"I was there," John said. "I'll never forget it. The white people carried Ted out of the ring on their shoulders. The Negroes just watched Luther Fuller lie there and bleed, like he'd let them down or something. I've never seen so much blood in all my life."

"That's not why I hired Luther's son," Ted snapped. He was still pinching the bridge of his nose.

"We know that, Ted," Harvey said. He turned back to Will. "Luther's now a foreman and union steward at the Buick plant in Flint, and let's just say there are a few people in high places who aren't too fond of him—or of Ted's decision to hire his son."

"Because they're Negroes?" Will said. The squirming duplicity of Northerners on racial matters amused him no end.

"I'm sure that's got something to do with it," Harvey said. "But the real problem is that Luther was one of the leaders of the 1937 shutdown of our Flint assembly plant. I'm sure you're aware it led directly to unionization. Some people will never forgive Luther Fuller for that."

Will could hear them now, rattling their iced gin in the country-club men's grills of Grosse Pointe and Bloomfield Hills, thundering that the National Guard should have broken into that barricaded Buick factory and beaten the living shit out of every last one of those unionizers. After all, they were breaking the law. They were trespassing on General Motors property. They deserved whatever they got.

"I hate to ask a silly question," Will said, "but is Amos Fuller any good at his job?"

"Oh, yes," John said. "I had my doubts at first, but he's coming along nicely. The kid's got loads of talent."

Now Harvey turned to Ted. "The problem is that if someone has been leaking our design secrets to the competition, it's going to take some awfully severe measures to find out who it was. If we go ahead and tap the phones, bug the building, hire spies, and then find out there wasn't any leak in the first place . . .

well, I think you can imagine the kind of morale problem we'd have around here."

"Mutiny," John said. "They wouldn't be able to hit the door fast enough."

"Jesus." Ted stared at the list. "Maurice Wilkerson, Norm Slenski, Claire Hathaway, Rory Gallagher, Amos Fuller."

"Yep, they're some of the very best," John said. "So what happens next?"

"I wish I knew," Ted said. "I've got Red Van Hooven working to get someone on the payroll at Kelsey-Hayes. I think I'll pursue that before I do anything with this list." He folded the sheet of paper and slipped it into his jacket pocket. "Let's not let any of this leave this room." They all nodded. "Now, Will, let's you and me take a little spin through the studio. My mood needs improving."

$\mathcal{C}$laire Hathaway was beginning to hate her sketches of the 1957 taillights. They reminded her of gargoyles. The lights were set in backward-slanting slabs of chrome, fat wedges of shiny silver metal that rose to sharp points, as though they'd been sculpted by the wind and the forward velocity of the car. Chrome gargoyles. There was so much chrome around the lights Claire wondered how a mere car would be able to support all that weight. But that was a problem for the boys in engineering. John Nickles was delighted with the way the sketches were progressing. "You're getting there," he told her. "Harvey says to lay that chrome on with a trowel." So she consoled herself that these pointed chrome monstrosities were actually Harvey Pearl's fault, the fruit of his fascination with the twin-tailed P-38 airplane from the war. She'd heard a rumor that the '57 Cadillacs and Chevys had already sprouted fins. *Fins!*

"Verrry nice."

The man's voice startled her, and she spun on her stool. "God damn you, Norm—oh, Mr. Mackey! You scared me half to death!"

He was standing inside her cubicle with his PR man. They were dressed in charcoal-gray suits, their shoes blazing black. They looked like a couple of bankers, or undertakers. Ted leaned over her drawing board. "These must be the taillights for the '57."

"Yes. And they're giving me fits."

"Well, I think they're very nice."

He was so close she could smell him. He no longer smelled like wood smoke. He smelled like talcum powder and shaving lotion, a strange saltwater scent. The silver hair was swept back. The collar of his white shirt was stiff with starch. He looked at his flack, whose hair was as black and shiny as his shoes. "Could you give us a minute alone, Will?"

The man drifted across the studio, and suddenly Claire wished she had taken more time with her hair that morning, hadn't just grabbed it in her fist and tied it back before racing out the door, ten minutes late. Now she wiggled her feet back into her brown penny loafers.

Ted glanced over his shoulder. "I've been meaning to tell you how happy everyone is with the front end of the new Century. The dealers absolutely love it. I found out this morning we moved more than ten thousand units again last week, and every dealer I've talked to says that front end is one of the big selling points."

"Well, thanks, but a dozen of us worked on the front end, you know."

"I'm well aware of that." He looked over his shoulder again. Over the wall of her cubicle he could see the entire Buick studio. Everyone was toiling over sketches of taillights, dashboards, hubcaps, bumpers. New cars were blooming before his eyes. He looked down at her. "Let's take a little walk." As she followed him across the studio she could feel every eye in the place on her. She knew she'd be in for a merciless ribbing when she returned.

The linoleum floor in the corridor was so bright it hurt her eyes. She matched his pace, his slow, measured pace, and waited. His hands were clasped behind his back. "Let me get right to the point, Claire. I've got a problem and I need your help. I don't want you to breathe a word about this to anyone. Do you understand?"

"Sure."

He looked over his shoulder and lowered his voice. "We think someone in this studio might be leaking our designs to the competition. I don't need to tell you how serious this could be. If you don't mind, I'd like to talk to you about it. In private."

"You don't think I would—"

"No, no, no," he chuckled. "You're not a suspect, for God's sake. That's why I need to talk to you. Over dinner. Is Monday night good for you?"

"Umm . . ."

"Strictly business."

"Gee, I—these sketches are due first thing Tuesday morning. Is there any way I can get a rain check?"

"Not if you want to have a job on Tuesday."

"Well, in that case my answer is yes."

"A wise decision. Eight o'clock Monday night at the Detroit Club."

She strolled back to the studio alone. When she tried to go back to work on her sketch, she found she couldn't concentrate. She kept thinking of their kiss at the New Year's Eve party and of his remark—"Strictly business"—and she had the uneasy feeling that a man in his position would offer such a reassurance only if he had something quite different from business in mind. And yet, to her surprise, she was glad she'd accepted his invitation.

Nine

*I*n Yiddish a schlemiel is a person who is forever spilling hot soup, a bungler. A schlimazel is a person on whom hot soup is forever being spilled, a victim. Morey Caan figured that made him a schlemiezel, a person who was forever spilling hot soup on himself, a self-victimizing bungler. But he rarely noticed when he spilled soup, or anything else, on himself, and when he did notice he tended not to care. He figured that was why men wore neckties: to keep food off their shirts.

None of this was lost on Charles Prentiss, *Life* magazine's Washington editor, who had brought Morey to the Press Club to discuss a list of story ideas. Prentiss was a dapper bachelor, a lover of food and wine. When he ate he tucked his napkin under his chins and smoothed it across the vast arc of his gut. Now he patted his bright red lips with the tip of his napkin and said, "Young man, there's a tie in your soup."

Morey looked down. "It's my tie, Charles."

"Yes, it is *your* tie in your chowder. Surely that's no reason to leave it there."

Morey took his tie out of his chowder and wiped it with his napkin. Now it was a two-tone brown tie. He considered it an improvement.

"I swear," Prentiss said, "I can dress you up—to an extent— but I positively cannot take you out. Not even to the Press Club."

"I'm sorry, Charles."

"I've got a twelve-year-old son who's neater than you are."

"I don't doubt it, Charles."

"Unfortunately he's not half the writer you are. In fact, no one in this sorry town is."

"I'll take that as a compliment, Charles."

Prentiss patted his lips, sighed, said, "Please do."

Just as every rebel secretly craves authority, so Morey Caan —free-lancer, free spirit, confirmed bachelor and aspiring author—craved these encounters with Charles Prentiss. Along with a handful of other magazine editors, Prentiss was as close as Morey had come to having a boss since he quit the *Post* two years ago and struck out on his own. While Morey was proud to be one of the rare souls who swam against the current, at times it could get lonely, even spooky, working by yourself in a vacuum, in your dark little Georgetown garret with nothing but sandwich rinds and stained coffee cups and Fat Boy for companionship. Charles Prentiss made Morey feel he was in touch with the world. He also had an unlimited expense account, so lunch with him always meant the best free food money could buy. Morey, who ate out of cans at home, followed Prentiss's lead today and ordered the filet mignon.

As the waiter cleared their soup bowls, Prentiss surveyed the dining room. "Isn't that Walter Lippmann having lunch with Drew Pearson at the corner table?"

"Yes, it is."

"Why don't you wave to them? They're very famous and they both appear to be sober."

"Because Lippmann doesn't know me from Adam, and Pearson hates my guts."

"Oh? Why's that?"

"I think because I scooped him with my Iran story last year. Also, I called him an asshole to his face in here years ago."

"Ah, the pettiness of the anointed."

When the filet mignon and the second bottle of beaujolais arrived, Prentiss got down to business. He always thought best when he was eating and drinking on the expense account. "I'm turning you down on the story about Ike's caddy," he said.

"Why?"

"Because the poor man—Ike, that is, not his caddy—he's been in office barely a year and there are two things people are already sick of hearing about."

"Namely?"

"His golf swing and his wife's sleeping habits." Prentiss burped into his napkin. "Now as for the Detroit story, I'm very intrigued with the idea of car designers, the process they go through to bring a car to life. It's very mysterious—no one understands it. I certainly don't. I think the way to approach it would be to pick a particular car, then write the story of how it starts as an idea and becomes a machine—sort of like a biography."

"That's it!" Morey cried. "Biography of a Buick!"

Drew Pearson looked up from his martini and glared at Morey. Morey smiled and waved. Then he said to Charles, "So that means yes?"

"That means maybe. You say you have a source at GM?"

"The PR guy for the whole Buick Division. I've known him for years. He's already agreed to cooperate—in fact, the story was his idea."

"That's what I like about you, young man. You truly are an incurable opportunist."

"Does *that* mean yes?"

"Yes, that means yes."

Ten

The snow began to stick just as Will Lomax turned north toward home. Two cars in front of him promptly corkscrewed into a ditch. He narrowly missed them, negotiated the treacherous turn from Plymouth Road onto Southfield Road, then gripped the Buick Century's basketball-hoop-sized steering wheel and eased the car toward the suburbs.

The sudden skin of snow and ice on the roads was merely the latest in a string of insults that had been accumulating since early that morning. First there was the phone call to Morey Caan, then the meeting with Ted Mackey, who spent half an hour ranting about the importance of finding the spy in the Beauty Parlor before offering his lukewarm praise for the Red Van Hooven report. It was uttered in passing, almost grudgingly, as though he hated to admit that someone had come close to meeting his exacting standards. It convinced Will that Ted's power came from his ability to make his subordinates feel chronically inadequate, reducing them to a constant rat-like frenzy to do more, to work harder, to do whatever was necessary to win that elusive pellet of praise. When Will glanced in the rearview mirror, he saw eyes that were ashen with fatigue and worry. Had he already joined the other rats in the maze?

He skidded to a stop at a yellow light at Eight Mile Road, the Detroit city limit, the birth of the suburbs. Waiting for the light to change, he felt a stab of longing for the raffish life of the newspaper reporter. In newspapers, if you botched it today there was no need to worry because you would always get another chance to botch it again tomorrow; at General Motors, at least in his new job, if you botched it today there might not be a tomorrow.

The light changed and he gunned the Buick into the storm. The snow was coming out of the North, coming straight at him, falling faster, a blur in the headlights. This kind of snow could fall all night, maybe for days, maybe the drifts would pile up to the windows of his house, then up to the roof, and there wouldn't be any work for days and days. He could sit by the fireplace and read. But no, Ted would show up for work if he had to ride a dogsled, and he would expect no less of his staff. Suddenly Will thought of the two towering magnolia trees in the front yard of his boyhood home in Virginia. He'd seen them covered with snow just twice, and that snow had looked like sugar. This snow, somehow, did not.

Will settled into the line of crawling cars. After the meeting with Ted, Will had talked with Red Van Hooven, which was kind of like trying to communicate with a lug wrench. He managed to convey to the Flying Dutchman that he was to get someone—preferably a woman with a gift for gab and a collection of tight sweaters—on the Kelsey-Hayes payroll. After that there was lunch with some sales people who had the delightful habit of talking in numbers—("We might have to quarter-point them for the rest of the bi-weekly in order to double quota")—and then a long afternoon of phone calls from the Detroit *Free Press* and the *Automotive News* and the *Wall Street Journal* about Buick's brisk early sales. Finally, at eight-thirty, long after everyone else had left and the night janitors had arrived, Will ignored the ringing phone and shuffled out of the office.

Now, creeping toward home, he could see that the conversation with Morey had set the tone for the entire rotten day. When Will confessed that he'd been so busy he hadn't given a thought to The Book, Morey had snapped, "So what's the matter? You already forget about your trip to Washington last year?"

Low blow. Of course Will hadn't forgotten. How could any man forget the moment when he first suspected he might have made a colossal blunder, when everything he'd decided to do with his life—change careers, get married, pull up stakes, make babies, buy a house, press his nose to the corporate grindstone—had suddenly, sickeningly, begun to feel like a bad joke?

That moment had come almost exactly one year earlier, when he had been summoned to assist in a most delicate operation: the confirmation hearings before the hostile Senate Armed Services Committee of President-elect Eisenhower's nominee for secretary of defense, former GM president Charles "Engine Charlie" Wilson, one of the richest of the very rich men who'd been tapped for a cabinet that was already being called "the Millionaires' Club."

Will had been called to Washington for two reasons. Since he'd worked as a newspaper reporter on Capitol Hill, it was decided he would be the perfect person to tutor the nominee on how to deal with the Washington press corps, a group Wilson referred to as "those pricks"; and Will, like the majority of the Armed Services Committee—indeed, like most of the powerful members of Congress—was a Southerner. Car people from Detroit tended to view Southerners as some sort of foreigners, cunning at best, mean-spirited at worst, and definitely not to be trusted. Most of them were Democrats to boot. So Will was supposed to tutor a volatile, outspoken, Republican Yankee industrialist on how to stay on the good side of a bunch of hostile, cunning, Southern Democrats while television lights blazed and "those pricks" circled overhead like buzzards in the press gallery. Landing a B-29 in heavy fog probably would've been easier. Yet Will relished the assignment. He was already turning heads in Detroit, and if he could do any little thing to ease Engine Charlie's passage from private industry to government service, his name would be made back home.

He arrived in Washington on a rainy January afternoon in 1953 and went straight up to the GM suite on the top floor of the Shoreham Hotel. There he spent two days and two nights closeted with Charlie Wilson and a small army of bluesuits— White House liaisons, congressional aides, Secret Service men, representatives from the GM Salary and Bonus Committee, corporate lawyers, GOP lawyers, Washington lawyers, tax lawyers. Phones rang constantly, and the air was blue with smoke. Most of the fuss was over what Charlie Wilson would do with his vast collection of GM stock and his upcoming bonuses now that he was about to be put in a position to swing millions of dollars of business GM's way.

When the hearings began, things turned sour almost immediately. The culprit was the senator from Texas, Lyndon Johnson. Will had interviewed Johnson many times, and he'd learned not to be fooled by the syrupy drawl or the face that looked like melting wax. Lyndon was already a very powerful man with the ambition to become a much more powerful man; and this, Will knew, made him valuable as an ally and dangerous as an enemy. He was one of the most relentless and ruthless operators in Washington—there was talk he'd stolen votes to win the 1948 election—and this alone seemed to qualify him for higher office, make it his virtual destiny.

As soon as the niceties were out of the way, Johnson asked if Wilson had any documents to offer the committee. Wilson handed up a pack of resignations from the boards of oil companies and banks, along with a letter outlining the cash and the 1,737 shares of GM stock bonuses due him over the next four years.

"And what do you intend to do with that cash and those stocks as they become available to you?" Johnson asked.

"Why, I intend to keep them."

A ripple passed through the press gallery, and Johnson's face brightened at the smell of blood. "What is the value of that stock, the par value?"

"The par value is five dollars," Wilson said. "The market value is about sixty-five or sixty-six dollars, something like that. Some of you probably have some. I doubt if I'm the only man in this room who has any."

"Well, I do not have any," Johnson said, pausing for effect. "And if I did, I would know what it's worth."

Snickers in the press gallery. Will had to admire Lyndon. He actually made Engine Charlie turn pink. Happily, Wilson bit his lip and fielded a few innocuous questions from Senator Leverett

Saltonstall. Just when things were beginning to move along smoothly, Senator Robert Hendrickson, a Republican trench warrior from New Jersey, said, "Mr. Wilson, I am interested to know whether—if a situation did arise where you had to make a decision that was adverse to the interest of your stock in General Motors—could you make that decision?"

Wilson leaned toward his microphone. Surely, Will thought, he would hit this puffball a mile. "Yessir, I could," Wilson said firmly. "But I cannot conceive of such a situation because for years I thought that what was good for the country was good for General Motors—and vice versa. The difference did not exist. Our company is too big and powerful. It goes with the welfare of the country. Our contribution to the nation is quite considerable."

The pencils in the press gallery were racing now. What a gem! "What's good for the country is good for General Motors." For better or for worse, Engine Charlie Wilson had just made Washington headlines for the first time.

After that bombshell, the hearings were adjourned until after the inaugural festivities. Will had never seen so many glossy faces and limousines, so much blue hair and mink. The next day, he learned from one of the GM lawyers that during the inaugural ball Dwight Eisenhower, his presidency less than half a day old, had taken Charlie Wilson aside and told him he'd had a change of heart. Given the uproar from the opening round of confirmation hearings, Ike wanted Wilson to bite the bullet and sell all of his GM stock and the bonus shares as soon as they became his property. Wilson turned pale at the thought of paying $200,000 in capital gains tax, but he agreed.

Even Will thought they were home free now. But when the hearings resumed, Richard Russell of Georgia joined Lyndon Johnson in pressing Wilson on how he intended to handle his forthcoming bonus stock. Wouldn't it be possible, they wondered aloud, for the secretary of defense to make decisions that would boost the value of the GM stock and thus fatten his long-term bonus? Though Wilson offered to donate any increase in the value of his bonus stock to charity, Johnson was not satisfied. Then Wilson reminded him that they were discussing a moot point: since GM policy prevented him from selling any of the bonus stock until it was awarded to him in four yearly increments, he couldn't sell any of it now even if he wanted to. Johnson still was not satisfied. They had reached an impasse, and one of GM's lawyers suggested a brief recess.

Will would never forget what happened next out in that marble corridor. The whole crew of bluesuits from the Shoreham Hotel huddled around Wilson. "What do I have to do to satisfy that prick?" he hissed. "Forfeit the whole fucking bonus?"

"Of course not," one of the corporate lawyers said.

"Isn't taking a $600,000 pay cut and paying $200,000 in capital gains tax enough of a sacrifice for that redneck asshole?"

"It's more than generous," one of the tax lawyers said.

"Then what the fuck am I supposed to do?"

Everyone studied everyone else's brilliantly shined shoes. It was at that precise moment that Will Lomax could feel the bottom falling out of his stomach. He had few illusions about the importance of money to these people. He'd sat in on too many contract negotiations with the UAW, heard too many perfectly rational arguments for closing an inefficient factory or jacking up the price of cars. Money talked in Detroit. Fine and dandy. But now Will was standing in the Senate Office Building, in the very corridor where he used to hang around waiting for rich men to come out of locked rooms and tell him lies, and he was listening to the former president of the largest corporation on the planet agonize over whether going into government service would leave him a very rich man or a very little bit less rich very rich man. This was the way the world worked in 1953. This was the GM way, the GOP way. This was the caliber of man Will had decided to go to work for, the caliber of man who was about to take over the United States government. This, Will concluded, was horseshit.

"Gentlemen," he said, "may I make a suggestion?" Every head snapped in his direction. "Since Mr. Wilson is scheduled to receive, what is it, seventeen hundred shares of stock over the next four years?"

"It's seventeen hundred and thirty-seven shares," sniffed one of the lawyers.

"Then why doesn't the Salary and Bonus Committee just allow Mr. Wilson to convert those shares of stock into cash at today's market value? That way he'll get some money—though not as much as he deserves, of course—and he'll be free of even the appearance of any possible conflict of interest. If I know Senator Johnson, he'll jump at a deal like that."

No one moved or spoke. Finally Engine Charlie said, "Young man, I think you just might have hit on something there."

When the hearing resumed, Wilson announced the extraordinary step the Salary and Bonus Committee had agreed to take. Lyndon Johnson, who knew there was no such thing as total victory in politics, was satisfied at last. The committee voted, 15–0, to approve Charlie Wilson as secretary of defense.

And now, a year after that trip to Washington, Will Lomax had been promoted to the top PR job at Buick and he was driving a company car into the teeth of another blizzard and he felt utterly, blackly lost. The problem, as Morey had reminded him on the phone this morning, was that his big breakthrough was also the beginning of the end.

He guided the Buick off Southfield Road into his driveway. A foot of snow had already fallen. He shut off the headlights but left the engine and heater running. The white frame house looked like a gigantic sugar cube, or a huge square igloo. Even the lights burning in the kitchen and in the spare bedroom upstairs did little to make the place look cozy. This is what I'm busting my ass for, he thought. It took him half an hour to work up the nerve to shut off the car and go inside.

But the house was warm, miraculously warm, and quiet. After a day of jangling telephones, meetings, arguments, traffic and snow, the deep warm silence seemed magical. He stood in the kitchen and listened to it: just the faint ticking of the grandfather clock in the foyer and the faraway murmuring of a television set. Only then did he realize how exhausted he was.

He took out a tall glass and filled it with ice cubes and Old Crow. It was good brown liquor, the kind his father used to drink, and Will hoped it would burn the chill out of him. It did. As he poured another drink he noticed a new appliance beside its box on the countertop—a Hurri-Hot Electri-Cup. It had a removable egg rack and could boil twenty-three ounces of liquid as well as baby bottles, instant coffee and eggs. It cost $14.95 and looked like some sort of stainless steel toadstool. Next to it was an unopened box that contained a device called the Power-Chef Mixer. He opened the box and discovered mixing bowls, a juice strainer, a ten-speed mixer that doubled as a meat grinder. It cost $45.95. Just the other day Margaret had suggested that winter was the perfect time to buy an air conditioner for their bedroom window, and she just so happened to have found a Westinghouse model for less than $400. Hurri-Hots, Electri-Cups, Power-Chefs, air conditioners, TV dinners, color TV. What would be next—color TV dinners? He laughed, but no sound came out.

He walked through the darkened dining room, past the softly ticking grandfather clock, into the living room. The lights were off and the TV was on and Margaret was asleep on the sofa, bathed in blue light. God, Will thought, please don't let her be pregnant again. She always slept a lot during the first months. Her bathrobe had fallen open to reveal her legs up to mid-thigh. Not so very long ago the sight would have inspired him to start tearing off his clothes, but now it did nothing for him. Is that what marriage does to a man? On the TV screen, a Rolls-Royce drove onto a stage, made two circles and stopped, and a giant pink egg rolled out of the back seat. It broke open and out popped the piano player Liberace in a pink feathered cloak. Will wondered how this guy made a living before the invention of color TV. He realized he was wondering about a lot of things but not coming up with any answers.

The house creaked as he tiptoed upstairs to check on the children. It seemed that the only times he got to see his son and daughter during the week were in the chaos of the breakfast table and these nightly visits to their rooms. A wedge of light slanted from the spare bedroom into Robbie's room. The boy had climbed out of his crib again and was asleep on the little mat in the corner. A climber, Will thought, already impatient, headstrong, determined to do things his way. He was convinced the boy climbed out of the crib night after night simply because he knew he wasn't supposed to. Good for him, Will thought, wish I could still say the same for myself. He leaned close to the sleeping child and smelled Ivory soap, cotton, cough syrup. The little tongue clucked and a bubble of spit burst on his lips. Will touched the soft white hair. It was terrifying, such vulnerability.

The baby's room was even worse. Will had never been comfortable around infants, was scared of dropping them or waking them or doing something that would trigger a long wail and bring on understanding, competent Mom. He had changed a diaper only twice and had botched it both times. Two-year-old Robbie was fragile enough; eleven-month-old Lisa was almost more than he could bear. He didn't dare go into the dark room, so he stood in the doorway until he could make out her rhythmic breathing. Satisfied, he started downstairs.

When he reached the landing, something in the spare bedroom caught his eye. At first he thought it was yet another new appliance, but when he stepped into the room he saw it was the big fat gray Remington typewriter he'd taken from his father's office after the funeral. It was pudgy and massive, covered with dust. He cranked a sheet of paper into the carriage and typed the first thing that came to his mind:

"Young man, I think you just might have hit on something there."

In the quiet house the clacking of the keys sounded like gunshots. The old machine still had a nice action. He looked around the room at the naked, knotty-pine walls and the empty bookshelves. Six months after the move his books were still in boxes. The only things on the desk besides the typewriter were a few newspaper clippings, GM annual reports, press packets and magazine ads. Morey would be appalled; this was supposed to be Will's refuge, the place he came to work on The Book. Margaret kept threatening to turn it into a sewing room. He looked at the words he'd just typed and thought of his conversation that morning with Morey. He thought of his trip to Washington last year and how it felt when the bottom fell out of his stomach.

Quietly, careful not to wake Margaret or the children, he started unpacking his neglected notes and files and arranging them on the empty shelves.

Eleven

*M*orey Caan was frantic. He was running late for his interview with Senator McCarthy, and he knew that the only thing the Great Red Hunter hated more than a Commie in the State Department was a reporter who kept him waiting. As Morey fumbled with the key to his apartment, his phone rang. Cursing, he unlocked the door and raced back in. Fat Boy darted under the sofa. "Yello?"

"Morey! Pete Hoover here returning your call how the hell you be?"

"Pete, I was just on my way out."

"Got a message you tried to reach me. What's up?" There was a rustling sound, then a muffled "Go fuck yerselves!"

"Come again?"

"Nothing. These pricks playing poker in the back think they own the joint. Fuck 'em."

"Where are you, Pete?"

"Bill's Grille—home of the world's tastiest Gibson."

Bill's Grille was a grim, smoky little hole-in-the-wall in Alexandria's Olde Towne. When Morey worked for the *Post* he dropped in there two or three times a week to peruse the local rummies, retired military boys, Pentagon paper pushers and the occasional disgruntled spook like Pete Hoover. The bartender was a guy named Rudy. His nose looked like a bulb of broccoli, and he wore a burgundy vest with gold buttons and rolled the sleeves of his starched white shirt right up to his elbows. He was known as a good listener and as a maker of potent martinis and Gibsons. The way guys in middling positions of power sat in there getting stoned and swapping national defense secrets, it was a wonder the Russians hadn't put Rudy on their payroll.

"Reason I called, Pete, was to see what you were doing on the South Lawn the other day."

"Jeez, you crazy little bug-eyed bastard, you don't miss a trick, do you?" He coughed. Then he sighed. "Aww, what the hell. This is supposed to be top secret, but fuck it. Y'aren't gonna believe this one."

"Try me." Morey took out a notebook and pen.

"About a month ago the agency asked me to go on a mission in Guatemala—very similar to the job we did in Iran last year, but with one major difference."

"No shah?"

"Not only that, but no popular military support for the stiff we're backing. The agency's been burned before doing this, but I made the mistake of thinking the people who run this fucking government are capable of learning from history."

"You're losing me, Pete."

"I turned down the Guatemala job. Told 'em it stinks. So they decided to fix my wagon—assigned me to the White House and told me to shoot the fucking squirrels."

"Did you say shoot the *squirrels?*"

"Shoot the *fucking* squirrels is what I said. They've got me shooting the fucking squirrels!"

"Why?"

"That's the best part. The way I heard it, the American Public Golf Association built the putting green for Ike on the South Lawn last year. A way for him to keep his short game sharp and all that shit. Course he loves it. But there's a small problem."

"Fucking squirrels."

"Bingo. See, when Truman was in the White House he liked to feed the squirrels, so by the time he left town the little fuckers were so fat and sassy they'd eat right out of your hand. Now they bury their nuts in Ike's new putting green. About a month ago he hits a perfect putt and right before it goes in the hole it hits a bump and bounces wide. He blows a fucking gasket and tells his butler, this little Filipino fag named Moaney, to shoot the next squirrel he sees. But Moaney's terrified of guns, see, so he contacts the Secret Service and they contact the FBI and they contact the agency. Since I didn't wanna play ball in Guatemala, my bosses decided squirrel duty'd be just the thing for me."

Morey didn't know whether to laugh or cry. Even by American standards, going from the cutting edge of international espionage in Iran to squirrel-shooting duty on the White House lawn was an astonishingly swift fall from grace. And which was worse— a President who loved animals but had it in him to drop two atomic bombs, or a President who loved golf but had it in him to shoot squirrels for fucking up his putting green?

"Pete, I'd like to get together and talk more about this, but right now I've got to get down to the Hill for an interview."

"I'm here every afternoon from five o'clock on. Corner bar stool."

"One last thing. You heard anything about Eisenhower starving a lot of German POWs to death in '45?"

There was a rumbling, phlegmy laugh. "You really are a piece of work, you know that?" The laughter faded. "You come on down here some afternoon and we'll have us a little talk."

That, in spook speak, was as good as a yes. Morey's skin was tingling. As soon as he hung up the phone it rang again. McCarthy's secretary was calling to say the senator had just left for an emergency meeting and wanted to reschedule the interview. Right, Morey thought. Joe probably had an emergency urge to suck off some cute congressional page.

When he hung up the phone he heard footsteps out on the stairs. He'd entered the apartment in such a rush he hadn't closed the door behind him, and now he saw his neighbor, Ann Wilson, trudging up the stairs with a bag of groceries in each arm. What a pleasant coincidence, he thought. No sooner am I off the phone with the man in charge of shooting squirrels for the President than I run into the woman in charge of orchestrating his daily schedule. When Ann Wilson had arrived from Ohio with the invading Republican horde and moved into the apartment directly above Morey's, he told her his name was Morty and he worked as a loan officer at a bank near DuPont Circle. Shortly before Christmas she'd invited him up for an eggnog, and she spent half an hour railing against his article in the *New Republic* about the coup in Iran. She said the CIA agent who leaked the story should be shot for treason. Morey said he'd never heard of the magazine, then asked where Iran was.

Now he watched her broad hips and tree-trunk ankles driving up the last steps to the landing outside his door. She had a pretty face, creamy skin, big green eyes. Morey figured all she needed to do was lose about seventy-five pounds.

"Need some help?" he said, stepping out onto the landing.

"Oh, Morty," she huffed, "be a doll and come take one of these bags. I'm about to give out."

Gladly! He snatched one of the bags from her. She smelled marvelous, like talcum powder and expensive perfume and sweat. He told himself: You sleep with her and she rolls over on you in the middle of the night and you never wake up. He led the way up the last flight of stairs because he supposed any woman with a backside as broad as a Buick's didn't appreciate having men follow it at eyeball level.

While she put away the groceries in the kitchen, he pretended to thumb through a magazine in the living room. Actually he was looking for her little brown diary. He'd first noticed it that day she'd had him up for an eggnog. While she was in the bathroom he'd opened it, not realizing what it was, and read a few pages. It was a gold mine. A few stray jottings from the President's appointments secretary were all Morey needed to realize that his wildest fantasies about Ike were not nearly wild enough, that no satire could possibly outdo the reality, if that was the word, of Ike's world. Like the phone call from Pete Hoover, this was both thrilling and disturbing, but at least it had shown Morey that he was on the right track, that the best way to write his book was simply to record the things that came out of Ike's mouth.

While Ann whistled merrily in the kitchen, Morey dug under the magazines on the coffee table until he found what he was looking for. Using a magazine as cover he opened the diary to the first entry:

Jan. 23, 1953: DDE had long phone conversation with Gen. Omar Bradley about Korea situation. When he hung up he said to me, "Ann, I've just learned a lesson. Life's going to be different from now on, I'm afraid." Asked him why. He said, "Omar's been calling me Ike for years. On the phone just now he called me 'Mr. President.' "

Amazing. You had to get elected President to realize it's lonely at the top? What did you expect the White House to be like—some kind of officers' club with better food?

"What are you doing?" Ann was standing behind him.

"Nothing! Reading!"

"You were talking to yourself. I could hear you. What's that you're reading?"

"This . . . magazine. I've never heard of *Sports Illustrated*."

"That's the very first issue. I thought you hated sports."

"I do." He got the diary safely back to the coffee table. "But I love magazines."

"What happened to your necktie?"

He looked at it. The tie was beige originally, but now, thanks to the Press Club chowder, the bottom four inches were the color of fudge. "Oh, it got in my soup at lunch the other day. Actually improved the taste."

She laughed. She had a lovely laugh, the way she flashed her teeth and tossed her head back. "Oh, Morty, you're such a mess. I swear, you need a woman to look after you."

Remember, he told himself, she rolls over in the middle of the night and you're dead meat. "So how's your boss getting along?"

"Just fine. He and the First Lady are going to Gettysburg for the weekend. He's having a few of the guys up to play bridge."

"Doesn't Mamie play bridge?"

"Not with the President."

"Why not?"

"Because—she says he yells at her whenever she makes a bad bid."

Morey made a mental note to write down that quote and the

Omar Bradley quote as soon as he got downstairs. "I hear Ike's pretty good at bridge."

"I hear he's fantastic. That's another thing that really bugs me about the press. People write that he's such a dummy—well, if he's so dumb, how come he's such a good bridge player?"

Spoken like a true Buckeye. "Good question. I honestly hadn't thought of it like that before."

She was full of interesting information. He'd already pried out of her that she made six thousand dollars a year, shared a drab yellow cubicle with Ike's correspondence secretary, kept a cocked mousetrap under her desk and thought nothing of working fourteen-hour days. So much for the trappings of power.

"Enough shop talk," Ann said. "Why don't you stay for supper? I've got all the fixin's for beef Stroganoff."

Morey had never heard of beef Stroganoff. He imagined it was some shiny Midwestern delicacy that caused hard arteries and thick ankles. "I've already got plans tonight," he said. "In fact, I'm booked up till Sunday."

"Sunday it is, then. Eight o'clock sharp."

"Sounds great." He stood up and started working his way toward the door. "Can I bring anything? Dessert? Wine?" Bromo Seltzer?

"Just bring your adorable self and your appetite. And please wear a clean necktie."

Twelve

*W*hen her husband phoned to say he wouldn't be home for dinner—something about having to take some salesmen out on the town—Milmary Mackey was sitting at the kitchen table studying the snapshot she'd dug out of the attic on New Year's Eve. It was a picture of a young pilot, a dark-haired, athletic man, sprinting toward the camera as a gray airplane, its nose in the dirt and its twin tails in the air, burned in the distance. Ever since she'd shown it to Harvey Pearl on New Year's Day, that snapshot had been humming in her mind. She even dreamed about it once. It seemed to have fictional possibilities, to contain secrets that demanded to be deciphered and written down. And now at the age of thirty-eight, in the dead middle of a winter day, in the dead middle of her life, Milmary sensed, with the canniness of the truly desperate, that solving the riddles inside that snapshot was a chance, possibly her last chance, at salvation from a life that had become little more than an endless cycle of cocktail parties, hangovers, Garden Club meetings, bridge games, station wagon rides with her sons, cookouts and requests to canvass door-to-door to help fight tuberculosis, diabetes, heart disease, cancer and gout.

She stared at the snapshot. The startling thing about it, she now realized, was that the man's face gave no indication he was in any danger or that he was afraid. The face was brimming with the glad abandon of a boy. He could've been dashing down a beach or a football field instead of running away from a crip-pled, burning airplane, a plume of smoke curling from the cock-pit into the sky. The gray of that sky struck Milmary as the perfect depiction of how the sky had actually looked that day —grainy and evil and hot. The memory actually made her shiver. She hadn't felt that sensation in years, not since the 1930s when she fled Detroit and plunged into the humid little New York world of writers and radicals and painters and poets. Compared with provincial Detroit it was an exotic, exhilarating world, full of raffish characters. A few were geniuses, some were middling talents and most were outright fakes, but they all came to refer to Milmary Cavanagh as "the virgin."

The label was not meant to be flattering. She was then fresh out of the University of Michigan and had just published her first short story in *Collier's*. Her talent may have been unformed, even ordinary, but her looks were not. Just about everyone wanted to bed this Irish beauty with the auburn hair and the long, splendidly carved legs, the smoldering emerald eyes and the reputation for having turned her back on a vast fortune somewhere in the Midwest in order to pursue her writing career. And just about everyone tried to bed her. But they all, to a man, failed.

She had just enough talent to make the fawning of established writers believable, and she was just naive enough at first to believe they invited her to their parties and up to their shabby apartments and studios in order to discuss the finer points of characterization and dialogue and plot. It became a kind of game to see who would be the first to break through. No less a heavyweight than Eugene O'Neill gave it his best shot. After taking Milmary to see *Mourning Becomes Electra*, usually a sure path to an aspiring author's treasures, he got her up to his apartment, plied her with theater talk and red wine, actually got her blouse unbuttoned—then watched in horror as she sprang from the sofa, buttoned her blouse, smoothed her hair and vanished into the Greenwich Village night. O'Neill went straight for the whisky in the kitchen. Three quick shots and he was off on an epic spree, a bout that lasted three days and three nights and left him facedown, cold as an iced fish, on the Fifth Avenue trolley tracks. He was dragged to safety by a passing pedestrian. Six months later, he was awarded the Nobel Prize for literature.

Similar scenarios were repeated, with less grandiose finales, dozens of times. She was forever breaking hearts by making herself seem available, then refusing to put out. "The virgin" was downgraded to "the tease." She sold a short story to *The New Yorker*, but her pile of rejection slips grew taller and she had to go to work as a receptionist at the magazine and the romance of New York began to wear thin. Like many Americans, she was rescued from purgatory—in her case not a purgatory of bread lines and relief checks but one of drunken parties, dull poetry readings, rejection slips and pushy men—by the bombing of Pearl Harbor. Her father pulled some strings and got her a job writing press releases and publicity copy for General Motors' new War Production Office; and so, feeling like that most pulverized of American fauna, the failed writer, she left New York in the spring of 1942 and moved into an apartment building her father owned in Windsor, Ontario. She didn't have to pay rent and she had a sweeping view of downtown Detroit across the river and, a little farther downwind, the belching, newly active industrial sinews of the city.

She was lonely and miserable and so she plunged into her new job. One of her first assignments was to write a pamphlet about the Wildcat fighter plane GM was building for the Navy. To her surprise, the more she learned, the more she wanted to know. She was shocked to find that American planes were vastly inferior to the enemy's, particularly the Japanese Zero and the German Messerschmitt; and she was amazed, almost horrified, when she began to understand how feverishly American industry was working to design and build better, faster, deadlier warplanes. So many companies were involved—GM, Grumman, Northrop, Lockheed, North American, Boeing, Bell—and of course dozens of other companies were cranking out bullets, jeeps, tanks, cannons, land mines, rockets, machine guns, battleships, aircraft carriers, submarines and bombs, always more bombs, you couldn't have too many bombs. She met a man who was writing a book called *Bullets by the Billion*, about a Chrysler munitions plant. She was beginning to comprehend the true power of America and the true madness of this war.

Her first interview for the Wildcat pamphlet was with the head of all the design teams working on GM's defense contracts, a man so important she had trouble finding him. His office was tucked away at the end of a corridor behind an unmarked door in a drab warehouse in Wyandotte. From his imposing title and rich voice on the telephone, she'd expected someone big and solid, probably in uniform. What she found behind that unmarked door was a man barely five feet tall with a flattop haircut, suspenders and a bow tie. His mustache looked like a frayed whisk broom.

"Harvey Pearl?" she said, shaking his hand.

"No, actually I'm Clark Gable. This is a disguise."

She liked him instantly. Here he was in charge of hundreds of designers and millions of dollars' worth of deadly machinery—and still able to joke about the fact that he looked like Caspar Milquetoast. She'd known more than a few artists in New York who could've used a dash of his humility.

Harvey led her through a sparsely furnished office to his studio, a large, white, sky-lit room not unlike the studio of every struggling artist in New York. But these walls were covered with meticulous sketches and blueprints of an airplane, a curious, cigar-shaped airplane with two propellers in the nose and a cockpit so far forward it looked like it was about to tip over. In New York studios she could always hear the honking of taxis and the hissing of radiators and the dripping of leaky faucets; here she could almost hear the roar of powerful engines and the rattle of machine guns.

"So," she said, "this is the mighty Wildcat?"

"No. The Wildcat's history as far as we're concerned. It's already in production at our plant in Linden, New Jersey. These pictures are the new XP-75 interceptor, the Eagle. I hate it. It's a mongrel."

"Sure doesn't look very menacing."

"I agree. I wouldn't want to go up against a Jap Zero in one, either. But at least it's better than what we've got now, and soon enough there'll be plenty of them." He rummaged in a box under his drawing table and dug out a photograph of a single-seat, twin-engine plane with twin tail booms. It was dazzling silver, and the engines and nose cones sharpened into points. The plane didn't rest on its tail like the Eagle, so even on the ground it seemed to float, light and springy, eager to fly.

"Now this," Harvey said softly, "is a true work of art. The Lockheed Lightning, the P-38, an absolute masterpiece of design."

"It's . . . pretty."

"She's *beautiful.* Compared to her, these other things we're cranking out are dogs." He gazed at the picture as though it were of a lovely woman. He whispered, *"Der Gabelschwanz Teufel."*

"Der what?"

"Der Gabelschwanz Teufel—the Fork-Tailed Devil. If you happened to work for the German Luftwaffe these days, that's what you'd call her. I suspect she's going to do even better in the Pacific." He snapped his fingers. "I've got an idea! They're training to fly the P-38 up at Selfridge, not far from here. We could drive up tomorrow and see the plane in action and you could interview a GM employee who's training to be a pilot. Trust me, it'll make a much better story than the Wildcat."

*T*hey left early the next morning in Harvey's yellow-and-green 1927 Cadillac La Salle, one of his trademarks, the first car he designed after Lawrence Fisher fetched him to Detroit from Los Angeles. Though he considered it a slab-sided, stiff-shouldered, top-heavy crock even by wartime standards, he had a deep love for this car. It was his first crude attempt—*the* first crude attempt—to make an American car look longer and lower than its contemporaries. It was the car that led to one of GM's most lucrative innovations, what some called "the annual model change" and others called "planned obsolescence." Harvey didn't much care what people called it. It had made the engineers subservient to the stylists, it had become an American institution, and it had made him a very rich and powerful man.

Milmary Cavanagh loved the car for different reasons. She loved the purr of the big V-8 engine and the way people looked at them when they drove past; she loved the plush leather seats. They smelled like money. For the first time she was relieved that her days as a starving artist were over.

Instead of taking Gratiot, the most direct route, Harvey agreed to take Jefferson out of downtown because Milmary wanted to see water. The morning was already hot, the sky silver with the humidity that had clung to the city for weeks, and she was happy simply to be moving, getting away. Anyplace was better than Detroit in August.

They traveled past the sugar-white Belle Isle Bridge, over the shattered pavements near the Chrysler plant, quickly through the blossoming slums of the East Side and then, as though someone had waved a wand, they entered Grosse Pointe. Suddenly the houses were far apart and the lawns were broad and smooth and shaded by towering hardwood trees. When they reached Lake Shore Drive, Milmary gazed at Lake St. Clair off to her right. The water was the color of green glass, smooth and lifeless, and there wasn't a sailboat in sight. Freighters crawled along the horizon, their bellies swollen with coal and iron ore to feed the blast furnaces and coke ovens and assembly lines. Off to her left the houses looked like fortresses, their lawns unfurling right down to the road. It occurred to her that this could have been Newport, Rhode Island, except that here there was no saltwater and you could hear the humming dynamos, smell the axle grease, taste the ash in the air.

When they approached the stone palace where her parents now lived, she kept gazing at the lake. Soon the road curved through some dreary second-rate suburbs and they were in the land of roadhouses and bait shacks and shabby marinas. The air was cooler out here. Milmary sank back in the seat and looked over at Harvey. He could barely see over the dashboard, and he had to stretch to turn on the radio. A newscaster was saying, "And the War Relocation Authority announced yesterday that it has opened a tenth relocation center, bringing to more than one hundred thousand the number of Japanese-Americans now housed in the centers. Separation of loyal and disloyal evacuees is scheduled to begin sometime next week. In other war news—"

Harvey snapped off the radio. "The whole goddamn world's gone mad! And we're just as guilty as the Germans and the Japanese!"

Milmary was startled. "What on earth are you talking about?"

"The internment camps. We talk about fascists and Nazis—and then we throw thousands of innocent people into concentration camps!"

She didn't know what to say. She hadn't given it much thought. She turned and watched the willow trees whipping past. Neither of them said a word the rest of the way.

Selfridge Field was a platter of dirt fringed with scruffy pine trees and dotted with Quonset huts, barracks, hangars, a single forlorn wind sock. Harvey parked in the shade near the radio shack and lowered the top. To Milmary, everything looked dry and dusty. Even the P-38s, so sleek and dazzling in the photograph, looked drab as they rolled out of the hangars. The only bright touches on the planes had been provided by the pilots who, like most men, especially men about to go off to war, had developed a fondness bordering on physical love for their instruments of death, and so had painted various terms of endearment near the machine guns in the nose cones—things like "Miss Virginia" and "Stinky 2" and "L'il." As the last plane thundered past, lifted into the sky and banked over the trees by the lake, Milmary noticed there was nothing painted on its nose cone.

"That's our boy," Harvey said, watching the plane's graceful ascent. Soon they could hear the crackle of machine guns. "Those are half-inch Colt-Brownings. The plane's so beautiful I sometimes forget how deadly she is."

By the time the first plane reappeared, a breeze had sprung up and the wind sock was horizontal. Sand skittered across the airstrip. Harvey put a pair of binoculars to his eyes and studied the planes as they approached. Milmary thought they looked awkward as they touched down, twisting and bouncing, a sharp change from their effortless departures.

"That breeze is fooling them," Harvey said. He focused the binoculars on the final plane as it came in over the trees. "Easy, boy, easy. Keep your nose up. I said *up*, dammit—*keep the nose up!*"

The plane hit the ground hard, bounced once, then slammed down with such force the landing gear under the nose cone buckled. Both propellers snapped off, spraying metal, and the plane went into a nose-first skid. Sparks showered the cockpit. When the plane came to rest just short of the fence, a fire truck sprang from one of the Quonset huts and raced down the airstrip. The plane started to burn. The cockpit popped open and the pilot hopped out, slid down the wing and hit the ground running. When the fuel tank exploded he was knocked down, but he got right up and kept running.

Harvey stood on the Cadillac's front seat and snapped three pictures. Then he joined the pilots and mechanics hurrying out to meet the pilot. Milmary was paralyzed. The fire truck was already pouring water on the crippled plane by the time the men reached the pilot. They crowded around him, and Milmary could hear whoops and laughter.

Harvey guided the pilot over toward the Cadillac. Even in his lumpy flight suit Milmary could tell by his thick wrists and broad shoulders that he was solidly built, an athlete. Standing next to

Harvey, he looked like a giant. He was holding a kerchief to his nose, and Milmary saw he was bleeding badly. When he peeled off his helmet and goggles, she gasped.

"Milmary Cavanagh," Harvey was saying, "I'd like you to meet—"

"Ted Mackey!"

Both men stared at her. Finally the pilot, still stunned and bleeding, said, "Milmary? Billy Cavanagh's sister?"

"You two know each other?" Harvey sounded miserable.

"We certainly do," Milmary said. "We met years ago in Ann Arbor Hospital. My idiot kid brother wound up there after spitting beer in this gentleman's face and calling him a quitter for leaving the Wolverine football team."

"I can't believe you already know each other," Harvey croaked.

"Well, Ted," she said, "I see now that your football career's over you've taken up a nice safe line of work."

He smiled. He had perfect teeth to go with the oft-broken nose. "Oh, that," he said, glancing at the smoldering airplane. "I've still got a lot to learn. We all do."

"Milmary," Harvey said, "Ted has to report to his commanding officer. Maybe we could come back tomorrow for that interview."

"Or maybe Ted comes to Detroit from time to time."

"Every chance I get. We're free on weekends."

"Wonderful. I'll buy you dinner Saturday night at the Detroit Club. Upstairs dining room at eight o'clock."

Harvey drove along the fence, parked near the charred P-38 and shut off the engine. The plane looked like it was trying to bury its nose in the dirt, a great crippled insect, and Harvey let out a whistle. "He's a lucky man." He turned to Milmary. "In more ways than one."

"That almost sounds like a compliment."

"It is. I can honestly say I've never seen a woman go after

something the way you just did. Very impressive. I think the two of you would make a very handsome couple." He shifted in his seat and cleared his throat. "You've probably been wondering about my little outburst on the way out here—about the internment camps."

That wasn't what she was wondering about at all, but she could see that he needed to explain. "Yes . . ."

He took a monogrammed handkerchief out of his pocket and patted the sweat from his forehead and upper lip. He stared straight ahead at the P-38. "Ever since I was old enough to dream of faraway places, I've dreamed of going to Japan."

"Why Japan?"

"It's pretty simple, really. When I was eight years old my family moved from an apartment in Hollywood to a big brick house in Pasadena. My father ran a custom carriage business, and thanks to the motion picture industry, times were good. My parents hired a Japanese girl as a live-in domestic, which was the thing to do in Pasadena in those days. Her name was Taka Matsuda. She started a garden in the back yard, and the house was always full of fresh-cut flowers. She had a kid brother who was my age almost to the day—Ichiro Matsuda—and I became a sort of surrogate kid brother to her. She wore silk kimonos and hung scrolls of haiku on the walls of her room at the back of the house. Pretty soon I started getting in trouble at school for drawing in the margins of my textbooks—airplanes, automobiles, ships, locomotives, anything that moved. For my tenth birthday, I'll never forget it, Taka gave me a calligraphy set. She loved my drawings and told me to ignore my teachers. She was the first person to tell me I had a gift. She said, 'In my country one is not scolded for drawing. Artist is revered man.' After I looked up *revered* in the dictionary, I knew I had to go to Japan."

"Have you ever been?" The urgency in Harvey's voice had made her forget about Ted Mackey.

"Never got the chance. I finished high school early, then graduated from Stanford in three years and moved back home and went to work for my father. He put me in charge of custom rebuilding, and soon I was making cars for people like Fatty Arbuckle and Charlie Chaplin. But I was miserable."

"How come?"

"Because at college I grew six inches and suddenly Taka wasn't a big sister to me anymore. When we stayed up late talking, I got very uncomfortable. I couldn't take my eyes off her mouth. It made me think of a flower, a carnation, or a bright red rose, and it always seemed poised for a kiss."

"Did you kiss her?"

"Once."

"And?"

"Nothing—except that she was terribly upset. So was I. About a week later Lawrence Fisher—you know, the Fisher Body Company here in Detroit—visited our shop. He said Alfred Sloan wanted to change General Motors designs every year, and he offered me the job of head stylist. I jumped at it—anything to get away from Taka. This car we're sitting in was my very first assignment."

"What happened to Taka after that?"

"I saw her once or twice a year when I went home for holidays or vacations. After Pearl Harbor my father pulled some strings and got her safe passage back to Japan, just before the government started rounding up everyone of Japanese descent and herding them into camps. I haven't heard from her since."

Then Harvey lowered his head and softly, almost happily, began to cry.

*W*hen the waiter brought snifters of cognac to their booth in the corner of the Detroit Club's upstairs dining room, Milmary Cavanagh popped the question she'd been dying to ask all night: "So tell me, Ted, why didn't you have anything painted on the nose of your plane?"

"Simple. All the other pilots are married or have a steady girl—except me. I considered putting my own name up there, but I was afraid the other guys might get the wrong idea."

Again she laughed. She had laughed so much during dinner that her ribs ached. The evening had been just what she'd hoped for—one of those times when the rest of the world melts away, when war and work disappear, when everything seems to happen in the glow of the candle at the center of the table and everything feels right and there's no place on earth you would rather be. She knew it was going to be that kind of evening when Ted Mackey entered the dining room ten minutes late wearing a white dress uniform, his white hat tucked under his arm. He had a garish purple shiner, but his bearing was ramrod straight. Every head in the room turned as the young officer strode to the corner booth. What a difference, Milmary thought, from the slobs I wound up with in New York.

For the next three hours the waiter filled the table with raw oysters, chowder, London broil, fresh asparagus, and bottle after bottle of French burgundy. It didn't take either of them long to forget there was a war going on, or that he'd soon be fighting in it. And after the first bottle of wine it didn't take much prodding for him to recount his adventures since that day they met in Billy Cavanagh's hospital room. Mostly Ted talked about finishing college and going right to work for General Motors, the years of riding trains and buses up and down the East Coast to sales meetings, dealerships, conventions. His engineering degree was quickly forgotten when it became apparent he was a born salesman. He traveled thousands of miles a year and slept in more fleabag hotels than he cared to remember. But he knew, even then, that he was on his way.

He also told Milmary about his boyhood on the wrong side

of the tracks in Detroit's Corktown—the fights, the streets, the day he played hooky and snuck into Briggs Stadium to watch Ty Cobb play his last game. "All of us in the neighborhood worshiped Ty Cobb," he said.

"Daddy said he was a redneck and a cheat. Why on earth would you worship a man like that?"

"I guess because even though he was a Southerner he was pure Detroit, just like us. He used to sharpen his spikes like razors, and he thought nothing of gouging opponents when he slid into a base. If the other guy wanted to fight, well, Ty was always ready for a fight. He even had the grounds crew soak the grass in front of home plate before every home game—we called it Cobb's Lake—so his bunts would die in the grass and infielders would slip trying to field them. That's what I liked about him, even when I was a kid. He knew where the margins were, and he wasn't ashamed of playing them."

Ted looked up and seemed surprised to see that the dining room was empty and their waiter was standing by the door, yawning, checking his watch. "Guess we'd better be going."

"I wish we could stay forever." Milmary put her hand on his.

"I've been doing all the talking. You've hardly told me anything about what New York was like."

"Ah, next time."

*F*or the rest of that brutally hot summer Ted Mackey spent his weekdays at Selfridge Field mastering the P-38 and his weekends in Detroit pursuing Milmary Cavanagh. After his crash he seemed to lose all fear and was soon the hottest jock in the 1st Pursuit Group, somehow able to coax the plane into the steepest dives and hold on just a little longer than the other pilots before pulling out and soaring back up to cruising altitude. It was this daring maneuver, which he executed to perfection, that would help write the legend of the P-38 in the Pacific.

Though his aim with the 20-millimeter Hispano cannon in the nose cone was erratic, he once nailed a running dog at three hundred yards with the half-inch Colt-Browning machine guns.

Mastering the P-38 was a snap; it was the pursuit of Milmary Cavanagh that was driving him to distraction.

He took her on boat rides at Belle Isle, to Tigers games, to movies, to dinner, even to the symphony once. But at the end of every evening she gave him a handshake, maybe a peck on the cheek, then she hopped into her big black Plymouth and roared away. Never before had a woman denied him like this, and never had he kept coming back for so much disappointment.

One night in early September when the city felt like a blast furnace, he took her to the "climate controlled" Fox Theater to see Eddie Albert and Robert Stack in *Eagle Squadron*. It was about a bunch of Americans who join the RAF to help fight the Nazi scourge, and though it had some excellent aerial combat scenes, Ted's mind kept wandering. He had received big news that afternoon, and he was trying to decide how to break it to Milmary. After the show, out under the glaring bulbs of the marquee, he said, "Milmary, there's something—"

"Save it. Tell me after I've made you the best martini you'll ever drink."

It was the first time he'd set foot in her apartment. While she fixed the drinks in the kitchen, he sat on the sofa and gazed across the river at the Penobscot Building and the lesser stalagmites of downtown Detroit. Ships loaded with raw materials or finished weapons slid back and forth on the black water. He still had no idea how he was going to begin.

"Voilà!" She set a silver tray with a shaker and a bowl of green olives and two brimming glasses on the coffee table. "Here's to my idiot brother Billy. He may not have taught me much, but he did teach me how to make the world's best martini."

They clinked glasses and drank. The gin burned Ted's throat

pleasantly. She turned off all the lights and sat beside him and rested her head on his shoulder. They sipped their drinks in silence and watched the lights of downtown and the Ambassador Bridge and the passing ships wobbling on the water. When his glass was empty, he cleared his throat. "Milmary, there's—"

"Wait! You haven't eaten your olive yet. It's the best part."

She popped the olive into his mouth. When he bit into it there was an explosion, a delicious blaze on his tongue.

"I soaked them in gin. Just for you."

How long had she soaked them? Days? Weeks? Ever since the day he crashed his plane? As his tongue burned with the taste of pimento, olive, salt and gin, he understood that she was in control of everything, that she'd thought everything through, planned ahead, soaked the olives, encouraged his desire without ever satisfying it because she understood, as he was only dimly beginning to understand, that her power came from being desired. He saw that the only way for her to avoid feeling abandoned when he went off to war, the only way to make sure he would come back was to make herself the unattainable object of his desire.

She placed fresh olives in the glasses and filled them to the brim. Then she stood up and held out her hand. "Come with me."

To his surprise, he felt himself being lifted off the sofa and led down a dark hallway. Suddenly he was standing beside a large white sugar cube of a bed; it actually glowed in the reflected river lights. His lust of past weeks was gone. The main thing he felt was confusion, a riot inside his skull. She took his glass and set it beside hers on the night table; then she pulled him down onto her. The only thing she said was "Please be gentle."

He felt like he'd been pushed off a cliff and was falling into the softest velvety blackness imaginable, a fall he hoped would last forever. They made hour after hour of vicious bloody love, pausing only to catch their breath, to sip icy gin and munch salty olives.

Once, as he fumbled for cigarettes on the night table, she said, "Do you always smoke after sex?"

"I don't know. I never looked."

It took her a moment to catch the joke, and when she did she laughed as she'd never laughed before, deep, racking, ragged laughter. A whole new humming bundle of nerves had been awakened inside her, and lying there, still sticky and fragrant, she realized she had crossed a threshold. She was a woman now. She had surrendered something precious, something a great many men had tried to take from her, something she had been saving all her life. Now it was gone forever. And now she would be repaid.

When he stubbed his cigarette in the ashtray, she ran her fingers through his dark, sweaty hair. He sounded very far away when he said, "So this is your first time."

"Yes."

"And you like it."

"I like it very much." She was astonished how much she liked it. Her girlfriends had led her to believe the first time was usually painful and always disappointing.

"Our orders came today," he said.

"Your what?"

"Our orders. We ship out for New Guinea tomorrow. I tried to tell you earlier. . . ."

After a long silence she said, "It's funny, but somehow I knew."

"It's funny, but somehow I believe you."

"Make me a promise."

"Anything."

"Promise me you won't get your gorgeous self killed—and that you'll come back for me."

He promised. And then, since there wasn't much else to say, they made love one last time. Finally, limp and exhausted, she drifted off to sleep.

He went into the kitchen and put two ice cubes in a tall glass and filled it with scotch. He sat by the window in the living room to wait for dawn. Ships were still sliding back and forth, and the factories downriver were still pouring yellow smoke into the sky. It never stopped. For months he had impatiently awaited the moment when he would go off to war, and now that it was here he didn't want to go. Now, suddenly, he had something to lose. He sat there naked, smoking one cigarette after another, sipping scotch until a gray light came on at dawn. *Promise me you won't get your gorgeous self killed—and that you'll come back for me.* He put on his uniform and kissed her on the forehead without waking her. Then he went back to Selfridge Field to pack.

*M*ilmary awoke late that morning, bloody, sore, alone and terrified—that she was pregnant, that he would never come back, that she would be disowned by her family, abandoned, disgraced.

But exactly three weeks later her period arrived right on schedule along with the first of many letters from Ted Mackey. "My darling Mil," the letter began. "We had our first contact with Japanese Zeros this morning. . . ." She'd been so scared and so lonely she'd forgotten the danger he was in. The letter woke her up; it also introduced her to a whole new world of worry.

She received that first letter two weeks after it was written. At the very moment she was reading it, a young Japanese pilot, Flight Petty Officer Toshiki Ishihara, was striding onto the flight deck of the aircraft carrier *Ryujo*, which was anchored halfway around the world just north of the Admiralty Islands, virtually on the equator. The morning was dazzling and hot, and Toshiki

Ishihara could not have been happier. This was the day he had been waiting for all his life. This was the day he would fly his very first combat mission in a Zero-sen, a brand new Mitsubishi A6M2 Model 21 fighter, the pride of the Japanese Navy.

Toshiki Ishihara felt a flutter in his stomach as he strapped himself into the cockpit. He was glad he had taken an extra sake, the prerogative of raw pilots going into combat for the first time, because the talk of some of the seasoned pilots that morning had unsettled him. They all spoke of how the American pilots seemed to be getting better, how their new planes dove more steeply and fired more ammunition more accurately, how there seemed to be more and more of them. All of this was said casually, mixed in with the usual chatter about baseball and the weather and girls, but Toshiki Ishihara had taken a second sake anyway. He hoped the other pilots hadn't noticed that his hands were trembling.

His was to be the seventh plane to leave the flight deck that morning, which meant he would probably be among the last to encounter enemy fire when they reached the target, a new airstrip on the northern shore of New Guinea. When the mechanic flipped the propeller and the engine coughed to life, all of Toshiki Ishihara's worries vanished. It was, if nothing else, a beautiful day to die.

The squadron of Zeros never made it to their target that day. As they crossed over Rooke Island, the cockpit glass shattered above Toshiki Ishihara's head and a hole appeared simultaneously in the plane's floor between his feet. He looked up and saw dozens of black dots falling toward him, then he heard his flight commander's voice in his headset ordering all pilots to take evasive action.

He banked hard to the right and saw a spray of silver bullets sail past, just missing his propeller. As soon as he came out of the turn he was amazed to see a twin-engine, double-tailed American plane passing directly in front of him. It was the most beautiful plane he had ever seen. He fired both machine guns and watched, in dismay, as the bullets sailed high. It should have been an easy hit.

When he yanked his stick to get up above the American plane, his engine sputtered and nearly died. He was losing oil pressure and he could smell smoke. He radioed to his flight commander that he was on fire and was heading back to the *Ryujo*, but his flight commander did not respond.

As he banked he saw that his fellow pilots were engaging the Americans in dogfights, the nimble Zero-sen's strength. But he could count only three of them. Where were the others?

His oil pressure had stabilized, but he was almost out of fuel. Bullets must have punctured his fuel tank. He calculated he would not be able to make it all the way back to the carrier, which meant he would have to land on one of several islands designated as emergency landing fields, then wait for help. One of these, Hermit Island, was not far away, off to the right.

To Toshiki Ishihara's horror, just as he was making his approach to the broad white beach, one of the silver American planes swooped down on him from behind. The air sang with bullets. He tried to climb but didn't have enough speed. He lost control as soon as his wheels touched the beach; the Zero skidded through some brush and palm trees, flipped, and landed upside down in a large turquoise pond. Toshiki Ishihara's neck was snapped by the impact. He died instantly.

Ted Mackey, the pilot of the P-38, made a wide loop and watched the plane settle belly-up in the pond. One of the landing gear had been sheared off, and the other two were sticking up in the air. The wheels were still spinning.

Ted hurried back to the airstrip. When he returned with a helicopter crew, they discovered that the Zero was intact except for the bullet holes in the fuel tank, the shattered cockpit glass and the missing landing gear. Without realizing it, Ted had bagged one of the great early trophies of the war in the Pacific.

Ever since Pearl Harbor, the Zero had been acquiring an aura of invincibility in the minds of the Americans. Wickedly agile and well armed, they could cover vast stretches on a single load of fuel, there seemed to be no end to the supply of them, and their pilots had no fear. Until that day, any captured fragment of a Zero had been considered a prize as American intelligence teams struggled to unlock the secrets of this mythical fighter.

Now, suddenly, they had one that was virtually fresh from the factory. It was shipped back to California and exhaustively dissected. The Americans were astonished to learn that the Zero was in some ways quite primitive. It lacked a self-starter, so someone had to flip the propeller to fire the engine. While Americans were learning to thicken the armor around their pilots— P-38s were regularly returning from missions with dozens of bullet holes in them—the Zero proved to be thin-skinned, surprisingly vulnerable. It even lacked a self-sealing fuel tank, which made it easy to ignite. Intercepted radio transmissions soon taught the Americans that the Japanese pilots had started calling the planes "Zero lighters."

Ted Mackey was the sudden hero of the 1st Pursuit Group, but he didn't get to bask in his glory for long. Two months later, on the day he downed his third Zero, his left engine overheated and caught fire. He limped along with one engine, escorted by Major Richard Bong, who was well on his way to racking up forty kills and who on this day saved Ted's life by chasing away two Zeros that descended, like vultures, on the crippled P-38 with "Mil" painted in bright red letters on its nose cone. By the time Ted made it to the airstrip, the heat inside the cockpit was so fierce he could barely hold the control wheel. He came in too fast and the right landing gear snapped, sending the plane into a corkscrewing skid—a maneuver, he joked later, that he'd perfected at Selfridge Field. He was pulled from the plane unconscious, his left kneecap shattered, his left foot badly burned. After flying fifty-two combat missions, downing three enemy planes and being awarded the Distinguished Service Cross and the Purple Heart, Lieutenant Ted Mackey was on his way home to Detroit.

*T*ed Mackey and Milmary Cavanagh were married in Blessed Sacrament Cathedral in Detroit on New Year's Day 1943.

The cavernous church had never been so visibly split in two. On one side of the aisle were Ted's people, the shanty Irish, his gimp-legged father, his stout, doughy mother, his siblings and in-laws and their litters, a badly done-up gang of wage slaves, union men, wife beaters, boozers and juvenile delinquents. On the other side were Milmary's people, the lace Irish fresh from the salons of Grosse Pointe, blue-haired dowagers, tycoons, debutantes, politicos, a well-tailored, heavily perfumed, lavishly coiffed and brutally barbered bunch.

William Cavanagh, his white hair bristling like quills, had made no secret of his displeasure with his daughter's choice of a mate. "He just won't do," he kept telling her, and even made mention of his will. But Milmary was not about to be bullied, and once it became apparent he couldn't hope to win this fight, William Cavanagh, a born politician and the newly announced Democratic candidate for governor of Michigan, donned tails and white gloves and paraded his daughter down the aisle of the cathedral. He wasn't about to pass up a chance to get his picture on the society pages.

Though he didn't dare admit it to his daughter, William Cavanagh was secretly afraid Ted Mackey was after his money. But his fears were groundless. Ted wanted to make his own money and, even more, to acquire his own power—not the abstract, ward-heeler variety but the kind that existed at General Motors, power you could touch and feel and smell, the power to make millions of shiny new cars and be boss to thousands of people and run your own fiefdom in the world's largest industrial empire, maybe run the whole show someday.

Though no one in the Cavanagh clan would have believed it, Ted was marrying Milmary because he loved her, because she lit an erotic furnace in him he didn't even know existed, because she was beautiful and brainy and had sent an avalanche of long steamy literate life-saving love letters across the Pacific to him when he was stuck out there on the parched rim of New Guinea, bored one minute, terrified the next and, as one of his fellow pilots so poetically put it, "hornier than a nine-dicked billy goat."

In the end, none of her family's objections mattered. Milmary was going to do what she was going to do, just as she had done all her life. She didn't want to go on a honeymoon because she loved her new job working directly for Harvey Pearl and didn't want to miss a day of work. Ted didn't object because he'd been put in charge of procurement for GM's lucrative new defense contracts. The newlyweds moved into a modest frame house in Birmingham, a northern suburb far from the machinations of Grosse Pointe.

When William Cavanagh died in his sleep a year later, it turned out he left Milmary a bundle of GM stock and dozens of apartment buildings in slums all over Detroit. The buildings weren't much, but they were commanding handsome rents because more than a quarter of a million people had swarmed to Detroit since 1941 looking for work in the defense plants. This sudden windfall freed Ted to take jobs that might pay a little less but would hasten his climb to corporate headquarters; and it allowed Milmary to quit her job on New Year's Day 1945, their second anniversary, the day she learned she was going to have a baby.

And now, nine years later, sitting at the kitchen table in the big white house on Mirror Lake, the mother of two boys, the wife of a man who had made good and was determined to make even better—now, suddenly, Milmary Mackey found herself wondering what to do about a snapshot that was like a taunt, a nasty reminder that she'd given up her dream of being a writer too easily and had settled for too little in life. The shivering sensation was gone.

She put the picture of the sprinting pilot and the burning plane back in the box. She watched the children skating on the lake. She was terrified, so terrified her hands were actually trembling. The most terrifying thing of all was what she would have to do to make the trembling stop.

Thirteen

Claire Hathaway awoke at seven o'clock the next morning with a jackhammer jabbering inside her skull. The pain was a hot, angry throb behind her eyes, and her mouth tasted like a squirrel had crawled into it in the middle of the night and died.

She didn't dare move. She opened her eyes and saw the picture of the 1954 Buick on the wall at the foot of her bed. It had a creamy yellow body and a white top and a flaming red interior. It was the first '54 Buick to roll off the Flint assembly line, and she had to admit it was a stunning departure from the stodginess of cars from the '40s and early '50s, a car that announced the war was now ancient history, so let the good times roll. The car was sleek and low-slung—two of Harvey Pearl's prime objectives—and it looked like it was in motion even when parked. Yes, that was what made Claire proud of the '54 Buick Century: It looked like it was always in motion.

The '57s were going to be a different story. John Nickles wanted the tail light sketches finished in time for a design review first thing this morning. As quitting time passed Monday evening, she wasn't about to tell him, "Sorry, gotta run. Got a dinner date with Ted Mackey." So she hadn't left the Tech Center until well after eight o'clock, and racing downtown she tried to imagine what the division g.m. could possibly want from her. If she was in trouble, he wouldn't have invited her to dinner; if it was strictly business, he wouldn't have promised it was strictly business; if it was something unsavory, he wouldn't have arranged to meet at a bustling, snooty place like the Detroit Club.

By the time she pulled up in front of the brownstone fortress she was so nervous she sat in the car with the engine idling and debated whether to get out or drive straight home. But a Negro doorman in a green cap and long green overcoat whipped the car door open. "Good evening, miss," he said with a smile. "You can leave it running. We'll take care of it for you."

Inside, it was even worse. Beveled mirrors fractured the light, and every time she rounded a corner she was confronted with herself. Her hair looked awful. After trying to do something with it in the ladies' room, she paused outside the library and watched the old men in high-backed red leather chairs smoking cigars and reading newspapers on bamboo sticks. They were all studying the stock quotations. Every last one of them looked like he had so much money he would never have to worry about money. But wasn't that one of the first things Detroit had taught her—that there's no such thing as having too much money, and the more you have the more you want, and the more you want the more you worry?

The maitre d' in the upstairs dining room smiled and bowed as though he'd been awaiting this moment and now his evening was complete. She could feel every eye in the room on her as she followed him to the far corner.

Ted Mackey was sitting in the corner booth with a single candle burning and the *Wall Street Journal* open to the stock quotations. He stubbed out his cigarette and stood up; he, too, seemed delighted by her late arrival. She was so uneasy she ordered an Old-Fashioned from the maitre d' before she sat down. Ted didn't seem to object. In fact, by the time she finished her second drink and began to relax, she realized he'd been drinking two to her one.

He ordered an expensive bottle of French burgundy with dinner and drank most of it as he told her about growing up poor in Detroit. As he talked she remembered one of the truths about men her mother had passed on to her: they are their own favorite topics of conversation. So whenever he started to stray, Claire steered him back to his autobiography. She soon found herself mesmerized by his voice, as smooth and soothing as the wine they were drinking. He obviously loved telling this story, and he sprinkled it with details that came back to her now: the night he fought Amos Fuller's father for the city Golden Gloves title and was so scared he vomited on his own father's back on the way out to the ring; the legendary arm of Chick Hewitt, who could throw a rock and make a seagull explode in midair; the favorite neighborhood pastime of lobbing bricks over the fence of the Cadillac plant on Michigan Avenue until a windshield shattered and the guards gave chase; the night he saw a bloated Negro corpse wash up on the beach at Belle Isle.

As his story unfolded, Claire realized that nothing in her childhood could match the glamour and struggle and sheer action of his. What could she come back with? The way a girl's reputation in Ames, Iowa, was ruined if her date stopped for gas at the Hudson station because everyone knew there was a condom machine in the men's room? Or a description of a typical night drinking Cokes and eating pork tenderloin sandwiches at the Rainbow Cafe? Or maybe the way teenagers cruised the Dairy Dreme and the Ranch Drive-In? Nothing in Ames ever exploded, shattered, or washed ashore.

Claire sat up in bed now, and bolts of pain shot through her head. She couldn't possibly make it to work—but she couldn't call in sick because she had to run the review of the '57 tail light sketches. She got out of bed, shuffled into the bathroom and turned on the shower. She swallowed four aspirins that almost came right back up, but two tall glasses of water kept them down. Standing very still under the stream of hot water, she remembered Ted asking if she thought the stylists she'd worked with on the '54 Century were loyal to the company. What a strange question. He sounded like Joe McCarthy. What did *loyalty* have to do with designing cars? He had leaned forward as he asked the question, his face close to hers, warm and orange in the candlelight, the wiry eyebrows dancing. Those eyes were full of mischief, and they reminded her of another thing her mother had tried to teach her about men: Don't trust them.

Claire had always ignored this piece of motherly advice because its origin was so obvious. What woman whose husband had gone to the corner for a pack of cigarettes and never come back *wouldn't* warn her daughter to beware of the devils? Hadn't her mother's entire life since that day been devoted to proving that men aren't even necessary? She'd gone back to work teaching freshman English at Iowa State to support herself and her children, and she'd snubbed every suitor who stepped up onto their broad front porch. Yet how could the woman expect her daughter, especially a bright, headstrong girl like Claire, to grow up in a small Iowa town where every girl had a father and every father was kind and affable (even if he didn't seem to be home all that much) and not have that daughter begin to suspect that men could be trusted and that they might even be something to be desired?

Instead of going to cheerleading practice with the other girls, Claire took to hanging around the garage of their next-door neighbor, an eccentric sports-car buff named Don Chadwick, who worked at the Synchrotron, a clump of gray buildings on the edge of town where men in white coats smashed atoms for a living. She helped him take a British MG-TC apart bolt by bolt and put it back together, and as payment he taught her how to drive—on a stick shift with the steering wheel on the right side, no less. Nothing in her life to that point had come close to the sensation of sailing down a country road in that green MG with the top down and Mr. Chadwick at her side in his snap-brim cap, the cornfields whipping past and the road unfurling ahead of them forever. She was so thrilled when she'd pulled off on the shoulder of the road to turn around that she even let Mr. Chadwick kiss her on the lips.

Soon she was designing her own cars, and while other girls were dreaming of some boy's ID bracelet or the Welsh Box Social or which Easter dress to buy at Younkers, she was rebuilding a 1939 Buick she'd bought from a chicken farmer for twenty-five dollars.

No boy had the nerve to ask her out. She felt the same scorn for high school boys she'd always felt for high school girls, and she didn't try to hide it. The only things boys seemed to worry about were sports and cars, which wasn't much better than shopping and hair. To escape she started devouring the fat novels her mother assigned—*Crime and Punishment* and *Jane Eyre* and *Madame Bovary*.

During Christmas vacation her senior year she went out with Charlie Craig, a high school classmate of her brother's who'd come home from Cornell for the holidays. They went to the Rainbow Cafe and ordered pork tenderloin sandwiches and talked about *Madame Bovary* for three hours. Claire was elated. Besides her mother, he was the first person she'd met who had even heard of the book. It was her favorite, not because she understood how adultery could cause such a fuss but because she, like Emma, was suffocated by small-town life and felt a powerful need to re-invent herself. While Emma, the daughter of a Normandy peasant, imagined herself a great lover and romantic, Claire, the daughter of an Iowa teacher, imagined fleeing to some faraway college and then getting a job in some faceless city where no one would know her and all things would be possible. This urge became tangible that winter night at the Rainbow Cafe with Charlie Craig, who'd just read *Madame Bovary* for a literature course at Cornell taught by a crazy Russian who collected butterflies in his spare time and wrote obscure novels. Then and there Claire decided she had to meet this man who could make Emma Bovary's plight so compelling to his students. But when she announced she wanted to go to Cornell in the fall, her mother said, "You're being impetuous again. We have a perfectly good college right here in town." That settled it. She would go to Cornell and find this Russian named Vladimir Nabokov.

The shower was beginning to go cold. She shut it off just as the telephone rang. Wrapped in a towel, dripping and shivering, she picked up the receiver in the living room. "Hello?" Even talking was painful.

"Did I wake you up?"

"Mr. Mackey! No, I was just getting out of the shower."

"It's *Ted*, remember? How you feeling?"

"God-awful. I just ate a whole bottle of aspirin. What on earth did we drink last night, battery acid?"

He was chuckling. "I'm in pretty rough shape myself. So tell me, what did you decide about lunch?"

"Lunch?"

"You promised you'd let me buy you lunch this week."

"Oh, right."

"How does Friday sound?"

"Fine, I guess."

"This time you get to do all the talking. And please give some thought to the other thing we discussed."

"What other thing?"

"The people you worked with on the '54, particularly the front end—you know, whether or not you think they can be trusted."

"Oh, that."

"You will give it some thought, won't you?"

"Sure, I'll try."

"Don't try, Claire. *Do* it."

There was a thrilling edge to the command. "Okay," she said, "I'll do it."

Fourteen

*J*ews were not ordinarily welcome at the National Presbyterian Church, but then Morey Caan was not an ordinary Jew. The only things that could get him inside a church or a temple were a wedding, a funeral or a chance to get a glimpse of President Dwight Eisenhower.

Morey arrived that Sunday morning half an hour before the eleven o'clock service. He was carrying a borrowed Bible and wearing a clean necktie, a white shirt, a dark suit. He supposed none of the ushers or Secret Service boys would give a second thought to the very un-Presbyterian black curls that boiled on top of his head or the very un-Presbyterian hook of his nose. He was right. He breezed in and took a seat about ten pews behind the roped-off presidential section.

He was always amazed by how successfully the high Protestants had managed to bleed the color and passion from their churches. He'd once visited a Congregational church in Vermont and thought he was in a hospital operating room. Though he hadn't visited many temples—his parents were much too busy on Saturdays running their pawnshop in Memphis—he did think Jews had the advantage of an ancient, top-heavy tradition; and at least the Catholics went in for some flash and hocus-pocus and the poorer Protestant churches down home, particularly the

Negro churches, rocked with some serious hooting and hollering. But this high Protestant shit! Morey supposed Ike chose this particular church because it was appropriately grand and bland, all sandstone and granite and frosted windows, no marble or stained glass or clouds of incense, no wild singing, no bloody statues like the ones Morey had seen in Mexico. No nothing. Just right for Ike and Mamie.

Morey knew that Ike had not attended church during his entire adult life and that he'd joined a church in Washington only because he felt it was important for the President to set a good example. The denomination didn't matter to Ike. Theology was a subject about which he knew little and cared less. God wasn't what brought him here every Sunday.

Morey pretended to read the Book of Ecclesiastes and tried to remember where Truman had gone to church when he was in office—or if he had gone to church. It was an intriguing question. On the one hand he could imagine Truman believing in God even as he committed one of the most monstrous acts of murder in the history of mankind; on the other hand he could imagine Truman not having much use for man-made religion and, in that case, not bothering to pretend he did. That was one thing Morey liked about Truman. He was the butt of a lot of jokes, but at least he did what he thought was right and never apologized and never looked back. Morey doubted Truman ever lost any sleep over Hiroshima and Nagasaki, and in Morey's mind he would forever be associated with those bombings, just as Eisenhower would forever be associated with the swarming, blood-soaked infantry assault on Normandy. To Morey it was simply a question of the degree of evil because he believed that men with that much power invariably did the evil thing. That was the nature of power, and as far as Morey was concerned the difference between Truman's and Eisenhower's most famous acts was the difference between performing surgery with clean, sharp instruments and performing an amputation with a dull, rusty hacksaw. One involved the risk of half a dozen American lives, the other required the sacrifice of thousands—including Morey's only brother, who died during Operation Tiger, Ike's aborted dry run for D-Day. Richie Caan and more than seven hundred other American soldiers perished in the English Channel when their landing crafts were torpedoed in a surprise attack by German E-boats. Many of the raw recruits, including Richie, drowned because they hadn't been told that their "Mae West" life vests went under their arms instead of around their waists. Ike hadn't bothered to tell them that—or to watch for a surprise attack. Richie Caan was fished out of the English Channel the next morning. He was floating upside down.

Even the stories of Ike as D-Day approached, chain-smoking Chesterfields, munching chocolates, reading pulp westerns and staring for hours at the night sky (the loneliness! the valor!)— none of it washed the blood from his hands. The man had been all too happy to play the role of clumsy butcher. His whole life had pointed toward that moment. And now there was talk that he had deliberately starved a million German POWs to death during the occupation in 1945 . . . a *million* Germans. If Morey could dig that story out, it would be the ultimate justification for his chosen mission in life.

Not that he needed it. On the day in 1952 when the United States had detonated its first hydrogen bomb and a Gallup poll had predicted Eisenhower would win the November election, Morey had made a vow: He would do everything in his power to avenge his brother's death by getting Ike run out of town before his first term expired. Failing that, he would do whatever he could to make Ike's life in Washington so miserable that he and his stupid wife wouldn't be able to get out of town fast enough after his successor's inauguration in 1957. The more Morey thought about it, in fact, the more he liked the second scenario. Make Ike bleed slowly into the plush White House carpets just as Richie Caan and hundreds like him had drowned slowly in the choppy, bloodstained waters of the English Channel.

Suddenly there was a rustling at the back of the church. Morey turned and watched as Ike and Mamie came strolling up the aisle. Even these rock-ribbed Presbyterians turned and gawked. When the Eisenhowers reached the front pew, Mamie paused to acknowledge the people sitting nearby. Morey thought she looked a bit puffy. Of course! This was the only day of the week she rolled out of their king-size bed before the crack of noon.

The service was even more boring than the building and the people in it, and Morey dozed off. When he awoke, everyone was standing and singing a hymn. He decided to slip outside and get in position for the presidential exit.

Out front, the Secret Service boys gave Morey a good raking with their eyes. He pretended to admire the sunny morning and was careful to keep his back to the reporters and photographers roped off on the far side of Ike's limousine. He heard the familiar rustling and turned just as Ike and Mamie came through the doors, down the steps and into the sunshine. They chatted with their fellow Presbyterians, they smiled, they gave the photographers an opportunity to snap a few pictures. Morey eased into the crowd of churchgoers and worked his way up close. It would be so easy to kill him, Morey thought. Then he felt someone pressing him from behind, and when he turned around he was looking into the chest of an Aryan linebacker.

"Morning!" Morey said. The Secret Service man nodded. "Wasn't that a terrific sermon?" He nodded again.

Half a dozen people were talking at once to Ike and Mamie, and they both stood there beaming, nodding, not saying a word. Then Ike held out his arm and said, "Dear, we have to run along now."

Mamie sighed as though this were the worst news she'd heard in a week. Then, to a woman in a mink stole with a blue cloud of cotton-candy hair, she said: "You should tell him what I told him when he asked *me* that question."

"What was that?" the woman said.

"I said, 'Mr. Pearson, I *do* have a job. I have a full-time job —and his name is Ike!' "

Christ, Morey thought, what a way to make a buck. There was a ripple of adoring laughter as Mamie and her full-time job disappeared into the limousine. Walking away from the church, Morey jotted the quote in his notebook. It was rich, certainly usable, though spending two hours with a bunch of Presbyterian Republicans and Secret Service goons seemed like a mighty high price to pay for a single rough-cut gem.

*W*ill Lomax was in his upstairs study reading old newspaper clippings about David Dunbar Buick when the telephone rang. He'd just had the phone installed so he could conduct interviews while sitting at the typewriter. He set the clips down and picked up the phone. "Hello?"

"Just wanted to let you know I did like I promised," Morey Caan said. "Went by the Buick dealership on Wisconsin Avenue after church this morning."

"And?"

"And I gotta admit that Century's pretty wild. I had no idea you guys painted 'em like jelly beans."

"It's a fun car, son, a sports car the whole family can enjoy, a car that—did I hear you say you went to church today?"

"Yes."

"But this is Sunday. Your Sabbath was yesterday."

"I go to National Presbyterian every Sunday to eavesdrop on Ike and Mamie."

"You're sicker than I thought you were."

Morey laughed. "I'm telling you, this book just keeps getting better and better. I couldn't make this shit up if I tried. By the way, how's The Book coming?"

"Not too bad, for a change. I was just reading about how David Dunbar Buick invented a technique for enameling cast-iron bathtubs at the turn of the century that broke a German monopoly."

"Bully for him."

"Actually, it's tough finding time to work on this. Mackey's been running my ass ragged. There's a big convention coming up in New York and he's had me working on his speech for two weeks. Plus he's shitting bricks because he thinks someone's been selling our design work to the competition, so he's got me hiring spies and every other goddamn thing."

"Jeez, sounds just like Washington."

"Don't laugh. The man is totally obsessed with your magazine article. Can I please tell him when you're coming to town?"

"Yeah, that's why I called. I just got the green light from Charles Prentiss."

"So when can you get here?"

"Soon. First I've got to go upstairs and eat dinner with a fat girl."

"You're much sicker than I thought you were."

"She's Ike's appointments secretary."

"Much, *much* sicker."

"She's full of interesting information."

"You've got no shame left."

"None whatsoever. That's the key to my success."

The best Will could do was get Morey to promise he'd try to show up sometime in the next two weeks. Then he went back to reading how David Dunbar Buick made the fortune that enabled him to build his first automobile.

*M*orey was amazed by how much he liked Ann Wilson's beef Stroganoff. She was amazed by how much he could pack away. He actually ate more than she did. It just wasn't fair the way skinny people could eat all they wanted and never gain a pound. She considered saving the German chocolate cake for herself, but she didn't want the evening to end just yet.

"I'm going to clear these dishes and put on some coffee," she said when he finally stopped eating. "You just relax. There's dessert yet!"

Swell, Morey thought—and who scrapes me off the ceiling when I explode? But he wasn't about to object. All through dinner he'd been eyeing Ann's diary. It was on the coffee table in the living room. When he arrived, he'd casually dropped the sports page of the Washington *Evening Star* on it. Now, once he heard water running in the kitchen, he made his move. He slipped the diary inside the sports page and strolled down the hall toward the bathroom.

"Where do you think you're running off to?" Ann called from the kitchen doorway.

"Just need to visit the bathroom."

"What's that you've got?"

"The sports page."

"As much as you ate, you sure you don't want *War and Peace*?"

He could hear her cackling as he locked the bathroom door and turned on the cold water and sat on the toilet seat. He took out the pen and paper he'd brought and opened the diary:

Jan. 12, 1954: Had to remind President about his press conference tonight. How he hates to face the press! What he doesn't like he tries to forget.

Jan. 17, 1954: President told me this morning that when he was president of Columbia University he never went out for a walk without his service revolver. He understands better than anyone I've ever met that in this day and age it's impossible to be overprotected.

Morey skipped to one of the most recent entries. It jumped out at him because of his conversation with Pete Hoover. He copied it verbatim:

Jan. 20, 1954: President allowed me to sit in on a meeting with J. F. Dulles, A. Dulles, Henry Cabot Lodge, Bobby Cutler—all of us with financial stake in United Fruit in Guatemala. JFD reported Operation Success moving along, money now flowing to colonels and generals and convincing them Jacobo Arbenz is a communist.

Ann started banging on the bathroom door. "You didn't fall in, did you?"
"Be right out."
"Dessert is served!"
He kept scribbling:

CIA's Howard Hunt has decided Castillo Armas is the best man to lead the uprising against Arbenz. A. Dulles agreed, though J. F. Dulles raised some objections.

Ann banged harder on the door. With her, apparently, dessert was serious business. Rather than risk having her put her shoulder to the door, Morey flushed the toilet and turned off the faucet. As he stood up, he skimmed the last entry:

President told me to cancel his appointment with Col. Philip Lauben, a member of the German Affairs Branch during the occupation in '45. When I asked him why, he said, "That old ninny. He's still worried about what we called Other

Losses. He seems to forget we had 17 million extra Germans
to feed and that we were under orders to treat 'em rough.''

When Morey emerged from the bathroom he was in a trance.
He hadn't had time to copy that last entry, and he was trying
to commit it to memory: "Col. Philip Lauben . . . Other Losses
. . . 17 million extra Germans to feed. . . ."

Ann was waiting right outside the door. "You see a ghost in
there?"

"No, but I did talk to God." The diary was inside the sports
page, and he clutched it to his chest. "What's the secret ingredient
in your Stroganoff—castor oil?"

"I never reveal my recipes. Come sit down, the best is yet to
come. And give me that newspaper. I swear you men are all
alike—can't get through a meal without thinking about sports."

"That's okay," he said, holding the sports page out of her
reach and backing toward the coffee table. He replaced the diary
safely, but when he sat down to dessert his heart was pounding.
He'd stumbled onto something big, maybe huge. He hadn't felt
his heart race like this since he first heard about the CIA's deal-
ings in Iran.

The cake was delicious, and Morey surprised himself by eating
a whole piece. Ann surprised him by cutting each of them a
second piece. She stunned him by eating all of hers. "Where'd
your appetite go all of a sudden?" she said. She sounded hurt.

"My appetite? You sound like my mother—'Darling, eat your
fruit!' I haven't eaten this much in one sitting since I won a
goldfish-eating contest in college."

She laughed so hard she inhaled a lump of cake. He pounded
her back until tears ran down her cheeks; she made a horrible
sucking sound, and he pounded harder. He wondered what he
would do if she started choking to death. Perform mouth-to-
mouth resuscitation? Call an ambulance? Let her die so he could
steal her diary?

Finally the cake dislodged and she was able to breathe again. She patted the rivers of mascara on her cheeks and croaked, "That's what I get for trying to laugh and eat at the same time."

When he was sure she'd recovered, he got up to leave. There was still two-thirds of a cake to finish, and he supposed that was why he got away without too much of a struggle. She did kiss him goodnight at the door, nibbling his bottom lip, pressing herself against him. When he tried to return her gentle hug, he discovered his arms didn't reach all the way around her torso. As soon as she released him, he skipped downstairs, raring to get on the phone and start digging into the strange doings in Guatemala and the whereabouts of one Philip Lauben, the old ninny who seemed to have forgotten that Ike had seventeen million extra Germans to feed in 1945 and that he was under strict orders to treat 'em rough.

Fifteen

*B*efore she left the Tech Center to meet Ted Mackey for lunch, Claire Hathaway spent half an hour in the ladies' room—not the little closet at the back of the design studio they'd added for the three women stylists, but the plush lounge off the reception area where the secretaries and typists spent their coffee breaks smoking cigarettes, chewing gum, gossiping and primping in front of the tall mirrors. Claire had even brought some makeup. As she applied mascara with an unsteady hand, she congratulated herself for telling John Nickles she was taking the rest of the day off. If she came back from lunch all done up like this, she'd never hear the end of it, especially from Norm Slenski and Amos Fuller. As she spread on lipstick, one of the secretaries asked, "You applying for that typing job in the blueprint room, honey?"

"If you are," said a big blonde with a gravelly voice, "just be careful. John Nickles likes to pinch bottoms."

There was a burst of raucous, knowing laughter from the women. Claire packed up her things and left without a word.

Driving south, she had the uneasy feeling she was losing control. Even her '39 Buick, which had been running rough, sailed down Jefferson so swiftly she had to keep hitting the brakes. When she reached Grosse Pointe the houses were suddenly larger, farther apart, done up like wedding cakes and castles. She was sure Ted had suggested meeting here because it was far from the usual corporate and Tech Center lunch spots.

The Country Club of Detroit's fairways were blanketed with snow; the driveway was lined on both sides with tall, naked elms. The clubhouse, a clump of bricks tricked up in the Tudor style to resemble a British manor, seemed to her a weirdly appropriate playpen for a bunch of car tycoons who would always have more money than taste. Professor Nabokov, whose latest letter lay open beside her on the front seat, would take one look at that pile of brick and exposed timbers and tall chimneys, and he would cry *"Poshlost!"* The cry would be full of both scorn and admiration, a condemnation and an embrace of this falsely beautiful, falsely grand monument to wealthy men's egos. That was something Claire—and very few others—understood about Vladimir Nabokov. Most people at Cornell assumed that since he was so eccentric, he was a snob. Shortly after arriving in Ithaca, Claire learned that nothing could have been farther from the truth. His latest letter simply reinforced what she'd learned years ago. When she took the envelope out of the mailbox this morning and saw the Ithaca, New York, postmark, she thought instantly of this lunch date with Ted Mackey. Then she felt a shiver of guilt—the first indication that she was not in control of what she was doing. Typically, the letter was elliptical and cryptic and brief:

> *Claire, darling,*
>
> *It has been too cold to write in the Buick, but, undaunted, I will soon bring Lo home. Then her troubles will surely begin, for there are only two other themes I can think of that could be more repugnant to an American publisher: one, of course, is a Negro-White marriage which is a glorious success resulting in scores of children and grandchildren; the other, I suppose, is the atheist who lives a happy and useful life and dies in his sleep in the back seat of his Buick at the age of 106.*
>
> *Love always,*
Volodya

"The back seat of his Buick"! The sly old dog—how he loved to slip in his little reminders of that crisp October afternoon during her freshman year when she'd finally gotten up the nerve to accept his invitation to tea. That semester he was renting a Swiss-style chalet with yellow trim and jagged shingles from a professor of agriculture who was on sabbatical studying crop rotation in Java. When Claire arrived, Professor Nabokov was in the back yard, sitting in the back seat of an emerald-green 1939 Buick. It was in far worse shape than hers. It was scarred with rust, had no engine or tires, and it hovered on four stacks of bricks. Though the lawn was neatly barbered, weeds pressed against the floorboards.

Claire stood at a distance, afraid to approach. He was sitting on the sofa-sized back seat writing on a yellow legal pad. He was wearing a dark overcoat and a white silk scarf. Again she was surprised by his face. When she'd first arrived in Ithaca a month earlier, one of the first things she'd done was to seek out the man who brought *Madame Bovary* to life for Charlie Craig. She first glimpsed him as he swept up the steps, overcoat and scarf flying, into the stout stone castle where he gave his legendary lectures. She had expected a dashing, athletic figure, a man who would look as comfortable on the back of a horse as in front of typewriter. But he looked soft, strangely puffy, and his face reminded her of General Douglas MacArthur minus the sunglasses and the corncob pipe.

He was known on campus as "Prof Vlad" because there didn't seem to be an undergraduate who knew for sure how to pronounce his name, and there definitely was not one who dared to ask. After listening to a few of his lectures, it was easy for Claire to imagine him sensing his students' consternation and enjoying it hugely, just as he must have been delighted to learn that his popular "Masterpieces in European Fiction" course was known to undergrads as "Dirty Lit" and his most beloved novel as *Madame Ovary*.

She never missed his lectures. She was amused by the way he stood stiffly at the podium reading from typed pages, never looking up at his rapt audience. Occasionally he would stop reading and take out a pencil and revise a sentence, as though he were alone in the room. She devoured every book of his available in translation.

Getting invited to his house for tea proved easy enough once he realized she was a serious student and a fan. Summoning the nerve to approach the hovering Buick was another matter. As soon as she saw that ugly chalet, she knew he was not the aloof snob everyone believed him to be. True, he had few intimate friends and several strange habits—concocting chess puzzles, for example, and writing crossword puzzles in his native Russian, and butterfly collecting, which he called "lepidopterology." But Claire was convinced these eccentricities were at least partly a mask, and she was determined to find out what lay behind it. She stood there for half an hour, watching him scribble on his legal pad. Yes, he really did look like Douglas MacArthur gone to seed.

Suddenly the rear door on the far side of the Buick opened with a squeal. He still had not seen her. He gathered up dozens of legal pads and tucked them under his arm, climbed down out of the car and started walking across the lawn. Claire noticed for the first time that a fire was burning heartily in a small incinerator in the far corner of the back yard. When Professor Nabokov reached it, he just stood there, legal pads under his arm, staring into the flames. She watched for a long time, possibly an hour, as darkness leaked through the trees, blackened the sky and the lawn, turned him into a bulky black silhouette against the orange flames. Finally he turned and marched toward the house, white scarf flying, legal pads still tucked under his arm. He entered the house by the back door.

She walked around to the front porch and pressed the bell. A series of gongs sounded, but no one came to the door. The gongs were so hideous she was afraid to press the button again. Just as she turned to leave, the door opened behind her. He was standing in the doorway in a baggy brown cardigan with a bright red ascot flaming at his throat. "Claire! So glad you made it. Do come in."

The house was even uglier inside. She followed him across shag carpets, through a sunken living room, down a hallway crowded with gewgaws that must have come from Mexico or some roadside stand on an Indian reservation—painted wooden statuettes, silver bracelets, hairy masks, stone arrowheads. Professor Nabokov settled into a lounge chair by the fireplace, and Claire sat on the sofa. Through sliding glass doors she could see the incinerator. The fire was almost dead.

She had officially been invited for tea, and after mentioning that his wife was away in New York, he did produce a pot of tea. Then he launched into the most astonishing monologue she had ever heard, telling her in vivid detail about the grisly murders of two cab drivers he'd read about that day in the New York *Daily News*; the endearing personality quirks of his favorite character in the "L'il Abner" comic strip, the irrepressible Earthquake McGoon; the reasons he considered Marilyn Monroe a marvelous actress; the key to a chess puzzle he'd solved that morning after tearing at his hair for three days. He showed her a beautifully illustrated book on hummingbirds. He showed her a rare specimen of butterfly, a "painted lady," that he had netted the previous summer in Wyoming. He talked with equal ease about beetles and Buicks and Milton Berle. He compared Swiss hotels to American motels and decided he preferred the latter, especially "tourist courts." Finally he taught her the meaning of the Russian word *poshlost*—not only the obviously trashy, but also the falsely important, the falsely beautiful, the falsely clever and attractive. He opened an issue of *Life* to an ad for a new car and told her the photograph of the gleeful mom and dad and their kiddies jumping for joy beside their shiny Tucker was a textbook illustration of *poshlost*.

Finally, after he tossed fresh logs on the fire and broke out a bottle of brandy, she got up the nerve to ask a question. "When I first got out here this afternoon, I saw you walk out to that incinerator. Do you mind me asking what you were doing?"

His eyebrows shot up, and for once the words did not come out in a smooth rush. "I was . . . Actually, it was getting . . ."

"Please tell me the truth."

She could tell by his expression that, suddenly, he was seeing her in a new light. His mask was gone. She felt she was being regarded as an adult for the first time in her life. He said, "I do believe you want to know the truth."

"Yes. Very much."

"I was about to plop the manuscript in the fire."

"Burn it?"

"That would have been the intention."

"How come?"

"How *come*?" He grinned at the Midwesternism, and she blushed.

"I mean, why?"

"I suppose because it took me forty years to invent Russia and now, at the age of fifty, I'm faced with the task of inventing America—and on days such as this it all seems perfectly hopeless."

"So why didn't you burn it?"

"I'm not sure. I suppose because when I got to the shadow of the leaning incinerator there on the innocent lawn I was hit by the thought that the ghost of the burnt book would haunt me for the rest of my life."

Two days later she learned what the troublesome novel was about. She arrived again for tea late in the afternoon and again found him in the back seat of the Buick, writing feverishly. This time, however, she stepped right up to the car. He was in a trance, and she waited until his head snapped up. "Claire!" He seemed startled. "Won't you join me?"

She opened the squealing door and climbed in. The interior was identical to hers, right down to the blue-striped upholstery and the smell—like a forest after a storm, like mulch, rotting and dank, sweet.

"Roll up the window," he told her. "You've been wondering about the book that nearly drove me to that act of desperation at the incinerator the other day."

"Yes." She was scared, but she had no desire to flee.

He shuffled the legal pads until he found the one he wanted, then started reading the opening of the novel: " 'Lolita, light of my life, fire of my loins. My sin, my soul. Lo-lee-ta: the tip of the tongue taking trip of three steps down the palate to tap, at three, on the teeth. Lo. Lee. Ta.

" 'She was Lo, plain Lo, in the morning, standing four feet

ten in one sock. She was Lola in slacks. She was Dolly at school. She was Dolores on the dotted line. But in my arms she was always Lolita.

" 'Did she have a precursor? She did, indeed she did.' " He looked up from the legal pad.

"Don't stop," Claire said. "Please."

"I have no intention of stopping," he said, dropping the legal pad and pulling her to him. They kissed, a slobbery, clumsy mashing of lips, until the Buick's windows were fogged. Then he nimbly unbuttoned her blouse and popped her left breast out of the unnecessary brassiere and feasted on the hard brown nipple. When she could hear what sounded like a bonfire roaring in her ears, she heard him say, "You are a virgin, aren't you?" It was all she could do to nod her head as she felt her panties being whisked from beneath her pleated skirt, which was held together by a large gold pin. "Up we go," he said, and she straddled him as he sat there in the middle of the huge seat, surrounded by legal pads and crumpled sheets of paper, his pants down around his ankles. She lowered herself slowly onto his pink penis, felt a knifing pain, felt herself being filled, then heard herself screaming with pain and pleasure as she bucked against him there on the blood-soaked blue back seat.

Curiously, after that day they never repeated the exercise or so much as spoke about it. Some vital function had been performed for both of them—for the émigré Russian who above all else wanted to be an American writer capable of writing convincingly about an American nymphet; and for the virgin who wanted desperately to grow out of a sheltered upbringing in a brain-dead Midwestern burg and who sensed, without surprise or shame, that the place to begin was on the steamy back seat of a Buick with a man who was old enough to be the father she never had.

And now, Claire thought as she hurried across the frozen parking lot into the Country Club of Detroit, Volodya was finally about to bring Lo home and become an American writer. His letter sounded so sunny, so full of hope. He was the last man in the world who would want to inject guilt into her life now. She was free to do as she pleased, just as she—and he—had been free that October afternoon, floating above the smooth innocent lawn.

*T*ed Mackey hated to be kept waiting, and he especially hated to be kept waiting by an employee. But this employee was different. This employee could get away with unheard-of things. The only question in his mind was: Did she know it yet?

He sipped his coffee and looked out across the vast dining room. Only one other table was occupied. In the far corner Henry Ford's kid brother, William Clay Ford, was drinking martinis and regaling a group of men, no doubt Ford executives, with a tale about a recent round of golf in Florida, something about a miraculous hole-in-one on a par four. Ted had read somewhere that envy is the hatred of something you want, the resentment of something you admire. If so, the sight of a man who was born rich and grew effortlessly richer every day of his life was enough to make Ted seethe with envy. He wanted to rise to the very top of General Motors, yet he despised most of the board members, men like William Clay Ford who flaunted their inherited money and their Eastern school ties or, worse, tried to dress up their provincial Midwestern souls with such emblems of sophistication as golfing trips to Florida or a passing familiarity with opera or some exotic red Italian sports car that cost a small fortune and rarely left the garage.

Ted resented all of them for their polish, their wintertime suntans, their utter lack of shame or self-doubt. They went through their days, their liquid lunches and love affairs and conference calls and golf games, believing they deserved it all. It was bad enough when their polish was store-bought because it reminded him that his was, too; it was worse when it was inherited, genuine, worn naturally, because no man named Ford would ever allow Ted Mackey to forget that he was different, that he had grown up poor and had worked hard for everything he had. That was what Ted resented—the way such men would never allow him to forget his past. Yet even as he resented them he understood that he wanted the world to think he was one of them, and he wanted his sons to learn to play tennis and soccer and golf and grow up to seem just like their sons.

So be it, he thought, looking out at the hard white glare of the golf course. He was not slowed by the realization that he hated what he craved, resented those he admired. If anything, his envy fueled his ambition, convinced him that he was right to enlist a very bright and very pretty young designer in his campaign to plug a potentially disastrous leak.

"Did you want to go ahead and order, Mr. Mackey?" James Hudson, a great bullfrog of a man, one of six gold-jacketed Negro waiters who stayed on through the winter, stood above him.

"No, Hudson, but I will have some more coffee."

As he poured, Hudson said, "Will Mrs. Mackey be joining you for lunch today?"

Ted loved the way these waiters, inner-city Negroes who'd spent long lives serving rich white folks, had developed extraordinarily sensitive social radar. They trafficked in information. It might be useful, even profitable, for Hudson to know whether the general manager of the Buick Division was having lunch with his wife, or with a Chrysler executive, or with some other woman.

"I'm waiting for one of my stylists to show up, Hudson."

"Very good, sir."

Ted turned and gazed out the tall windows. The sky had cleared, and the golf course sparkled as though it had been dusted with diamonds. Why was it that seeing things out of season always depressed him? A snow-blanketed golf course, a grassy ski slope under a hot summer sun, a deserted beach pelted by icy rain—these things always brought on monstrous gloom, a sense that his own life was hopelessly out of sync. It had happened just last night, when he'd wound up gazing out different windows at a different snow-blanketed golf course and a swimming pool half full of ice.

He'd taken Milmary to dinner at Oakland Hills Country Club, a private act of penance for having stayed out so late with Claire Hathaway. The evening started out as a refreshingly civilized get-together of half a dozen old friends, a chance for Jack and Audrey Winters to talk about their trip to Japan, a chance for Hank and Helen Schmidt to describe the new house they were building on Wing Lake, a chance for Milmary to dazzle everyone with her knowledge of how Saul Bellow had written *The Adventures of Augie March*, recent winner of the National Book Award, while wandering all over Europe, in cheap hotels in Paris, in a castle in Salzburg, in cafes in Florence, on a balcony in Rome, at the Crystal Palace Hotel in London, then in New York, Seattle, Saratoga Springs and Princeton.

"My Gawd," Audrey Winters chirped, "what on earth was the man writing about in all those places?"

Milmary paused, blinked twice, and said, "Why, Chicago of course!"

Ted laughed loudest because he knew that none of these people had ever heard of Saul Bellow and because he understood that Milmary didn't simply read a book, she lived it, breathed it, learned everything she could about the writing and the writer. She did it because books mattered to her and because she had once believed herself capable of producing her own, serious literary books, novels. Though she hadn't written anything in years, to his knowledge, she still devoured novels, short stories, *The New Yorker*, the *Paris Review* and half a dozen obscure literary magazines whose names Ted could never remember.

Even if she had slipped some, had quit writing and started drinking in recent years with a fervor neither of them chose to acknowledge, Milmary was still special. She was a woman who had traveled, who spoke French and rode horses, who knew how to give dinner parties. She was born with more style and grace, more class, more of the Ford variety of class, than Ted would be able to pick up or buy in a lifetime. It showed in everything she did, even in the way she sat there—"Why, Chicago of course!"—the laughter still echoing, her elbow on the table, wrist cocked, two long fingers holding a smoldering cigarette. Her lips were bright red and her blue dress was cut to reveal her neck and the string of pearls—tiny, creamy, perfect pearls from the Persian Gulf or the Bay of Bengal or the South China Sea or whatever it was the cagey salesman at Tiffany's had said when she'd eyed them in the glass case and had announced she wanted them. Ted didn't give a damn if they came out of Detroit River oysters and cost a month's salary—of course she could have them if they made her skin flush and her eyes flash that way.

Her literary discourse was the highlight of the evening. There hadn't been a whisper of that dreaded Detroit social staple—car talk—and Ted hadn't given a thought to design leaks, sales quotas, dealer conventions or Marilyn Monroe. But after dessert Milmary suggested the party repair to the upstairs lounge for "a little nightcap," and she promptly ordered a second brandy, then a third, then switched to scotch and milk, which meant her ulcer was acting up and she intended to get good and drunk. Suddenly Jack Winters stopped talking about bonsai trees and geisha girls and started in on Toyota and Nissan, which, he said, were two companies to watch out for. Ted didn't want to hear it again. The Japanese Zero had convinced him that "made in Japan" spelled trash, and he couldn't imagine why any sane American would buy a tin can when gas was so cheap and it was so easy to afford a big, beautiful Buick.

The evening continued to slide out of control. Hank Schmidt, a Buckeye from Akron, and Leon Hirt, who played tight end for the Michigan Wolverines, got into an argument about a clipping call in the fourth quarter of last year's Ohio State–Michigan game. Audrey Winters started crying into Ted's armpit because her eldest son had dropped out of Columbia and was running around Greenwich Village with a bunch of "beatniks and dope fiends." Ted didn't even bother to ask her what a beatnik was.

It was then that he'd noticed Milmary. She was dealing a hand of poker to three strangers at a corner table. The men had their jackets off, shirtsleeves rolled up, cigars stoked. Milmary's eyelids were at half-mast. The pearls were gone from her neck. Please, he thought, let them be in her purse. She had a cigarette plugged into the corner of her mouth, and she was yelling at one of the Negro waiters, "Lee-roy, hon, bring me a fresh drink," even though the man's name was Leon Trotter and she'd known him for years. The woman was Jekyll and Hyde when she drank. Ted knew from experience there was no sense in trying to get her to leave; she would make a scene, would embarrass him, maybe throw her drink. Then, in the morning, she would act as though nothing had happened.

So he positioned himself in the shadows at the far end of the bar while everyone else played poker and argued about a clipping call and fretted about their kids. He ordered a brandy and stared down at the golf course and the frozen swimming pool. He remembered how magical it had been to watch Ben Hogan's one-iron approach shot bounce up onto that sun-splashed 18th green three summers ago. Ted was sitting on this very bar stool. The grassy hummocks around the green looked like velvet, as soft and inviting as a woman's thighs. Hogan patrolled the checkered putting surface with the authority of a man who was aware he had arrived at the absolute pinnacle of his powers. He was wearing his trademark snap-brim cap and black-and-white

shoes. Something in his bearing, in his obliviousness to everything but the task before him, told Ted that after this moment
Hogan's life would begin its inevitable, slow decline. It was at
once horrible and beautiful to watch. Hogan calmly drilled the
sixteen-foot birdie putt to complete what was still considered
the single finest round of his career, the round that brought this
monster of a golf course to its knees and won him the 1951 U.S.
Open.

That moment now seemed to Ted like some sunny boyhood
memory. He brooded there in the shadows at the end of the bar,
high above the snowy golf course and the frozen swimming pool,
finishing two more brandies he didn't need and coming to understand, in a new way, why he was suddenly so intrigued by
a woman who was a little more than half his wife's age.

*T*he clubhouse was so empty and quiet that Claire
Hathaway felt like a trespasser. Of course, she told herself, at
this time of year the men who can afford to belong to clubs like
this are in Florida chasing golf balls and each other's wives.

Ted Mackey was sitting alone on the far side of the dining
room gazing out a wall of tall windows. She moved toward him,
her footsteps muffled by the thick carpets. He was wearing a
dark blue double-breasted suit and a scarlet necktie. With the
sun flooding down on him he looked shockingly handsome; he
also looked worried. When he saw her coming he jumped to his
feet. "Did you get lost?" he said, helping her with her coat,
guiding her into her seat.

"No, your directions were perfect. Am I late?"

"No, no, right on time."

Something about the way he said it, something about the look
on his face as she approached the table, told her this was not
going to be a casual, boozy get-together like their dinner at the

Detroit Club. She saw that he was drinking coffee, and she ordered a cup, black.

When the waiter left, Ted took a good long look at the golf course. Then he looked her in the eye. "You remember me asking you to think about the people you worked with on the '54s?"

"Yes."

"And whether or not they seemed loyal?"

"Yes."

"Well?"

She paused until the waiter poured her coffee and withdrew. "I can't imagine any of them doing what you talked about— giving away our work, or selling it. It matters too much to everyone."

"That's what I figured you'd say." He sounded disappointed. "That's why I asked you here today, Claire. Will you do me a favor?"

"I guess."

"Would you see if you can find a reason why anyone who worked with you on the '54s might sell us out? It could be just about anything—a debt, a grudge against the company, a bribe, a girlfriend, greed, anything. All I'm looking for at this point is a motive. Once I get that, I'll take it from there myself."

"Are you sure about this, Ted? I mean, you say the Plymouth's front bumper looks like ours, and I guess maybe it does in a way. But the resemblance isn't all *that* close."

"Let me explain something to you." He lit a cigarette, and suddenly she felt like a child who was about to receive a lecture. "We're the second-largest division in the largest corporation in the world. When you're that big, when you've got that much to lose, you can't afford to take any chances. It may not seem like the end of the world to you if a piece of a competitor's car resembles a piece of one of ours. But if there's a reason for it other than pure coincidence, then I damn sure better find out—

otherwise I won't be around for long. Right now this business is built on the annual model change, and the annual model change is built on secrecy. It's the number-one thing we sell. If your secrets start getting away from you, you're in deep shi— excuse me, you're in serious trouble. That's why I can't afford the luxury of sitting around and wondering. Maybe I'm going overboard, but I've got to assume the worst. I've got to act, and I've got to act now. Do you understand so far?"

"Yes."

"You don't have to get involved in this. I'm asking you as a personal favor."

"What happens if I say no?"

He looked away. "Nothing happens. I've got other irons in the fire."

She looked out the window. This was not what she'd expected when she came racing down Jefferson. Already she could see this was a mess. On the one hand, she took fierce pride in her work and didn't like the idea of someone stealing it; on the other hand, she wasn't ready to put herself in a position to ruin a friend's career. What if it was Amos Fuller, or Norm Slenski, or Rory Gallagher?

But what if she turned Ted down? Surely there wouldn't be any more of these intimate meetings in expensive restaurants. Surely a whole world of tantalizing possibilities—not the least of them a sudden boost to her career—would be closed to her. She thought of something she'd read recently by E. B. White: "Don't come to New York if you're unwilling to be lucky." The same could be said of Detroit, and Claire was willing, even eager, to be lucky. Here she was, sitting in an exclusive dining room with one of the most powerful men in the business, and he was asking *her* for a favor. He didn't seem like the type of man to ask a favor or take a snub lightly. Only a fool would turn him down. Besides, it was easy enough to work up a little righteous indignation if someone was indeed selling her sweat and blood to the highest bidder.

"Tell me what you're thinking," Ted said.

"A couple of things. I still find it a little hard to believe that someone would actually sell our designs."

"Believe me, it's been going on for years. Ask Harvey. When you've got something that's valuable, there's always going to be someone who'll try to get something for it. It's the oldest story in the book."

"Suppose it's true and I help you find out who did it. What's in it for me?"

He looked down at his hands and smiled. "I like that," he said.

"What do you like?"

"I like a person who isn't afraid to look out for himself."

"*Her*self."

"Yes, herself." He was still smiling. She imagined it was a smile of triumph. He squeezed her hand. "Believe me, Claire, I've got big plans for you. You help me get to the bottom of this and you won't be sorry. That's a promise."

Sixteen

*S*now flurries scurried across Will Lomax's headlight beams as he drove north toward home. He had the feeling he'd spent the past six months driving home in snowstorms in the dark thinking about nothing but numbers. Eight Mile Road. The Buick Century. Ten thousand cars a week for fifty-two weeks comes to more than half a million cars. Who's number one, Ford or Chevy? Who's number three, Buick or Plymouth? The numbers, like the snow, kept coming. If 1904 was the year David Dunbar Buick, a bathtub designer in Flint, produced his very first car, then 1954 was Buick's fiftieth anniversary, the precise midpoint of the Buick Century, the approximate midpoint of what some people were calling the American Century. . . .

He turned on the radio. Anything to get rid of this obsession with numbers. He had loved being a newspaper reporter, telling stories that were more or less true. That, he supposed, was why he was becoming more and more absorbed with his research for The Book. The story of David Dunbar Buick's rise and fall fascinated him, but even that served to remind him that General Motors was now the land of the bean counters, where numbers were what truly mattered because they could be measured, quantified, controlled. As he drove into the storm Will understood that people were pleased with his Thrill of the Month Club ad campaign—people joined the "club" simply by test-driving a new Buick—but he realized he was under pressure to come up with some numbers of his own, a catchy phrase, a slogan, a gimmick that would send Buick past Plymouth, all the way to number three.

When he finally made it home, Margaret kissed him and slipped on an apron and poured him a drink of Old Crow. The meatloaf she served him had been warming in the oven for hours, and it tasted like sawdust. If it hadn't been overdone meatloaf, it would have been overdone beef stew or overdone chicken pot pie or overdone steak. It wasn't her fault; it was his fault because when you worked for Ted Mackey there was never any way of knowing how late you'd get away from the office. Tonight he was so hungry he asked for a second helping of sawdust.

As he ate, Margaret recounted the events that made up her day. There had been nights recently when her litany had brought on a kind of sadness without end, a feeling that their years together, all the striving and bloodshed, the accumulation of homes and gadgets and toys and babies, the sense that things would always keep getting better and better—all of it felt like a stupendous waste. But tonight he listened as she recounted the day's dog bites and nosebleeds and bridge game and fender bender, and he thought of how he'd been possessed by numbers during the drive home, and he realized that her glad chatter did not bring on the sadness without end. He realized he envied her, realized he missed living in a world full of little stories that in their way amounted to much more than his world full of men who thought of everything in terms of numbers.

"That may be the best meatloaf I ever ate," he said, pushing the plate away.

"Stop it, you."

"I mean it. Loved the onion."

Margaret took his plate to the sink. He believed that spending the day with the children, cooking his supper, watching him eat, washing his dish—somehow all these little things combined to make her happy. Maybe she'd figured out something that he, in his frenzy, had completely missed. She was wearing the dress he'd given her for Valentine's Day last year, no doubt the dress she'd worn to that day's bridge party. It looked good on her. It clung to her hips, which were beginning to broaden but were still one of her best features.

"What are you looking at?" she said, turning from the sink, blushing as she'd blushed the first time she caught him staring at her at a buffet table in the Washington Press Club years ago.

"Nothing—just thinking about how well that dress fits you."

"It's getting tighter. And you're getting to be a dirty old man."

"That's true. And to prove it, I think you should slip into something a little less . . . red and meet me in the bedroom. I'm going to check on the kids and make one quick phone call. Then I'm going to show you something."

"Will Lomax, you're such a bird." She was smiling. "I'll be right up."

The children were asleep. Both of their rooms smelled of Vicks VapoRub. He detested that menthol smell because it made him think of the suffering of helpless children. He left both doors ajar in case they should cry out in the night, then he went into his study and closed the door and dialed Morey Caan in Washington. The room's walls were covered now with books, and there was a fat file on the desk beside the typewriter: "David D. Buick and Ransom E. Olds, the Early Years."

Morey answered with a groan on the seventh ring: "Rrrr."

"It's Will. Did I wake you up?"

"S'okay. I had to get up to answer the phone."

As he often did while talking on the phone, Will started doodling. He wrote "50 for 50," Ted Mackey's legendary 1950 sales campaign that allowed people to drive away in a new Buick after making a down payment of just fifty dollars. Then Will started adding zeros to the numeral 50. "When are you coming out to start your interviews?"

"Soon," Morey said. "I'm onto something very hot about German POWs and Guatemala."

"The war's over, son. And what's Guatemala?"

"It's a country in Central America that the CIA's into up to their armpits. I'd tell you more, but I'm afraid this line's bugged."

"You're getting paranoid. You ought to quit hanging around creeps like Joe McCarthy."

"Maybe so—but he's so damn cute."

"Let me run something by you real quick." Will looked at his doodles. The numeral 50 had become 500,000. "We're hoping to sell half a million Buicks this year."

"You have my condolences."

"After you do your backgrounders, how would you feel about coming back later in the year and maybe following the five hundred thousandth Buick down the assembly line—then on to the dealership and the proud new owner?"

"Hmmm . . . half a million Buicks. Not a bad angle. It's got possibilities. I'm going back to sleep now."

"When are you coming out?"

"Soon."

"I need a date."

"Call me tomorrow. Over and out." And he was gone.

Will hung up the phone and studied his doodles. Buick's second half-century . . . the Buick Century . . . half a million cars. . . . Maybe it *was* a good idea, Will thought. He liked the way it had just popped into his head. This room had a way of doing that, of helping him make associations he would not have made even a few weeks ago.

He turned out the light and went down the hallway to the bedroom. Of course all the lights were out, and modest Margaret was under the covers, naked, warm and waiting. As soon as he joined her under the heavy patchwork quilt, he knew exactly what would happen. As always, they started kissing, and within seconds he was on his back and she was astride him, grinding away, biting her lower lip, trying not to make any noise, trying not to wake the children. Soon she shuddered and gasped, sagged against him. Then, as he knew she would, she rolled onto her back and guided him toward his own climax, which would come in a few—

"Waaaaarrrrgh!" It was Lisa, the baby.

"Hurry, honey," Margaret whispered.

But it was no use. "That's okay," Will said. "You go see if she's all right."

In one smooth motion Margaret slipped into the robe and out the door. Will lay there on his back in the dark, listening to the wind rattle the windows. At least this session had ended differently. Each time they repeated these ritualized hydraulics, he felt that changing them was a little more impossible. Then, when he realized he'd gotten more excited talking to Morey about the half-millionth '54 Buick than he had in his wife's arms, he suddenly felt the familiar sadness without end. It was as black and vast as the Midwestern night, and he felt powerless to do anything about it.

Seventeen

On the two-hour flight to New York, Ted Mackey was so distracted he couldn't even concentrate on the newspaper accounts of Joe DiMaggio and Marilyn Monroe's honeymoon. He looked across the aisle at Will Lomax. He was surrounded by note cards and was chewing a pencil as he polished the speech Ted would give that evening to the Buick Dealers Association of Greater New York. Ted intended to deliver the speech dozens of times by the end of the year, and he wanted it to be just right—part pep talk and part declaration of war, a pat on the back and a stick of dynamite up the ass, the official announcement that the good old days of the seller's market were history and the power was shifting from the dealerships to the factory. From now on, Detroit was calling the shots. And Ted Mackey wanted the world to know that he was Detroit.

He looked out the window at the flashing silver propellers. For days he'd been wrestling with doubts. After all the trouble he'd gone to—putting a spy on the payroll at Kelsey-Hayes and enlisting one of Buick's top stylists as an in-house spy and bugging the Tech Center and tapping the phones—what if it all led nowhere? What if Plymouth's front bumper was just one of those weird coincidences that happen from time to time in the car business? Impossible, he told himself. He'd had his ear to the ground, as always, and he'd heard the rumblings. People in high places were murmuring that the Buick Division had turned into a sieve. Such talk could be deadly, and it was probably already placing his dream car, the Wildcat, in jeopardy. So now that word about the spying and bugging was out, Ted saw that his mission was clear: He had to come up with an explanation for the Plymouth's front bumper, something plausible and harmless that would put the doubts to rest and restore confidence in his powers as a manager. If he couldn't come up with something, then he would have to make something up. And he would have to do it soon.

He ordered another scotch from the stewardess and turned back to Sidney Skolsky's story in *Photoplay*. After spending fifteen hours in the Clifton Motel in Paso Robles on their wedding night, the newlyweds had continued on into the mountains above Palm Springs, where they hid away in a friend's cabin. "There weren't any other guests," Marilyn told her favorite gossip columnist. "Joe and I took long walks in the snow. There wasn't even a television set. We really got to know each other. And we played billiards. Joe taught me how to play."

The very thought of Joe DiMaggio spending his honeymoon teaching Marilyn Monroe how to play billiards struck Ted as all wrong. If DiMaggio had anything to teach Marilyn Monroe, it was that even the most ecstatic cheers can turn to boos in the wink of an eye. Perhaps no other man in the world was more intimately acquainted with the fragile nature of fame and power. In 1938, after two brilliant seasons with the Yankees, young DiMaggio had demanded a pay hike from $15,000 to $40,000 for his third season, a whopping sum in a country still grinding through the Depression. The Yankees were then owned by a rich and dapper beer baron, Colonel Jacob Ruppert, who ruled the club with an iron fist and shuddered at the thought of his young star sending players' carefully restrained salaries through the roof. If DiMaggio got $40,000 in 1938, what would an established star like Lou Gehrig demand in 1939? The colonel made a final offer of $25,000. DiMaggio stuck to his demand. Negotiations broke off, and the great holdout began.

Like millions of Americans, Ted Mackey, then a twenty-seven-year-old regional sales manager covering the southeastern states for Buick, found he could not resist the sports pages that spring. Wherever he went, from Detroit to Atlanta to New Orleans, he devoured every scrap of news about the holdout. And there was plenty of it. The newspapers had jumped into the battle, generally siding with the colonel and helping tilt public opinion against DiMaggio—not a very tough job in a day when $25,000 was a small fortune and $40,000 seemed like the pipe dream of a greedy young man. The tide turned against the Yankee Clipper.

Two days after the season began, DiMaggio swallowed hard and accepted the colonel's offer. But when he returned to the vast pasture of center field in Yankee Stadium, the star who'd grown accustomed to adoring cheers suddenly heard boos and catcalls for the first time in his life. One day a rotten tomato splattered on the back of his head. It so unnerved him that he took to smoking a whole pack of cigarettes before every home game. When informed of this, Colonel Ruppert was delighted. "Let the kid sweat," he said. "He made his bed, now let him sleep in it." Life would never be quite so simple or so pure for Joe DiMaggio. He would go on to have great seasons, but he would always be haunted by that tomato and the echo of those boos.

And now, instead of passing that lesson on to Marilyn Monroe, a fragile beauty on a precarious pedestal, he had spent their honeymoon teaching her to play billiards. Ted tossed the magazine onto the pile of newspapers. Now he had one more reason to make his move on the Wildcat and Marilyn Monroe as soon as he got back to Detroit.

*A*t the Essex House that night, the Buick dealers of New York gave Ted Mackey a hero's welcome. They loved him. His "50 for 50" campaign had made several of them rich, and they viewed him as one of their own, a salesman at heart, a marketing genius, someone in Detroit at long last who spoke their language and returned their phone calls.

Ted's after-dinner speech opened with one of his trademark zingers: "It's not a cheaper car that people want—it's an expensive car that costs less. And that's just what we're giving them with the new '54 Century!"

But as soon as he'd warmed up the crowd, his tone began to change. This was not a typical Ted Mackey pep talk. "The seller's market is a thing of the past, a wonderful little fantasy that died in the summer of '53. From now on, nobody will be able to sell Buicks at full price. Nobody." He paused. "We're gunning for number three this year, and our production quotas are up ten percent. That means you're going to have to move a hell of a lot more iron. Forget the big markup. The name of the game now is high volume. You may need to sell three cars this year to make the profit you made on one sale a year ago, and that's the way it's going to be for a good long while. We spent forty-five million redesigning the entire line this year, and the Century in particular is walking out of showrooms. If you can't sell what we ship, then maybe we'll have to put another store a few miles down the road from you—because we *will* sell every car we make this year. And next year. And the year after that."

By the end of the speech the lobster and filet mignon were sitting uneasily in more than a few stomachs. Later, in the hospitality suite, after the wives had gone to bed and the whisky had begun to flow, the dealers' mood shaded toward panic. Ted worked the room, jacket off, tie loose, shirtsleeves rolled up, drink in his fist, pure Detroit. He argued, he cajoled, he teased, he flattered, he bullied, he threatened. In other words, he did the very things to the dealers that they did to their customers, because he knew from long experience that car dealers had larceny in their hearts, and he knew that if he could fuel that larceny with panic, Plymouth didn't have a prayer.

As always, Ted stayed to the bitter end, until the air was stale and blue and the bartenders had left and the diehards had started pouring their own drinks and stirring them with their index fingers. They pleaded with Ted not to dump cars on them, and he promised he wouldn't, though of course he knew they knew he was lying. He watched, delighted, as they staggered out the door one by one, shaking their heads, muttering to themselves.

Finally, around three o'clock, Will Lomax weaved down the hall and Ted found himself alone with a guy in an electric green suit and yellow necktie. The suit had a shine to it, and it was so brittle that whenever he moved it flashed and changed colors—olive green, lizard green, forest green, back to olive green. It was a nigger suit if Ted had ever seen one, but the guy was as white as bread and had a crewcut and black-rimmed glasses.

"Lose your room key?" Ted said.

"Naw." He even had buck teeth. He held out his right hand. "I just wanted to say hello, Ted. We've never met, but I'm Hayes Tucker, Jr. I'm originally from—"

"Richmond, Virginia!"

"I guess you knew Daddy."

"Knew him? I set your father up in business in the spring of '38, back when DiMaggio was holding out from the Yankees. I think he and I were the only two people in the country on DiMaggio's side. He was one of the best damn salesmen I ever met—and hardest drinkers, too. How's he getting along?"

"He passed last year, I'm afraid."

"I'm sorry to hear that." A fifth of bourbon a day will catch up with a man, Ted thought.

"I guess you knew Daddy retired back in '51. Said it couldn't get any better than 1950."

"Yeah, I heard. So what brings you to the big city, Hayes?"

"I just opened my own Buick dealership out on Long Island,

and I wanted to let you know that what you said tonight makes a lot of sense. If I have a problem, it's keeping enough cars on my lot, especially that new Century. She sure is a beaut! A lot of my customers are my neighbors out in Levittown."

"What's Levittown?"

"You never heard of Levittown? It's the best darn little community on all of Long Island, a place where a kid can grow up with grass stains on his pants and people help each other out and—you might find this hard to believe, but on my block we got six houses and every single one of those folks either owns or has ordered a new Century from Tucker Buick."

"God damn."

"Ain't that something? More than once I've thought to myself what a picture that would make, all those new Buicks out in front of that neat row of houses. . . ."

"Go on."

"Well, it's like you said in your speech. The power's in Detroit now. The way I see it, with the money and muscle you factory people have, you could put together one heckuva campaign just from my block on Lindbergh Street."

"Hmmm." Suddenly Ted felt the full weight of the long day, the flight, the food, the speech, the drinks. "It . . . uh . . . it does sound interesting, Hayes. You got a business card?"

"Here you go." He gave Ted a card and pumped his hand. "Well! Guess I better be turning in." Buck teeth blazed. Ted watched the green suit flash out the doorway. He made a note on the back of the card to mention Hayes Tucker, Jr., and Levittown to Will on the flight back to Detroit. This was war, and Ted knew he had to take any ally he could get—even if the guy wore an electric green suit and came on like a bowl of scalding grits.

Eighteen

*M*orey Caan was crossing the tarmac with the other passengers when the snow began to fall. By the time he'd climbed the steps, found his seat and fastened his safety belt, snow was sticking to the airplane's propellers and wings, and the runway was white. The way my luck's been running, he thought, this plane's headed straight for the bottom of the Potomac.

The run of bad luck had started when Pete Hoover was suddenly yanked from squirrel duty on the White House putting green. This story, some savvy aide suggested to the President, was political dynamite. So traps were set, and the trapped squirrels were set free somewhere in Maryland; Pete Hoover was reassigned somewhere in Virginia, and Morey never got to print the story.

Then Harrison Chalmers, one of his best sources at the State Department, refused to discuss the CIA's operation in Guatemala. Just before he'd hung up, though, Chalmers said a very intriguing thing: "I wouldn't even waste my time with Guatemala right now if I were you. It'll be months before anything breaks down there. Oppenheimer's about to become a much hotter story."

"Robert Oppenheimer? The scientist?"

"His friends call him Bob."

"What about him?"

"You read the papers. You've got a nose. Think about it—how smart do you think it is to be against development of the H-bomb in this country today?"

"What are you trying to say, Harry?"

"I'm telling you to look into it. This Oppenheimer thing's

going to break a lot sooner than Guatemala. That's all I can tell you. Bye."

To Morey's surprise the plane's engines came to life, and he soon found himself being lifted smoothly into the storm, through angry purple clouds, into a miraculously blue sky. The sun was shining. And there he was—frustrated and now teased—on a plane headed to Detroit to research a story about a car when certain people in Washington were quietly plotting to overthrow Central American governments and others were trying to railroad scientists who didn't have the stomach for the hydrogen bomb. He had the sickening feeling he was barking up all the wrong trees.

Then he picked up the *New York Times.*

The story was in the bottom-right corner of the front page under the headline ATOM BLAST OPENS TEST IN PACIFIC; NO HINT OF HYDROGEN PLAN GIVEN. The story included a brief statement from the tight-lipped bastard who ran the Atomic Energy Commission, Rear Admiral Lewis Strauss, who said only that the AEC had detonated an "atomic" bomb in the Marshall Islands. The idea behind this, Morey could see, was to make it sound like the AEC was doing the press and the public a favor. When the AEC had detonated the first hydrogen bomb in 1952, there had been no official announcement, but word leaked out from sailors and fishermen in the area who wrote letters home, frequently embellishing them with harrowing drawings of an explosion that obliterated an entire island and ripped a mile-wide crater in the ocean floor. Some of those drawings, to the dismay of the AEC, made their way into newspapers and magazines. So Strauss's statement was an attempt to control information and prevent hysteria. The *Times* did mention the speculation Morey had heard floating around Washington that a variety of hydrogen bombs would be exploded during this series of tests. But that was all.

Morey ordered a bourbon from the stewardess, a rare daytime

indulgence unless he was flying or worrying. Now he was doing both. He was frustrated and twice teased—and he was flying in the wrong direction. When the plane dipped through the clouds, he saw that a cold rain was pelting Detroit, coating the city with gray slush. He permitted himself a bitter laugh: Better to be in this slushy hell than out there on some coral reef in the South Pacific when the blood-red mushroom cloud sprouted from the turquoise sea.

*J*ust as Will Lomax was gathering up his hat and coat and umbrella to leave for the airport, Red Van Hooven walked into his cubicle and handed him the long-awaited report on the inner workings of the Kelsey-Hayes Tool & Die Company. It wasn't bad, but Will knew it wasn't what Ted Mackey wanted to hear. "Nice job, Red," he said. "Very nice."

"You really think so?" The eyebrows shot up.

"Yeah, I do. Let's go show it to Ted."

The eyebrows collapsed. "I was kinda hoping you might . . ."

"Naw, I think you should give it to Ted yourself. It's your baby."

Ted read the report without any show of emotion. Then he stood up and started pacing—"like a caged puma," Will jotted in the notebook he now carried with him at all times, just like the good old days in Washington.

"Let me make sure I've got this straight," Ted said. Red Van Hooven shifted in his chair. "You've had this Miss Honeycrotch—"

"Honey*cutt*," Red said.

"You've had this Miss Honeycutt on the payroll at Kelsey-Hayes for the past two months—"

"More like six weeks."

"Quit interrupting me, goddammit!"

"Yessir."

"And all she's been able to come up with is that there are two, maybe three people who could possibly have been in a position to slip our front bumper designs to Plymouth?"

"That's about the size of it."

"Is she sucking the right dicks?"

"Gee, Ted . . . I'm not . . . I don't know that she's sucking *any* dicks."

"Well you tell her to start sucking tomorrow!" Ted thundered. "And if she doesn't know how, you send her up here and I'll give her a lesson she'll never forget." Red Van Hooven turned the color of a radish, and Will had to bite his hand to keep from laughing out loud. But Ted wasn't through. "I want results, goddammit. Those pricks in accounting are all over my ass with questions about the money I'm paying that broad. I don't want to hear any more of this 'two, maybe three' shit. I want a name, and I want it in the next two weeks or she'll be back so deep in that typing pool she'll wish she'd never come up for air. You got that?"

"Yessir."

"Now get the hell out of here. Will, you stay put."

Will watched Red dart for the door. He was getting to know Ted well enough to understand that the tongue-lashing was nothing personal and that it had achieved the desired effect: All steam had been blown off, and he was ready to start acting like a human being again. "When's that writer from *Life* due in town?" Ted said.

"I'm on my way to the airport to pick him up right now."

"I've got something I want you to run by him. At the convention in New York I met a dealer who lives in some housing development out on Long Island. Lewis—uh, Lever—"

"Levittown?"

"That's it. Apparently all five of his neighbors have just bought new Centurys from him."

"Good God."

"We've been chatting on the phone and he tells me they've sold the last vacant house on the block to some Korean vet. This dealer—you've got to meet this guy, I swear he could sell a fucking Buick to Henry Ford—he thinks he can sell this war hero a Century."

"Seven Buicks in a row. That's almost scary."

"Think about it. We could arrange for the new neighbor to get the five hundred thousandth '54 Buick."

"A Century, naturally."

"Of course. And we have a second-generation Buick dealer in the story—I set this weirdo's father up in business in Virginia during the Depression."

"And a whole block of Buick owners."

"And a Korean vet."

"And suburbia."

"There's only one thing missing," Ted said.

"What's that?"

"A Negro."

"Are you kidding? The *Saturday Evening Post* just did a big article on Levittown. Negroes aren't even allowed to buy homes there."

"Well, maybe that's where Amos Fuller comes in. It's still a helluva good story. Give this guy a call when you get back from the airport, and mention him to your writer friend." Ted wrote down Tucker's phone number; then he swiveled in his chair and pondered the rain. This, Will knew, meant he was dismissed.

*J*ust as Will had feared, Morey was a million miles away when he got off the plane at City Airport. He was muttering about the bumpy flight, the guy in the next seat who got airsick, the H-bomb, the tuna boat.

"Tuna boat?" Will said as he guided the Buick into the rain and headed for the Tech Center.

"Haven't you heard? Apparently there was some Japanese fishing boat downwind from the blast—the wind was supposed to be blowing the other way, but it shifted—and now the AEC's saying nobody got hurt. You believe that you need to get your head examined."

Will had been so busy he hadn't even read the papers. He hadn't heard about the H-bomb test, let alone a tuna boat that might have been showered with radiation. Of course he wouldn't admit that to Morey. He knew that Morey, much like Ted Mackey, needed to blow off his quota of steam, and Will's job, as a good friend and a good PR man, was to sit tight and endure these therapeutic blasts.

To Will's delight, the Tech Center succeeded in taking Morey's mind off the coming apocalypse. He was instantly agog, like a kid who'd been turned loose in the world's most exotic toy store: rooms full of life-size clay cars, studios cluttered with drawings of fantastic futuristic bubble cars, sketches of hubcaps, door panels, glove boxes, bumpers, windshields. There were plywood skeletons of cars. There were hand-fashioned metal skins of new cars. The place was more like a laboratory than a factory, and everyone Morey saw was an artist. And there were hundreds of them.

They found Harvey Pearl in the Trim Studio. "Come in, come in," he said. "We were just discussing whether these tail lights make the '57 look like it's about to become airborne—and whether that would be good or bad."

There were polite chuckles from the designers gathered around the air-brushed drawings. Morey recognized it instantly as the same flattering laughter college students use to win the favor of a popular professor. As Harvey Pearl described the virtues of the P-38 airplane, Morey scanned the assembled stylists. There were three dozen of them, and they looked less like artists than like eager young accountants—close-cropped hair, conservative suits, shiny shoes. There were only two women and one Negro in the room. Morey could see that the Negro wasn't paying attention to the lecture. He was doodling.

When the session broke up, Morey chatted with each of the stylists. He was amazed by the complexity of the design process, by how long each sketch took and how specialized every task was. There were hubcap specialists, dashboard specialists, bumper specialists. And though each stylist may have made only a small contribution to each finished car, they all took fierce personal pride in their achievements. "That's *my* hood ornament," they would say, or "That's *my* windshield slant." Morey had never thought of this before. He'd always assumed that cars just popped out of someone's mind whole, like a chick emerging from the egg. But cars, it turned out, were the handiwork of dozens and dozens of stylists toiling under deadlines and harsh white lights for weeks, months, even years. Morey had learned long ago that the two things you don't want to watch people make are sausages and laws. He now added cars to the list.

Yet it was fascinating. When Morey approached the Negro shortly before quitting time, the kid looked up from his drawing board and said the strangest thing: "You impress me as the kind of cat who appreciates a good cartoon."

"Yeah . . . well, sure," Morey said.

What a curveball! The Negro reached into a drawer and furtively removed a sheet of paper. Morey recognized the drawing instantly. It was from *The New Yorker*, and it had made him laugh so hard when he first saw it that he'd clipped it out, sent a photostat to Will and taped the original to his refrigerator door. A huge chrome barge of a car—a parody of a Cadillac, perhaps—is parked at a gas pump with the engine idling. As the attendant pumps gas into the tank he shouts to the driver, "Hey, shut the motor off. You're gaining on me!"

At the bottom of the cartoon, in small block letters, was the name A. Fuller.

"You drew this?" Morey said.

"That's me, Amos Fuller. But keep it quiet. Anyone finds out and my ass is back out on the street. They got no sense of humor round here."

Morey had his man for the article, a street-wise Negro who dressed like an Ivy League freshman—gold-rimmed spectacles, tweed jacket, flannel slacks, his hair cropped short and worn natural. And a cartoonist to boot. Yes, Amos Fuller was perfect.

"So tell me," Morey said, "how did you manage to get a job in here with all these nice college boys?"

"There's a five-dollar word for what got me this job."

"Testicular fortitude?"

Amos grinned. One of his front teeth was gold. "I wouldn't know nothing about that. No, man, I got the job the good old-fashioned way. Nep-o-tism. My old man's a foreman in Flint now, and he used to box against the boss of the whole show."

"Ted Mackey?"

"Yep. Way I heard it, when the Great White Hope put a whuppin' on the best prospect to come out of Paradise Valley since Joe Louis. . . . Well, I think Mackey felt so bad he made sure the man's baby boy got a nice clean job soon as he got out of Cass Tech."

Yes, Morey had his man. Riding to the airport late that night with Will, he was thrilled with the story. It was no longer about a car; it was about human beings—about one particularly unique human being. Morey rambled on and on about how eager he was to come back for more interviews, the manic opposite of the gloomy mumbler who'd arrived from Washington. When they turned into the airport parking lot, he realized Will hadn't said a word since they left the Tech Center. He had a glazed, faraway look in his eyes.

"You all right, old man?" Morey asked as they trotted through the drizzle to the terminal.

"Yeah, fine."

"Bullshit. What's wrong?"

"Nothing."

They were late, and they walked briskly to the gate. "Will, this is no time to start holding out on me. What's wrong?"

"It's just that . . . I knew it was a gamble bringing you in on this story, and I've finally realized just how big a gamble it is." They made the first call for Morey's plane. "You met Mackey. You saw what a ball-breaker the guy is."

"Total prick."

"You know, it's funny. I've never admitted this to anyone—I was barely able to admit it to myself—but I'm terrified of the guy. Scared shitless. He's the first person I've ever met who's been able to make me imagine how it would feel to fail." Will shook his head. "Ain't that something?"

"Christ, Will, the guy's so full of shit his eyes are brown."

"Maybe so. But there's something you don't understand. If I do fail, if I do get demoted or fired—"

"You'd have a job at the *Post* in less than twenty-four hours."

"You're missing the point. I don't want to go back to the *Post*. I want to succeed at *this* job—I want it more than anything else in the world. When I think about losing it I wake up in the middle of the night sweating."

"But why? It's a fucking PR job."

"I'll tell you why—and it took me a long time to get to the point where I could say this. It's because of The Book. It's really taking off now, and I don't want anything to happen that'll cut me off from my sources."

"Ah, I get the picture. You want me to write a nice puff piece about the new Buicks."

"No, no, no." He laughed. "I know you better than that."

They heard the final call for Morey's plane.

"So," Morey said, "all of a sudden you've got something to lose. How does it feel?"

"It's scary, but it feels good. Damn good, in fact. It's been a while."

"Well, don't worry. I'm not going to write anything that'll get your legs chopped off."

"Promises, promises. That's what you told Joe McCarthy."

They laughed and shook hands; then Morey hurried out to the plane. As he climbed the stairs, he looked back at the terminal. Will stood there on the other side of the rain-streaked windows, his hands buried in the pockets of his raincoat. He looked small and alone. Morey waved, but Will must not have been watching because he didn't wave back.

Nineteen

*A*s she set out to find the spy in the Beauty Parlor, Claire Hathaway kept thinking of Ted Mackey's words that day at the Country Club of Detroit: "When you've got this much to lose, you can't afford to take any chances."

He was right, of course, and he'd made her realize that though she was just a small cog in a monstrously powerful and complex machine, the fate of that machine would, in a very real sense, be her own fate. Accepting this mission was like crossing a line, an admission that she could no longer pretend to operate above the grubby world of commerce.

The spying started innocently enough. One night, when everyone was working late to meet a morning deadline, Claire decided to open with grapeshot. "Is it just me," she called out, loudly enough for the dozen nearest stylists to hear, "or is the front bumper on this year's Plymouth a spitting image of ours?"

"Hadn't noticed," Rory Gallagher said.

"Me neither," Emily Buhner said. That didn't surprise Claire. Emily hadn't noticed that her lipstick was smeared a quarter of an inch beyond the edges of her lips or that there was a gravy stain shaped like Africa on the front of her pale pink blouse.

"Well, I noticed," Amos Fuller said. "When I seen them two bulbs, I figured their stylists must be a buncha tit men, just like us."

Through the laughter Emily said, "Amos, you're disgusting. For your information, I am not a tit man."

"Y'ain't telling me something I don't know!"

Another gale of laughter erased Emily from the conversation.

"Come on, you guys, I'm serious," Claire said. "The Plymouth has a Dagmar bumper exactly like ours." But no one took the bait, not even Norm Slenski, who was always the first to weigh in with a pointless opinion on any subject. Even when she got her co-workers alone—at lunch, in the Tech Center corridors, at parties—she got nowhere. And she continued to get nowhere until the night Norm offered to take her on a guided tour of the gambling dens of Hamtramck.

One of the most purely Polish neighborhoods west of Warsaw, Hamtramck was a wide-open, deliriously corrupt, blue-collar Catholic city-within-a-city that had earned the nickname "Wild West of the Middle West" back when Norm was growing up. The tour began at ZZ's, which was on the top floor of the Public Safety Building, just across the railroad tracks from Dodge Main. Shortly after midnight, when the second shift got off, the place changed from a sleepy social club into a gigantic, rollicking crapshoot. Claire couldn't believe her eyes. Assemblyline workers in grimy overalls dropped their paychecks on the plywood tables and tossed the dice. Winners scooped up piles of cash and paychecks with both arms, and still some spilled on the floor; losers tossed off shots of whisky. The place filled with smoke and cursing and laughter and polka music, with roars of joy and wails of despair. One loser actually wept on Norm Slenski's shoulder. "My old lady's gonna murder me! Norm, buddy, spot me a fifty till Monday!"

From ZZ's they went to the Kosciuszko Club, the Knights of Columbus and a joint with no name, just a single yellow light bulb burning over the front door. Everywhere they went the men eyed Claire approvingly and gave Norm a wink, and he kept winning. He played poker, darts, craps, rummy, punchboards; he even flipped a guy for fifty dollars, called heads—and won. By four o'clock he was just getting warmed up, but Claire had seen enough. Any man who gambled like that could certainly wind up in need of some quick cash. This was, at least, a possible motive.

"Don't these joints ever close?" she said when they stepped out onto the sidewalk and stood under the yellow light bulb.

"Why should they? They'll be packed again as soon as the graveyard shift gets off."

She could see the jagged roofline of Dodge Main a few blocks away, could hear the whir and clang and hiss of the assembly line. "So," she said, "that's where they make the damn Plymouths, eh?"

"Whatta you got against Plymouth? If it wasn't for Dodge Main there wouldn't be no Hamtramck."

"I'll tell you what I've got against Plymouth. They've been stealing our designs right out from under our noses."

"Says who?"

"Says me. Says a lot of people. Come on, Norm, you've been around longer than anybody. You've seen the '54 Buick and you've seen the '54 Plymouth. Does their front bumper look like an accident to you?"

"Who cares?"

"I do. It makes me furious. I'd like to know who's selling us out."

"What's it worth to you?" He was grinning. He leaned against the wall of the building and started twirling a strand of her hair between his fingers. In the yellow light his round face reminded her of a harvest moon in Iowa. He was such a moron—and yet he'd come up with the perfect question, the only question: What was it worth to her? She hadn't even asked herself.

"It's worth plenty."

"How much is plenty?" He kept twirling the strand of hair.

"Cut the crap, Norm, and tell me what you know."

"Not till you tell me why you want to know so bad."

"I already told you—it makes me furious. I bust my ass, I take pride in my work, and some yo-yo comes along and starts selling my work to the highest bidder."

"That's bullshit. Somebody put you up to this. Who was it?"

How had she let this big, dumb, moon-faced Polack paint her into a corner? "Okay," she said, "I'll make you a deal. You tell me what you know and I'll tell you who told me to ask."

"You got a deal. Let's go over to my cousin's apartment and talk it over. It'll be more comfortable."

"I'm perfectly comfortable right here." He was still toying with her hair. She waited. "Well?"

"It's your move," he said.

"All right. It was Harvey Pearl."

"I figured. You tell Harvey that Plymouth sent their whole design staff to his stupid Motorama at the Waldorf-Astoria the past two years, and if he can't figure it out from there he's dumber'n I thought he was."

"How do you know that?"

"You live in Hamtramck you hear things about Dodge and Plymouth. No big mystery. Come on, let's go over to my cousin's place. He's hunting in the U.P. and he gave me the—"

"Some other time, Norm. Your wife's probably waiting up for you."

"No she's not. This is my night out with the boys."

"Then go play with the boys." She walked around to the

driver's side of her car. In the yellow light the oxidized paint was as iridescent as lizard's skin. She opened the door. "By the way, Norm, do you gamble like that every weekend?"

"No," he croaked, "sometimes I lose."

When she started the car, his jaw sagged. He watched in disbelief as the bulky old Buick rumbled around the corner. When the street was quiet again, he went back into the club. He needed a drink in the worst way.

*A*t lunch in the Tech Center cafeteria the next day, Amos Fuller noticed Claire Hathaway was acting even friendlier than usual. She bought him lunch and roared at his latest cartoon. It showed two neighbors working on their lawns on opposite sides of a picket fence. The first neighbor is pushing a mower, huffing, mopping sweat from his brow; the second neighbor is spraying a canister of No Weed on his lawn. He says, "You ought to give it a try. It's guaranteed to kill everything but the grass, and there's a chance they could be wrong about that, too."

Why did Amos find it so endearing when a beautiful woman laughed until her eyes watered and mashed potatoes squirted between her lips? When Claire got hold of herself, she rummaged in her purse and pulled out a color postcard and set it on the table. "Recognize this?"

"Sure," he said. "It's the Temple of Dawn in Bangkok. It sits on the banks of the Chao Phraya River."

"Nobody else had a clue. You're really something, you know that?"

She was always amazed by his knowledge of geography, chess, architecture, history, jazz, the duties of a corner man during a boxing match—any of the things he had come to know from twenty years of living, reading, hustling, being in touch with the streets. Though he never let on, he resented the amazement of people like Claire Hathaway. Young Negroes, they seemed to be saying, weren't expected to know very much. "Who's the postcard from?" he said.

"My brother. He's a pilot in the Air Force."

"What the hell's an Air Force pilot doing in Thailand?"

"Beats me. Go ahead and read it."

He turned the card over:

Dear Claire,

Earthquake and I are on R&R here in the Venice of the East. Best thing yet was an outdoor kick-boxing match. It poured down rain, we were knee-deep in mud, lightbulbs kept exploding in the ring. Having a ball.

Love you,
Wallace

Amos turned the card back over and gazed at the Temple of Dawn. "Sounds like your brother got his hands on some of that Thai reefer."

"Nothing would surprise me with Wallace."

Amos kept staring at the postcard. "Man, I've always wanted to go to Bangkok. It's almost exactly halfway around the world from this salt mine. . . ." He also dreamed of visiting the pyramids, the Taj Mahal, the Mayan ruins in the Yucatán, Rio during Mardi Gras and dozens of other places he'd explored in the picture encyclopedias in his parents' living room. But the farthest he'd ever ventured from Detroit was a bus ride to Flint to tour the Buick plant where his father was foreman.

"So," Claire said, returning the postcard to her purse, "when are you going to take me out to hear some jazz?"

Amos almost choked on his cherry pie. For two years he'd been trying to work up the nerve to ask her out. For two years he'd assumed a corn-fed beauty from the grain belt would sooner die than be seen out on the town with a Negro. And just like that, she'd popped the question herself.

"How 'bout Saturday night?" he said.

"It's a date."

And so on Saturday afternoon Amos glided into Berry Gordy's 3-D Record Mart, bursting to break the news. There were no customers in the store, as usual, and Ornette Coleman was squawking and honking on the hi-fi. "So," Amos announced, parading in front of the neighborhood crew sprawled on ratty sofas and chairs in the back of the store, "the youngest buck of the bunch got hisself a gray piece to go out with to-night!"

Everyone whooped and hollered at the kid—everyone except Howard Russell. His freshly processed hair was curing in a dew rag. He'd gotten laid off three days earlier from a job riveting floorboards into Ford Fairlanes at River Rouge, and he'd been drinking Night Train wine steadily ever since. "Amos," he said, "you works for the man and you dresses like a motherfuckin' perfesser. Why some white bitch gonna go out wi' choo'?"

Everyone laughed even louder—everyone except Berry Gordy. Amos was like a baby brother to Berry. They'd grown up next door to each other on Grand Boulevard, not far from General Motors headquarters, in the largely Negro, middle-class West Side. Amos had worked as a water boy when Berry was fighting his way up through the Golden Gloves brackets, from flyweight to bantamweight to featherweight, eating like a horse, working out, dreaming a familiar Detroit dream. Jackie Wilson had done it. Joe Louis had done it—had started out working in a Ford factory and was now heavyweight champion of the world. If they could do it, Berry Gordy told himself, he could do it too. Luther Fuller kept reminding him how long the odds were, how foolish it would be to pursue a professional boxing career. When that failed, he tried to persuade Berry at least to finish high school.

But Amos knew that nothing would keep Berry from his

dream. He knew Berry hated being tied down in one of his father's small businesses—the plastering and carpentry operation, the printing shop, the Booker T. Washington Grocery—and that he preferred shining shoes out on a street corner. So it didn't surprise Amos when Berry dropped out of high school and tried to make it in the ring. What did surprise Amos was that after three years of fighting in Detroit's Olympia and then in California, Berry came back home and announced he was giving it up. When Amos asked him why, he said, "One day in Los Angeles I was standing on a street corner, and I noticed two posters stapled to a phone pole. One was for a Battle of the Bands, the other was for a boxing card. The boxers were twenty-five years old and looked fifty. The musicians were fifty years old and looked twenty-five. That did it."

Five years later, after serving a hitch in Korea and working briefly in a rear-axle plant, Berry opened the 3-D Record Mart on Twelfth Street, in the heart of Detroit. The bins were full of Charlie Parker and Miles Davis, Thelonious Monk and Sarah Vaughan, a little Nat "King" Cole and Della Reese, even some fringe stuff like Ornette Coleman. But few people outside Berry's circle of musicians and fellow jazz buffs who haunted Baker's Keyboard Lounge and the Paradise Club and the Minor Key ever bought the records. Detroit, a lunch-pail town never known for its sophistication, preferred raw, thwanking blues shouters like John Lee Hooker. The 3-D Record Mart had been open less than a year, and already Berry had admitted to Amos that it was doomed.

But Berry had learned something. He had a hunch that the way to success and power in the music business was not by selling Negro music, especially cerebral Negro music like jazz, to a Negro audience, but somehow by fusing the various strains of Negro music that flourished in cities like Detroit—gospel, blues, R&B—into an entirely new sound, then selling it to a mass audience of Negroes and whites. And it was Howard Russell's putdown of Amos Fuller that Saturday afternoon in the back of the 3-D Record Mart—"you works for the man and you dresses like a motherfuckin' perfesser"—that helped Berry Gordy verbalize his hunch for the very first time.

"Say, nigger," he said to Russell, "what you do makes you so great?"

"Me, I drinks wine." The only laughter came from Charles Baker, who'd also been laid off from River Rouge and was working on a major jag of his own.

"You drinks wine," Berry said. "And you works for the man in a car factory—sometimes. So you gonna sit there and put down Amos for being clean and using his artistic talent and making a decent living—just cause he works for white folks? Who you think owns River Rouge? When you gonna wise up, nigger, and realize ain't nothing wrong with the white man's money—and there's a hell of a lot more of it?"

"Amen." Everyone turned. It was Bill Robinson, a kid with light skin and reddish processed hair who'd started hanging around the store when he discovered the fine selection of records by his favorite singer, Sarah Vaughan. He was younger than Amos, but he had a fine falsetto voice and he'd already written dozens of songs for his vocal quartet, the Matadors. He even had a stage name. He called himself Smokey.

"What's that s'posed to mean, little boy?" Russell said.

"Amen means amen," Bill said. "Berry's right. Who cares who's paying you so long as you're doing what you love to do?"

Amos sensed an edge in the air he didn't particularly like, so he said he had to swing by the cleaner's to pick up his gold lamé pimp suit, something nice and conservative to set this white girl at ease. Everyone howled as he left—everyone except Howard Russell and Charles Baker.

At Baker's Keyboard Lounge that night, Amos couldn't take his eyes off Claire Hathaway. He'd never seen her wear so much makeup or tease her hair so high, had never seen her wear pearls or a strapless dress that exposed her shoulders and throat. The regulars nodded their approval when Amos led her into the rich gloom and steered her to his favorite table in the corner farthest from the bandstand. Bill Robinson, sitting alone at the bar drinking a Coke, winked at Amos as they passed.

Claire seemed nervous at first, but after a couple of drinks she started bouncing along with the music. She was mesmerized by the mirror that hovered at an angle over the organ, giving everyone in the room a reflected view of Jimmy Smith's hands as they flashed across three tiers of keyboards. When the first set ended, she turned to Amos. "If you don't put your tongue back in your mouth, young man, I'm going to have you thrown out of here for indecent drooling."

He clapped his hands and laughed his goofy gold-toothed laugh. Yes, he thought, she was remarkably cool, considering she was from Iowa and probably saw her first Negro the day she arrived in Detroit and surely had never set foot in a mixed-race nightclub. This could be his lucky night.

As the musicians climbed down off the bandstand, she said, "Amos, I've been hearing a rumor."

He considered telling her yes, it's true, we really do have bigger cocks. But he didn't want to press his luck just yet, so he said, "Oh?"

"I hear someone's been slipping our design work to Plymouth."

"You what?"

"I hear someone's been slipping our design work to Plymouth."

"Who'd you hear that from?"

"A couple of different people. That's not important. What's important is that some people are very worried about it. If I were you, Amos, I'd do myself a favor." She took a deep breath.

"Now don't get the wrong idea. I'm telling you this because we're friends and I care about you."

"Right."

"First of all, it's no secret that one of the reasons—I said *one* of the reasons—you got hired into the Beauty Parlor—"

"Is because of my father's relationship with Ted Mackey. Yes, Claire—now tell me something I don't already know."

"Don't start getting defensive."

"I'm not getting defensive. Get to the point."

"The point is that if you know anything about this, you ought to say so right now."

"Oh? And why's that?"

"Because—this is what I'm trying to tell you, Amos—if it comes out later that you knew something and didn't say so, there are people who'd love to use that as an excuse to get rid of you. Not to mention the egg on Ted Mackey's face."

"Since when did you get so worried about me getting fired?"

"I don't know—a while ago. You *are* my friend, you know."

"Bullshit. And what's this shit about egg on Ted Mackey's face? You tippin' in on Ted Mackey?"

" 'Tippin' in'?"

"Come on, Claire, cut the naive shit. You may be from Iowa, but you ain't dumb, and I may be twenty years old but I'm a nigger off the street and I ain't exactly dumb either. All of a sudden you're worried about my job and Ted Mackey's pretty face. Why don't you just go ahead and tell me what this is all about."

"I've already told you. I'm sorry I brought it up. Let's drop it."

"No, let's not drop it. Let me tell you something. You say there's a rumor going around that somebody's been selling us out to Plymouth. It could be true, for all I know. But have you ever met my father?"

"Of course not."

"Well, my father's built like a Roadmaster—and he's a whole lot meaner than one. If I ever did anything—*anything*—to mess up this job after all the shit he's been through in his lifetime, he'd whup my black ass so bad I'd wish I never picked up a pencil and learned to draw. You hear what I'm saying?"

"Yes. Case closed."

"Good. Now—you tippin' in on Ted Mackey?"

"I'm going to smack you, Amos Fuller. I am not *tippin' in* on anybody. The only reason I mentioned any of this is because I don't want to see you get hurt. It shouldn't come as a big surprise to you that plenty of people out there are just itching to stab you in the back—not only because of the color of your skin but because of how you got your job. If you can't accept that, then I guess we're not really friends after all."

"Okay. Thanks for the warning. Now I'm going to get us two more highballs, and when I get back we're going to talk about something besides cars, something nice and light. Like the hydrogen bomb, maybe."

But when Amos returned with the drinks, Bill Robinson was sitting in his chair. The little bastard spent the rest of the night running his warbly mouth, telling Claire about his singing group and the new record label their friend Berry Gordy was trying to start. He even sang her his new song, and she forgot all about Jimmy Smith. Amos, unable to get a word in, proceeded to get glumly drunk. He had some trouble driving, and when he pulled up in front of the Huntington Arms apartments, Claire didn't invite him in. She didn't even kiss him goodnight. Driving home with one eye closed, he decided, with the irrational clarity of the wounded male, that Claire Hathaway was indeed tippin' in on Ted Mackey.

Twenty

As the last of the ice on Mirror Lake melted and the days grew longer and warmer, Milmary Mackey saw less and less of her husband. That suited her fine. She realized their marriage had arrived at its long, dry afternoon, that time when the prospect of having more children had been quietly, mutually abandoned and the pulse of passion was growing fainter and neither she nor Ted had the energy or the desire to do anything about it.

Milmary had stopped drinking in the afternoons, and she turned down dozens of invitations to cocktail parties, backyard cookouts and country club dances. She didn't tell Ted about the invitations or bother to send regrets. She simply tossed them in the trash and forgot them. Ted was so preoccupied with work he didn't even notice.

Almost every afternoon now, after spending the morning at her typewriter in the back bedroom, she went for a long ride on one of Carl Frierson's quarter horses. He was a whiskery old bachelor who'd built a cabin on the far side of the lake years ago, long before the post-war car boom hit and the auto executives started planting their gaudy monuments in the trees. He rented his horses by the hour. They weren't much, at least compared with the polished jumping horses Milmary had ridden in Grosse Pointe as a girl; but now she took an almost erotic pleasure in riding them through the woods, which were suddenly fuzzy with flowers and buds. She could feel her legs growing stronger by the day, and as her senses sharpened, her appetite returned. She loved the smell of the woods, the spongy soil bursting with buds and laced with Indian bones, the smell of the beginning and the end of life. What she loved best, though, was the musty smell of the horses and the barns, the iodine burn of hay and leather and manure. When Frierson saw her brushing a sweaty horse, he grunted, "You don't gotta do that, Mrs. Mackey. I got a nigger to take care of that." But she insisted. The little rituals of feeding and grooming the horses put her back in touch with the physical world, the world of the senses that had seemed to disappear beneath the winter's ice and snow and her own self-induced blur of drinking and forgetting.

One afternoon, after Betsy had gone home to Pontiac and the boys were still at Little League practice, Milmary came in from her ride and went upstairs to shower and change. She had pushed the horse hard the last mile, and her legs were still trembling. She was proud that the jodhpurs she'd worn as a teenager still fit perfectly, a claim few women her age could make. The insides of her thighs were dirty from the saddle, damp and warm. Passing the boys' bedroom, she noticed it was even messier than usual, as though a grenade had gone off in there. She was picking her way through the sneakers and sweat socks and dirty T-shirts to open a window, at least let some of the radioactivity out, when she noticed that the space under Tommy's bed was crammed with what looked like newspapers. She reached down and pulled out a handful of comic books—*Green Lantern, Little Iodine, Superman, Flash*. She had no idea her sons read such trash, let alone that they hoarded it beneath their beds like buried treasure. Men in capes and masks who possessed supernatural powers were doing combat with villains capable of destroying the universe. She was transfixed. So this was what fueled her sons' overheated imaginations, this was how they spent their weekly allowance. She took half a dozen of the comic books and put them on her desk in the back bedroom.

Through the wall of windows she could see a solitary man in a red canoe paddling slowly across the lake. The lake looked like a blob of mercury, silver and still. She studied the gallery of strange objects on her desk: the old black Royal typewriter; the snapshot of Ted sprinting away from the burning plane; *Superman* and *Green Lantern* and *Flash*; the first pages of her short story about a World War II pilot known for his courage in combat but tormented, when earthbound, by unspeakable doubts and fears. The writing had been agony so far, but she was encouraged. It was a start.

In the bathroom she peeled off her riding clothes. Just as she was about to step into the shower she noticed a folder on top of the magazines Ted kept beside the toilet. It was marked "Wildcat." He must've forgotten it on his way out this morning. She opened it and was greeted by another surprise—dozens of newspaper clippings and photographs of Marilyn Monroe.

This had been quite a day of revelations, Milmary thought as she stepped into the shower. First she'd learned that the protagonist of her story, the P-38 pilot, was plagued by private doubts about such things as what his wife was doing while he was away at war; then she had learned about her sons' heroes; and now she had learned of her husband's mysterious interest in a blond movie star. So boys and men shared an attraction to the outlandish, to the preposterously powerful and beautiful. Was there a similar thread to their doubts and fears? The answer, she knew, would have to come from her short story, from the fate of the brave but tormented pilot of the legendary P-38.

Twenty-One

*M*orey Caan gazed out the train window at the petrochemical badlands of New Jersey. He'd been unable to shake the feeling that this trip was unwise, a waste of time. Big news was breaking every day in Washington, such a steady staccato of sensational stories that he almost wished he was still working for a daily newspaper. Almost.

It had started with the hydrogen bomb mishap in the Pacific. Then Oppenheimer was suspended by the Atomic Energy Commission and a "blank wall" was placed between him and all classified information. Now the Army-McCarthy hearings were under way, and Ike had just unveiled the "domino theory," his fear that if the United States allowed the French to lose Vietnam to the Communists, then a whole string of calamities would ensue—the fall of Laos, then Cambodia, Thailand, Burma, Malaysia, Indonesia, eventually the Philippines, Formosa and Japan, possibly Australia and New Zealand and finally, no doubt, New Mexico and New Jersey. Looking out the train window at the flames spurting from the refineries, Morey thought getting rid of New Jersey might not be such a bad idea.

Already he missed the intoxicating roll he'd been on, beginning with last week's press conference starring Ike and Lewis Strauss of the AEC. After a brief opening statement, Ike turned the podium over to Strauss, a short, natty bundle of energy who'd made his fortune by advising the Rockefellers how to manage theirs. Now he was one of the most vocal proponents of the H-bomb and, therefore, a bitter enemy of J. Robert Oppenheimer, one of the bomb's most vocal opponents. There Strauss stood, balding, bespectacled, viciously precise, surrounded by maps and charts as he explained to the press that the "Bravo" test had gone almost exactly as planned.

"The wind failed to follow prediction that day and shifted south," he read from a prepared statement, "and the little islands of Rongelap, Rengerik and Utirik were in the path of the fallout. A Japanese fishing trawler, the *Fortunate Dragon*, appears to have been missed in our search of the area. But based on a statement from her skipper to the effect that he saw the flash of the explosion and heard the concussion six minutes later, it must have been well within the danger area."

The *Fortunate Dragon*! Magnificent irony for the atomic age, Morey thought as he scribbled in his notebook. Strauss went on to say that all 236 natives of the three islands had been evacuated and placed under medical supervision, that he had visited them personally and found them "happy and well." One woman gave birth to a healthy girl, which she named after Strauss's wife, Alice. Since the natives have no use for money, Strauss gave the woman ten pigs.

He claimed there was no contamination of any fish other than the tuna in the *Fortunate Dragon*; and while the radioactivity from the blast would dissipate quickly, the military gains for the United States would endure. Then he asked if there were any questions.

After taking care of the big hitters in the front row, Strauss pointed at Morey. "Admiral Strauss," Morey said, rising to his feet, "can you describe the area of the blast, the effectiveness of the blast, and give us a general description of what actually happened when the H-bomb went off?"

"The area," Strauss said, "if I were to describe the area specifically, that would be translatable into the number of megatons involved, which is a matter of military secrecy. You said 'the effectiveness'—I don't know what you mean by that."

"Many people have been groping for some information as to what happens when an H-bomb goes off—how big the area of destruction is. What I'm asking you for is some enlightenment on that subject."

"Well, the nature of the H-bomb is that, in effect, it can be made to be as large as you wish, as large as the military requirements demand. That is, an H-bomb can be made large enough to take out a city."

"A whole *city*?!" Morey realized every reporter in the room had cried out with him.

Strauss blinked. "Yes, a whole city—destroy a city."

"How big a city?" Morey said.

"Any city."

"*Any* city? New York?"

"The metropolitan area, yes."

"Washington, D.C.?"

"Oh, certainly."

Morey was drowned out as a dozen reporters started shouting questions. It was, he thought now as the train entered the tunnel for the final approach to New York, the finest moment of his career. The administration had spent a solid week back-filling and clarifying Strauss's remark, trying to quell a tide of hysteria about the power of this new generation of bombs. For a few glorious days Morey had actually made news instead of merely reporting it; for one heady moment the full power of the press was his own personal power. He was interviewed by several Japanese journalists and by John Cameron Swayze and Mary Messina of Associated Press. This he could learn to like.

The Oppenheimer press conference yesterday had provided a different kind of thrill. Morey showed up at the White House early and got a good seat in the third row. Stewart Alsop showed up fifteen minutes later and informed Morey that he was sitting in his reserved chair. Morey looked up at Alsop and said, "Fuck you."

Ike tried to make the investigation of Oppenheimer's security file sound like a routine matter. Everyone in the room knew better, and they all had the same question: If the man who directed the development of the atomic bomb isn't safe from the Red hunters, then who is?

Throughout the question-and-answer period, Morey kept waving his hand in the air. Finally, when Ike had taken care of all his pets and the heavyweights, he pointed at Morey. "Yes, you there in the red necktie."

"Mr. President," he said, "will Dr. Oppenheimer's past service to the country, particularly his contributions to the development of the atomic bomb, have a bearing on this investigation?"

Ike cleared his throat. "I have known Dr. Oppenheimer and, like others, I have certainly admired and respected his very great professional and technical attainments and this is something that is the kind of thing that must be gone through with what I believe is best not talked about too much until we know whatever answers there might be."

Morey could feel the stunned silence around him. Pens had stopped scratching notebooks. He was powerless to resist. "Mr. President," he said, "would you mind repeating that?"

He sat down to roaring laughter. Ike, who never forgot a slight and rarely made the same mistake twice, surely made a mental note never to call on that frizzy-haired asshole again. But Morey didn't care. He was ecstatic over getting the single best morsel yet for *Straight from the Horse's Mouth.*

But as the train pulled into Penn Station, that ecstasy was gone. Morey felt confused. Wasn't it possible that the biography of a '54 Buick might actually mean more to the American people than the recent avalanche of news about Oppenheimer, McCarthy, Vietnam and the Bomb? Will was forever saying that Americans nowadays were far more interested in what was parked in the driveway than in what was going on in Washington or some banana republic or jungle halfway around the world. Maybe he was right.

In the station Morey bought a copy of the New York *Herald-Tribune*, Ike's favorite newspaper. In a front-page story, John Foster Dulles hinted that the United States might use atomic force to prevent the collapse of the teetering French fortress at Dien Bien Phu. Morey laughed out loud. Atomic weapons in Vietnam! Everyone in Washington knew Ike wouldn't trust Dulles with a stick of dynamite to blow up a fish pond.

*R*iding in from La Guardia in the back seat of the black Buick limousine, Ted Mackey got started on the stack of

New York newspapers. They were loaded with accounts of Marilyn Monroe's reception in Japan.

DiMaggio had been invited there to conduct baseball clinics and smile for the cameras, an old and lucrative shtick for the ex-Yankee. Marilyn had gone along, according to Louella Parsons, after promising to stay in the background and play the loyal, faceless wife while her husband took his turn in the limelight. But when the Pan Am Clipper stopped in Hawaii to refuel, there was a crowd waiting at the airport for autographs and pictures—not of Joe, but of Marilyn. Reluctantly she obliged while he stayed aboard the plane. In Tokyo the press dubbed her "the honorable buttocks-swinging madam." Mobs pawed her. A throng camped outside their hotel around the clock. DiMaggio, upstaged and unhappy, was delighted when an Army official invited Marilyn to sing for the troops still stationed in Korea.

Her performances in front of thousands of homesick, horny soldiers were electrifying. Even after she agreed to tone down her act, reducing the writhing and cutting out a few of the more suggestive songs, the troops continued to rampage. "On two occasions," the *New York Times* reported, "troops rioted wildly and behaved like bobby-soxers in Times Square, not like soldiers proud of their uniforms."

The coverage stopped abruptly when Marilyn returned to Tokyo, where she and Joe shuttered themselves in their hotel suite. What Ted Mackey didn't know, what even the most industrious gossip columnists were unable to dig up, was that an exchange took place in the privacy of their bedroom shortly after Marilyn's return from Korea. Still flushed from the adoring cheers and whistles and applause, Marilyn, dressed in a pink cashmere sweater and black toreador pants, rambled on and on about how wonderful it was to feel so desired, so loved. "Joe," she said dreamily, kicking off her shoes, sprawling on the bed, "you've never *heard* such cheering."

Joe DiMaggio had always been a man of few words. Once a sportswriter had sat near him and two other Yankees in the lobby of a Cleveland hotel and had noticed that the three ballplayers were watching other guests come and go without saying a word. Just for fun, the sportswriter decided to time their silence. After an hour and twenty minutes DiMaggio cleared his throat. One of his teammates said, "What's that, Joe?" The other said, "Shut up. He didn't say nothing." Then the three lapsed back into silence.

Now, looking down at Marilyn Monroe stretched out on the bed, DiMaggio cleared his throat again. This time he intended to speak. He believed he had many things to teach this woman, for he knew all about insomnia, ulcers and how cheers could turn overnight into catcalls and boos. He would never forget the last day of the 1948 season, for example, when the Yankees had fallen hopelessly behind the Red Sox and the manager sent a replacement out to center field for DiMaggio in the bottom of the eighth inning. Wracked by painful bone spurs in his feet, DiMaggio hobbled off the field as thirty-five thousand fans— *Boston* fans, in Fenway Park—stood and gave him a thundering ovation. He was crying by the time he reached the dugout.

DiMaggio did not tell these things to his wife now. He wouldn't have known how. Instead he fixed her with his heavy-lidded Sicilian stare and said, "You think I never heard such cheering? You need to think again."

It was a pivotal moment in their marriage. If she understood what he meant, she didn't let on. Already she was thinking about their return to the States. She'd had enough of ironing his shirts and learning Italian cooking while he played golf all day and hung out at night with his cronies. Though she didn't tell him, she'd already decided to move from San Francisco back to Los Angeles and take a role in the movie *There's No Business Like Show Business*. She had the power to drive crowds wild. It was crazy not to use her greatest natural gift.

*T*hat night Ted Mackey threw a dinner party in the back room of Toots Shor's for the top ten New York–area Buick dealers and the stylists he'd brought from Detroit for the opening of the year's first Motorama. Ted loved this restaurant because Toots called him Theodore and the clientele consisted of just enough show-biz types, sports figures, bookies, newspapermen and ticket hustlers for Ted to feel he was in touch with the real New York.

As the party was breaking up, Ted drew Claire Hathaway aside. "There's something we need to talk about," he said. "In private. Take a cab and meet me at El Morocco. It's on East Fifty-fourth Street. The cab driver'll know the place. I'll be waiting out front."

"But I'm supposed to go down to Greenwich Village with Amos and—"

"Tell them you've got a headache. I'll see you in fifteen minutes."

Twelve minutes later, Claire walked into El Morocco. She'd never seen anything like it. Out front, limousines were double-parked; inside, women were dressed in white satin and plunging necklines and glittery gowns. The men wore tuxedos, loud suits or dinner jackets. There were papier-mâché cactus plants and palm trees hovering over the black tables and zebra-striped banquettes. An orchestra was blasting, and on the jammed dance floor all the couples looked like they were glued together.

The maitre d' seemed to know Ted, and he led them to a small round table in the corner, under a canopy of palm fronds, far from the orchestra. Claire was wearing her best charcoal-gray dress, but this crowd made her feel like a librarian. A woman in pink pulled up a chair at a nearby table, hiked her skirt up over her knees and started pounding along with the orchestra on a pair of bongos.

"This is some place," Claire said. Not since the day she got off the bus at Cornell had she felt like such a hayseed.

"I figured it was about time you saw how the other half lives," Ted said, fixing drinks from the bottle of Johnnie Walker scotch, the ice bucket and seltzer bottle the waiter brought without having to be told. Ted handed her a drink and raised his glass. "A toast to . . . to finally seeing you outside the city limits of Detroit, far from the prying eyes of the world."

"I'll drink to that."

Ted started talking about the opening of the Motorama in the morning, but she couldn't take her eyes off the crowd. She thought she saw Cary Grant come out of the men's room.

". . . don't you agree?" Ted said.

"Yes. No. I'm sorry, what were you saying?"

"That I've been trying to reach you at home all week, but you're never in. Very bad form, don't you agree?" There was a trace of fatherly reprimand in his voice.

"I've been working a lot of late nights."

"You could've called."

"I guess the reason I haven't is because I haven't come up with much on anyone in the Beauty Parlor. About the only thing worth mentioning is that Norm Slenski gambles like a drunken Indian. I'm not much of a spy, I'm afraid."

Ted's hand fell on hers, casually, almost as though by accident. But it stayed there. She looked at the blue veins snaking through the soft black hairs, the gold wristwatch peeking from the starched white shirt cuff. It was such a strong hand, so warm.

"Don't apologize. That information about Slenski could come in very handy. As a matter of fact, he's one of our prime suspects." She felt him squeeze her hand. She squeezed back. "Enough shop talk," he said. "Let's dance."

"God, no! I'd die of embarrassment!"

"We'll wait for a slow number. I'll lead. There's nothing to it."

The next thing she knew she was being tugged toward the dance floor and they were melting into the mob. She was surprised how light he was on his feet, how easy it was to follow his lead. He held her close, and she rested her cheek on his shoulder.

Suddenly they twirled and her head snapped upright and she was looking straight into his face. "You're not falling asleep, are you?" he said.

"No, I was just thinking—this is nice, and it feels good to be out of the spying business. I'm really awful at it."

"Quit apologizing. I appreciate what you did."

"*Didn't* do is more like it."

"You did plenty. You proved something to me."

"Like what?"

"That you can keep a secret and that you can be trusted. Those are two very valuable characteristics in an employee— especially an employee who happens to be a beautiful and talented young woman."

He kissed her gently on the lips. When he pulled away she pulled him back to her, held his lips an instant longer, just as they had done at his house on New Year's Eve.

Suddenly the orchestra's drummer started pounding out a raunchy jungle rhythm and the dancers obediently began to rumba. Bongos thundered, drawing fresh couples to the dance floor, whistling, shouting, clapping, snapping their fingers in the air.

"Let's get out of here," Claire said, and yanked him back to their table. Now they sat pressed against each other on the zebra-striped banquette, holding hands under the table, talking nose to nose. From time to time they kissed.

"I almost forgot," he said. "I've got some news for you."

"Good news?"

"Excellent news. So excellent, in fact, that it requires

champagne—which just happens to be on ice right now in my suite at the Plaza."

She didn't say a word. She simply stood up and held out her arm.

*B*y the time they left Birdland, Will and Morey were so brightly lit they didn't even notice the drizzle. They walked back to the Plaza, jabbering all the way. When they burst into the lobby their clothes were wet, their hair scrambled, their eyes on fire. "Two blazing dinosaurs!" Will said to one gaping bell-hop. Then he told Morey to order them a nightcap in the Oak Room and sit tight while he fetched the man he identified only as "the missing link in the biography of a Buick."

Morey sat at the bar and ordered two brandies and brooded over how much he missed Will. Tonight's prowl through the streets and bars and jazz joints had reminded him of their college days and their life together in Washington; it made him feel old. Suddenly a conversation at a corner table escalated from loud to angry. It was half a dozen of the Buick dealers from Toots Shor's, and it was obvious they hadn't stopped pounding home the booze since dinner.

"That's horseshit and you know it, Tobin," snapped a burly guy with a pink face and yellow hair. "I've been selling Buicks since the Depression and I've had good years and bad years— but I've never seen anything to equal this. And the whole problem is that those boneheads in Detroit are making too goddamn many cars."

"He's right," said a man with waxy skin and a black suit. He looked more like an undertaker than a car dealer. "It's killing me too. They're determined to outsell Plymouth. Fine and dandy. But I'm selling more cars than ever—and I'm *losing* money!"

"Absolutely," said pink face. "And I'll tell you something else,

Tobin. The only reason you're having a halfway decent year is because you're at the busiest intersection in Scarsdale, where all the sheenies live, and you're bootlegging the living piss out of those Roadmasters."

Tobin was wearing a blue-and-yellow checked sportcoat, and he stood up so fast his chair crashed to the floor. The bar fell silent as he started waving a cigar in the pink face. "Now you lissena me, Jack Mayhew. You start accusing me of breaking the law and you're asking to get your ass whipped."

"Who's gonna whip whose ass?" Mayhew said, rising to his feet.

The bartender hurried over and stood between the two men. Then the undertaker eased them back into their chairs. Morey wrote on a cocktail napkin: "Bootlegging? Dealers losing money? Detroit making too many cars?"

"Quiet, please! Writer at work!"

Morey spun on his bar stool and was face to face with a man in a guacamole green jacket, buzzcut black hair and a pair of black-rimmed glasses. The guy stuck out his right hand. "My name's Hayes Tucker, Jr. Guess you know yours."

"Hayes," Will said, "is the top Buick dealer on Long Island."

Morey shook the hand. Did car dealers have some secret warehouse where they hoarded the world's ugliest sportcoats? Will was giving Morey a look meant to remind him that they were both getting paid good money for this.

"So," Hayes said, "Will tells me you're coming out to Levittown."

"Maybe so."

"I spent most of today on the phone with a real nice fellow who's just bought the last house on our street."

"The Korean vet?" Will said.

"Turns out he's no ordinary Korean vet. He got frostbite so bad they had to amputate his left foot and give him the Purple Heart. Wouldn't you know it, he's driving a '42 Plymouth and thinks maybe it's time to step up to a Buick. If he does, that'll make seven Buicks in a row on our block! Wouldn't that be something?"

"That'd be something, all right," Morey said.

Hayes fished a stack of snapshots out of his pocket and fanned them across the bar: an endless maze of streets and cul-de-sacs dotted with identical houses. Moving vans were parked in several driveways. Off in the distance, bulldozers were skinning fresh earth to make way for more houses. Morey could almost smell the sawdust, hear the tattoo of hammers, the barking of dogs, the cries of children. "So that's Levittown," he said. "Looks a little barren."

"It used to be potato farms," Hayes said. "But don't worry about that. Big Bill's spending eight million smackers on trees and shrubbery. It's gonna be a jungle before you know it."

"Big Bill?" Will said.

"Big Bill Levitt. He's the genius who put this baby together. Sold me my house for eight thousand bucks—with a down payment of ninety bucks and a handshake. That was all the cash I had on me the day I drove out to see the place. That's Big Bill for you." He scooped up the snapshots. "So what do you think, Morey?"

"I think seven new Buicks on one block could make an incredible little story."

"Then you'll be out to see us?"

"We'll see, Hayes. It's going to be a while before they make that half-millionth Buick, you know."

"Right you are!" He sprang to his feet. He reminded Morey of a jackrabbit. "Guess I'll be turning in. Don't want to miss the opening of that Motorama tomorrow."

Will walked him to the elevator. Now we're getting somewhere, Morey thought, now we're getting in touch with the essence of American sickness. Suddenly happy, he sipped brandy and looked out the huge window at the horse-drawn carriages lined up across Fifty-ninth Street. A cab pulled up beneath the window. Ted Mackey climbed out, followed by a much younger woman—the stylist Morey had interviewed, Claire Hathaway. She took Ted's arm and they hurried up the steps through the hotel's side door. No way, Morey told himself. Mackey's married, and she's young enough to be his daughter—and they work for General Motors, for chrissakes.

"Everything all right?" Will said, sliding on to the next bar stool.

"Two blazing dinosaurs." They laughed. "I just saw the damnedest"—careful, he told himself—"I just thought the damnedest thing."

"What's that?"

"I hope Hayes Tucker never tries to sell me a car."

7ed poured champagne to the brims of the glasses to make sure some would spill. He handed Claire a glass. She was sitting on the sofa by the window, with the lights of Central Park strewn behind her. They clinked glasses and drank.

"I can't stand the suspense," she said. "What's this excellent news?"

He kicked off his shoes and tossed his necktie and jacket on a chair. "The news is that I have a proposition for you."

"Mister Mackey! What kind of girl do you think I am?"

"I'll show you what kind of girl I think you are." He leaned down and kissed her, his tongue flickering in her mouth. He pulled away and walked across the room, spilling champagne. "I learned from Harvey yesterday that the Engineering Policy Group is ready to vote on the Wildcat. Since the Century's looking like such a smash, Harvey thinks the vote's going to be yes."

"Ted, that would be wonderful."

"Yes, it would. And I'd like to know if you'd be interested in heading the design team—*if* it goes through."

"You're kidding."

"I'm not kidding. I couldn't possibly be more serious. I told you that if you helped me out, I'd make it worth your while. Besides, you're perfect for the job."

"Do you really think I could handle it?"

"There's no doubt in my mind. I wouldn't have asked if there were."

She swallowed the rest of her champagne and put the glass on an end table, then stood up and slipped her arms around him. He dropped his glass, a thunking splash on the carpet. Then he felt himself being pulled down onto the sofa. As they kissed they tore at each other's clothes.

"After long and careful deliberation," she said, "my answer is yes."

"I forgot the question."

They laughed and kissed and wrestled on the sofa. It would go on like that for hours, on the sofa, in the chairs, on the bed in the other room. At dawn they wound up sunk in hot suds in the huge bathtub, sharing the last bottle of champagne and watching the tiles glow with the first blue light. They hadn't spoken in more than an hour. As she watched the blue deepen on the tile walls, Claire thought of the sky, of flying, and of her brother.

"Weren't you some kind of pilot in the war?" she said.

"Yes, a very average pilot."

"I heard you got a medal."

"Two, actually. One was for dumb luck, the other was for wrecking a plane and messing up my leg."

"My brother's a pilot." She looked at Ted. His eyes were closed. "He's in the Air Force. I got a postcard from him the other day, from Bangkok. I think he's on some kind of secret mission."

Ted wasn't interested in this vague story about some brother off on a shady mission. He wanted this spell—this lovely young woman in this hot foamy water, these blue tiles, this burning champagne—to last forever.

The phone rang.

Groaning, he wrapped himself in a towel and went to answer it. Hayes Tucker, Jr., obviously well into his second pot of coffee, wanted to buy Ted breakfast and tell him about the Korean vet. Ted heard water splashing in the bathroom. He agreed to meet Hayes in twenty minutes in the restaurant at the Waldorf-Astoria.

"Who was it?" Claire called from the bathroom.

"The technical director of the Motorama. They've got a last-minute crisis, as usual. I've got to run down and meet them. You get some sleep and I'll see you this afternoon."

He was dressed in five minutes and, after bending over the tub to kiss her, he was gone.

Boiled

Shrimp

and

Anthracite

One

On the first leg of the flight to Los Angeles, Harvey Pearl took the window seat and promptly turned his back on Will Lomax. But every time Harvey got lost in his thoughts, got lost staring at the mushrooming thunderheads, Will would ask him a question. "Is John Nickles having any luck tracking down that leak?"

Harvey turned from his thoughts and his glorious view and looked at the man in the aisle seat. He was so polished, so young and eager, that Harvey didn't have the heart to tell him to shut the hell up. "I believe he is," he said.

"I pity the poor bastard who did it. Ted takes these things personally."

"Yes, he does. We all do."

"Ted sure was on cloud nine this morning, though."

"I know. I was at his house celebrating last night." Harvey looked back out the window. The thunderheads looked like plants—evil, gorgeous, dangerous plants. He wondered if he would be able to sleep after the stop in Chicago, since he hadn't slept at all last night. After breaking the good news to Ted about the Wildcat, after helping Ted and Milmary drink two bottles of champagne, Harvey had invited her down to his house for a nightcap. He was afraid he was making a terrible mistake; but as he paced the house after she left, listening to Franz Schubert, drinking gin, then black coffee, then more gin, Harvey understood that he had no choice. He had to tell his secret to someone.

It was unbearable. And Milmary was the only person he knew who might even begin to understand. Looking at the thunderheads now, he had to admit he did feel a sense of relief, an actual physical lightness, from telling Milmary that he went to Japan last year not to see temples and Toyota design studios but to track down Taka Matsuda.

He believed she was still alive somewhere in Hiroshima. That's where her last letters had been postmarked in the late forties and early fifties, cheerful, chatty letters that came to him once a week, then once a month, then once a year, then stopped coming altogether.

He spent his first two days in Hiroshima knocking on doors in Taka's old neighborhood. He showed everyone a photograph of her he'd carried since the day she left California. All he learned was that the makeshift building on the site of the old Matsuda home, a hodgepodge of scrap wood and sheet metal, was occupied by fourteen people named Shioji who spoke no English and were openly suspicious of this foreigner. On the second afternoon, exhausted and frustrated, Harvey sat on a park bench and buried his face in his hands and started laughing. If only the boys at GM could see me now, he thought. While they're in Florida drinking gin and playing golf, I'm halfway around the world on a wild goose chase in a city that just a few years ago was a heap of rubble and ash.

Eventually he stopped laughing, stood up and started walking. He walked for two days, aimlessly, in a haze, drinking everything in. The picture of Hiroshima that would stay forever in his mind was a famous news photograph taken hours after the bomb was dropped. The only building standing was the shell of a Western-style church with Gothic arches, its stained-glass windows melted, its roof gone. The other buildings looked like rotten teeth, or tombstones. All the trees were scorched and leafless, and the rubble was smoking. There were no people in the picture.

But as Harvey walked the streets he was amazed by how

quickly the Japanese had rebuilt. In no time they'd slapped together a city of cardboard and scrap wood and stucco and tin,
and now they were busy replacing those makeshift shelters with
solid new homes and offices and shops. He was amazed that the
public parks were ablaze with young trees and lovingly tended
flowers. He was amazed that, in a country where order was so
highly prized, so many drunk businessmen would weave merrily
down the sidewalks at the end of the day. Finally he was amazed,
almost appalled, at the brazen way people would gather as he
passed, giggling, pointing at a foreigner, whispering, *"Gaijin!
Gaijin!"* He was ready to go home.

Before leaving the next morning for the train that would take
him to the airport in Tokyo, he made one last visit to Taka
Matsuda's old neighborhood. As he snapped a few pictures, a
boy with black bangs chopped perfectly across his eyebrows
walked out of the Shioji house. Without a word, the boy took
Harvey by the hand and led him up the street to the shabby
restaurant at the corner.

The only person in the place was a man slouched at a corner
table smoking a cigarette and reading a newspaper. On the television behind the bar Ronald Reagan, dressed as Lieutenant
Brass Bancroft, was getting ready for a bayonet fight with a
German soldier. The sound was turned off. The man reading
the newspaper didn't stand up when Harvey approached—a
shocking breach of Japanese etiquette. He simply held out his
right hand and said, "Mr. Pearl, please have a sit."

Harvey shook the hand, a cold and tender hand, and sat down.
The man was wearing glasses. Harvey guessed he was in his mid-
thirties, but he looked weary beyond his years. Surely he wasn't
a businessman because he wasn't wearing a suit, he needed a
haircut, his shirt was untucked, and at eleven o'clock in the
morning he was slouched in an empty restaurant reading a newspaper. Harvey waited. After the boy ran off, the man said, "I
understand you have looking for my sister."

"Then—you must be Ichiro Matsuda!"

The man laughed, a thin laugh that turned into a cough. "No, Ichiro-san dies honorable for his country in great war, shot down by America plane much superior Zero-sen."

"I'm sorry to hear that." Taka had not said anything in her letters about losing a brother during the war.

"Not to sorry." He laughed again, this time merrily. He lit a fresh cigarette from the butt of the last one. His hands were trembling. "So. You like Hiroshima, yes?"

"I find it fascinating."

"Very so."

"Then you must be Taka's other brother, Tetsuo?"

"Very so. Now—you have come to see Taka, yes?"

"Yes. Is she still alive?"

"She is home. Kagoshima. She is expect you. We go now?"

Just like that Harvey found himself on a train headed not north to Tokyo and the airport and home, but south to Kago-shima, where Taka Matsuda had lived briefly as a girl, where her brothers were born and her father died. Tetsuo, sitting in the window seat, produced a pint bottle of Seagram's 7, took a slug and passed it to Harvey. Harvey took a longer slug and waited for the burn to hit. He could feel the disapproving stares of the other passengers, mostly women and children at this hour, but he didn't give a damn. He took another slug. Something told him he was going to be needing it.

All the way to Kagoshima, Tetsuo Matsuda rambled on about the Nissan strike. Even if his English had been good, it would've been difficult to follow his disjointed tirade about how the company had crushed the union and installed one of its own, how he'd been railroaded out of a job, fired, blacklisted, left to die. When Harvey tried to ask about his sister, all he said was "She very better." Then he went on ranting against his fellow union organizers for caving in to Nissan. Harvey figured it was the whisky talking.

When they stepped out of the train station in Kagoshima they were swallowed up in the brawling traffic of the waterfront. Cranes that looked like monstrous insects swung the city's wares—porcelain, silks, tin—into the holds of waiting ships. The street smelled of brine, car exhaust, frying fish. Harvey snapped a few pictures while Tetsuo Matsuda tried to flag a cab. The very first stories Taka had told Harvey in her room in the back of the big house in Pasadena had been stories about Kagoshima, her birthplace, a city of repeated devastations—civil wars, volcanos, epidemics. During the last war, Harvey had heard, it had been badly blistered by American incendiary bombs made of magnesium and jellied gasoline.

The cab carried them away from the waterfront, up steep green hills, past a university. Many of the buildings were old, older than anything in Hiroshima, but there were also reminders of the war—scorched buildings, vacant lots. The cab stopped in front of a house on a block of one-story wooden houses. Harvey paid the driver and followed Tetsuo through a gate, across an immaculate courtyard, into the cool, dark house. Tetsuo flopped on a sofa and said, "Taka is in back." Then he fell asleep.

Harvey walked down a long, dim hallway to a bedroom. The shades were drawn against the afternoon sun, and the room was filled with an eerie orange glow. The only furniture was a chair, a small dresser and a bed. When Harvey reached the doorway he could see a woman sitting on the edge of the bed with her hands folded on her lap and the bottom half of her face wrapped in a gauze mask, the kind the Japanese wore when they had a cold so they wouldn't pass germs on to others. It took Harvey's eyes a moment to adjust to the orange light. As soon as he was sure it was Taka Matsuda, he started toward her with his arms open.

"No!" she cried, raising a hand as if to ward off a blow. "Sit. We must talk first." Harvey sat in the chair. She cleared her throat. "You are very kind to come, but you have upset me terribly."

"Your letters—"

"Please just listen. I will tell you everything and then you will understand why I stopped writing." She stared at the wall and took a deep breath, as though preparing for a painful recitation she had already made many times. "It was a Monday morning. The sky was blue, and it was very hot and humid. Like everyone else in Hiroshima, I was to help with the house-clearing that day because they were afraid of the fire bombs and they wanted to make breaks to keep the fires from spreading. Since it was hot and the work was hard, I wore gloves and a straw hat with a broad brim."

"So you *were* in Hiroshima. . . ."

She ignored him. "I hadn't been working fifteen minutes—I was trying to move a large rock from the foundation of a house—when the girl beside me said, 'Look, Taka. B-chan!' I have often laughed at that. She spoke as though the B-29 was a harmless pet. I looked up and saw the silver plane with the white line coming out behind it. The next thing I knew the air was on fire."

Harvey had started moaning softly, but she kept staring at the wall and talking in the same flat tone of voice. "When I woke up it was dark and I was alone. I tried to walk but could see only a few feet in front of me and couldn't tell where I was going. But then I came into daylight and realized I had been in a cloud of smoke or dust. I was by the river, so I slid down the bank and sat in the cool water. Many others were in the water. Everyone was burned and their faces were swollen. My eyes were closing and it was becoming hard to see so I tried to walk, but my legs did not work. So I sat there beside the river."

She ignored Harvey's moaning.

"I woke up on a straw mat. I was in an elementary school that had been made into a medical center. Everyone around me cried for water. On the third day I heard someone call my name. I tried to open my eyes but I could not, I had to use my fingers to open them. It was Tetsuo. Do you know what I said to him?"

Harvey shook his head.

"I asked him if he had any mandarin oranges!" She laughed. "Then Tetsuo brought me here. I have been here since. Tetsuo mailed my letters to you from Hiroshima."

"Why did you stop writing?"

"Because . . ." She looked at her hands. "I had surgery but it did not help. I tried to get a place with the Hiroshima Maidens but was not accepted. When I knew I would never be the same I did not want you to know, because I did not want you to be ashamed or feel guilty."

The Hiroshima Maidens. Harvey remembered seeing something about them on television, something about a group of atomic bomb survivors being brought to the United States for plastic surgery. Until now he hadn't given them a second thought.

"So," Taka said, "you are ready to see me now?"

Harvey nodded. She reached up and began to unravel the gauze mask. He kept telling himself it wasn't going to be so bad. After all, her hands and high cheekbones and wide, dancing eyes had not been damaged. But as the last of the gauze came off, he heard himself gasp. The pretty little snub nose had been mashed, like warm clay pressed in by a thumb, and all that remained were two black holes and a lump of cartilage. The mouth, once the flower he dared to kiss, was twisted, the lips and flesh melting down over the jaw, all of it red scar tissue that even now looked angry and hot.

Harvey started weeping. The tears seemed to come from inside his bones. He realized in that instant that his safe, orderly, monkish life had come to an end, that all the years of walling out the world, of burying himself in his work, all the years of routine and order and carefully orchestrated flamboyance, his almost

Japanese blending of his work into his life—it was all over. Eventually—he had no idea how long he wept—Taka rested her hands on his shoulders. "Stop now, Harvey. It is over. Now you must go."

He stood up and rubbed his face and eyes with his handkerchief. She had replaced the gauze mask. He hugged her and felt her go limp in his arms, but then she pushed him away. "Tetsuo will take you back to Hiroshima," she said. "Thank you for coming. Please go."

She eased him out of the bedroom and closed the door behind him. Tetsuo was waiting on the front porch, smiling, obviously refreshed by his nap. On the train he produced a fresh pint of Seagram's 7, but Harvey waved it away. "So," Tetsuo said, "what you do think of my sister?"

Harvey had been staring out the train window at the people stooped like statues over the rice paddies. He swung toward Tetsuo. "What do I think? That's a hell of a question."

"What you are going to do to my sister? Something?"

Harvey studied the smiling face for a glimmer of irony, but he saw none. "You mean for. What am I going to do *for* your sister."

Tetsuo lit a cigarette and shrugged off the distinction. Harvey wasn't sure if he failed to understand it or if he understood it perfectly but saw no real difference, at least not coming from an American.

"I'm not sure what I'm going to do," Harvey said. "Something needs to be done, though, wouldn't you say?"

Tetsuo shrugged again, took a belt of whisky, offered Harvey the bottle. This time Harvey took the bottle and drank until the tears once again sprang to his eyes.

*W*hen the triple-tailed TWA Constellation made its scheduled stop in Chicago, a businessman took the seat between

Harvey and Will. Some sort of salesman, Will guessed. He was impeccably groomed, his hair wetted and combed straight back, brown suit, brown shoes, a necktie that didn't shout. His face was round and it repeatedly broke into a smile that revealed a gap between the front teeth, a smile so big and sincere it seemed to generate heat. When the plane reached cruising altitude, the man ordered a double scotch from the stewardess and said, "You fellows from Detroit?"

"That's right," Will said.

"Then you must be in the car game."

"That's right. I work for Buick."

"I've always been an Oldsmobile man myself, but I gotta admit that new Century is one sharp-looking little car."

"Glad you think so."

"Me, I'm in the Multimixer game."

For the first time since the plane took off, Harvey stopped staring out the window. "What on God's earth is a Multimixer?" he said.

"Why, it's the best little milkshake maker on the market—can handle up to five at a time. I'm on my way out to see two brothers who have eight of the devils in their hamburger stand."

"You mean to tell me," Harvey said, "that one hamburger stand does so much business they need to make *forty* milkshakes at a time?"

"That's exactly what I said! I gotta see it to believe it!" He lowered his voice. "Just between the three of us, the real reason I'm going to see these brothers is because they're on to something. I'm going to study their operation—then I'm going to put the hamburger on the assembly line."

Will stood up and walked to the rear of the cabin. Here he was on his first business trip with Harvey Pearl, a perfect chance to get an anecdote about David Dunbar Buick for The Book—maybe learn where Harvey got the inspiration for putting fins on cars—and not only is Harvey remote and distracted, but now along comes this beaming, moronic milkshake-maker salesman who wants to mass-produce hamburgers. Will spent the rest of the flight reading magazines in the rear of the cabin, returning to his seat only when the captain announced their approach to Los Angeles. Now the salesman was promising Harvey he would rent a Century at the airport and give him a full report during their return flight. Harvey looked terrified.

*T*he salesman's name was Ray Kroc, and the Buick Century he rented at the airport had a white roof, a canary-yellow body and a red-and-black interior. The color scheme was a little fruity, he thought, but there was nothing fruity about the way the two hundred-horsepower V-8 plowed into the hot afternoon. He had a couple of hours before his first sales call, so he decided to take a spin up the coast.

He drove north toward the lavender Santa Monica mountains. He had always loved those mountains because they tumbled right into the sea while the mountains off to the east could be framed by palm trees and covered with snow. The afternoon was glorious, and he breathed the scent of eucalyptus and salt air and waited for a straightaway to see what the Buick could do. It walked up to fifty, sixty, seventy, eighty miles per hour without breaking a sweat. Magnificent! At Malibu, Ray took one of the canyon roads and was surprised how well the car handled the spaghetti curves. When he got on the Arroyo Seco Parkway, traffic was so light he got in the far-left lane and fed her the gas again. It was thrilling, it was positively sexy, to get your guts shoved against your spine as the world whipped past, faster and faster, as fast as you wanted to make it go.

He took the Hollywood turnoff and parked in a lot off Sunset. As he rolled his display case across the parking lot he felt the full force of the heat for the first time; it bounced off the asphalt at him, baking his bones. His face was shiny with sweat by the time he reached the service entrance to Schwab's Pharmacy, the legendary Schwab's, where starlets were discovered every day and absolutely everybody who was anybody hung out. Ray had dreamed for years of making this sale. Milkshake maker to the stars . . . He mopped his face with his handkerchief and pressed the button by the service elevator.

Nothing happened. Then he heard a strange noise. Was it a saxophone? He kept listening. Yes, it was a saxophone, all right, but the damnedest saxophone this former dance-hall and radio and whorehouse piano player had ever heard. Ray pressed the elevator button again, but the weird saxophone music kept drifting down the elevator shaft to him—disjointed, fractured scales, all jumbled and torn apart and thrown back together in crazy ways. And yet, as wild as it was, it sounded almost sweet. Yes, Ray thought, it was disjointed and crazy and a little angry, but somehow it managed to come out sweet.

After pressing the button a third time and realizing the elevator was frozen on the third floor, which was where he needed to be in five minutes, Ray started lugging his display case up the stairs. When he reached the third floor, flushed and sweaty and out of breath, he came upon the saxophonist. There, bathed in yellow sunshine, was the craziest Negro he'd ever seen. His hair was long and unkempt, kind of electrocuted-looking, and he had a bushy beard; he was dressed in a Hawaiian shirt, khaki pants, sandals, no socks. His name was Ornette Coleman. He was booked to play McKee's Disc Jockey Lounge in Hollywood that night, and he was trying to polish his newest composition. From where he was sitting he'd been able to watch the salesman pull up in the yellow-and-white car, and as the man pounded up the stairwell toward him, Ornette had imagined the footsteps were the ticking of a metronome, and he quickened the tempo of his playing to match the footsteps. Much better, he thought, as the footsteps grew nearer and louder and his playing grew louder, harder, wilder. Yes, he told himself, that's *it!*

"Are you the elevator boy?" the salesman snapped.

Ornette stopped playing the saxophone, a white plastic alto he favored because each note came out distinct, detached, almost as though he could actually see it. He said, "Yup."

"What's wrong with the elevator?"

"Ain't nothin' wrong with the elevator."

"Did you hear me ring?"

"Three times."

"Then why the hell didn't you come down and get me?"

" 'Cause I got to do what I got to do. Right now I got to practice." He put the saxophone back to his lips and started toodling a fractured version of "Yankee Doodle Dandy." The salesman scowled and pushed his display case down the hall. He was drenched with sweat, breathing hard, ready to strangle the next person he saw—not the ideal state to be in when you're about to make the most important sales pitch of your career.

Again Ornette used the man's footsteps on the linoleum floor as a metronome for "Yankee Doodle Dandy," figuring the goofy white salesman was so worked up he wouldn't even realize he was being shucked. He was right. Ray Kroc had entered that exalted state he always got into before a major sales pitch, and he barely heard the honking as he approached Bernie Budnick's door.

Ray had sold hundreds of Multimixers without working half as hard as he worked that day, without the arm-waving, the table-pounding, the anecdotes, the testimonials from satisfied customers. But Bernie Budnick was not impressed. He relit his wet green cigar and shifted his rump on the foam-rubber donut that kept his hemorrhoids from burning a hole clear through his chair. "Ray, Ray, Ray," he said, "I hear everything you're saying. But Schwab's isn't a drugstore. It's an institution. And institutions by definition aren't supposed to change. We're perfectly happy with things just the way they are."

"But think of your customers!"

"That's exactly what I'm doing. Our customers are the happiest people in the world. Bill Holden was in this morning. Ronnie Reagan's down at the fountain right now. Beautiful guy. Loves our chocolate malteds. The other day he told me himself, he said, 'Bernie, you ever change a *thing* in this place and I'll never set foot in here again.' "

Even Ray Kroc knew when he was licked. When a potential customer starts telling you that a star like Ronald Reagan likes things just the way they are, you're licked. He packed up his display case and rolled it out of Bernie Budnick's office.

At the elevator the Negro was still playing the white horn. "What the hell is that you're playing?" Ray said.

"It's a saxophone. An alto."

"I know that, dammit. I mean what's that piece of music?"

"I don't have no name for it yet. I'm just trying to play what I feel. Today I felt beat—till I heard you coming up the stairs."

"You mean it's your own music?"

"Yup."

"I've got a title for you. Why don't you call it 'Ray's Pitch'?"

Ornette tugged at his beard. "Ooooh, I like that. My bass player's named Ray. How come I should call it 'Ray's Pitch'?"

"Because it's got a snowball's chance in hell of making it—like the pitch I just made down the hall."

"Ha!" Ornette stood up. Without removing the saxophone from around his neck, he opened the elevator door, slid the grate back and rolled the display case into the cage. As they descended he said, "What's in the box?"

"Multimixers. They're milkshake makers."

"I know that, dammit." Ornette was smiling, and Ray, still dazed from the beating he'd taken in Bernie Budnick's office, found himself smiling too. Ornette said, "You sell them things for a living?"

"Hundreds of 'em. All over the country, coast to coast."

"Wow."

"What's that supposed to mean?"

"Just wow. Everything is everything. You and me is just alike."

"You coulda fooled me."

"No, I mean in here." He pointed toward his heart. "We after the same thing. We both understand that we gotta do what we gotta do."

"Whatever you say." When they reached the ground floor, Ray rolled his display case back out into the blazing afternoon. The asphalt radiated heat, like a bed of coals. When he was halfway across the parking lot, he turned. The Negro was standing in the doorway, waving and smiling. Ray understood then that the guy had been serious, and to his surprise he found himself thinking that maybe he and this wild Negro *were* after the same thing.

This, Ray told himself, had to be the unlikeliest encounter he'd had in all his years of crisscrossing the country. But that was exactly why California had been put on the map. Quirkier than hell. Instead of feeling deflated by Bernie Budnick's snub, he felt inspired, ready for the next challenge. And he knew he had an oddball saxophonist to thank for his sudden eagerness to get to San Bernardino.

A few miles away, in the ballroom of the Bel Air Hotel, Will Lomax studied the young men and women—dancers, actors, actresses and singers—who'd answered the call of GM's local casting director. The line stretched the length of the ballroom and out into the peach lobby. Will had never seen so many beautiful people in one place. Did they breed them out here at some huge genetics lab and stud farm? Or was it something in the water?

"Mr. Lomax!" One of the GM staffers who'd met Will and Harvey at the airport, a blond kid with a whiskerless face, was trotting across the ballroom. "They're about to start going over the pictures upstairs!"

Will almost laughed in the kid's face, but he understood why he was so breathless. This Motorama was Harvey Pearl's baby, and when he displayed the pictures of the cars he'd selected for this year's show, all the technical people, the director and stage manager and choreographer and dozens of others, would be in attendance. It was *the* meeting. Though there wasn't anything for the "corporate liaison" to do, Will was expected to put in an appearance. He followed the blond kid across the ballroom.

"I'm not believing my sorry eyes. Is that you, Will Lomax?"

A woman broke from the line of auditioners and approached him. She had blond, almost white hair, nut-brown skin and blue eyelids.

"Don't give me that big dumb look," she said, clasping his right hand in both of hers. Bracelets jangled. "It's me, Cecelia Griffin from the University of Virginia. Class of '44? Tri-Delt?"

"Cecelia! You don't—I didn't—"

In college Cecelia Griffin had coal-black hair and fair skin, and either she wore looser blouses then or the past decade had been a boon to her bust. She was one of the most sought-after coeds on campus, but she was always on the arm of some Neanderthal linebacker or some pretty boy who drove a sports car and came from a respectable Virginia family and had a good start on a drinking problem. Will looked closer and noticed that the roots of her hair along the part were black. He thought of the old joke: "Why would a woman with such beautiful blond hair go and dye her roots black?"

She seemed to read his mind. "So I dyed my hair. Big deal." She motioned toward the people waiting in line. "You think all that blond hair's natural? For that matter, you think all those perfect tits and flat tummies and straight teeth are God-given?"

Will laughed. "No, I suppose not. What are you doing here?"

"I'm trying to get work. The question is, what are *you* doing here? I thought you and Morey Caan were going to be famous Washington newspaper reporters."

"We were. I mean, he still is. We—"

"Mr. Lomax!" The blond kid was holding the door open.

"Are you working on this show?" Cecelia said.

"Sort of. I'm doing PR work for General Mo—"

"Mr. *Lomax!*" the kid hissed.

"I've got to run," Will said.

"Could we get together for a drink?"

"Sure . . . I don't see why not."

"Call me tonight. I'm in the book. West Hollywood."

*I*t promised to be another flawless California day, so Ray Kroc got up early, shaved, showered and left for San Bernardino.

The Buick hummed toward the rising sun. We both understand that we gotta do what we gotta do, he kept thinking. Ray couldn't be sure about the Negro, but he knew exactly what he had to do that day. And there was no doubt in his mind that he would succeed.

The Buick loved the open road. He pressed harder on the throttle and raced toward the fat red sun in a flaming orange-and-raspberry sky. He got to San Bernardino with time to spare and decided to do a little exploring. He drove up and down the main drag, then tried a few side streets. He didn't see a tree taller than any of the houses. Sagebrush bounced across the streets. He crunched sand between his teeth and felt the first hot stirrings of the Santa Ana wind. Even the mountains, so lavender and lovely in Los Angeles, looked baked and evil out here. Already the sun had turned yellow, and it pulsed with heat.

Ray wondered why anyone would voluntarily move to such a flyblown tank town to set up a business. He'd done enough

homework to know that Richard and Maurice "Mac" Mc-
Donald, the owners of the busiest hamburger stand in San Ber-
doo, had left their native New Hampshire and come to southern
California just in time for the Depression. They kicked around
at a variety of grunt jobs in movie studios, but they kept their
eyes open. They noticed that the canyon roads around Los Angeles were lined with bustling stands that served barbecue and
hamburgers and chicken. So Dick and Mac bought the cheapest
piece of land they could find, which happened to be in San
Bernardino, and erected an octagonal building. But they soon
realized their drive-in hamburger stand needed to be different,
so they fired their carhops, slashed prices and streamlined the
preparation process. The idea was to serve a hamburger in
twenty seconds instead of twenty minutes.

Ray pulled the yellow-and-white Buick onto the parking lot,
found a scrap of shade and shut off the engine. Through the
sweeping panorama windshield he could see the first workers
arriving. They all wore spiffy white uniforms and white paper
hats. Ray liked that. He also liked the way everything was spot-
less; no trash blew across the lot, and even the trash barrels
were painted bright white. The sign on top of the building was
gigantic, easy to read for motorists passing on Route 66:

1 5 Cents
—McDonald's Famous Hamburgers—
Buy 'Em by the Bag!

Soon the parking lot began to fill. By the eleven o'clock opening, a dozen people were waiting in line at each of the windows;
by noon, twice as many. Ray got in one of the lines. "Say," he
said to a swarthy man in a seersucker suit, "what's the big
attraction?"

"Never eaten here before?"

"Nope."

"You're in for a treat. You'll get the best hamburger you ever ate for fifteen cents. The shakes are good and thick, too. But the part I like best is you don't have to wait around or mess with tipping anybody."

"You mean the food's already cooked?"

"They're probably grilling my hamburger right now. It'll be ready by the time we get up to the window."

Brilliant, Ray thought. He noticed that most of the people carried their bags of hamburgers to their cars and just sat there and attacked the food.

Finally, when the sun was high in the sky and cleanup began, Ray walked through the employees' entrance. He didn't see a single fly. Rounding a corner, he bumped into a man with a flat, broad face and apple cheeks. He was wearing a white uniform and a white paper hat.

"You must be Mac," Ray said, sticking out his hand.

"No, he's my brother. You want to speak to him?"

"Then you must be Dick."

"Yep."

"I'm Ray Kroc from the Multimixer company in—"

"By the Jesus!" He shook Ray's hand and hollered over his shoulder, "Mac, get back here! Mr. Multimixer's here from Chicago!"

Another man with apple cheeks and a white uniform and white hat came jogging from the kitchen, wiping his hands on his apron. "Well, if it isn't Mr. Multimixer! We heard from your local salesman that you was coming out to see us."

Ray was surprised and delighted by the welcome. The brothers gave him a tour of the operation, and it didn't take long to appreciate the beauty of it all. Everything had been reduced to a science. Even the french fries were portioned in wire baskets and stacked, production-line fashion, alongside the fryer vats. There were indeed eight five-spindle Multimixers. Henry Ford would've loved it. When Ray offered to buy the brothers dinner that evening, they eagerly accepted.

Dinner wasn't very productive from a sales standpoint because the McDonalds, taciturn to begin with, didn't like to talk while they were eating. It was as though one task at a time was all they cared to take on. But after dinner they took Ray to meet their architect, and as he studied the drawings of the fifteen franchises they'd already sold he realized he'd arrived at the perfect moment. The ball was already rolling. The buildings were covered with red and white tiles, and they had slanted roofs and big windows. The crowning touch was a pair of soaring yellow arches that shot through the roof and suggested the letter M. Ray could foresee problems keeping fluorescent bulbs lit inside those towering arches, but he said nothing.

On the way back to their house, Dick and Mac went on and on about the Buick's plush interior. Ray wasn't even listening. He was gathering his thoughts for the final sales push. When he pulled into the driveway beside the McDonalds' white frame house, neither of them spoke or moved. The brown mountains loomed behind them. Down at the bottom of the hill stood the octagonal hamburger stand and the town of San Bernardino and, snaking off into the desert, Route 66. A coyote howled. A hot rod roared off into the night.

When it occurred to Ray that the brothers might just sit there admiring the view forever, he said, "I still haven't tasted one of your famous hamburgers."

They offered to buy him lunch the next day, and he accepted. That would be the perfect moment to cement the deal.

*W*ill Lomax took Cecelia Griffin to dinner at a place on La Cienega that was done up like a cross between a Polynesian whorehouse and a Polynesian temple specializing in human sacrifice. Cries and shouts could be heard every time the kitchen door swung open. The cocktails, smoking potions served in hollowed-out pineapples, had Will and Cecelia relaxed and thick-tongued long before the food arrived. Once he got over his suspicion that he was eating wickedly overpriced dog meat, Will found himself enjoying the meal. Best of all, GM types wouldn't be caught dead in a place like this.

After dinner they decided to have one brandy for the road. Until then the conversation had been highly upright, Will giving a capsule history of his newspaper days in Washington and his sudden move to Detroit, Cecelia telling him about her jobs since arriving in L.A.—a Palmolive soap commercial, a TV game show, her first speaking part in the Doris Day movie that started shooting next week in Burbank. When the brandies were half gone, Will decided the time had come to lay his cards on the table. He pulled out snapshots of his wife and children.

"They're beautiful kids!" Cecelia said, and she sounded like she meant it. "Where did you say your wife's from?"

"West Virginia." And right now she's in Detroit, he thought, and she doesn't have blond hair or nut-brown skin and her hand doesn't keep brushing against my thigh. "How about your husband—where's he from?"

"First of all, he's my *ex*-husband. He's from Jefferson City, Missouri. I met him in college. I thought anyone with a dick that big couldn't help but keep me happy the rest of my life. Guess again."

Now that families, marital status and penis size were open topics, Will suggested a ride in the Skylark convertible. He put the top down and drove up the hill to Sunset, then east toward Hollywood. He didn't have any particular destination in mind. He was just drinking in the soft night air, glancing now and then at Cecelia's bare bronze shoulders and blue eyelids and bright pink lips; he was having very little trouble forgetting he had a wife and two children in a house two thousand miles away. When he stopped for a red light at La Brea, Cecelia asked if he liked jazz. "Love it," he said, though he hadn't listened to any of his records since he left Washington.

She directed him to a parking lot off Santa Monica Boulevard. As he was putting the top up she said, "I just know that anyone who lived with that goofy Morey Caan has got to be a smoker." He was about to tell her he hated the taste of tobacco when he saw her lighting a fat, hand-rolled cigarette with twisted tips. "Shut the door," she said, inhaling deeply. "A girlfriend of mine brought this back from Baja last weekend. She said it grows wild on the side of the road and it'll rip your head off."

"Sounds like fun." He shut the door and took a puff. He coughed up the smoke, tried again, managed to hold it in.

"That suit and tie didn't fool me," Cecelia said. "Here, why don't you relax a little. . . ." She loosened his necktie and undid the top button. By the time the reefer was gone he was tingling all over and he had the strangely pleasant sensation that his hair was on fire.

The club was less than half full, dimly lit, with candles in little red bowls on the tables and a small bandstand at the back of the room. A woman with an orange dress and skin so black it almost disappeared in the gloom came to the table and took their orders. Will had never seen skin so black. A man in a sharkskin suit stepped onto the bandstand and said into a silver bulb of a microphone: "Good evening, ladies and gentlemen, and welcome to McKee's Disc Jockey Lounge. We're pleased to have the Ornette Coleman Quartet with us again this evening. Tonight Ornette has brought along an old friend. Please welcome the Ornette Coleman Quartet—with Mr. Sonny Rollins!"

The shouting and whistling startled Will. He was amazed by the crew that came from behind the sparkling silver curtain, squinting into the spotlight, bumping into chairs and music stands. There was a Negro with a wild beard and wilder hair and a Hawaiian shirt and a white saxophone; a bass player who looked like a chauffeur; a piano player with an orange sharkskin suit and alligator shoes; a fat drummer; and finally the only one Will recognized, Sonny Rollins, one of Morey's idols. The only indication that the musicians were aware of other people in the room was a mumbled announcement by the guy with the white saxophone: "This first tune's somethin' brand-new. We call it 'Ray's Pitch.' "

They all hit it at once, an instant shrieking traffic jam, then the saxophonist broke away on a wild sprint, flashes of what sounded like nursery rhymes and popular songs, "Billy Boy" and "Yankee Doodle Dandy," followed by a long, lush and much more digestible solo by Rollins. Will felt plugged directly into the instruments, his heart throbbing along with the bass, the cymbals tickling his hair roots, his skin shivering with the sax runs, shimmering flat-out duels as Coleman and Rollins turned the song into a blistering conversation. Will's right foot stomped along with all the other feet in the room and he forgot where he was and time went away. The only thing that mattered was that everyone was plugged in with him, everyone feeding off the same heartbeat.

Between numbers there was wild applause, and Will whispered in Cecelia's ear, "I can actually *feel* this music!"

"I told you that stuff would rip your head off. So how does it feel?"

"Wonderful."

"How does this feel?" She ran a hand up his thigh.

"Not bad. Don't stop."

Each song was hotter than the last, the crowd louder, wilder, urging the musicians on. They were gone into their own world. Will had never heard music like this before, and he got lost inside it, socking a fist into his palm and stomping the floor. When the first set ended, the musicians stood up and, without so much as a thank-you or a goodbye, wandered off behind the curtain.

Now Will looked around and was surprised to see that the club was packed, people sitting on the bar, on tables. A bunch of white kids were playing bongos down by the stage; there were elegant Negro couples, Mexicans, guys in berets. Cecelia's hand was still on his thigh. "I hate to be a party pooper," she said, "but will you be a doll and run me home? I've got that audition at ten in the morning and I really need to get some rest. It's not far. You can come back."

To the rhythm of bongos they floated out to the street. He paused to admire the pink neon martini glasses in the club's windows, the hot-pink gas that sputtered and sizzled in the tubes. She laughed and slipped her arms around him. Then they kissed right there on the sidewalk, in the warm pink glow, with neon buzzing in their ears.

*I*n his darkened room at the Route 66 Motor Lodge in San Bernardino, Ray Kroc lay in bed listening to the trucks grinding back and forth. How appropriate that I should wind up here at the edge of the continent, he thought, where so many journeys begin and so many end. Sleep was out of the question. He had a vision of fluorescent lights dotting the roadside night, an endless string of yellow arches stretching across the bulky land, all the way to the other ocean, with thousands and thousands of Multimixers chugging away in the red-and-white buildings and sending a steady stream of cash into his pockets.

As the night wore on, his fantasy became more specific. The name "McDonald's," he decided, was crucial. "Kroc's" just wouldn't get it. This idea had less to do with the M-shaped yellow arches than with a born salesman's intuitive feel for what will sell. He also agreed with Dick and Mac's decision to do away with carhops and let the customers come to the windows. To hasten turnover and cut down on loitering, there must be no pay phones, no vending machines, no jukeboxes. Each new franchise must also live up to the McDonald brothers' strict standards of cleanliness. Nothing could be left to chance in the drive for absolute uniformity and predictability. Yes, Ray promised himself, every McDonald's would be exactly the same.

*O*ff to the east, behind the snow-dusted mountains, the sky was beginning to turn pink. Soon the lights of Los Angeles, that pulsing bed of coals, would begin dying one by one.

It was Cecelia who suggested they drive up here, somewhere in the Hollywood Hills, to share her last bottle of champagne and her last joint. They'd spent the past five hours thrashing the sheets on the sofa bed in her studio apartment, and the way Will was feeling now she could have suggested he tie a rock around his neck and jump off the Santa Monica pier and he probably would've done it. His bones had melted. He was as alive and happy as he'd ever been.

She was resting her head on his shoulder. She'd unbuttoned his shirt halfway and was scratching his chest hair with her dangerously long, pink fingernails. His jacket and tie were balled up somewhere in the back seat. He looked down at the lights and drank champagne straight from the bottle. "You know something?" he said. "I'm going to scream if I hear another word about glass headlight bubbles or venetian blinds in rear windows or fiberglass fender skirts or scoops or fins—"

"What are you talking about?" She started nibbling his earlobe.

"The Motorama. It's the biggest bunch of crap you've ever seen. The big news at that meeting yesterday was that Harvey's pulling the Wildcat prototype out of the show because he doesn't want to overexpose it. The director threw a screaming fit. I swear, these people . . ."

"There's big money in those silly scoops and fins."

"I know that. But do they have to give the cars names like Vega and Espada and El Camino?"

"Maybe they've got some poor Mexican locked up in a basement cooking them up."

"I wouldn't put it past them. I wouldn't put anything past
them." He laughed, drank champagne, watched the lights fade
as the sky brightened. He had never been drunk like this before,
drunk not with alcohol or love but with unabashed lust. The
woman flat loved to make love and she didn't need a blueprint
and she wasn't ashamed of it.

"You know," he said, "I could put in a word for you this
morning with the director of the Motorama."

"Please don't."

"It might actually do some good, believe it or not."

"I'm sure it would, but I really wish you wouldn't."

"Why not? Connections make the world go—"

"Please, Will!" She snapped into a kneeling position and
gripped his shoulders. "No good words. I mean it."

"Why not?"

"Because I don't want it to look like . . . I mean, let's face it,
this town's full of girls who got to the top by lying on their
backs. Look at Marilyn Monroe. They say she was the best
cocksucker in Hollywood when she was on her way up."

"Is that a fact?"

"I'm being serious." She was gripping his shirt in her fists
now. "Promise me you won't."

"Okay, I promise. No good words."

She let go of his shirt and kissed him. She really was serious.
Then the absolute purity of this night hit him: She hadn't bedded
him for anything other than the sheer joy of it. Any lingering
twinge of guilt vanished with that realization. Then, as if to add
an exclamation point, her head slid down toward his lap. In the
course of the night they'd done many things, but not this. He
leaned back and looked up at the dying stars, the perfect mirror
of the city's dying lights. He heard his zipper coming down, felt

himself growing in her mouth. He tried to count the stars, but it didn't do any good.

*A*t dawn Ray Kroc was in the lobby of the Route 66 Motor Lodge typing a one-page contract on the office typewriter. At noon he was sitting in his rented Buick Century watching customers march up to the McDonald's windows. At three o'clock he was in Dick and Mac's tiny office finishing off a cheeseburger and french fries and chocolate milkshake, a meal that would have cost him fifty-four cents if the McDonalds had allowed him to pay. Ray wiped his mouth with a napkin and shivered.

"You cold?" Mac said.

"I could close a window," Dick said.

"Don't bother," Ray said. "I'm just a little excited." He went over his business proposition point by point, talking very slowly, then wrapped it up by saying, "It'll be a gold mine for all three of us!"

"I dunno," Dick said.

"See that house up on the hill?" Mac said.

Ray nodded.

"See that big front porch?"

Ray nodded.

"That's our home and we both love it. We sit on that porch in the evenings and watch the sun set and we look down on our place here. It's peaceful. We don't need any more headaches."

"Right," Dick said. "More places, more problems."

They might as well have been speaking Greek to this Bohemian plunger from Chicago. But after the Schwab's debacle and the encounter with the wild-looking Negro, Ray was not about to take no for an answer. If these thick-skulled Yankees couldn't see that they were sitting on a gold mine, then by God he would *make* them see.

"I hear what you fellows are saying," he said. "You've worked hard all your lives and you don't want any more headaches. But how about if somebody else took all the headaches and you still got your share of the profits?" He let that sink in, then he started in with the questions that would generate easy answers and positive thinking. "You guys like money, don't you?"

"Yep."

"Sure."

"And you hate headaches, right?"

"Yep."

"You bet."

"Okay. So what would you say if you could get somebody else to open the other places for you while you stay right here, working in your restaurant and sitting on your porch in the evening watching the sun go down? No risk to you. No cost. Pure profit just for letting somebody use your name and your system. What would you say to that?"

"Aw," said Mac, "who in hell'd be crazy enough to do that?"

This, of course, was exactly what Ray wanted to hear. At last he'd gotten the brothers right where he wanted them. "Who'd be crazy enough? *Me*, that's who!"

The brothers gave each other a long, hard look. Before they could say anything, Ray jumped to his feet and dropped his one-page contract on the table. The time had come to shoot the moon. "Wait! Don't say a word! I'm going to take a little stroll into town to buy a paper. I want you to read this contract over. It's very simple. Talk it over. Sign it by the time I get back and we're in business together. Otherwise, I'll be on my way and you fellows can finish cleaning up."

When he got back half an hour later Dick and Mac hadn't budged. Their expressions hadn't changed. "Well?" Ray said.

Dick pushed the contract across the table as though it carried deadly germs. Ray was afraid to look at it. He studied the brothers' granite faces. Nothing there. Finally he looked down and saw two signatures scrawled on the bottom of the contract. Ray wanted to kiss them, but he calmly folded the piece of paper and slipped it into his pocket.

"You never did say how you liked your cheeseburger," Mac said.

Ray thought of the swarthy guy in the seersucker suit he'd talked to yesterday outside the hamburger stand. "It was the best damn cheeseburger I ever ate for nineteen cents."

When the second Motorama of the year opened that night in downtown Los Angeles, the Wildcat was missing. In its place was the Firebird, a weird little three-seater job with a glass bubble top, a pointed nose cone and a single fin rising from the trunk lid. Everything came off beautifully. The orchestra blared, the fountains spurted, the dancers kicked, the lights blazed, the cars twirled on huge turntables, and the press and public poured in to marvel at Harvey Pearl's futuristic dream machines.

To the surprise of all the GM people, Harvey spent less than half an hour at the show. Once he saw that everything was running smoothly, he slipped out a back door and climbed into his lime green Cadillac and drove south, toward the airport.

He arrived almost an hour before the flight was due. It was to be one of the longest hours of his life. He wound up in the corner of the cocktail lounge pouring down some liquid courage, then chewing gum to mask the smell of the gin, then pouring down some more and chain-smoking cigarettes. Finally the plane arrived. He stood by the customs gate watching the passengers file past the agents, open their luggage, receive stamps on their passports. Friends and family awaited most of the travelers, and after they cleared customs there were yelps and tears, hugs and kisses. Just as Harvey had feared, there was no woman with a gauze mask on her face.

He drove back to the Bel Air and told the desk clerk to hold his calls. In his room he turned off the lights, drew the curtains and sat on the edge of the bed, drinking scotch straight from the bottle until he passed out.

*A*s the TWA Constellation lumbered down the runway, Will Lomax found he was unable to stop staring at Harvey Pearl. He'd never seen him look so bad—a day's growth of whiskers, crumpled suit, pink eyes, the distinct aroma of booze. Harvey stared out the window as the sun-shocked world tilted, receded, then disappeared.

Ray Kroc, seated to Will's left on the aisle, was still dressed in a crisp brown suit, was still bug-eyed and beaming. "What's your poison, fellas?" he said. "Drinks are on me all the way to Chicago."

Harvey turned from the window and looked at him for the first time. "You celebrating something, Ray?"

"You bet I am." He patted his breast pocket. "I've got a signed contract right here that's going to make me a rich man."

"Doing what?"

"Selling hamburgers—thousands and thousands and thousands of 'em. And this time I'm not going to let a bully like Ernie Hemingway run me out of business."

"You mean Ernest Hemingway?" Will said. "The author?"

"I guess I heard somewhere that Ernie wrote some books. I'll always remember him as the neighborhood bully who smashed my lemonade stand and ran me out of business in the summer of 1908—and taught me the value of stick-to-itiveness. I'll never be able to repay *that* debt."

Will looked at Harvey and said, " 'Wrote some books'?" Harvey gave him a blank look. Will turned to Ray. " 'Wrote some books'? The guy's a shoo-in for the fucking Nobel Prize this year!"

"If you say so," Ray said. "Personally, I like Norman Vincent Peale. And biographies—you know, true stories."

"Excuse me." Will stood up and climbed over Ray's knees. He couldn't listen to another word. *Wrote some books!* He wandered to the rear of the cabin. Wasn't Frank Lloyd Wright also from Oak Park, Illinois? What other country in the history of mankind, Will asked himself, has produced a single town that produced an Ernest Hemingway, a Frank Lloyd Wright and a Ray Kroc? That realization bred another. Ray Kroc would undoubtedly sell thousands of hamburgers and become a rich man because he had all the necessary ingredients for success—"stick-to-itiveness," an appetite for the writings of Norman Vincent Peale and an unswerving faith that he was destined to meet with success. It was quite a locomotive. Will realized he was as envious of people like Ray Kroc as he was horrified by them. They weren't even guilty of the sin of greed, because money, for them, was almost beside the point. The point was that they were free to dream their absolutely brilliant, absolutely demented American dreams.

The restroom door opened, and the boy who emerged looked a little green around the gills. Will locked himself inside, lowered the toilet lid and sat down. He felt like hell, which wasn't surprising, since he'd missed an entire night's sleep and had stayed up late last night drinking with a bunch of Buick dealers. To his horror he could still smell Cecelia's perfume on his hands. Without standing up he washed his hands with hot water and Ivory soap. He realized he was not doing this out of guilt. If anything, there were a dozen reasons he wished he was still sitting beside Cecelia in that Buick convertible watching the red sun squirt out of the mountains. The jazz, the marijuana, the exuberant fucking, the view of the jeweled city just before dawn, the feeling of floating outside time—a few years ago it would've added up to a memorable night. Now it was a crisis. He smelled his hands again, breathed the reassuring fragrance of Ivory soap. There was nothing more innocent than the smell of Ivory soap.

Someone knocked on the door. "Sir?" came a female voice. "Is everything all right?"

"Be right out." He ran water in the sink, dried his hands again and stepped outside. A stewardess with hair as blond as Cecelia's and an even better suntan was standing by the door. She cocked her head and looked up at him. Was this the motherly look they teach in stewardess school—or something more? Christ, he thought, if every woman's glance is going to be loaded like this, maybe I should go ahead and get the thing surgically removed and save myself a lot of trouble. The stewardess was smiling. "Everything okay?"

"Yes. Fine, thanks." Most of the cabin lights had been turned off. They were flying into the night. A low murmur of conversation was barely audible above the humming of the propellers. "I could probably choke down a bourbon," he said.

"I'll run get it. Wait right here."

He tried not to, but he couldn't resist watching the twitch of her hips as she moved up the aisle. Was this how these things worked? The irrepressible skirt-chaser decides to settle down, gets married, starts a family, remains faithful for five years—then one night the dam bursts and all hell promptly breaks loose? He walked up toward his seat. Ray Kroc had moved into the middle seat and was leaning into Harvey's face, saying, ". . . the hamburger bun, for example. It takes a certain kind of mind to see the beauty in a simple bun. But when you get right down to it, what's the difference between a hamburger bun and, say, a car bumper?"

"Not much, I suppose," Harvey said.

"Of course not! Personally, I think we need to find a bakery that'll pre-slice our buns for us."

Will retreated to the rear of the cabin. *Pre-sliced hamburger buns!* Where would it end? He smelled his hands again. He would have to take a shower and wash his hair as soon as he got home, send the clothes he'd worn that night with Cecelia to the dry cleaners. This was no time to start getting sloppy.

On the night he decided to take the PR job with General Motors, he'd stayed up till dawn with Morey Caan. Sure, he'd said, anybody can live a pure, uncluttered life out there on the fringe, in what he and Morey used to call Edge City. The true challenge was to plug in—be a husband, father, homeowner, taxpayer, flack—and still maintain your hunger, still be a "real" writer capable of producing The Book. The problem, Will could see now that he was twenty thousand feet over Arizona, was not that he'd sold his soul to the corporate devils. No, the reason he kept smelling his hands was that he was afraid of having it all blow up in his face, of wrecking his marriage, losing his job along with his access to the inner tickings of General Motors, the mother lode of raw material. Yes, that was the lesson Cecelia had taught him. He didn't feel ashamed of his decision to plug in to GM any more than he felt guilty for spending the night with her. But now he could see what an elaborate Rube Goldberg contraption his life had become. Each part was related to every other part, and either it all worked or none of it worked. If he hoped to finish The Book, then he would somehow have to keep the whole wobbly thing together. No, this was no time to start getting sloppy.

"Here's your drink, sir."

He jumped. "Oh, thank you." He expected her to go mother other passengers, but she leaned against the magazine rack and slipped off her shoes. Anything would have sufficed, he supposed, but he heard himself say, "Where'd you get that terrific tan?"

"On the beach in front of my house. I live in Malibu."

"Must be nice."

"It is. I love it. Where are you from?"

"Detroit."

"Those gentlemen you're sitting with . . . the one who took your seat, he's really something."

"Yes, he's going to sell thousands and thousands of hamburgers."

"He sure is wound up about it. And what do you do?"

Will felt like he had a ring in his nose and was being led to the slaughterhouse. "I'm in public relations with General Motors."

"How interesting. Do you travel much in a job like that?"

"Quite a bit."

"Do you get out to L.A. often?"

"I'll probably be back in a few weeks."

She smiled, and her teeth glowed in the low light, hard, perfect teeth. "Do you mind my asking—are you married?"

"No." Welcome to the slaughterhouse.

"That's funny. I would've guessed you were."

He slipped his left hand into his pants pocket. "Why's that?"

"Because you seem preoccupied. Married men are so preoccupied."

"Oh, I'm just . . . tired. We've been under a lot of pressure the past couple of days. How about you?"

"It's not bad. The girls gripe a lot, but this job's actually pretty easy."

"No, I mean are you married?"

"Oh!" She laughed. White teeth blazed. "As a matter of fact I live by myself at the beach. . . . And I was wondering . . . maybe you'd like to come out for lunch or take a swim next time you're in town?"

"Sounds great."

A buzzer sounded. "Damn," the stewardess said, "time to go back to work. That drunk in 4-D's vomiting again. By the way, my name's Cindy." She wrote her name, phone number and address on a paper napkin and handed it to him. Her hand-writing was florid and girlish. "Let me know when you're back in town."

He watched her hips twitch back up the aisle, and it occurred to him that she hadn't even asked his name. He put the napkin in his shirt pocket, close to his heart, an open possibility.

When the plane landed in Chicago, Ray Kroc exchanged business cards with Will and Harvey. His had a drawing of a giant milkshake maker above the slogan. "It's a crazy mixed-up world . . . thanks to Multimixer!" They watched him trot across the apron.

Harvey grunted. "That son of a bitch wore me out. I'm exhausted."

Just then Cindy the stewardess walked past, smiled at Will, and winked.

Two

*M*orey Caan was itching to get home. At last, after being granted an audience with Senator McCarthy, he could finish off the long-overdue article on the "Joe Must Go" move-ment and get the *Saturday Review* editors off his back. Then he would be free to devote his full energy to the biography of a Buick. He was willing to stay up all night. Anything to wash Senator Joe out of his belly.

At least the worst of it, the face-to-face encounter with the Great Red Hunter, was over. When the receptionist had ushered Morey into McCarthy's office, the senator was on the telephone. A fan twirled overhead. The room was so cool and dark and musty that Morey felt like he was in a bunker—which, in a sense, he was. McCarthy kept tapping the telephone's mouth-

piece with a pencil, a technique for jarring the needle of a listening device, and he talked like someone in a low-budget
gangster movie: "Yeah, yeah, I can listen. I can listen all day
and all night, but I can't talk. Follow?" He glanced at Morey.
He tapped the mouthpiece. "Sure thing. Just mention this stuff
sort of casual to Echo Papa Two and get his reaction." He tapped
the mouthpiece. "Yeah, I'm with you. Sounds good. Don't call
here. I'll call you tomorrow, usual time." Instead of copying all
this down in his notebook, Morey wrote: "5 o'clock shadow
. . . ferret-eyed . . . looks even meaner than Nixon."

The interview lasted less than half an hour. McCarthy talked
like a man on top of the world instead of someone who'd been
hanging himself out to dry on national television for the past
six weeks. He said the Army-McCarthy hearings were going
"splendidly." He called Roy Cohn a "great patriot." He dismissed the "Joe Must Go" movement as the shenanigans of a
bunch of demoralized Democrats with proven Communist sym-
pathies. "A very patriotic American named Roman Reuter, a
mink rancher and a candidate for state commander of the American Legion, has launched a counter-attack supporting me. Roman's who you should be writing about, not those commie
crybabies." That suggestion, delivered with a blow of his big fist
to the desk top, told Morey everything he needed to know about
Joe McCarthy. Until that moment Morey knew only what he'd
read in the papers and seen on TV and heard at the Press Club
bar—that McCarthy had a flaming belly, trembling hands, trou-
bled sinuses, bursitis, allergies and, according to more than a
few people, a severe drinking problem and an eye for young
boys. From what Morey saw and heard in that bunker, all of it
was true. In other words, he wasn't all that much different from
most of the politicians in Washington; he just had a little more
power, which made him a little more dangerous.

When the bus finally made it to Georgetown, Morey trotted
home. He wanted to take a shower—McCarthy actually made

him feel physically unclean—before getting down to work. Fumbling with his keys, he saw a note on the door: "Call me immediately. Pete H." As soon as he got inside, Fat Boy started braying for food. Morey ignored him and dialed Pete's number. The phone rang a dozen times, and just as he was about to hang up he heard the familiar "Yello."

"Pete, it's Morey. What's up?"

"You just caught me on my way out the door. The bastards gave me an ultimatum—I go to Guatemala or I hit the fuckin' road."

"So what're you going to do?"

"I'm on my way to Guatemala. Be working for Howard Hunt and his boys. Man, you've got no idea what's going on down there. This one stinks to high heaven."

"So why are you going?"

"Because somebody's got to blow the whistle on these bastards. They're totally out of control. As far as I can tell, this whole thing's about a bunch of Eisenhower's buddies getting screwed out of some land down there. Some fruit company."

"I've heard some names." The only names he knew were the ones in Ann Wilson's diary.

"The usual fat-assed Republicans. Anyway, we gotta make it look like the country's about to go Communist. My boss told me this morning, 'I'd rather fight 'em in Guatemala than at the Alamo.' "

"The Alamo?"

"I'm telling you, this is rich. But I've gotta run or I'll miss my plane. I'll call as soon as I get back, and we can sit down and have one of our little de-briefing sessions. You follow?"

"Yeah, just like Iran." Morey felt like he was talking to Joe McCarthy again. "One last thing, Pete. About those German POWs who starved to death in '45—do you know someone at the agency named Walter who's working on it?"

There was a sigh, then a long pause. "You don't know where you heard this, right?"

"Of course."

"You remember Walter Carruthers over at State?"

"Sure. He talked my ear off about the coup in Iran last year. I thought he'd never shut up."

"Well, McCarthy's investigating him right now—leaning on him pretty hard from what I hear. Something about a socialist organization Walter belonged to when he was an undergrad at Columbia."

"So what's that got to do with Ike in '45?"

"Walter worked directly for Ike during the occupation. Kept very good notes on some of Ike's practices, so they say. Now that McCarthy's got the heat on, Walter thinks he might have to use what he knows about Ike to save his own neck."

"I'll be damned. Walter Carruthers. You reckon he's willing to talk?"

"Ask him. And remember—you don't know where you heard this."

After Morey hung up, he took a shower, made a pot of coffee and got to work washing Senator Joe out of his belly once and for all. It took him all night. By sunrise he'd finished his article and was ready to go after the biggest fish of all, the President of the United States.

Three

*M*ilmary Mackey had spent the entire afternoon at her typewriter and had produced just one paragraph. But after bringing her fictional pilot back from a bombing run that left whole blocks of Tokyo in flames, she had discovered something valuable about him. She had discovered the source of his dread.

When the phone rang, she knew it was Ted calling to say he wouldn't be home for dinner. They hadn't had dinner together in weeks. After the usual small talk he said, "Darling, we just got the preliminary second-quarter sales figures and I need to—"

"I understand. I might be asleep when you get in."

"We'll go to the club Friday, have a nice quiet evening together."

"That'll be fine."

"Everything okay?"

"Just fine."

"What you been up to?"

"I've been writing."

"Riding? What, Frierson's horses again?"

"No, *writing*. On the typewriter. My new short story."

"Oh." There was a pause. "Wasn't today your bridge day?"

"I've stopped playing bridge."

"Oh. The boys all right?"

"Yes. They're still at Little League."

When she finally got him off the line, she knew the spell had been broken. But when she re-read the paragraph, she was delighted. She'd come to see that her main character dreaded coming down out of the deadly sky because he was due to go on R&R in Australia and he dreaded freedom far more than he feared death. He dreaded anything—the barracks, the officers' club, R&R, a big city, brothels, money—that tore him away from the orderly business of killing and staying alive, anything that presented him with messy options. His name was Jason Stone. Dropping incendiary bombs on a Japanese city full of women and children was simply his job, his duty; negotiating the social intricacies of barracks or brothel was terrifying because it forced him to make choices, to decide right from wrong, to make a stand. Would he report Captain Jenkins for leaving formation and causing two planes to get shot out of the sky? Would he go with the boys to the whorehouses in Sydney and have one more secret to keep from his fiancée back in the States? Milmary was beginning to think of Jason Stone as twentieth-century man himself, afraid not of dying a pure and simple death but of living in an anxious world full of bad choices. Afraid not that the Bomb would fall but that it wouldn't—thus sentencing him to a long life filled with anxiety and pointless dread.

Suddenly—and it was these white flashes of insight that justified entire afternoons spent sweating out a single paragraph—suddenly she understood the inevitable moment her story was leading to: the moment when Jason Stone would turn his dread to ash by volunteering to fly the *Enola Gay*, the B-29 that would drop the world's first atomic bomb on Hiroshima.

She stood up and turned off the desk lamp. She looked at the *Green Lantern* and *Flash* comic books beside her typewriter. While she scorned her husband for being so out of touch with his own family, she had to admit she knew very little about her sons' lives. Only recently had she stumbled upon their pulp heroes. Did they have tree forts and secret tunnels? What were their Little League baseball games like? She'd always told herself she stayed away from their ballgames because they asked her to; there was no greater humiliation for a boy, they said, than to have his mother standing in the bleachers like Wendell Thornberry's mom, screaming at umpires, coaches and bumbling ballplayers. So she stayed away and told herself she was doing so out of love. But now she knew better. Now, standing before the typewriter and the comic books and her unfinished story, she felt she was missing something important that would soon be gone forever. She couldn't have said why, exactly, but her new understanding of her fictional bomber pilot made it essential for her to go, right now, to see her sons play Little League baseball.

She told Betsy not to plan on Ted for dinner, then went out

and started the Buick station wagon. As she drove down the gravel lane she noticed a man on a tractor digging a hole in the lawn between Harvey's house and the lake. She stopped the car and motioned to the man. He climbed off the tractor and waddled up the hill toward her. He had a sunburned face and a stomach that strained his dirty T-shirt. He took off his cap. "Ma'am?"

"Excuse me, but I live next door, in the white house. What are you doing down there?"

"Digging a hole."

"Yes, but what's it for?"

"One a them bomb shelters, s'far as I know. I just dig the holes."

"I see. Thank you."

So Harvey was jumping on the bandwagon. Only then did Milmary realize she hadn't heard from him since his trip to Los Angeles, and she had no idea if Taka Matsuda had arrived safely, or even if she was still alive.

Claire Hathaway and her crew were working late again. The Wildcat was giving them fits. They'd been given the standard three years to redesign the 1954 Buicks, but now she and her team were expected to create a new car from scratch in half that time. If working long hours under impossible deadline pressure was what made Claire happy, then this should have been the happiest time of her life.

But this time there was a difference. This time there was a doubt in the back of her mind. Ted Mackey had formally offered her the job of heading the Wildcat design team one night at the Hotel Book Cadillac—in room 415, to be exact—as they lay in the scrambled bedsheets, still sticky from their second lovemaking session. She felt she deserved the job, of course, but his timing made it impossible for her not to wonder.

"Sheee-it yes!" came Amos Fuller's voice over the top of her cubicle wall. It startled her. Only now did she notice the murmur of the transistor radio he had tuned to the Tigers game.

"What happened, Amos?" Norm Slenski called out.

"Kaline just hit a two-run homer off Bob Feller. Ain't nobody on the team can hit that badass except Big Al."

"What's the score?"

"Indians three, Tigers two. Bottom of the second."

Their banter broke Claire's concentration. She stood up and walked over to Rory Gallagher's cubicle. He was working on the Wildcat's wheel-well cut-outs.

"Rory, what are you doing? We've got to have the front bumper finished by Friday morning—not the wheel wells."

"I know, Claire, but I get off on these tangents. Look. What do you think?"

She studied his drawing. Instead of the predictable semicircular cut-outs around the tires, his flared toward the rear of the car, adding to its sense of motion. It was a small but brilliant touch. Then she noticed he'd taken it a step further. The metal inside the wheel wells was white instead of the traditional black. Coupled with the wide whitewalls on the tires, this gave the car remarkable airiness and buoyancy—two of the prime design goals John Nickles had set for the crew. This, Claire knew instantly, was a perfect stroke. It would be a major feather in Rory's cap.

"Very nice," she said. "Now get back to work on that front bumper."

Walking back to her cubicle, she consoled herself that Rory's breakthrough was not a threat to her, was actually one of the reasons she was in charge of this team. Drones like Rory Gallagher and Norm Slenski could always be counted on for the incremental advances—a wheel well here, a roofline there. But besides me, she thought, Amos Fuller is the only person in this studio who can see cars whole, with the vision to pull all the parts together. That's why I'm in charge of this crew, she told herself, and that's why someday I'll be in charge of the whole show.

Her phone was ringing. Probably John Nickles calling from a dinner party, half pickled again, to check up on the troops. "Hello?" she said.

"I told you working late one or two nights a week was fine —but five nights is above and beyond the call of duty."

"Ted! What time is it?"

"Almost eight. Time for you to knock off and let me buy you a drink."

"I really need to get home. Hello?"

"I'm right here."

"What was that clicking noise?"

"Beats me."

"I really have to get home. My mother's supposed to call at nine."

"Then I accept the invitation. Your place in half an hour. I'll bring the champagne."

"But I've got to finish this front bumper sketch—"

"Half an hour. That's an order."

She heard the clicking noise again. "Okay, you win. My place in half an hour. Do you remember how to get there?"

"How could I forget?"

*M*ilmary parked behind the wooden bleachers along the third baseline. Sure enough, there were a dozen women in the bleachers, and one of them was wearing a bright pink sun hat and had her hands cupped to her mouth. "Open your eyes, ump!" she bellowed. "You're missing a great game!"

Milmary stood in the shadow of the bleachers. She had no idea which positions her sons played or even the name of their team. All she knew was that they wore yellow T-shirts and blue caps with the letter G above the brim. Betsy had ironed the letters onto their caps.

The boys in the field were wearing yellow shirts and blue caps, so she studied them one by one. Despite the uniforms, each boy was unique: the first baseman was pudgy and ham-faced; the second baseman was olive-skinned and cat-quick; the catcher looked like a fire hydrant and kept chattering at the batter trying to rattle him; the pitcher was tall and—it was her first-born. She was surprised how much taller Tommy was than the other boys. He cupped the ball in his mitt at his belt buckle, rocked back on his heels, dropped his right hand behind his back and then, in a blur, fired the ball toward home plate. The ball smacked the catcher's mitt like a gunshot. It was astonishing— these miniature men were so skillful, they could be taught to do anything. She thought of her husband learning to fly a warplane, the sight of him running from that crippled P-38, the black smoke curling into the sky.

The first batter struck out on three pitches. The second batter hit a line drive straight at Tommy. Milmary gasped, but he casually raised his glove and speared the ball right in front of his face. Approving cries rained from his teammates and the bleachers.

When the third batter walked on a full count, Tommy kicked the dirt. Just like his father. The next batter, a burly boy who handled the bat like a twig, lofted the first pitch high over the second baseman's head, way out into right field. All the spectators and all the players on both benches leaped to their feet and started shrieking. Milmary didn't know much about baseball, but she knew when the sound of panic was battling the sound of jubilation. Then she saw why. The right fielder, a skinny boy with glasses, was trotting uncertainly toward the ball as it fell out of the sky. The screaming grew louder as the baserunner rounded second and the batter rounded first. It was apparent the right fielder had no idea where the ball was, but he kept squinting at the sky, kept wandering toward the infield, his glove open. The ball hit the grass a few feet in front of him, bounced once, and smacked him on the chest. He sat down as though a chair had been yanked from under him and watched the ball dribble to a stop a few yards away. The center fielder was there to pick it up and throw it to the second baseman, the cat-quick kid, who spun and threw a bullet toward third base. The ball arrived when the batter was a good fifteen feet short of the base. He was so shocked to see his home-run ball waiting for him in the third baseman's glove that he didn't even bother to slide. When the umpire called him out, the woman in the pink sun hat screamed: "About time you made a decent call, ump!"

Apparently the game was over because all the boys in the yellow shirts raced out to right field, where the boy who'd blocked the ball with his chest was still sitting in the grass. They picked him up and pounded him on the back and carried him on their shoulders to the bench. They lobbed paper cups full of dirt into the air. They whooped and danced.

Only then did Milmary realize the boy they were carrying was her baby, John.

The way he'd sat down when the ball hit him—the unarguable logic of it, the pure response to the physical world—filled her with a sudden terrible love for the boy. While Tommy was clearly the star, capable of striking out batters and spearing line drives, John had bad eyesight and thick glasses and had been banished to the outfield, where he wound up getting knocked down by mystifying fly balls.

"Atta boy, number nine!" one of the mothers hollered. "You saved the game for us!" Then she turned to the woman in the pink sun hat. "He never saw it. Luckiest play I've ever seen."

Milmary drove home slowly, taking back roads, watching the sun turn orange and slip into the trees. She didn't want this to end. She was trying to commit it to memory, the way it felt to understand new things about her sons—and to realize they were virtual strangers. Then she realized there was another reason she was driving so slowly on an indirect route: She was in no hurry to get home and spend another night alone, another night of keeping astonishing discoveries to herself.

"*I* sure hope that thing works!"

Claire had to chuckle as she watched Ted's penis shrink inside the slippery white condom. She was fascinated by its smell of rubber and brine and blood. Not two minutes earlier, he'd been on top of her, flailing away, cursing, and now he lay there on his back, his barrel chest heaving for air, his cock shrinking before her eyes. Such a fickle weapon. No wonder men were so insecure.

"You hope it works?" he said. "I could've sworn I heard you yelling your head off not thirty seconds ago."

"No, not *that*. I know that works. I mean the rubber thing."

"Yes, we all hope that works."

She walked over to the desk and picked up the postcard her brother had sent from Thailand. She could feel Ted watching her, but she didn't care. He was always complimenting her. He complimented her so lavishly and so often that she had stopped feeling ashamed of her body, was even beginning to feel almost proud of it.

"Here," she said, flopping on the bed and handing Ted the postcard. "Recognize this?"

"I'd say it's Disneyland if I had to guess."

"What's Disneyland?"

"It's an amusement park Walt Disney's building near L.A. It's supposed to open next year—and some of the buildings are almost as horrendous as this. What the hell is it?"

"It's the Temple of Dawn in Bangkok, Thailand. It's from my brother. I already told you he's an Air Force pilot."

"What's an Air Force pilot doing in Thailand?"

"Go ahead and read it."

Ted read the stunted account of the outdoor kick-boxing match. It reminded him of the Japanese prisoners he'd seen having kick-boxing matches during the war. They were so vicious Ted started carrying a loaded revolver whenever he flew a mission. He vowed those animals would never capture him alive.

"Excuse me one second," he said, handing Claire the postcard and rising from the bed. He took his pants into the bathroom and closed the door. He flushed the condom down the toilet, washed himself in the sink, slipped into his pants. Since Claire wasn't wearing perfume, he decided to shower when he got home.

When he emerged from the bathroom she was watching him. "Come back here and lie down."

He lay beside her. His breathing had returned to normal. She was staring at the postcard, and though he wanted to get away he said, "So who's this guy Earthquake?"

"He's my brother's copilot. His real name's Jim McGovern, but he's so crazy they call him Earthquake McGoon." She was delighted that her brother's copilot was named after Professor Nabokov's favorite character from "L'il Abner."

Ted reached for his shirt. "I'd still like to know what American pilots are doing in that part of the world."

"Do you have to leave already?"

"Afraid so. Gotta tuck the boys in."

Claire pulled the sheet up to her chin and watched him dress. As he was knotting his necktie she asked a question she'd never dared ask before: "So what do you tell your wife?"

He slid the knot up to his throat. "I tell her I'm working late. I've got a meeting or a dinner engagement. I tell her what I tell her."

"Do you think she suspects anything?"

"God, no. If she did I'd certainly know about it."

"You better comb your hair again."

She loved to watch him comb that silver hair. It reminded her of sitting with her brother on the edge of the bathtub and watching their father shave—the masculine ritual of the brush, the lather, the razor strop, the way a new man emerged from the white foam.

Ted bent over to kiss her. She wanted to run her fingers through his hair, pull him back onto the bed, but she knew she couldn't. There were so many things she couldn't do.

"A few of us will be coming out from headquarters tomorrow," he said. "Everybody wants to see how the Wildcat's coming along. So have the troops shipshape, eh?"

"Is that all?"

He looked around the room and patted his pockets. "Oh yes, there is something else. Will you be seeing Slenski tomorrow?"

"If he doesn't call in sick with another hangover."

"Could you do me a favor?"

"It depends."

"Could you try to find out just how big his gambling debts are—and who he owes the money to?"

"I could try. Why?"

"Let's just say he's become the prime suspect. It would be helpful to know a little more about his debts. I can't tell you exactly why just yet. Okay?"

"Sure. Fine. Is *that* all?"

He leaned over and pecked her lips. "It was wonderful, better than ever. We'll do it again soon. Get some rest and I'll see you in the morning."

She watched him slip out the door. She stared at the door as his footsteps faded down the stairs, as the big door in the lobby squealed and slammed shut, as he walked down the sidewalk and started the Roadmaster and drove off to the suburbs, off to his big white house and his sons and his wife. When the night was quiet again, she picked up the glass ashtray from the bedside table and threw it at the door.

*A*t the dinner table Milmary Mackey asked her sons, as casually as she could, how the game had gone that afternoon.

"We won six–five," Tommy said. "I pitched a two-hitter for three innings and got a double and a triple. Can I have some more macaroni?"

"What do you say?"

"*May* I have some more macaroni. *Please.*"

"Yes, you may. How about you, John?"

He was trying to slip his peas under his place mat. "No more macaroni and cheese for me, thank you."

"How did you do in the game today?"

"I struck out twice and grounded out."

"Is that all?"

He looked up at her. His eyes were huge behind the lenses, fish eyes. "What do you mean?"

"I mean, is that all you did?"

"I fouled off twice but I already had two strikes so I got to keep batting. Then I struck out."

"Don't you play in the field somewhere?"

"He plays outfield with Wendell *Thorn*berry," Tommy said.

Milmary gave him a look that put him back to work on his second helping of macaroni and cheese. She said, "Where do you play in the outfield, John?"

"Right field."

"Did they hit any balls out there?"

"One."

"Did you catch it?"

"No."

"Did you drop it?"

"No."

"It knocked him on his butt!" Tommy cried.

"That's enough, young man. Eat." She turned back to John. "Did it hurt when it hit you?"

"A little. May I be excused now?"

"In a minute. What happened after the ball hit you?"

"Wendell Thornberry picked it up and threw it to Tony Longo and he threw the guy out at third."

"Yeah," Tommy said through a mouthful of macaroni, "it saved a two-run homer. It saved the whole game for us."

"That's great, John!"

John studied her with his fish eyes. "How come you're asking so many questions about Little League all of a sudden?"

"Because I'm . . . interested, that's all. Now, who has room for a piece of chocolate cake?"

The boys' eyes widened. "What's the cake for?" Tommy said.

"Yeah," John said. "It's nobody's birthday."

"We'll just call it a victory cake. As soon as you clear these dishes I'll bring it out."

They sprang into action, and Tommy was first into the kitchen. John dropped a fork. After he picked it up he said, "Where's Dad tonight?"

"Your father had to work late."

"Again?"

"Yes, again."

"I haven't seen him in almost two weeks."

"He's very busy these days. He works hard for you, you know."

"Nobody else's dad works late every night."

And yours probably doesn't either, she thought. John dropped his fork again, picked it up again. She wanted to hug him, hold him to her, but she didn't dare. He was perceptive beyond his years, and he was already suspicious. A show of affection and he would probably think she'd been drinking again. As she watched the boys wolf down the cake, it was all she could do not to cry.

Four

*E*arthquake McGoon was talking about the fight they'd seen in Bangkok, but Wallace Hathaway was too scared to listen. He was so scared he could smell himself. He smelled horrible, like diesel fumes and onions and sweat. It was the smell of holy terror, and he was concentrating hard on keeping a tight asshole.

"My favorite part," Earthquake shouted above the engines, "was when those fucking light bulbs kept exploding on the mat. Those little boys with the brooms were too much."

Wallace Hathaway didn't hear a word he said. He'd come halfway around the world hoping to see some action, and now shells were whistling past the cockpit like screaming babies, tracers, machine-gun and rifle fire pinging against the skin of their unmarked C-119 Flying Boxcar, a target even a blind man could hit at this range. Wallace and Earthquake had flown the plane together many times, usually lacing the jungle with napalm to rob the Vietminh of their treasured cover, but they'd never flown into the teeth of anything like this. The jungle was alive with fire.

"Steady does it," Earthquake said, finally acknowledging that they were no longer knee-deep in mud watching the world bantamweight title fight. "I do believe somebody down there doesn't want us to land this little beast."

At last Wallace saw the red flares that marked the Dien Bien Phu airstrip, and he lowered the landing gear. As soon as the wheels were down, a rocket shell tore into the right engine, and pilot and copilot lurched forward, like a pair of marionettes, then slammed back into their seats. It almost knocked the wind out of Wallace. He could taste blood, and when he looked down he saw four pink teeth in his lap. Black smoke started gushing from the right engine and seeping through the cockpit floor. Both men started coughing. A bullet popped through the glass by Wallace's left ear, then exited, making a slightly bigger hole in the glass by Earthquake's right ear. "Well, fuck you too!" Earthquake roared, and punched a hole in the glass to let the smoke out.

Both of them knew it was too late to pull out of the landing. "Guess we might as well drop these goodies off now, eh, Wally?" Earthquake said. The "goodies" in the Flying Boxcar—food, medicine, ammunition—were part of a U.S. aid package that now covered about 80 percent of France's expenditures in this aggravating little war. It was a bizarre war, too. President Eisenhower had recently given the French ten bombers and two hundred U.S. Air Force personnel to service them; then he'd thrown in some Flying Boxcars and pilots; meanwhile, the Communist Vietminh were fighting with American weapons seized by Chinese Communists from routed Nationalist Chinese supporters of Chiang Kai-shek.

The French had decided to make a stand on the broad, flat, mountain-fringed valley of Dien Bien Phu, in the northern reaches of Vietnam. The densely wooded hills and jungles around the valley would make the fortress virtually unassailable, the French believed, and so they set about planting land mines and stringing barbed wire around the perimeter, digging trenches, building bunkers, an airstrip and three artillery bases. These were named, as only the French would think to do, after Colonel Christian de Castris's three mistresses: Gabrielle, Béatrice and Isabelle.

The French believed their superior firepower would make short work of the enemy's expected siege. What they failed to anticipate was the resourcefulness of the Vietminh general, Vo Nguyen Giap, or the dedication of his troops. For three months, as the French dug in on their isolated, exposed plateau, Giap moved fifty thousand troops through the jungle to the rim of the valley; another twenty thousand were strung out along his communication and supply lines. Even more astonishing, cannons were dismantled and carried piece by piece on soldiers' backs through the jungle, then reassembled and trained on the French emplacements. Suddenly the jungle was a wicked enemy: it cut the French off from reinforcements and resupply and gave the enemy superb cover.

And so on March 13 the siege had begun. The French were stunned by the ferocity and accuracy of the enemy's artillery fire. Beatrice fell immediately, and Gabrielle went the next day. Isabelle, it turned out, was too far away to launch a counterattack. That night Colonel Charles Piroth, the one-armed French gunnery expert, declared, "I am completely disgraced." At dawn he drank a cup of black coffee, smoked a cigarette, then pulled the safety pin out of a grenade with his teeth.

The next day, the Vietminh started storming the perimeter in waves. Even veterans of this ugly little war were appalled. Fresh waves charged over a carpet of corpses until they had pierced the outer defenses. Each night a cease-fire was called so the dead and wounded could be removed.

Wallace Hathaway and Earthquake McGoon knew none of this as they tried to land their Flying Boxcar in a heavy rain of fire. The smoke in the cockpit was now so thick that Earthquake was having trouble seeing the flares on the airstrip. He couldn't stop coughing, and his eyes were burning and watering. "I said let's drop these goodies off, eh, Wally?"

Wallace Hathaway didn't answer. He had stopped coughing. Earthquake looked over and saw that he was slumped forward in his harness, chin sagging, two dark red stains spreading on his chest. His front teeth were missing. Then the plane slammed into the ground and exploded.

When the C-119 came to rest, no French soldiers came out

of their trenches or bunkers to rescue the American pilots. The fire from the Vietminh was too fierce. So the unmarked Flying Boxcar sat out there on the mortar-pocked airstrip, full of medicine and ammunition and food, and it poured orange flames and black smoke into the sky. Eventually the other fuel tank exploded. After dark, when the fires had burned themselves out and the day's cease-fire went into effect, two French soldiers were sent out to inspect the wreckage. All the supplies had been incinerated, and the two American pilots were charred beyond recognition.

Five

*C*laire Hathaway walked up behind Norm Slenski and looked over his shoulder at his sketches of the Wildcat's hubcaps. He was experimenting with spoked wheels. Give him a small enough task, she thought, and he'll always give you big results. He didn't see her standing there, and she considered walking away. But she'd spent the past week reliving the night she hurled the ashtray at the door after Ted left her, and she had come to her senses. She realized she didn't want to be anything other than the other woman in Ted Mackey's life. Even his wife was playing a distant second fiddle to his career. Who needed that? So she had decided to go ahead and do him this small favor. It would be nice, for once, to hold a bargaining chip.

"Love those spokes, Norman."

"Christ!" He spun on his stool. "Don't sneak up on me like that!" He smelled of booze. It was his first day back on the job after a week-long bout with the cocktail flu.

"You feeling any better?" Claire said.

"I feel like shit. I was at ZZ's last night—remember, I took you there?"

"How could I forget?"

"Not such good luck last night." He shrugged. "But that's the way it goes. This time last year things was even worse."

"Maybe you need your old good-luck charm back."

"Maybe so. But first I need to come up with a couple grand real quick. Like yesterday." He tried to laugh, but his face clouded with pain.

"I might be able to help you out some," Claire said. As she'd hoped, his face brightened. "I've got a little set aside—it's not a couple thousand, but it's something."

"It wouldn't be for long. . . ."

"Of course I'd need to know where my money was going."

Suddenly he looked angry. "Don't start that bullshit again, Claire. Has Harvey got you buying information for him now?"

"Fuck you, Norman. You're the one who brought it up." She turned and started to walk away.

He grabbed her arm. "I'm sorry, Claire. It's just that—you got no idea how bad this is. These guys play hardball."

"I can probably get you eight hundred by tomorrow." She was sure Ted wouldn't flinch at such a sum. "Will that help?"

"God, yes! It'll keep me off the bottom of the Detroit River for the next couple of weeks."

"I'll have it by noon tomorrow. Who do you owe the money to?"

"You wouldn't know them—a couple of Hamtramck hoods named Jimmy Kowalski and Shep. I don't even know Shep's real name. I don't wanna know it, either. He's the badass. They say he's killed upwards of fifteen people. Men *and* women."

"Norm, you're an even dumber Polack than I thought you were."

"Tell me about it." He hung his head like a dog, a very hung-over, very remorseful, very scared dog. Claire actually felt sorry for him, felt the prickly beginnings of shame over what she was doing. But wasn't she also keeping him off the bottom of the Detroit River?

"Claire!" Amos called from across the studio. "Telephone, line three." She decided that if it was Ted she'd insist they meet tonight. She would ask him for the money then.

But it wasn't Ted. It was her mother calling from Iowa to tell her Wallace had died in a freak plane crash in the Philippines.

Six

On the day Harvey Pearl bought his plane ticket to Tokyo, a letter with a Kagoshima postmark arrived from Taka Matsuda. Typical, he thought. As soon as you express desire, as soon as you become a man of action, you're reminded that it's all vanity. Maybe there was something to those Buddhist texts Taka had discussed with him years ago in the back room of the big house in Pasadena.

He brewed a pot of tea and took the unopened envelope out to the porch, where he could see the lake and the comforting hump of earth, the roof of his new concrete-walled, fully stocked bomb shelter. It had cost him $30,000 and it was worth every penny. It had a chemical toilet, an independent oxygen supply, duplicates of all his favorite design books and an anthology of haiku. There was enough canned food and enough bottled water to last two people three months, and there were two cases of hard liquor. Though never much of a drinker, at least by Detroit's standards, Harvey had little trouble imagining that three months underground might inspire a powerful thirst. He was delighted to see that a green bearding of grass had already sprouted on that hump of earth. Soon his little insurance policy would be all but invisible.

He wouldn't have built it if he hadn't gone to Japan. Before he'd seen Taka's melted face, the Bomb had seemed like a good enough idea. He barely gave it a second thought. Sitting on his porch now and gazing at his secret, he felt a chilly warmth: this was as secure as the world allowed a man to feel today.

He sliced open the envelope. The letter opened, as he knew it would, with an apology:

Dear Harvey,

I am so sorry to miss the airplane to Los Angeles. You are very generous to offer. But something terrible has happened. My brother Tetsuo, as you know, has had a hard life. He was the union leader at Nissan and he was once very powerful but the company hated the union and my brother and his friends were fired. Tetsuo was never the same. A graduate of Todai, Tokyo University, our best school, he was a proud man and he went apart. He took things from this house and sold them in pawnshops. The day before my plane to Los Angeles he commits suicide. I have felt too guilty and too ashamed to write until now. I am so alone and so scared. Harvey, please tell me what to do.

Taka

He phoned his travel agent and told her to change the ticket from a round trip for him to a one-way for Taka—Tokyo to Honolulu to Los Angeles to Chicago to Detroit. Then he called Henry Ford Hospital and rescheduled her appointment with the plastic surgeon. His telegram to her read: TICKET ON WAY. DON'T MISS THE PLANE THIS TIME. TERRIBLY SORRY ABOUT TETSUO. LOVE, HARVEY.

Seven

*I*t had been a typical summer day in Washington, a nonstop steam bath, so Morey Caan decided to change clothes when he got home from Arlington National Cemetery. As he packed for his trip to Detroit and Memphis, he kept thinking that Wallace Hathaway and James McGovern had received mighty lavish funerals for a couple of pilots who died on a routine training mission in the Philippines.

At the cemetery, the two black horses were lathered with sweat by the time they started pulling the caisson with the twin flag-draped caskets down the gravel path from the chapel to the graves. The procession moved through a thicket of trees and out into a rolling meadow. Morey had never seen so many tombstones, identical bone-white crosses stabbing the turf in perfect rows, stretching on forever. Suddenly he wished he hadn't agreed to do Will Lomax this favor. He wished he was at home waiting for Pete Hoover to call from Guatemala instead of here in the cemetery walking behind the caisson with Claire Hathaway on his left and her mother on his right. He knew Claire only slightly and her mother not at all. Besides, the sight of all those bone white crosses reminded him that he had never done well in cemeteries. Maybe it was just as well his brother was buried in a common grave somewhere on the coast of England.

But today, after the initial shock of seeing how many bodies had been planted at Arlington, Morey got hold of himself. The snare drums, the horses, the flag-draped caskets, the ghostly playing of "Taps" followed by the crack of the rifles—it was, he had to admit, potent theater. As the echo of the rifle reports galloped over the tombstones, Morey glanced at Claire and her mother to see how they were holding up. Claire was staring into the distance, eyes dry, jaw clenched. Her mother, a parched little woman who wore no makeup and hadn't said a dozen words on the way out from the airport, did the strangest thing. She looked at her wristwatch.

Heading out of his apartment now, Morey checked his mailbox. The new *Saturday Review* had arrived, and his McCarthy article got a minor mention on the cover. The hearings, mercifully, were grinding to a close, and Morey sensed he wasn't the only person who was sick of the whole circus. Besides, the "Joe Must Go" movement now seemed a bit like shooting a horse just to make sure its leg was broken.

Morey hailed a cab at DuPont Circle. As it raced along the banks of the Potomac, he looked across the river at the silver hills of Virginia. So many bones already in the soil, so many more arriving every day even though the country wasn't even at war. At least the day hadn't been a total waste. Claire was so grateful for his support that she offered to show him the diary she kept during the creation of the '54 Buick Century, and she promised to go over it with him page by page when they got to Detroit. He sat back, let the hot wind blow in on him, and finished sweating through his clean white shirt.

*W*hen Claire got home from her brother's funeral that night, a dozen white roses were propped against her door. The card read:

Darling,
We're all praying for you and your brother. We went ahead and unveiled the Wildcat clay today at the Tech Cen-

*ter. It was a smash! Hotter than the Corvette, according to
Harvey! I'll call tomorrow.*

As ever,
Ted

Also in the envelope were eight one-hundred-dollar bills
clipped to a note: "These are for our friend Norm. We don't
want any harm to come to him—just yet."

Claire put the roses in her grandmother's green glass vase and
set them on the kitchen table. Only Ted Mackey would choose
white roses at a time like this. She'd never known anyone so
brash and confident, so unwilling to believe that the future would
be anything less than terribly bright. Her brother had been just
such a boy, and now he was dead at the age of twenty-five. But
maybe that was the best way to go through life and the best
way to go out—believing the illusion that you are both excep-
tional and invincible.

She started digging in the closet for the diary. It was somewhere under her college books. Lifting the boxes was a strain,
and only then did she realize just how drained she was by the
day's events. It had all been so strange, like a waking dream. As
she and her mother and Morey Caan had walked slowly down
the hill behind the caisson and the clopping black horses and
the chattering snare drums, Claire was astonished to realize she
felt happy. This was the last thing in the world she would've
expected at her own brother's funeral, but there it was. She felt
calm and light and happy—happy that Wallace had died the
way he wanted to die, happy that he was getting a funeral he
would've loved, happy to have a man at her side in that endless
landscape of dead men, happy that she and her mother were
holding up so well. Somehow, holding up well seemed important
in Arlington National Cemetery.

Of course her mother was probably delighted that there was

no longer a man in her life, no one left to fill her with wants and needs and then abandon her, die on her, pull what she called "the big vanishing act." Now it was just Ruth and Claire, mother and daughter. As she followed the caisson down the twisting path to the graves, Claire got the feeling her mother couldn't wait to get this over with so she could hurry back to Iowa, back to her quiet life of teaching and reading and living out her days alone, invulnerable at last.

At the airport, Claire tried one last time to persuade her mother to spend a few days in Detroit.

"I can't," she snapped, dully watching the planes rise into a sky that looked like a sheet of aluminum. Her hair, brown and brittle, was pulled into a severe bun. She wore no makeup. She hadn't smiled all day.

"Why not? Just for a day or two."

"I already told you. I've got summer school this year. They dumped all the illiterates who play football in my lap. I suppose it's their idea of fair punishment for flunking those idiots."

Claire knew the story from her mother's letters. As usual, she had flunked half of her freshman English students, including a dozen boys who were crucial to the success of the Iowa State football team. Some things never changed. All through high school Claire had helped her mother correct freshman English compositions, and they used to sit up late howling at some of the whoppers. To this day Claire remembered a girl named Susan Whitworth, the daughter of a chicken farmer from Boone, whose burning ambition was "to earn a degree in English and work as a journalist and win the Pullet Surprise." Even now, standing in the Washington airport less than an hour after her brother's funeral, Claire found herself smiling at the memory of Susan Whitworth.

"What on earth could possibly be funny at a time like this?" her mother said, watching the sky.

"Nothing. I'm sorry."

"And one more thing. Watch out for that Jewboy."

"That who?"

"That Jewboy, Caan. He wants to use you. I can smell it."

Remarks like that reminded Claire why she had fled Iowa, why she was having an affair with a married man, why one of her best friends was a Negro, why she was preparing to share a cherished diary with a journalist who happened to be a Jew. If her mother had told her she looked good in heavy makeup, she probably would've scrubbed her face with Octagon soap.

At last she found her diary. She set it by the front door and turned off the lights. On her way to bed she smelled the white roses. Already they had begun to rot.

Eight

*H*aving Morey back in town was just what Will Lomax needed. He'd been learning unspeakable things about General Motors while doing research for the 1954 publicity campaign, things a savvy company man would not even admit to knowing. At last he had someone he could share them with. After Margaret and the babies went to bed, Will and Morey took a bottle of Old Crow and two glasses up to the spare bedroom and turned on the fan. Will did most of the talking while Morey sipped whisky and listened, studied the books and the stacks of typed notes and manuscript pages. He was stunned by what he was seeing and hearing.

In studying the early history of the corporation, Will had become fascinated by the lives of the automobile pioneers. Not William Durant, who pieced GM together, or Henry Ford, whose life had been twisted by friends and enemies into an outlandish myth, or even Alfred Sloan, Jr., the architect of the modern corporation. No, Will was drawn to the men he called "cowboy entrepreneurs"—Ransom E. Olds, Louis Chevrolet, Henry and Clement Studebaker and, of course, David Dunbar Buick. He snatched an index card and started reading: " 'Buick was first of all a tinkerer. Produced and patented a lawn sprinkler, then a series of innovations in indoor plumbing. Finally perfected a process for enameling porcelain to cast-iron bathtubs that broke a German monopoly. Buick was directly responsible for the contemporary bathroom and architects were quick to use his ideas in Eastlake, Romanesque and Shingle type homes then in fashion.' "

"And all through college I thought Buick was a synonym for vomit," Morey said.

Will ignored him and kept reading: " 'By the turn of the century this son of Scottish immigrants had lost interest in bathrooms, had become fascinated with the internal-combustion engine, particularly the valve-in-head engine. In 1904 produced his first car, called it a Buick. On December 1, 1904, established the Buick Motor Company.' " Will flipped the card onto the desk. "By the way, that's the day—December first—that we're going to make the half-millionth '54 Buick."

"Fearful symmetry and all that."

"Right." Will picked up another index card. " 'In 1906 Buick traded in his GM stock. Got involved in oil speculation and a number of unsuccessful business ventures. Eventually had to take a job as an instructor at Detroit School of Trades at age 72. By 1928 he couldn't afford a telephone. GM then making two hundred million dollars a year but gave him nothing. Died penniless the next year, just before the market crashed.' "

"That's damn good material, old man. So much for being a cowboy entrepreneur, eh?"

"And now you've got guys like Ted Mackey who can barely read and write running the division. And guys like Charlie Wilson are secretary of defense. And Harvey Pearl, the Michelangelo of the Motor City, wants every car that comes off the line to have four-foot fins and enough chrome to anchor a fucking destroyer. You should hear these people talk. 'These are the golden days'—they actually say shit like that with a straight face."

"You think these car guys are bad, you should come back to Washington," Morey said, and the conversation raced on to Eisenhower, McCarthy, Guatemala, squirrel shooting, Ann Wilson's diary and German POWs. When Margaret got up to make breakfast, they were still sitting there by the fan. The sun was up and the bourbon was gone, but they were talking faster than ever. Margaret paused in the doorway, gave Will a dark look, then went downstairs.

"Whew," Morey said, "what was that all about?"

"Don't ask. We had a little misunderstanding. She'll get over it."

Or so he hoped. He'd already committed the very blunder he'd vowed to avoid. Shortly after the Los Angeles Motorama, he came home from work one night and found Margaret standing at the kitchen sink with her arms folded. When he tried to kiss her, she turned her face away. "Who's Cindy?" she'd said.

"Who's Cindy who?"

"Cindy from Malibu. I found her name and phone number and home address in your shirt pocket while I was doing the laundry."

"Oh, *that* Cindy! That's Cindy Warhover, our district manager in L.A. She helped us with the Motorama."

"Do all district managers give you their home phone numbers and addresses on cocktail napkins?"

He'd spent weeks on damage control—flowers, dinners, nights at the movies. But as her greeting this morning showed, he hadn't succeeded in melting her suspicions. As the smell of sizzling bacon drifted up the stairs, Will consoled himself that this recent marital chill had at least freed him to work on The Book. The

234 / MOTOR CITY

more intriguing the whole puzzle became, the less his marital troubles seemed to matter. This was like a drug, and he felt no desire to resist its pull.

Nine

The day the first-half sales figures hit his desk was a day Ted Mackey would never forget—not because the numbers looked so good but because it was the day he spoke with Marilyn Monroe for the first time.

"Hello? Mr. Mackey? Hello?" The voice coming through the transcontinental telephone static was surprisingly bird-like. He'd expected a husky voice, something from the bottom of a whisky barrel.

"Yes! This is Ted Mackey!"

"I can barely hear you. Can you hear me?"

"Yes, Miss . . . Mrs. . . . Shall I call you—"

"Call me Marilyn. That's my name." She laughed. Then there were several seconds of static. Ted had never in his life been struck dumb by a woman. Finally she said, "My manager tells me you have a very interesting proposition for me."

"Um . . . yes . . . Marilyn. We . . . I . . . What I wanted to talk to you about is actually a bit of a secret."

"Oooh, I *love* secrets."

"I'm afraid this one may not seem very juicy to you, but believe me, it's big news here in Detroit. Are you familiar by any chance with the Chevrolet Corvette?"

"You mean there's actually a car called a Carvette?"

"No, it's a *Corvette*. It's a two-seat sports car. Very sexy. A big seller, too. Here at the Buick Division we're coming out with a two-seat sports car of our own and—"

"You mean there isn't even a back seat?"

"No, just two front seats."

"What good is a car without a back seat?" Lusty laughter came through the static. Then Ted got it. He'd read in a tabloid that when Marilyn was married as a teenager, one of her favorite places to make love was the back seat of a car, preferably when it was parked on a city street. Once, when her husband protested that they might be discovered by a passerby, Marilyn supposedly cooed, "It's all right, honey, we're *married!*"

"I realize a car without a back seat is a little out of the ordinary," Ted said. "And to be honest with you, it's a bit of a gamble. Which is why I called you. I'd like for you to appear as the star of our advertising campaign for this new car—print, TV, radio, the works. We're calling the car the Wildcat, and I'd like you to be the Wildcat Girl."

"The Wildcat Girl. I like that, Ted. But I don't even have a driver's license."

"Somehow I think we can get around that."

"Well, I'll have to talk it over with my husband and my manager. We're in rehearsals right now for my new picture, so this isn't a good time."

"What's your new movie called?"

"*The Seven Year Itch.* We're supposed to do some location work in New York in the fall. Where are you located again?"

"I'm in Detroit."

"Is that near New York?"

"Not too far. I'm sure we could get together in New York if that would be convenient for you."

Someone—DiMaggio?—was yelling at her. "I've gotta run," she said. "Send us something and we'll talk again soon."

After that, the first-half sales figures were almost beside the point. Buick had sold 267,789 cars through June 30, exceeding even Ted Mackey's expectations and shattering all records.

Ten

*W*hen Hayes Tucker, Jr., saw the Bekins moving van drive past his house and back into the last driveway on Lindbergh Street, he went flying out his front door. He was on the Brunswicks' porch waving when Bob and Sally and their three kids and their dog drove up in the wheezing, mustard-colored '42 Plymouth.

"You kids finally made it!" Hayes shouted, bounding across the dirt yard. He opened the car door and grabbed Bob Brunswick's wrist and hoisted him up out of the driver's seat. Bob, crewcut and pot-bellied, dressed in a butterscotch sports shirt, almost fell on his face.

"Hang on a second, Hayes," he said. "Let me get my cane."

Hayes had forgotten about Bob losing his left foot to frostbite at Chosin Reservoir. He felt like smacking his forehead. How could I forget something like that, he asked himself, when it meant the guy couldn't operate a clutch and the automatic Dynaflow transmission was already sold?

The three kids and the dog were tearing around the house, laying claim to bedrooms and bathrooms. Bob Brunswick stood there by the Plymouth, leaning on his cane, squinting at the flat, treeless, honeycombed world surrounding his house. "Oh, this is my wife," he said. "Sally, this is Mr. Tucker from down the street, the gentleman I told you about who sells Buicks."

"Call me Hayes, Sally." She shook his hand but kept her left hand pressed to her throat. She looked exhausted and vaguely scared. Her curly red hair swooped up in front of her ears into twin tusks. A perfect car-buying couple, Hayes told himself. "I don't want to hear the word 'Buick' again today," he said, releasing her hand. "We've got to get you kids settled in first. And Sally—I want you to wipe that look off your face. I know exactly what you're thinking. You're thinking it all looks a little naked and the houses all look alike. I'll prove you wrong in about five minutes. Why, we've got us a regular engineering company on this block—Pete and Scotty and Zim. There's nothing they can't build or fix. They started adding on, changing things the minute they moved in. And Big Bill Levitt's spending eight million smackers on trees and shrubs."

Sally smiled. A crash inside the house sent her hurrying to investigate. As soon as she was out of sight, Hayes steered Bob around back to the electric meter. "I'm going to show you a little secret, Bob. There's a whole lot of surplus juice in those lines up there." Bob looked at the power lines and scratched his head. "Here's all you do. After they hook you up this afternoon, you take a screwdriver, unscrew this screw here, splice the black wire, put one end under this gizmo, one end back where it was, solder 'em up and you're in business—all you'll ever need, free of charge."

"You sure this is jake, Hayes?"

"Sure I'm sure. Everybody on the block's doing it. Let me tell you something, Bob. The first lesson you need to learn is that you just arrived in the land of milk and honey."

Bob Brunswick surveyed the neighboring yards. From back here the houses were anything but identical. Each had its own little addition, a porch here, a patio there, a deck or a tool shed or a carport or a sandbox. Toys were scattered everywhere. Drying racks and clotheslines sagged with laundry.

"You *do* have some tools, don't you, Bob?"

"Uh . . . somewhere. Everything's in boxes."

"I'll swing back this afternoon after the electric company's gone and help you fix her up."

They went into the house. It still smelled of paint. Hayes's wife, Virginia, had arrived on cue with sandwiches and potato chips and soft drinks. Scotty Decker and Jim Zimmer, each the proud owner of a spanking new Buick Century, had dropped in to say hello. The house was filling with furniture and boxes, and Hayes could see that Sally was already beginning to relax. The little black terrier kept yapping and nipping at the movers' ankles as they lugged things in from the van. When no one else was looking, Hayes saw one of the movers drop a box marked "Encyclopedias" on the mutt's tail.

Eleven

*M*orey Caan couldn't believe he was driving to Memphis in a pink-and-black Buick Century with a two hundred-horsepower V-8 engine. "I'm driving a car the color of boiled shrimp and anthracite," he kept saying. "I'm driving a car the color of boiled shrimp and anthracite." Somehow, writing about a powerful machine that combined the pure pink protein of the sea with the glittering black fuel that fed the coke ovens in brawny American cities like Detroit seemed to Morey the most perfect thing a man could do in 1954. Best of all, the Buick had come to him with magical ease. Will Lomax made a single phone call and there it was, gleaming, full of gas, ready to go.

It truly was a beautiful beast. Here, at last, was something Morey could imagine wanting to own. He was mesmerized by the strong yellow headlight beams, the perfume of vinyl and cold new steel, the wraparound windshield, the steering wheel as big as a basketball hoop, the chrome horn ring, the sleek hood ornament sitting out there pointing the way, urging him onward. He even liked the upholstery. The tops of the seats were pleated red vinyl, like the booths in diners and bowling-alley cocktail lounges, and the black fabric on the base was shot through with glinting silver threads.

After spending a week in Detroit going over Claire Hathaway's diary, he now understood that while this Buick looked and smelled and felt like some unattainable fantasy, it was the exact opposite. It was priced to sell, and more than half a million of them would be sold by the end of the year. It was, Morey had to admit, a wickedly ingenious piece of work.

He'd planned to stop overnight near Louisville, but he was making such good time and having so much fun he just kept rolling. Driving this car reminded him of the all-night drives from Charlottesville to Memphis when he was in college and didn't have a care in the world, when he was young and foot-loose, utterly free. The slightest pressure on the accelerator and he shot past cars and trucks as though they were up on cinder blocks. Once, when he pulled out to pass an old Chevy and was surprised by a truck that had topped a hill and came barreling down at him, he simply stomped on the throttle and felt the Dynaflow kick down and sweep him safely past the Chevy. Though the trip was mostly two-lane roads, he averaged better than seventy miles an hour. He wanted it to last forever.

When he crossed into Tennessee, he started to pick up the first fuzzy Memphis radio stations. He worked the pudgy tuning knob until the voice of some jacked-up street Negro cut through the static: "Say, bay-bee, where'd ya spend last night? Oh Lawd, dat wuz de Wolf! Howlin' Wolf! And dis is ole Dewey Phillips playin de red, hot 'n' blue comin' atchoo through WHBQ in de Ho-tel Chickso on de magazine flo-wah. . . ."

Hunh?! Morey turned up the volume and gunned the Buick harder into the bug-swarming night. WHBQ? He'd never heard of the station. Broadcasting from—what did the man say?—the Hotel Chickasaw?

"Yass, yass, we comin' atchoo tonight cuttasy People's Ferncher Company at 3 1 0 South Main Street, where ya jus' pay a little down and pay for it while ya wearin' it out—or they catch up witchya! Ha! Lissen to ole Dew now! Feelin' nervous? Gittin' a divorce? S'okay. Jus' tell 'em ole Dew sencha. Now we got a little sumthin' here by Sister Rosetta Tharpe, 'Strange Things Is Happ'nin' Every Day.' Ain't dat de truth!"

Out of the perforated steel speaker in the dashboard came a rollicking boogie-woogie piano beat, a driving syncopation in such perfect rhythm with the big V-8 that Morey kept it pegged right where it was, at seventy-seven miles per hour; then came the blaring siren voice of Sister Rosetta Tharpe, dripping sex, strange things are happening every day. . . . Morey understood then that he was locked in a race with dawn and that he owned this long slab of concrete with the dotted black line in the middle, the last miles of his long slide down into the west Tennessee riverbottom with Howlin' Wolf and Sister Rosetta Tharpe and B. B. King and Big Boy Crudup coming through louder and clearer with each passing mile, calling him home.

The orange sun was resting on the rooftops when he drove into Memphis. His eyeballs were on fire and his mouth tasted like gunpowder, but there was no question what he had to do. He drove straight downtown to the Hotel Chickasaw. The famous ducks were drinking out of the fountain in the lobby, and a bellhop yawned and pointed the way up to the mezzanine.

Morey arrived just as Dewey Phillips was packing up his gear. He wasn't a yellow-eyed Negro after all but a skinny white boy with a bulging Adam's apple and jerky movements, some malnourished, high-octane Benzedrine freak. And he was perfectly delighted Morey had enjoyed the show. "Y'ain't heard nothin' yet. Gotta check out Nat Dee's 'Tan Town Jamboree' show this afternoon."

"I'll probably be asleep," Morey said. He was beginning to hallucinate. Dewey's nose kept changing shape, and there were sparks shooting out of his hair.

"Listen in tonight, then," Dewey said. "Gonna have a wild-assed white boy on the show, live and in person, yessiree."

After promising to tune in at midnight, Morey drove down to Beale Street and parked in front of S&L Loans. The pawnshop looked shabbier than ever, and when Morey thought of his father working out his last years here, alone now, everyone dead or gone, he felt something beyond sadness or pity, something close to awe. How did Sammy do it, day after day, year after year? Because he knew no other life, Morey supposed, and he was unable to imagine wanting to. How lucky the man was, in a way. Sammy had never known the delirium Morey felt the day he broke the story about Iran, and so he had never known the agony of the inevitable hangover. Yes, Morey thought as he climbed out of the Buick, his father was a lucky man.

When Morey opened the pawnshop door, bells tinkled, the first line of defense against the hungry, broke, thieving, strung-out hordes who washed up here day in and day out. The saxophones and guitars were still lined up along the right wall; the rings were still in the long glass case in back where Big Joe could keep an eye on them—all the tawdry blazing pinkie rings and engagement rings and wedding rings, the wreckage of impossibly bunged-up, abandoned dreams. The walls were still lime green and still fuzzed with two generations of untouched dust. When Sammy saw him, he came out of the cage in back and trotted toward him, arms outstretched, an unlit stub of a cigar clenched in his teeth. The teeth were a little yellower, the hair in the ears and nostrils a little thicker, a little whiter. Sammy hugged his boy and stood back to examine him. "Son, you look like shit!"

"I know, I know—I drove nonstop all the way from Detroit."

"Joe, get out here and look at this nebbish son of mine!"

Big Joe heaved himself up off his stool behind the ring counter, an effort that did not thrill him so early on a hot July morning. Morey knew that sound so well, the weary wheeze of a man who was destined to spend the rest of his life in this prison. How old was Big Joe now? Fifty? Sixty? It was hard to say with a baby-faced, world-weary giant like him. Besides, it didn't really matter. What mattered was that Big Joe no longer felt any compassion for the bearers of saxophones, cluster rings, purloined hi-fis and moth-eaten minks who passed through the front door of S&L Loans. Morey supposed his nose was even harder than Sammy's by now, because he despised the shuffling, sniveling parade that came through that chiming door. Big Joe despised these people because he'd come to understand that he was one of them and would never be anything else. Being a Jew in the South was bad enough, Morey thought, but the colored really had it rough. Sammy, of course, never gave a thought to such things. He was too busy staying alive. He'd recently written Morey a letter expressing amazement that some of his best customers now were white boys, teenage thugs who came to buy the garish pimp clothes in the side room. Morey could imagine what Big Joe thought about white boys coming down here *voluntarily*. Surely he took it as an insult, as one more stab wound to his sour heart.

Big Joe slapped Morey's hand with his big black mitt, looked him up and down as if he were appraising stolen merchandise. "You need to get you a wife, boy. Fatten you up some."

"And you need to quit eating so much fucking fried chicken."

Big Joe smacked his belly and laughed.

"The day my only male child marries is the day I die and go to heaven," Sammy said.

"All right, all right," Morey said. "I drive all night and this is the welcome I get?"

Sammy hugged him again. He smelled like a thousand dead cigars. "So you took the overnight bus?"

Morey brightened. He'd forgotten all about the Buick. This, and this alone, would shut Big Joe up. He led them outside and gave a quick car salesman's rundown of the features—wrap-around windshield, tinted glass, automatic Dynaflow transmission, power steering, power brakes, two-hundred-horse V-8, four-barrel carburetor.

Big Joe's eyes were bulging. "Man," he said, "I likes them wide whitewalls and moon hubcaps. Where'd you get the bread to buy a motherfucka like this?"

"I didn't buy it. I've been in Detroit working on an article about General Motors. They just handed me the keys and told me to turn it in to the nearest Buick dealer when I got through—"

"Uh, excuse me, suh."

They all turned. A skinny white kid was about to go into the pawnshop. He was unlike anything Morey had ever seen. His hair was lacquered into a preposterous pompadour and he was wearing shiny black pants that were tight at the ankles, baggy at the knees and pleated at the waist. His shoes were pointy-toed and white, and the collar of his purple shirt was turned up. Red pimples flared on his cheeks. "I've come to pick up that shirt I had on layaway, suh."

Big Joe went inside to take care of the kid. "Did you *see* that?" Sammy said. "That's what I get in here nowadays—whites trying to look like the colored." He shook his head.

The bells tinkled and the kid came out of the shop with a red shirt under his arm. He ducked his head and started up the street, the heels of his shoes clicking as he walked.

"Say!" Morey hollered. "Excuse me!"

"Don't give him any trouble," Sammy said. "He's probably got a knife. They all got knives these days."

Morey walked up to the kid with his right hand out. "My name's Morey Caan. My old man runs this shop. You mind my asking—those clothes—are you a musician by any chance?"

"I'd like to be, suh." He was shifty-eyed and suspicious. White trash all the way, Morey thought, the bad skin, the bad diet, the loud clothes, the wild hair, good manners masking deep feelings of inferiority and resentment.

"What do you play?"

"A little git-tar. Mostly I sing."

"Who do you sound like?"

He looked Morey in the eye for the first time. "I don't sound like nobody you ever heard before."

"Do you happen to know Dewey Phillips, the disc jockey?"

The face broke into a smile. Morey was surprised to see that he had good teeth and an engaging, almost pretty smile. "You might could say I know him. I'm gonna be on his show tonight."

"With Dewey?"

"Yeah. You know Dew?"

"I met him this morning. He's pretty . . . wild."

"Oh, man, that Dew is gone, ain't he? I stay up late as I can ever night listening to his show." The kid looked down at his shoes, stiletto-toed, glossy and white; then he looked up the street. The smile was gone, and he seemed uncomfortable again. "Well, I better be gettin' to work."

"You've got a day job?"

"Yeah, I drive a truck for Crown Electric." He looked Morey in the eye again. "But not for long." Then he ducked his head and started up Beale Street, shoes clicking, checking himself in the store windows as he went.

"Say," Morey called to him, "what's your name?"

But the kid didn't hear him. He was hurrying up Beale Street, away from the river and toward the hot orange sun.

*M*orey slept into the afternoon, got up to make a sandwich, then went back to bed. Shortly before midnight he emerged from his boyhood bedroom to find his father asleep in the tattered yellow recliner in front of the television set; a cigar butt fumed in an ashtray at his elbow. Milton Berle was telling jokes and grinning like a hyena on the screen, but no sound was coming out. Morey decided to let his father sleep.

His instincts told him he needed to be at the Hotel Chickasaw, so he grabbed a camera and notebook and raced downtown, arriving on the mezzanine just as Dewey Phillips was introducing the first record of the night: "Gonna git things rollin' with a Big Boy Crudup number, yass, yass. But it ain't done by the Big Boy—it's done ri-cheer by a local boy we'll be meetin' di-rectly. Lemme hear ya say 'Das aww-*right!*' "

The song had a scraping, bluesy feel, like the stuff that had roared out of the Buick's dashboard the night before, not at all sophisticated or polished, but heartfelt, raw, a little raunchy. Morey felt his foot tapping along, and he noticed that Dewey's alligator loafer was tapping, too. He'd begun to sweat. "Where in the Sam hill is that boy?" he moaned. "I told him to be here fifteen minutes before midnight."

Just then Morey heard a great squawking down in the lobby. He looked over the railing and saw the ducks scattering as an odd little entourage charged past the fountain. Leading the way was the kid Morey had talked to outside S&L Loans. He was still wearing the white shoes and the black pants, but he had changed into his new shirt, flame-red and ruffled; his hair was lovingly sculpted and watered and looked like polished metal. He was followed by a dark-haired man and by a couple holding hands, all three of them trotting to keep up. They reached the top of the stairs just as the record was ending, and Dewey, without a word of introduction, was starting the flip side on the other turntable. Morey recognized the song instantly—Bill Monroe's "Blue Moon of Kentucky"—but it had been jacked up until it jumped with hormonal heat. It wasn't exactly blues and it wasn't exactly country, and suddenly Morey recalled the singer's remark that morning: "I don't sound like nobody you ever heard before."

" 'Bout time y'all showed up," Dewey said, mopping his face with a handkerchief. "Looky there." He pointed at the telephone. All the lights were blinking. "Yessiree, I do believe we got us a hot one on our hands!" He pulled a chair up next to his and slapped it. "Have a seat, son. Soon as this song's over I'm gonna inner-view ya."

The kid sat down. Morey wrote in his notebook that he looked like a scared bird.

"Mr. Phillips," the kid pleaded, "I don't know nothin' about bein' inner-viewed."

"Just don't say nothin' dirty, boy," the dark-haired man snapped. He had a ski-jump nose and dark, moist eyes that rolled constantly in their sockets like ball bearings. The other man and the woman were the boy's parents, Morey supposed—a pasty, beat-up pair. The man looked tired, vaguely suspicious of all this foolishness; the woman had dark bags under her eyes, and her arms and legs were grotesquely swollen. Yes, Morey thought as he scribbled in his notebook, white trash de luxe.

"Aw-right-o!" Dewey bellowed when the record ended. "Here he sits, live and in person, the young fella we just been listening to. What's your name, son?"

"Um . . . Presley, suh," he mumbled. "Elvis Presley."

"Speak up, boy! And this here's your first record?"

"Uh . . . no, suh . . . actually—"

"Y'ain't gotta 'no, suh' ole Dew. My wife don't even do dat!"

"Uh . . . no, Dew. I cut one a year or so ago at Sun Records with Mr. Sam Phillips. This is my first real good one, though. Least Mr. Phillips and I think so." The man with the ball-bearing eyeballs smiled and nodded.

"Y'ain't alone," Dewey said. "That phone's ring-a-ling-dingin' off the hook. Where'd ya pick up them threads, Elvis? The man is *sharp*. He's got on a shirt that could flat put a fire truck to shame."

"S&L Loans on Beale Street. They got a real nice selection down there."

Morey was writing frantically. A real nice selection! Pimp city!

"And where'd you go to school, Elvis?"

"Humes."

"Humes! Everybody hear dat?"

Suddenly Morey understood what was going on. Humes, where Morey graduated, was a white high school. Dewey Phillips was letting the world know that Elvis Presley, believe it or not, was white.

"Well hear dis," Dewey shouted. "Once again, it's a Big Boy Crudup number done ri-cheer by Elvis Presley from Humes High School. Lemme hear ya say, 'Das awwwwwww-right!' "

He flipped a switch and the record started playing again. He held out his hand to Elvis. "I wanna thank you for comin' down, son. You done just fine."

"I thought you was gonna inner-view me."

"Where ya been? I just done did. Dat was live on the air. Ha!"

Elvis's jaw sagged, and his mother had to lead him down the stairs by the arm. Morey decided to follow them out.

As they walked past the ducks in the lobby, Elvis's father turned to Morey. "Ain't that the damnedest thing you ever did see?"

Morey could smell whisky on the man's breath. "It damn sure was," he said.

"Live on the air! If that don't beat all."

"Your son's a hell of a singer."

"You really think so?"

"I certainly do."

"I think he sounds like a nigger."

"Well, he's going to make one hell of a magazine article."

The man stopped walking, and his look of disbelief hardened into suspicion. "You some kind of a writer or something?"

"I write freelance articles for *Life* magazine."

The man shook his head and stared at the floor. "*Life* magazine," he muttered. This, clearly, was more than he could bear.

But Morey got him to pose for pictures in front of the hotel with his wife and son. As the flashbulbs popped, Morey had the feeling, the warmest feeling a journalist ever knows, that he was capturing an odd, monumental moment of history. Best of all, this story was his and his alone.

Twelve

*A*s the summer wore on, a procession of hot, sticky days punctuated by late-afternoon thundershowers, Milmary Mackey grew more and more obsessed with two seemingly unrelated things: her sons' Little League baseball team and her short story.

At first she was disturbed by the strangeness of this pair; but she was rescued from this distress one morning when the literary quarterly, the *Paris Review*, arrived in the mail. It contained an interview with the British author Graham Greene. Instead of going up to her typewriter as she did at this time every morning, she sat in the living room and read the interview. One quote jumped out at her: "Every creative writer worth our consideration, every writer who can be called in the wide eighteenth-century use of the term a poet, is a victim: a man given over to an obsession."

Somehow, that helped. Somehow, understanding that she was a victim made her illogical dual obsession more bearable. There was nothing she could do except write her way out of it.

After reading that interview, she went gladly to her sons' Little League games as they marched toward the city championship.

She always arrived late, always parked down the block, always stood at a distance. She was delighted by Tommy's prowess as a pitcher and batter, the way the other boys treated him with awe; and she was enraged, as the team kept winning in sooty little parks all over the city, in Ecorse and Highland Park and Wyandotte, that the coach was less and less inclined to risk playing near-sighted John in right field. She wanted to say something to the coach. Wasn't he missing the point? But that was a line she'd vowed not to cross, and so she kept her distance and said nothing.

She was also delighted and enraged by her writing. She was delighted by the way her short story had grown, one agonizing word at a time, to its finished length of twenty-one pages and seemed to want to become a full-blown novel; and she was enraged by recent news reports that the crew of the *Enola Gay* had been suffering from a variety of mental disorders. Hadn't mankind—victors and vanquished alike—suffered enough? When would it end? But this disturbing news also brought her a sort of grim satisfaction. Life was imitating her art. As Jason Stone knew so well, today's world was indeed full of hollow victories and bad choices.

On the morning after she finished her story, Ted surprised her by sleeping late, then shuffling down to the kitchen in his bathrobe. It was after eight o'clock. His hair was combed but he hadn't shaved, and the bags under his eyes told her that whatever he'd done last night had been rough. She poured him coffee. "Taking the day off, dear?"

"I just might do that," he said, shaking the *Free Press* open. He grunted at a story on the front page. "Listen to this. 'Lucius Clay was appointed yesterday by President Eisenhower to head a hand-picked commission to study the nation's highway requirements.'"

"Who's Lucius Clay?"

"He's on the GM board. A Yalie. Helped pick Ike's cabinet, including Charlie Wilson."

"Guess he knows a lot of millionaires."

"You better believe he does. And now he's going to tell Ike we need federal legislation to pay for a completely new highway system."

"How do you know that?"

"Because he told me so last week. If he has his way, this country's roads will finally catch up with the cars we're building. Think what that'll do for sales."

"I hate to think."

"What the hell. I do believe I'll take the day off. What do you say we go to the club? Take a swim, eat some lunch."

"That would be nice."

While he was upstairs calling his secretary, Milmary went into the kitchen and fixed herself a Bloody Mary.

*A*t that very moment, John Nickles burst into Harvey Pearl's office at the Tech Center. He was carrying a tape recorder. Harvey looked up from his sketch of a Cadillac fin. "You okay, John? You look like a fish on ice."

"I feel like a fucking fish on ice. Listen to this!" He closed the door and switched on the tape recorder. The tape lasted about five minutes. Norm Slenski was talking on the phone to an engineer at Plymouth, telling him about the general configuration of the Wildcat, the wheelbase, the weight, engine sizes, passenger space, cost range, likely production dates, even some of the probable color schemes. They talked about how much money the information was worth, but didn't arrive at a figure.

When the tape ended, Harvey let out a low moan. "So," he said, "I guess we can assume Slenski's the guy who leaked our '54 bumper designs to Plymouth, too."

"Seems reasonable. Of course we don't have any proof of that."

"Okay, John, here's what you're going to do. You go out there right now and you call that asshole into your office and you close the door and call security. You play the tape for him. Then you throw him out. I want him out of this building in fifteen minutes. He doesn't even clean out his desk. And you tell him that if he ever sets foot on this property again, he'll be arrested. If he gives you any shit, you tell him you're doing him a big favor by giving him a head start on Ted Mackey." When John didn't move, Harvey snapped, "Get moving!"

"Um . . . there's one more thing." His eyes swept the room. "I really don't think we should talk about it here, though."

"Can it wait till tomorrow?"

"I guess so. It's another tape."

"Why don't you come out to my house tomorrow around seven."

"Yessir."

"Now go get rid of Slenski. I don't want to see his fat face again as long as I live."

*I*t was a hot, sunny morning. Though summer was far from spent, the majestic elms around the Oakland Hills club-house were already beginning to shade to gold. On this weekday morning there were only a few women lying in lounge chairs by the swimming pool. Ted Mackey stripped off his seersucker shirt and stretched out and let his thoughts drift—from the upcoming Michigan football season to Ben Hogan's recent putting woes to the taste of Claire Hathaway's cunt, the taste of cinnamon and salt.

"What are you thinking about?"

Milmary's voice startled him. He opened one eye and saw that she'd taken off the white blouse and was wearing a black one-piece bathing suit. She was brushing her hair. The coppery highlights flashed in the sun, and her cheekbones jutted sharply. She looked beautiful, yet hard and dangerous.

"I was thinking about what I'm going to say to Marilyn Monroe."

"You mean you get aroused just thinking about her?"

"Hunh?" He propped himself up on one elbow. She was staring at his seersucker swim trunks. He looked down and saw, sure enough, a noticeable bulge.

Now she looked him in the eye. "Is that why you wanted to spend the day out here—so you'll be brown and beautiful when you meet the object of your wildest fantasies?"

"Darling, please don't start."

"I've seen all the clippings and pictures of her you've been saving."

"It so happens we're trying to hire her for a major ad campaign."

"Will she be wearing a bathing suit? Or will she be nude for this one?"

"How many Bloody Marys have you had?"

"Two."

"It's not even noon yet. You celebrating something?"

"As a matter of fact, I am. I finished my story yesterday and sent it off to *The New Yorker*."

"Well . . . congratulations. You haven't even let me read it yet."

"You haven't asked."

"I wasn't sure . . . I didn't know if you wanted anybody to read it."

"You miss everything, don't you?"

"What the hell is that supposed to mean?" He sat up. One of

the women on the far side of the pool peeked over the top of her magazine.

"You had no idea I spent the spring and summer writing a story about a pilot during the war. You have no idea your sons are playing for the Little League championship tomorrow."

"They are?"

"You have no idea Harvey's Japanese friend is due to arrive tomorrow night—and no clue as to what the poor woman's been through."

"What the hell are you talking about?"

"And you're completely unaware that I haven't had a decent orgasm all summer long."

That did it. He'd come here to unwind, not to get flogged. He stood up, slipped on his shirt, wiggled his feet into his sandals. "Why don't you order some food. Maybe your mood will improve."

"My mood is fine. Where do you think you're going?"

"I'm going down to the driving range to beat the living shit out of some golf balls."

"Oh, that'll solve everything."

"Maybe if you laid off the sauce you'd be able to have a decent orgasm."

"I haven't been drunk in months. Try again."

"Go to hell."

"Oh, that's clever, Teddy. I should've listened to Daddy—he always warned me never to criticize a man for being a lousy driver or a lousy lover. So tell me something—and don't give me any more crap about Marilyn Monroe—what's her name?"

She hadn't planned this, but suddenly there it was, out in the open at last. She looked up at the perfectly combed silver hair, the boiling silver curls on his chest, the sweat wobbling on his brow. He looked menacing, but she drilled him with her stare until he looked away.

"What's whose name?" he hissed, picking up a towel.

"Is it someone at the office?"

"Order some food."

"Someone in the neighborhood?"

"Dammit, Mil—"

"Is it anyone I know? Just tell me who it is, Ted, and I'll forget it ever happened. I deserve to know, goddammit."

"I don't know what you're talking about."

"Jesus, Ted . . ." She pinched the bridge of her nose. She had vowed to herself long ago that when this moment came she would not allow herself to cry. "You know exactly what I'm talking about." She pinched harder, pinched until it hurt. "I'm so tired of living like this."

He flipped the towel over his shoulder and buttoned his shirt. "I'll send a waiter out to take your order. See you in an hour."

He stormed into the clubhouse. At his locker he could barely lace his golf shoes. He realized his hands were not trembling because he was angry; they were trembling because he was terrified.

Thirteen

The weather had turned suddenly cool and there was a taste of fall in the air. Mirror Lake was molten copper in the day's last sunlight. This was Harvey Pearl's favorite time of day and his favorite time of year. He leaned back in his chair and gazed down from his porch at the lake and his new bomb shelter. The grass had come in nicely. Everything seemed perfect, frozen in place. He found such stillness, such fragile peace, almost frightening.

John Nickles turned into the lane in a sky-blue Skylark convertible. He had the top rolled back. For such a mole, such a hard worker and bland dresser, the guy certainly had a taste for flashy cars. When the bell rang, Harvey hollered for him to come on in. After a curt hello, John started setting up the tape recorder, opened his locked briefcase, threaded a reel into the machine.

"You want a drink?" Harvey said.

"No thanks."

"Well, I'm going to fix myself one. Something tells me I'm going to need it."

"All right. Scotch on the rocks."

When Harvey returned with the drinks, John downed his in three quick gulps. What was with this guy? He said he didn't want a drink, then knocked it back like a longshoreman; he was one of the top designers in Detroit, but he lived in a split-level nightmare in Wyandotte that was painted baby-shit green and looked like it belonged to a hubcap salesman. Now, without a word, he switched on the tape recorder. Out came the voices of Ted Mackey and Claire Hathaway.

"Hello?" she said.

"I told you working late one or two nights a week was fine —but five nights is above and beyond the call of duty."

"Ted! What time is it?"

"Almost eight. Time for you to knock off and let me buy you a drink."

"I really need to get home. Hello?"

"I'm right here."

"What was that clicking noise?"

"Beats me."

"I really have to get home. My mother's supposed to call at nine."

"Then I accept the invitation. Your place in half an hour. I'll bring the champagne."

"But I've got to finish this front bumper sketch—"

"Half an hour. That's an order."

"Okay, you win. My place in half an hour. Do you remember how to get there?"

"How could I forget?"

John shut off the machine. "There's about half a dozen more. Pretty much the same stuff, though once or twice they get into some pretty juicy specifics. Seems Claire's developed a taste for what the French call 'soixante-neuf.' Want to hear them?"

"No, I think I've got the picture." Harvey looked down at the lake. The sun had set, and all the molten copper was gone. "Why is it that I'm not even surprised?"

"I sure as hell was. I thought Claire had better sense."

"You thought Claire had better sense," Harvey grunted. John wasn't trying to be ironic; he probably didn't know what the word meant. "Oh, this is truly wonderful," Harvey said. "Just grand. Here we are hip-deep in the design of a top-secret new car and the competition already knows more about it than we do and the head of the design team's fucking the goddamn division manager. John, I'm not believing this is happening."

They sat there without speaking until the last of the sunlight was gone. When Harvey finished his drink, he turned on a lamp. "Where are the rest of the tapes of Ted and Claire?"

"Right here in my briefcase."

"Let me have them. All of them." John unwound the tape from the machine and handed six reels to Harvey. "Now, John, these are orders. You don't breathe a word about this to anyone."

"Yessir."

"Has anybody else heard any of these?"

"Nosir."

"I'll take care of them. Remember, not a word to anyone."

"Yessir."

When John was gone, Harvey locked the tapes in his bottom desk drawer. A few years ago, even a few months ago, this would've seemed like the end of the world; now it seemed like a messy little bit of housekeeping. He understood why. It was because the most important thing in his life—the only important thing—was to be at the airport when Taka Matsuda's plane arrived.

The Worst

Sufferers

in These

Little

Affairs

One

It wasn't the rejection itself, it was the wording of the letter, its cold formality, that stung Milmary Mackey. She thought her years at *The New Yorker* before the war and her one published story in the magazine would at least win a close reading, maybe some detailed criticism. But the letter that arrived that chilly fall afternoon was the same little cough of bad news she'd mailed out to hundreds of writers when she worked at the magazine. It was signed by Beryl Windham, a name Milmary didn't even recognize. Though she'd never handled rejection well, this news sent her into a tailspin. She spent the afternoon at her desk, staring down at the lake, sipping scotch and milk, reading the letter over and over.

She tried to figure out why she was taking this so hard. After all, it was the first thing she'd written in years, and it had been turned down only once. She'd gotten dozens of rejections before selling her first story to *Collier's*.

As the sun sank toward the lake and the whisky warmed her, she began to see that this story was much more than a summer project or the return to an abandoned dream. When she considered the prospect of failing all over again as a writer and resuming her life as suburban mother and wife to an unfaithful, career-mad man, she felt claustrophobic, almost panicky. Since the confrontation with Ted at the Oakland Hills pool, their marriage, like any marriage that exists under the cloud of a recognized but unnamed secret, had slipped into an even deeper chill. It was all so predictable, so ordinary and predictable.

She thought again of the Graham Greene interview. At a time like this she needed to remember what she was—not a victim of the Bomb itself, like Taka Matsuda, but a victim of her obsession with the Bomb. The only one thing for her to do was to embrace her curse.

She went to the window and looked down the hill. A single light was burning in Harvey's house. She wanted so badly to tell someone about her resolve to get her story published. But no, she didn't dare call or visit, not with all Harvey and Taka had on their minds. It would be an hour, maybe more, before Ted arrived home from the office—or wherever it was that he stopped on his way—and then there would be cocktails, small talk, a joyless dinner, another loveless night. It was all up to her. She crumpled the letter from *The New Yorker* and threw it in the trash can, cranked a fresh sheet of paper into the typewriter and started writing to the editor of the *Atlantic Monthly*.

Two

*H*arvey Pearl heard the snow before he saw it. Somehow, a freak early snowfall fit his mood perfectly. It made him realize he was safe, virtually invulnerable. He was sitting in the bomb shelter with the door open, wrapped in an Army blanket and sipping ginseng tea, when he heard the first snowflakes crackle on the brown leaves. The tea was the same kind Taka used to make for him when he was a boy. She'd brought a bag of it from Japan along with some of the books she used to read to him at bedtime. His favorite was a collection of Hemingway's

Nick Adams short stories, and it was open now on his lap. He'd spent the entire afternoon out here sipping tea, reading and rereading "Indian Camp," listening to the crackling snow, a casual use of time that would have been unthinkable even a few weeks ago. But now, he realized with pride, everything had changed. Things like tail fins and fender skirts and windshield slants and design leaks now seemed like child's play; and he was consumed by things that had never crossed his mind, from the Cold War and plastic surgery to canned food and chemical toilets.

He was thrilled by Taka's reaction to the bomb shelter. As soon as she arrived she started decorating the interior, covering the shelves of canned food and bottled water with paintings she'd done since the war, watercolors of misty mountains and glassy ponds. These reminded Harvey of the simpler times they'd shared in Pasadena, and now the shelter seemed more like a link to a vanished past than a hedge against an uncertain future.

Harvey had started spending whole afternoons out here. It was so quiet the worries of work evaporated and he was free to think. He realized he'd read the Hemingway story over and over because it was the ideal way to prepare himself for the coming ordeal. He also realized he'd been so busy with Taka that he still hadn't told Ted about Norm Slenski or decided what to do about Ted and Claire's affair. On the one hand, he didn't want to damage Claire's promising career; on the other hand, Milmary was almost like a sister to him, and he didn't want her hurt. He had no idea what to do.

It was already time to leave for the hospital. As he locked the shelter with the tiny key—one of only two like it in the world —he saw the Mackeys' Roadmaster glide down the lane to the paved road. He realized that for the first time in thirty years he hadn't had a single thought about cars all day.

*T*ommy and John Mackey were in the back seat of the Roadmaster, punching each other and speculating with their father about who would tear whose head off at the Red Wings hockey game. The consensus was that Ted Lindsay, who had it in for Eric Nesterenko, would try to put him in the hospital before the end of the first period.

Milmary sat in the front seat beside her husband, swaddled in a knee-length mink coat. Though the heater was blasting her ankles, she felt as if her bones had turned to ice. She didn't like these trips to Olympia, the institutionalized brutality of hockey or, worse, the blood lust of the blue-collar fans. Once she'd seen a man toss a squid—*a live squid!*—over the glass after the Red Wings scored a goal, and everyone in the place roared merrily as it squirted ink at the opposing goalie until a man in street shoes skidded out onto the ice and scooped it up with a snow shovel. It was barbaric, and she didn't want her sons exposed to it, but she knew Ted would brush her objections aside with some quip about turning the boys into fairies, so she said nothing.

Besides, after she'd written to the *Saturday Review* the night before, a surprise cold front moved in and she built a fire and kept drinking. Then she had trouble falling asleep. Ted came in late again, shortly before midnight, and she swore she could smell perfume on him, but he denied it and told her she was drunk, which was true. Rather than argue she closed her eyes, but the bedroom started spinning. She went downstairs and tried to read a magazine by the dying fire. In the middle of the night she woke up on the livingroom floor with a throbbing head and a stiff neck. After breakfast she had a Bloody Mary, then took half a Nembutal and a nap. She drank Bloody Marys all afternoon, and now she was nursing the leather flask of straight scotch. Just like the good old days. She told herself this had to stop.

When Ted guided the Roadmaster off Southfield Road onto Grand River, she shivered.

"You cold, darling?" he said.

"No, but please slow down. The snow's sticking."

"I'm doing thirty-five. The roads are fine."

She took a belt from the flask and handed it to him. Instead of taking a drink, he slipped it into the pocket of his camel-hair overcoat. She said nothing and lit a cigarette. As soon as she exhaled, her power window zipped down three inches, compliments of a husband who could control all the windows and had recently quit smoking and now, in the self-righteous manner of the reformed, loathed the smell of cigarette smoke. Had his lover insisted that he quit? She reached for the button on her door and zipped the window shut.

"Darling, you know how smoke—"

"It's snowing outside! It's fifteen degrees! It's—oh, to hell with it." She lowered her window halfway—an icy blast—and tossed the cigarette sparking into the night. Then she closed the window and fumbled in his coat for the flask. This time she held on to it.

The boys had stopped wrestling in the back seat. No one said a word the rest of the way to Olympia.

Driving down Woodward Avenue to Henry Ford Hospital, Harvey was amazed how trashy the world looked—hamburger stands, drive-in restaurants, gas stations, bowling alleys, car washes, gaudy churches, tire stores, the commercial slag of a city devoted to motion. Something new and horrible seemed to be going up on every vacant lot. He thought of Ray Kroc, who'd just sent along a pack of snapshots of smiling, moon-faced Mr. Multimixer standing beside his new three-tone Buick Century. In the background workers were erecting what looked like a gas station. Huge plastic arcs sprang from the sides

of the building, positively one of the weirdest structures Harvey
had ever seen. This, Ray explained in his letter, was his very
first hamburger stand, and Harvey realized it would fit in perfectly here on Woodward Avenue. He'd spent his entire adult
life driving past these places without giving them a second
thought, but now they all looked like props from a nightmare.
It was almost enough to make him yearn for the scrap-wood
and sheet-metal terrain of Hiroshima. At least that city, unlike
this brash, blinking sprawl, had been purified by fire and light
and had come to understand the vanity of power.

Yet whenever he took Taka out for a drive, she expressed
amazement that bordered on delight. To her everything in Detroit was overwhelming—the trees so big and healthy, the electric signs so bright and cheerful, the roads so wide and so full
of big new cars. In fact, riding in the car, even more than sitting
in the bomb shelter, opened her up and made her once again
the storyteller Harvey remembered from his youth.

One afternoon, as they drove across town for a picnic lunch
on the shores of Lake St. Clair, Harvey had asked about her
plastic surgery in Japan. She launched into the story without
hesitation, and she told it almost eagerly, without bitterness or
shame. Four years after the war, she rode the train alone from
Kagoshima to Hiroshima, then took a bus to the hospital where
she was to meet a doctor friend of her brother's from Tokyo
University who claimed to have developed a method of plastic
surgery that was 99 percent successful. Taka had decided not
to tell him that her hair had fallen out and grown back several
times or that just a few weeks earlier a mysterious rash had
developed between her toes. The hair loss and the rash had
confounded her doctors in Kagoshima, who decided, in despair,
that these were just two more devilish manifestations of "the
atomic disease." No, from the surgeon in Hiroshima she wanted
no more confusion, no more doubts. She wanted just one thing:
her old face. She wanted her upturned nose instead of this

mashed lump of cartilage, her dancing mouth instead of this lipless hole, and she wanted to be rid of the flesh that had melted like red wax over her jaw.

To her dismay, the small private hospital in Hiroshima was grimy and reeked of disinfectant. The only bright spot was a small vegetable garden in the courtyard, where radishes, carrots and potatoes—the biggest, plumpest vegetables Taka had ever seen—were being harvested by two nurses. When she learned the garden had been planted to study the effects of radiation on plants, she understood in a new way how perverse this new Bomb was: It sickened and killed people even as it made plants flourish.

Taka found the surgeon's office at the end of a dark corridor. The nurse told her to sit down and wait, and she sat there alone with her hope and her terror for three hours before the doctor appeared. His white jacket was smeared with blood—like a butcher's, Taka thought. He looked tired, but at least he was pleasant as he led her into a small operating room with yellow walls and long wooden shelves that sagged with files on his patients. He asked about Taka's brother as he examined the burns on her face. His hands were cool and tender.

Since no general anesthesia was available at the hospital, the doctor stabbed her in the back three times with needles full of Novocain before picking up his scalpel. Taka closed her eyes. As the operation dragged on, she could tell from the way the doctor was lecturing his two assistants that there had been a terrible misunderstanding. The 99 percent success rate of this procedure was something he'd read about in an American medical journal. Like every other doctor she'd seen since the war, this one was groping, trying something he knew little about, hoping for the best. Under the circumstances, they all seemed to think anything was worth a try. At one point during the operation Taka opened her eyes and saw a strip of flesh from her back attached to a pair of forceps. It was draped over her shoulder, and it looked like a piece of pink-rimmed shoe leather. She needed all of her strength not to become sick.

Within an hour the doctor had grafted the skin from her back over the scar tissue along her jawline. By the next day the graft began to turn gray. The doctor gave her an injection to stimulate blood flow to the patch of skin, but it didn't help. Two days later, he removed the rejected graft.

She returned to that hospital four more times, but each operation failed and finally she gave up. When she heard about a joint American and Japanese venture to take about two dozen female atomic bomb victims to New York for expert plastic surgery, she eagerly added her name to the list of candidates. When she learned she'd been turned down, she returned to Kagoshima, resigned to living out her life indoors, in half-darkness, far from the prying eyes of a disapproving world, in the private purgatory of the *Hibakusha*.

Then last year, long after she had given up all hope, Harvey came looking for her. Now Taka lay unconscious in a recovery room at Henry Ford Hospital in Detroit, her face wrapped in damp bandages as Harvey hurried through the snowstorm and the neon hell of Woodward Avenue to be with her. He turned on the windshield wipers and for the first time in his adult life tried to imagine what it would be like to live outside of General Motors. Maybe twenty-seven years was enough. Surely John Nickles or, in true GM fashion, a dozen other men were perfectly capable of replacing him. One reason Harvey had never considered retirement was that there had never been much in his life besides work. Now, he realized as he pulled into the hospital lot, that was no longer the case. He parked and shut off the engine, but he didn't move. He waited until snow covered the car and obliterated the outside world. He sat there listening to his breathing. It took him half an hour to work up the nerve to get out of the car and go into the hospital.

*T*ed Mackey was happy to oblige his wife and stop by the Slapshot Club on the way to their seats. He figured he needed a drink worse than she did, though for different reasons. Last night, finance wizard Ned Schroeder from the finance committee and a couple of his bean-counting buddies from the Engineering Policy Group had stumbled upon Ted having dinner with Claire Hathaway at the Red Flame, an out-of-the-way steak house on Livernois. Being discovered in a dim corner booth with a beautiful female employee was not what Ted needed right now. Knowing how Schroeder worked, he figured their surprise encounter would be fed into the ravenous corporate rumor mill first thing Monday morning.

Then when they got back to Claire's apartment she'd thrown another of her tantrums, wailing that she hated slinking around town the way they did, hiding in the corners of restaurants, dreading the appearance of a familiar face. Why wouldn't he take her on a vacation to some faraway place where there weren't any car people? She wept as he wrestled with her clothes, wept as they made love on the bed, on the sofa, then, almost viciously, on the rug in the living room. She was still crying when he left.

To top that off, when he got home Milmary accused him of smelling like another woman's perfume. Luckily she was drunk and he was able to deny everything. But when he got in the shower he saw rug burns on his kneecaps and scratches from Claire's fingernails on his shoulders and arms. He couldn't ignore these signs any longer: as she demanded more, he felt himself falling for her; and as he fell he was growing careless. He wondered if deep down he wanted to get caught, wanted to live up to her escalating demands. No, he told himself, there wasn't room at the top of GM for guys who chased their dicks around town.

When they pushed through the turnstiles at Olympia, Ted let the boys go on ahead to the Slapshot Club. They vanished into the crowd, chasing each other through the forests of legs just as Ted and his brothers had done in this building years ago. It was a good, tough crowd—mostly men with tonic in their hair and grease under their fingernails and foaming cups of beer in their fists. Ted took it all in—the cigar smoke, the belly laughter, the rising electricity—as Milmary clutched her mink coat to her throat and steadied herself against him. He understood that this kind of crowd repelled her, probably terrified her; but the higher he rose at GM, the more he felt a need to stay in touch with this rough and raw part of his past. Every time he came here it seemed more people recognized him, hollered to him, clapped him on the back. Some men simply stepped aside and made way for this couple, this elegant woman with the mink coat and suede gloves and frosted hair and this ruddy, polished guy who walked as though he owned the place and obviously had the power to put hundreds, even thousands of these men out of work with a single phone call. The crowd seemed to part before them, and in no time they reached the Slapshot Club.

Tommy and John were already enthroned on bar stools drinking Shirley Temples, ginger-ale cocktails adorned with maraschino cherries and orange slices. While Milmary ordered drinks, Ted looked the room over: the usual mix of executives and their wives, everyone smoking cigarettes and gulping booze and shouting. Bob McNamara from Ford standing stiffly in the far corner, drinking coffee. Eggheads like McNamara probably come to hockey games about as often as I go to the symphony, Ted thought. Then he saw Ned Schroeder holding court across the room. Ted grabbed his drink and headed for him. This was a perfect chance to get him off to the side and let him know, in a casual way, that he'd been taking the Wildcat design team out to the Red Flame for one-on-one pep talks. When Schroeder saw Ted coming, his face lit up.

*A*fter pacing the waiting room for half an hour, Harvey bummed three cigarettes from a red-haired Negro and smoked them so fast he almost vomited. As the wave of nausea passed, he thought again of "Indian Camp," about the Indian who cuts his own throat rather than listen to the cries of his wife during childbirth. Later on, when Nick asks his father why the Indian killed himself, his father says, "He couldn't stand things, I guess."

Harvey walked to the end of the hall and looked down at the traffic jam on Grand River—hockey fans arriving for the Red Wings game, he supposed. "They're usually the worst sufferers in these little affairs," Nick's father had said just before he found the Indian dead in the top bunk.

How wise, Harvey thought, to understand the agony of being powerless to help when a loved one suffers. The agony was compounded, in the Indian's case, by the knowledge that he had physically helped cause his wife's suffering and, in Harvey's case, by the knowledge that he had been part of the war machine that had caused Taka's suffering. *He couldn't stand things, I guess.*

Harvey walked to the other end of the hall and looked south toward downtown and the river and Canada. A few blocks from the hospital, workers had carved a deep hole in the earth where the Ford Freeway and the Lodge Freeway would cross. A short while ago this sight would've made Harvey feel warm all over; now, looking down at the dark hole in the earth, he imagined he was seeing a huge open grave.

He felt a sadness beyond anything he had ever known. You devote your whole life to making long, low, beautiful cars, and at long last, just when the world begins to catch up with your vision, the zeal that made it all possible turns to cold ashes in your mouth.

*W*hile her husband talked shop across the room, Milmary drank scotch and milk and studied the glossy photographs of the Red Wing players that lined the walls. Though they were smiling and wearing their dentures, they were all pug-ugly, their faces scissored with scar tissue, a gang of swarthy and vicious Canadians.

"Those aren't their real teeth, you know."

When she spun around, Norm Slenski's face was inches from hers. He was holding an index finger to his lips. "Shhhhh!" He glanced over his shoulder. "Ted doesn't know I'm here. Have you heard the news?"

"No, Norman. What news?"

"I got canned. Doesn't Ted know yet?"

"He hasn't said a word about it. If he did know, he certainly would've said something. What in the world happened?"

Norm looked relieved. "It's a long story. I'll tell you some other time."

Wanda appeared at his side. "Hello, Mrs. Mackey," she said. "Would you like to see our new baby pictures?"

"Of course, Wanda." Milmary felt strangely grateful for this diversion. Anything was better than drinking alone or listening to people talk about hockey and cars. Most of the snapshots Wanda spread on the bar were out of focus, and the unlucky boy bore a strong resemblance to his father: same sleepy eyes, same round face, same look of middling intelligence. But Milmary said the things you're supposed to say when proud parents trot out their baby pictures, and she didn't ask why the kid drooled so much.

As she studied the snapshots, Milmary started feeling something strange and unexpected, something wonderful. Here was Norm Slenski, a draft horse who, according to Harvey, could always be counted on to do thankless jobs like designing floor mats but had not yet cluttered the world with a truly original idea; and here was his mousy wife, who was wearing a gingham dress and sensible tan shoes and probably cut her own hair by putting a bowl on her head and chopping away with dull scissors. Everything about them was aggressively plain.

Or was it?

Milmary knew the Slenskis' story, a classic Detroit story, better than she cared to. Norm and Wanda grew up on the same block of Joseph Campau, went to Kosciuszko School and Hamtramck High together, got married right out of high school and now lived in the double-decker between their parents' double-deckers. To Milmary, a refugee from claustrophobic Grosse Pointe, the arrangement sounded like a living hell.

But the longer Wanda cooed about her baby, the clearer it became to Milmary that this woman had something far more valuable than a mink, a house on a lake, original paintings and literary pretensions. Sure, she was as plain as a box of rocks and she was married to a glorified (and unemployed) grunt. But she had a big, ugly baby—and she was happy.

"So, Wanda," Milmary said when Norm went to get a fresh beer, "how long have you two been trying to have a baby?"

"Your memory's terrible, Mrs. Mackey. You know we're Catholics. We already have two girls. This is just our first boy."

"Yes, of course."

"But this baby's definitely been the best."

"How's that?"

"Maybe because it's a boy or something, but Norm's a new man. He's never paid so much attention to me. He hurries home from work every night. He even bought me flowers yesterday. Flowers! I feel ten years younger. Norm says we might even move to a bigger house with a yard and—"

The siren wailed out in the corridor, signaling the return of the teams to the ice for the opening face-off. Norm rushed up with a fresh beer and started chugging. When he saw Ted's group breaking up across the room, he put the half-empty glass on the bar, grabbed his wife by the arm and hustled her out the door. Milmary watched them join the river of fans heading for their seats, and she felt a pang she recognized as envy. She wanted to be as happy as those two lumpen Polish proles; and now, thanks to their fuzzy snapshots, she knew how to go about it.

*W*hen Harvey returned to the waiting room, the red-haired Negro was asleep on the sofa and one of the surgeons was talking to a nurse. "Ah, there you are, Mr. Pearl," the doctor said. "I was afraid you'd left."

"How is she?"

"Taka's resting comfortably." He had the sugary manner of an undertaker. "I want her to rest. Why don't you come back in the morning, say around ten. Her lower face will still be covered with bandages, but I'm sure she'll be eager to talk. I think it's best if you go on home and get some sleep."

The snow had stopped falling. Harvey dusted off the Buick's windshield and let the engine idle until the heater warmed up. Driving out Woodward, he remembered how his mother used to advise him to deal with an uncertain and unfair world: "Expect the worst and you'll never be disappointed." He had always been too much of a dreamer, too much of a believer in his own gifts and in the essential kindness of fate to live by such advice. But now, driving home alone on a cold and suddenly starry night, he chose, for the first time in his life, to expect the worst. It was the only way he would be able to make it through this night.

*A*s Ted eased the Roadmaster into the traffic flowing out Grand River, Milmary turned to check on the boys. Stuffed with hot dogs and Cokes, hoarse from screaming while Ted

Lindsay and Eric Nesterenko had slugged each other senseless, they'd fallen asleep instantly on the back seat. Now, as the traffic loosened and the car gathered speed, she noticed Ted had that glazed look, his famous million-mile stare. The three cups of black coffee she'd drunk between the second and third periods had cleared her head, and she was too buzzy and alert to ride all the way home in silence. "So what was on Ned Schroeder's mind?" she said.

Ted grunted. "Not much, as usual."

"You looked like you'd been punched in the stomach after you talked to him."

"Not a bad analogy."

"Well, what was it?"

"Just business."

"Something bad?"

He shot her a look and nearly sideswiped a parked Packard. "Why all this interest in my job all of a sudden?"

"Well, I've barely seen your face in the past month. I thought it might be nice to carry on an actual conversation for a change. Sorry I asked." She folded her arms and looked out the side window.

"I'm sorry, darling." He rested his right hand on her knee, worked the mink coat open. "Schroeder just had a little bad news—which he was obviously delighted to pass along."

"About what?"

"The Wildcat. Seems the car's in trouble all of a sudden. They're even talking about shelving it."

"But why? I thought it was your dream car."

"There were some leaks in the design studio. I swear, the next time I see that Slenski son of a bitch I'm going to kill him with my bare hands."

Milmary considered telling him about their conversation before the game, but thought better of it. She slid across the seat, rested her head on Ted's shoulder and put his hand back on her thigh. The boys dozed in the back seat. The car was warm against the icy, starry night. She couldn't wait to get home.

Three

*T*ed Mackey overslept the next morning. It was raining when the clock radio buzzed at six o'clock and the velvety voice of J. P. McCarthy started purring that Ernest Hemingway had been awarded the Nobel Prize for literature. Ted considered waking Milmary and telling her the news about a writer she loved to hate because, as she put it, "Anyone who puffs his chest up that much must be scared of *something*." But she hadn't stirred when the alarm went off. No wonder. She'd practically raped him when they got home from the hockey game, had ignored his protests about fatigue, a headache, too much to drink. As soon as he had the condom in place she'd climbed aboard and ridden him for half an hour. Even as Ted had drifted off to sleep he thought the whole exercise had been strangely businesslike, not at all romantic, not at all like Milmary. Yet it hadn't been unpleasant, either. . . .

Now he jerked awake a second time. Someone was knocking on the door. J. P. McCarthy was purring about the possibility of the rain lasting all day and all night. It was almost nine o'clock.

"Mr. Mackey?" Betsy called through the door. "Your office just called. Should I tell them you isn't feeling well?"

"No, goddammit! Tell them I just left."

He shot out of bed and almost tripped over Milmary's blouse and skirt and girdle and his own jacket and loafers. Johnny Reed and Tom Flanagan were due in his office at nine o'clock sharp, and he had to face the firing squad in the Engineering Policy

Group meeting at ten. He shaved in such a hurry that he had to use a styptic pencil and then stick scraps of toilet paper to his face to stop the bleeding. On his way out he grabbed two condoms from the dresser. Though he didn't expect to be needing them when he visited Claire Hathaway that evening, he knew that in these matters it was always better to be safe than sorry.

*S*trange, Will Lomax thought. Ted Mackey was usually the first to arrive in the morning and the last to leave at night. Even stranger than Ted's absence, though, were the two guys in his office. When Will had dropped off the press release about the third-quarter sales figures, one of them was sitting in the swivel chair with his feet on Ted's desk and the other was lying on the sofa smoking a cigarette. They both were wearing expensive overcoats and gray fedoras, but they looked tough, like boxers, their faces puffy and their knuckles hardened with scar tissue.

"Morning, gentlemen," Will said, dropping the press release on Ted's desk.

"Oh, you finished the report," the man in Ted's chair said. "Good job."

The guy on the sofa laughed. He was blowing smoke rings at the ceiling. "You seen Ted yet this morning? We was supposed to meet him at nine."

"His secretary tells me he's on his way," Will said. "Anything I can help you with?"

"Yeah," the man behind the desk said. "You can find this Slenski guy for us."

"Norm Slenski? I'm afraid he doesn't work here anymore."

"That's why we need you to help us find him." Both men laughed.

Miriam stuck her head in the door. "Ted's on your line, Will."

He took the call in his office. "I overslept," Ted growled.

"Took Milmary and the boys to the Red Wings game. Listen, I've got a nine o'clock meeting with—"

"They're in your office right now. Who the hell are they?"

"Coupla boys I grew up with in Corktown. They're going to do me a little favor. Tell 'em I'll be there in half an hour."

Will passed the message along. Then he dialed Hayes Tucker, Jr.'s number in New York. As the phone rang, Will realized he welcomed Ted's late arrival. It was one more chance for him to operate on his own, the latest in a string of golden opportunities as Ted became absorbed with the sales war and design leaks and as the rest of the PR brass geared up for the publicity binge for the fifty-millionth GM car. That historic vehicle would be produced sometime in 1955, a bread-and-butter Chevrolet Bel Air. There was talk of spraying the car with special gold glint paint, using upholstery shot through with gold threads, even plating hundreds of parts, from screws to trim, with 24-karat gold. It would literally be a golden car for the Golden Age.

While that campaign had already put Will's '54 Buick project deep in the shade, it also freed him to operate on his own. For once he was making things happen instead of writing newspaper copy about people who made things happen or writing their press releases and speeches. One phone call to Luther Fuller in Flint had set up the exact time the five hundred thousandth '54 Buick would make its way down the assembly line. One phone call, and he had dictated the rhythm of an entire factory. It was physically thrilling.

Finally the squeaky voice came over the telephone line: "This is Hayes Tucker, Jr. May I help you?"

"Hayes, it's Will Lomax in Detroit. I'm calling to let you know we're going to run the magic number down the line on December first."

"Any special reason?"

"As a matter of fact, there is. David Buick established the company on December first, 1904."

"Nifty! Fifty years on the nose! Say, where's Ted been hiding? Haven't heard a peep out of him in weeks."

"He's been swamped. Hayes, another reason I'm calling is I need to know how you're coming with that Korean vet."

"Super."

"Has he signed a contract yet?"

"Well, no. But I worked him over pretty good at a PTA meeting last night. Don't worry, he'll come around."

"Hayes, listen to me. We're counting on that sale. *Life* magazine's got a big spread scheduled for right after Christmas. We've got the production date locked on the car. We've *got* to have that sale nailed down—and soon, you hear me? If we don't, we'll have to go with our backup."

"Your backup?"

"As a precaution, I've lined up a fellow in Chicago who's starting a chain of hamburger stands. He's buying a whole fleet of Buicks for his managers."

"A backup?"

"It's just a precaution, Hayes. You're still our first choice."

"Look, Will, there's no need to panic. I'll have Bob's signature on a contract any day now. That's a promise."

When Will hung up, he had a warm feeling in his gut. Now that the chips were down, a man with as much larceny in his genes as Hayes Tucker, Jr., could be counted on to come through.

*T*he call from Will Lomax had been bad enough. But as soon as he hung up, Bob Lundt, GM's zone sales rep for Long Island, was on the line. Earlier in the year, Lundt's weekly calls had been jovial pep talks, but now they'd turned into daily torture sessions. Hayes was beginning to understand why his daddy had always referred to zone sales reps as Typhoid Mary. Since he had several dozen of these calls to make today, Lundt got straight to the point. "How many units did you move Saturday, Tucker?"

"Lemme see. One, two, three, four. Four, Bob."

"Four new cars?"

"No, three used, one new."

"Get on the ball, Tucker. I've got six hundred *new* cars to sell by the end of the month. I'm not enjoying this any more than you are, but Detroit's giving me these impossible fucking quotas—and that means I've got to pass them on to you guys at the dealerships. You with me so far?"

"Yes, Bob."

"You boys had your chance to make money during the first half of the year. Now it's the factory's turn to make some money—or so Mackey and everybody else in Detroit tells me, and that's what they're paying me to tell you. The power's in Detroit now. I wish I had a fucking dime for every time I've heard somebody say that. You may not like it and I may not like it, but that's the way it is. You still with me?"

"Yes, Bob."

"Now, if you can't move the iron we're shipping, there's a chance they'll stick another Buick store somewhere between Farmingdale and Levittown."

"*What?* Another dealership between—"

"It's just talk right now, but I want you to know which way the wind's blowing."

Through the one-way mirror that allowed him to survey his showroom and lot, Hayes saw a truck loaded with new Buicks pull up. "Pardon me for interrupting, Bob, but what's that truck I see pulling up out front?"

"Does it have four Centurys and three Roadmasters on it?"

"Looks more like four Centurys, four Roadmasters and two Specials."

"Good, they overloaded."

"Bob, I didn't even order those cars! I've already got thirty-six new cars sitting on my lot! What the hell am I supposed to do with ten more?"

"You're supposed to *sell* them, Tucker. Give 'em away if you have to. Just get rid of 'em."

For the first time in his life Hayes Tucker, Jr., went to lunch with no intention of returning to work for the rest of the day. He took the keys to a red Skylark convertible and drove straight to Farmingdale Liquors and bought a pint of Old Grand-Dad, his daddy's brand, then drove south until the road ended at the beach. Off to his right he could see the water tower at Jones Beach, a silver toadstool in a blue sky. He spent the afternoon sitting there with the top down, sipping bourbon and watching ospreys skim across the cold green water of Great South Bay. When he pictured what it would be like to have another Buick dealership down the road, he was suddenly able to imagine failing at business. His daddy would roll over in his grave. No, Hayes told himself. This is 1954. I am my father's son. I sell Buicks for a living. No.

He was awakened by a policeman. It was dark and bitterly cold; the Old Grand-Dad bottle was on the floor, empty. He felt like someone had driven nails into his eyeballs. "Musta dozed off!" he told the cop, trying to sound chipper and alert as he handed over his driver's license.

The cop studied the license, then said, "Take it slow going home, Mr. Tucker."

Hayes put the top up and drove with his head out the window and one eye closed. The cold air helped. He figured it must be late because there was hardly any traffic.

He parked in his driveway, afraid that opening the garage door might wake Virginia and the kids. In the kitchen he poured himself a glass of milk and ate nine chocolate-chip cookies. Christ, it was after one o'clock in the morning! How would he explain this one? Virginia had probably sent the police out looking for him. As he reached for the milk bottle, he knocked over a bag of sugar. Everything in the room was trying to spin and run away from him. He hadn't been this looped since New Year's Eve, when he jumped into Jim Zimmer's pool fully clothed and nearly came down with pneumonia. Now as he cleaned up the sugar an idea came to him, a perfectly brilliant inspiration that never would've entered his mind before Typhoid Mary blew into his life.

Hayes took the bag of sugar and slipped out the front door. The lawn was drenched with dew, and stars were winking in the cold black sky. He weaved down the sidewalk, careful not to trip over the tricycles, footballs or hula hoops. When he got to the end of Lindbergh Street he looked around. The neighborhood was dead asleep. He walked up to the '42 Plymouth in Bob and Sally Brunswick's driveway and poured the whole bag of sugar into the gas tank. Then he strolled home whistling at the stars. No way those bastards in Detroit were going to make a failure out of Hayes Tucker, Jr.

Ted Mackey had overslept that morning and now, long past midnight, he was having trouble falling asleep. He lay in bed looking at the half moon, at the skin of blue slush on the lawn, at the frozen lake. Milmary was snoring beside him. What had gotten into her? As an encore to last night's performance she was waiting for him tonight in a black teddy and black stockings and black high heels and a peach satin robe. The bedroom was lit, soft and orange, by candles; Oscar Peterson's piano was tinkling on the radio, and there were snifters of brandy on the bedside table. As soon as she had him undressed she knelt beside the bed and, without a word, took him in her mouth. She'd never done that before, had never taken charge, and it seemed to thrill her as much as it thrilled him. His excitement fueled hers and hers fueled his and an hour later, after some good old-fashioned missionary-position calisthenics, she was snoring softly and he was staring out at the half moon, the frozen lake and the blue lawn.

He poured the rest of her brandy into his snifter, flushed the condom down the toilet, then padded downstairs in a bathrobe and leather slippers. Some coals were still smoldering in the livingroom fireplace, so he dropped a log on them and sat down in the black BarcaLounger. He'd planned to stop by Claire's apartment on his way home, but she was working all night against a morning deadline on the Wildcat's dashboard bucks. Ted didn't have the heart to tell her she was almost certainly wasting her time.

Secretly he was relieved she was working all night. To think that after all these years of random coupling with stewardesses and secretaries, hookers and hostesses, neighbors and strangers, the mad mechanical fucking he thought of as "pure biology"— to think that someone from that long procession actually mattered now and was forcing him to make an impossible decision. To think that just up the stairs from where he was sitting his wife lay asleep, the pale blue vein throbbing on her neck, her smooth, speckled shoulders glowing in the dying candlelight. How had this happened?

He considered pouring his story out to Harvey. He'd be shocked, maybe pissed off because of his fondness for Milmary; but he was a man, he was a friend, he would understand. Then Ted asked himself what good it would do to tell Harvey, or anyone else. It might lighten his load of guilt and confusion, but it wouldn't tell him what to do.

As he sat there in the BarcaLounger sipping brandy and watching a second, then a third log turn to ash, Ted Mackey—lapsed Catholic, adulterer, self-doubter—came to a decision. The only way to sort out this mess was to bare his soul to a faceless stranger, with no fear of discovery and no expectation of forgiveness, and hope the admission somehow would unlock the mystery of what he must do, which woman he must hurt. A

Catholic priest would fit the bill as well as anyone. If that made
him a foxhole Catholic, then so be it. He'd seen dozens of men
take this desperate step during the war. But nothing Ted had
seen in the Pacific was half as terrifying as this.

Four

*E*ven when their ancient Plymouth was pronounced
dead on arrival by the mechanics at Tucker Buick, Bob and Sally
Brunswick didn't jump at the chance to buy a new Century at
a rock-bottom price. They casually toured the showroom and
lot with Bill Voisin, the dealership's top salesman. They joined
the Thrill of the Month Club by taking a spin in a black-and-
white Century four-door with a fire-engine-red interior. Then
they went into Hayes's office to tell him, almost sheepishly, that
they wanted to go home and think it over.

Hayes was stunned. Though he'd never tried it himself, his
father swore by the sugar-in-the-gas-tank trick, especially when
the prey was a married couple with three kids and one dead car.
But there they were, gimpy Bob and mousy Sally, standing in
his doorway asking if they could use his phone to call a cab.

Hayes insisted on giving them a lift home. Since Voisin, the
hardest of the hard-sellers, had struck out, Hayes decided to try
the soft touch. Sometimes, his daddy had taught him, if you
pretend selling a car is the farthest thing from your mind, it has
a way of selling itself. With Bob in the front seat and Sally in
back, Hayes pointed the red Skylark convertible south toward
the shore.

"Where are you taking us?" Sally said.

"I'm gonna show you folks the scenic route home. There's a

great little fishing spot down here where you've got to take those boys of yours."

"Bob, did you remember to take your medicine?" Sally said.

"What's the medicine for, Bob?" Hayes said.

"My foot." He blushed. "I mean, where my foot used to be. When the weather turns cool like this the stump gets sore. Sometimes it feels like my foot's itching, even though it's gone."

"How about that. Boy, I'll bet that Korea was no picnic."

"Drove some of the boys plain crazy. Course you don't hear much about that nowadays."

After fifteen minutes of war-is-hell chitchat, Hayes cried "There it is!" and pulled off to the side of the road. Through the swaying sea oats on their left, they could see a dozen men standing on the beach holding fishing poles; they looked like statues, frozen in place, each unaware of the others. The water beyond them was a sheet of silver. Gulls wheeled overhead. "They pull all kinds of fish out of that bay," Hayes said. "Bass, pike, bluefish, sturgeon. It's wall-to-wall clams and oysters." He didn't know what he was talking about. The only fish he'd ever caught in his life were the three goldfish he'd scooped out of the tank at Woolworth's last Christmas Eve. "It's one of the top fishing spots on all of Long Island—and hardly anybody knows about it. Best thing is, it's only fifteen minutes from home by car." He stepped on the last word ever so slightly.

Bob took a deep breath of salt air. "Sure is peaceful. I need to get that fishing pole of mine out of the attic."

"It's in the basement," Sally said.

"Well," Hayes said, "you dig that baby out and we'll come down here with the boys next weekend and catch us some supper. I'll be happy to drive."

As they rode back to Levittown, Bob went on and on about the fish he used to catch on Cape Cod in the summertime when he was a boy. By the time they turned onto Lindbergh Street, Hayes figured he had the sale locked up. But next time he wasn't taking any chances. Next time the reluctant Brunswicks would be subjected to the full glory of The System.

Five

*T*hree days after Taka's first round of plastic surgery, Harvey took her back to the hospital to have her bandages changed. He wanted to be with her when the bandages were removed. After all, he reminded her, this surgery was for her, not him; in his eyes, she would always be beautiful. But she insisted he stay in the waiting room, and now, looking down at the bulldozers working on the new expressway interchange, he was glad he'd relented. There was no hurry. There would be several more operations here and, if those failed, a whole new series at Mount Sinai in New York.

When Taka emerged from the doctor's office with the lower half of her face wrapped in fresh bandages, Harvey didn't say a word. He helped her into her coat, put his arm around her, and led her to the elevator. When they were alone inside, descending, he said, "What did the doctor say?"

"He says too early to tell. One more week."

"Did you look at yourself?"

"No, I do not need mirror."

"Why not?"

"Because—when time comes, you will be my mirror."

*H*alfway to the Shrine of the Little Flower, Ted Mackey started having second thoughts. What did he stand to learn inside a dark box that he couldn't learn out here on Woodward Avenue, waiting for the light to change while a fat boy holding a hamburger twirled in the purple sky?

By the time he reached 1 3 Mile Road, he'd made up his mind to swing by Claire's apartment first. It couldn't do any harm, and it might do some good. He checked his wallet. He still had the two condoms he'd taken from the dresser drawer.

He drove past the Shrine of the Little Flower and was so lost in thought he almost overshot Salem Street and had to jerk the wheel hard to the right. As he made the turn, he noticed in his rearview mirror that a car followed him off Woodward. Was Milmary having him tailed? He wouldn't put it past her. He pulled over to the curb, stopped and waited for the car to pass. It was a blue Kaiser with a man at the wheel and an old lady smoking a cigarette beside him. Not your typical private eyes, Ted thought with relief; but he would have to be careful.

After the Kaiser disappeared, he drove to the Huntington Arms. Claire's lights were off, and her new canary-yellow-and-white Buick Century was gone. Working late again, no doubt. This was all Ted needed to know. He had tried to take matters into his own hands, but obviously it was not meant to be. He drove back.

The last of the tour buses had left the Shrine of the Silver Dollar, and the place actually felt more like a church than a tourist trap. He wondered if his dear devout mother still came here twice a week to arrange the flowers on the altar and iron the choirboys' vestments. In a little shop off to the side of the vestibule, an old nun dozed amid the candles and crucifixes and Bibles and pictures of Father Charles Coughlin, radio preacher, celebrity, racist, millionaire and a god in the eyes of Ted's mother and millions like her. Was it the religion itself or its flawed human practitioners, Ted wondered, that had killed his faith? But this was no time for such questions. He'd come here to make a simple, straightforward transaction: I talk, you listen, and we both hope it does some good.

He chose a dark pew near the back of the church. Only a few people were waiting outside the confessional to his right—a terrified teenage boy, three old ladies and a young nun. No doubt a young priest was in the box doing the hot and dirty work while Father Charlie sat in the rectory preparing his Sunday rant and counting the day's take from the souvenir shop. Ted had a powerful urge to bolt, but the teenager made a fast escape, and the three old ladies and the nun were processed in quick succession. Suddenly Ted found himself pulling back the heavy velvet curtain and kneeling on a slab of wood in the dark.

He'd forgotten how dark these boxes were, but he instantly recognized the compounded smell of after-shave, cheap perfume, halitosis, hair tonic, body odor and floor wax. The little trap door slid open and he could see the dim outline of a man's arm through the screen. The priest sighed, waited.

"Um . . . forgive me, Father, for I have sinned," Ted said. When the priest sighed again, he got a whiff of whisky. "I can't quite remember how to begin."

"It doesn't matter. God's forgiveness is—is that *you*, Ted?"

Panic shot through him. "Father Coughlin?"

"Yes, it's been quite a long time."

"I suppose it has."

"What brings you to confession, my son?"

My son, my ass! Not only did this priest know who Ted was and how much he was worth, but he had a direct pipeline to Ted's mother, a radio audience in the millions and a big mouth. "Well, Father," Ted said, "I came to confession tonight because I wanted to tell you personally to stick it up your ass."

Ted could hear the priest's gasp. As he yanked the curtain open and strode out of the church, Ted felt better than he'd felt in weeks.

$\mathcal{T}$he lights in Claire's apartment were on. Ted parked the Roadmaster behind her new Century and shut off the engine. Now what?

Of course he could divorce Milmary and take up with Claire, even marry her. But that would have unknowable consequences for his career, so that was out. Besides, he knew deep down that he wasn't ready to abandon Milmary, break up his family, give up his life by the lake. He could tell Claire it was over and find her a new job elsewhere in the company, just try to put the episode behind him. But Claire had a temper and a jealous streak, and there was no telling how she might react to that. Maybe it would be best to let her know, through a third party—maybe Harvey—that she was no longer needed at GM, just get rid of her altogether. It would take a little doing, but it had a certain appealing finality.

When her bathroom light went off, he made himself get out of the car and walk across the lawn. The frosted grass crunched under his feet. He climbed the stairs and stood outside her door, listening. He could hear a jazz record, a trumpeter. Probably Miles Davis. Ted Mackey, a man who prepared for everything —every meeting, every phone call, every speech, every chance encounter at the water cooler—had absolutely no idea what would happen next. He knocked.

"Who is it?"

"It's Ted. You decent?"

The door flew open and Claire hurled herself at him, almost knocking him down. She was wearing her floppy, cocoa-colored robe, and her hair was a mess. She looked like she'd been crying. "I've been needing to talk to someone so bad," she said, hugging him. She licked his ear. The door across the hall opened, and Ted turned. An old lady with blue hair and a skull face said "Ack!" and slammed her door.

Claire took him by the hand and led him straight to the bedroom. She sat on the edge of the bed and started undressing him.

"I thought you needed to talk." His cock was swelling.

"In a minute. I want you inside me. Did you bring any of your things?"

He took a condom from his wallet and ripped the foil open. She was on top of him instantly, pinning his shoulders to the mattress and bucking as though she wanted to drive him right through the bed, through the floor, out of her life. It seemed almost angry. After she came, she collapsed against him. He couldn't tell if she was sobbing or just breathing hard. She was still wearing her robe; he was still wearing his sportcoat, his white shirt, his black necktie knotted right up to his throat, even his socks and garters.

When she let go of him, he went to the bathroom and flushed the condom down the toilet. Now that, he told himself, was a bona fide quickie. His amusement vanished instantly, and he went back into the bedroom. She was lying on her back, wrapped in the lumpy robe, staring at the ceiling. He felt silly. He took off his sportcoat and slipped into his boxer shorts and sat on the edge of the bed. "So what was it you wanted to talk about?"

"I went to church tonight," she said softly. "To confession."

"Oh? I didn't know you were a churchgoer."

"That's just it! You don't know a thing about me. You don't know who I am, you don't know what I want, what I—"

"Now, Claire." He tried to sound soothing, but he was thinking he'd had this very conversation with his wife not long ago beside the pool at Oakland Hills.

"Don't 'Now, Claire' me!" She snapped upright. Her cheeks were flushed. "You come down here whenever you please. You bump off a piece of ass, then hurry home to your wife in the suburbs. Do you have any idea how that makes me feel? I feel like a piece of property. Or a toy."

"If I'm not mistaken," he said, standing up, "it was you who just bumped off a piece of ass." He put his pants on and slipped into his loafers and sat in the chair beside the bed. "I came here to talk."

"Well, well, well—miracles never cease. What was it you wanted to talk about—your breathless rise to the fourteenth floor?"

"No." He looked at his hands. "I came here to tell you about . . . Marilyn Monroe." Of course! Why hadn't he thought of this sooner?

"What?"

"Marilyn Monroe. And the Wildcat."

"What the hell are you talking about?"

"The Wildcat's in serious trouble, Claire, and I think my only hope of salvaging it is to sign Marilyn Monroe to do the ad campaign."

"So what?"

"So I might have to shift everyone off the project for a while. Since you're in charge of the design team, I wanted you to be the first to know. I'm going to New York soon to meet with Marilyn and her manager and try to sell them on the ad campaign. It's a longshot, but I'm afraid it's my only hope."

"That's what you came here to tell me?"

"Yes. I wanted—"

"Bullshit. You're sitting there saying one thing and I'm hearing something entirely different."

She really was tough. "Yes, well . . . I suppose . . ."

"Quit fucking around, Ted. Just spit it out."

His mouth felt dry. She was sitting on the edge of the bed now, glaring at him, and he didn't have it in him to look her in the eye. He studied his hands. "Claire, what I suppose I'm getting at is that we've got to stop seeing each other. People are talking. It's only a matter of time before word gets out, and that would be very, very bad for both of us."

She sprang off the bed and stood over him. "Word gets out! Not *that*! Not an image problem for the division manager!"

"Claire, you're getting hysterical. This is much more serious than that. This would be very bad for you, too. Believe me. Now please sit down. We need to discuss this calmly."

"We do not need to discuss this calmly. You'd fire me if you had any balls—*if*. Or you'd transfer me for some phony reason like this Marilyn Monroe shit, then just go on with your life like nothing ever happened. You think you're so big and powerful that nobody can—"

"Dammit, Claire, I have no intention of firing you. But like I was trying to explain, it might be necessary to reassign the whole Wildcat team. If you wanted to work in another division, I'm sure we could arrange something."

"Oh, I'm sure you could. You can arrange anything. That's the trouble with you—you think it's all a matter of *arranging* things. Well, I've got news for you. If you try anything, I'll tell this whole fucking city what a cheating, two-faced bastard you are. I'll tell Harvey. I'll tell your wife—"

"Don't you threaten me!" he roared, jumping to his feet. He towered over her.

"I'll threaten you if I damn well please!" she screamed up into his face. "I'll be damned if I'm going to get shuffled out of the way because some executive got tired of screwing me! Get the hell out of here! Get out! *Out!*"

"Now, Claire . . ." He started backing toward the door.

"Get *out*! I'll see you at work, you bastard! I can't wait!"

He got out just before she hurled something against the door. All the way home he kept hearing the sound of her screaming and sobbing, kept seeing the skull face of the old lady across the hall, who stuck her head out of her door and cackled as he hurried down the stairs. It had been bad, worse than bad; but by the time he got home all he felt was relief. It was over. Milmary had a drink waiting for him. She asked how his parents were, and only then did he remember he'd told her he was going to Royal Oak to visit them. He said they were fine. Then he went into the living room to watch the evening news with his wife while his sons played checkers by the fire.

Six

*H*ayes Tucker, Jr., learned The System at the family Buick dealership in Richmond, Virginia. Instead of using the usual battery of salesmen on Bob and Sally Brunswick, though, Hayes had decided to handle this one by himself. When Bill Voisin, sensing he was about to lose a commission, asked why, Hayes told him: "Because those skinflints *owe* me this one."

When Bob and Sally drove onto the lot in the red Skylark convertible Hayes had let them borrow, Tucker Buick was buzzing with potential buyers, thanks to a week-long blizzard of TV commercials that showed Hayes out on the lot in his guacamole sportcoat slapping the hoods of shiny new Buicks and saying, "I dare you to come on down this weekend—and this weekend only—and steal these babies from me!"

Hayes watched them pull up through his one-way mirror, and he was out on the lot before Bob and Sally were out of the car. Since their Plymouth was sitting behind the service department, its pistons frozen in place with fermented sugar, there was no need for The System's lead-off batter, the "appraiser," the guy who determined the value of the trade-in. He might or might not take the car for a test drive, he might or might not have the mechanics look it over; but whatever he did or didn't do, he was to make that car disappear. Park it across town. Throw the keys on the roof of the shop. Have someone take it on an overnight, out-of-town "test drive." But under no circumstances was he to give the potential buyer a means of escape.

Since the bag of sugar had already taken care of that, Hayes now became the "liner." All he had to do was write a sales order, no matter how preposterous, and get Bob Brunswick's signature on the dotted line. Hayes ushered Bob and Sally into his office and had his secretary bring coffee. He'd already pulled the curtains over the one-way mirror. He chatted for a while about the dozen bass he pulled out of the bay yesterday, then got Bob talking about his sons' Little League team. When things were warmed up to his satisfaction, Hayes said, "Now look. We need to get you kids into a nice, roomy family car." He watched them shift in their chairs. "I've got an order form right here. Let's just talk about what you need. With those three kids, I know you're going to want a four-door. . . ."

Fifteen minutes later, a beaming Hayes Tucker, Jr., emerged from his office with Bob Brunswick's signature on an order form for a fully loaded seashell-pink-and-midnight-black 1954 Buick Century four-door. The penciled-in price was $1,500—more than $1,000 below the suggested retail price. Hayes would soon take care of that.

He led the Brunswicks into an office with a gold plate on the door that said ASSISTANT SALES MANAGER. This was the "closing office," and it had dozens of framed diplomas and certificates on the walls and a Friden calculator, known as "the Okie Charmer," on the desk. The office also was bugged. All salesmen used this office, and when they came in here they became the "turnover man," responsible for somehow busting the customer off the ludicrous deal the "liner" had written. Handsome commissions awaited those who succeeded.

As Bob and Sally sank into the sofa, Hayes licked his lips. He relished these rare opportunities to handle a sale all by himself. He went to work with the Okie Charmer. "Okay, let's see now . . ." The calculator chattered and chirped and spat out a piece of paper. Bob and Sally, thoroughly etherized, held hands and stared at the growing strip of paper. "Your thousand-dollar discount, that gives us a nice base price of fourteen

ninety-five. . . . Dynaflow transmission . . . runs you . . . two-
fifteen. . . . Tint on the windows . . . two-tone paint job . . .
hell, I'll throw in the paint job for free. . . ."

Bob squeezed Sally's hand; Sally squeezed back.

"V-8 with the four-barrel carburetor . . . hmmmm . . . okay,
okay, not bad at all. . . . Dual exhaust . . . Looks like we're
going to be able to get you kids into that beaut for under twenty-
six hundred!"

"But I thought—didn't—?" Bob sputtered.

Hayes slapped his forehead. "What's the matter with me? We
haven't even talked about the trade-in on your Plymouth! You
sit tight and talk it over and I'm going to run down the hall and
see what my trade-in manager says. I'll be back in a jiff."

But Hayes went straight back to his own office and turned on
the speaker. Sally was saying, ". . . had no idea all those things
cost extra."

"It's still a pretty good deal, honey."

"Yeah, but we need two cars. If we pay twenty-six hundred
for a new car, we won't be able to afford to get the Plymouth
fixed."

So that was it. Hayes picked up the phone and dialed his
service manager. "Hey, Jimmy, don't we have another old Plymouth out back, about the same model as that mustard-colored
'42 with the froze-up engine?"

"Lemme think. . . . Yeah, we got a black '41."

"The motor any good?"

"Motor's fine. Guy traded it in cause he blew the fuck out of
the rear end."

"Will it fit in the '42?"

"Oh, sure. They didn't hardly change nothing from year to
year during the war."

Hayes hung up and sprinted back to the closing office. Normally this was the time for the "stick man," the finance expert,
who had to figure out a way to raise the money for car payments

even if it meant using as collateral every stick of furniture the family owned. But Hayes knew that with Bob's electrician's salary plus overtime at Grumman, a $2,600 Buick Century was already affordable. Now he was going to make it irresistible.

He burst into the closing office. "Great news, kids! I just talked to my parts manager. He's already ordered the parts to rebuild your Plymouth's engine from the ground up. And you know what I'm going to do?"

They both leaned forward, as if pulled by a string.

"As a welcome-to-the-neighborhood present, I'm going to re-build that engine for free. You won't get anything in trade, but hey, you'll be a two-car family, and you're still getting a steal on a new Buick. Whaddaya say?"

Bob looked at Sally, the quizzical look of a man who knows better than to take so big a plunge alone. Hayes held his breath. Sally had the blank, compliant look of a wife who was willing to leave this one up to the man of the house. That look, Hayes knew from long experience, was money in the bank.

"Well," Bob said, rising from the sofa to shake Hayes's out-stretched hand, "I guess we got us a deal."

Seven

No one in Bill's Grille, not even Rudy, wanted to hear about Guatemala. But Pete Hoover wanted to talk about it, so he ordered a fresh Gibson and made his way through the cig-arette and cigar fog to the pay phone.

Morey Caan was frantically digging in his dresser for clean BVDs when the phone rang. "Hello?" He kept digging.

"Morey, ole pal, Pete Hoover here. Pull up a chair. Got a little story for ya."

"Pete, I'm due at the airport in fifteen minutes."

"Fuck the airport and listen up. First thing they had me do was visit all these fat-assed colonels and butter 'em up with some cash and tell 'em what a Commie prick Jacobo Arbenz was. Then they sent me across the border. So there I am in Honduras, right, with a bunch of Howard Hunt's flunkies, and my Spanish's so fuckin' good they put me in front of a microphone at this ratty-assed little radio station and next thing you know I'm broadcasting into Guatemala about all these major battles along the border. A regular Edward R. Fucking Murrow, if I do say so myself."

Morey found the clean BVDs. "Pete, I've really got to run."

"I'm almost through. So we walk back into Guatemala and wait for the gover'ment to fall on its ass. It was twice as boring as Iran. Just when we're all 'bout half asleep, in come a coupla Somoza's P-51s from Nicaragua for a raid on Guatemala City. I heard the planes were flown by CIA boys, but I'm still checkin' that out. Anyhow, Arbenz craps his pants and hits the road and the military takes over."

"And United Fruit gets its land back."

"Natch."

"And Ike wins another one."

"Right. Some story, eh?"

"It sure as hell is. Listen, Pete, I've got to get to the airport. But as soon as I get back we'll sit down and talk."

"Where you off to in such a hurry?"

"Detroit."

"What the fuck for?"

"I'm writing an article about a Buick."

"A *Buick*? Here I am calling you with the scoop of the year—"

"Pete, listen to me—"

"No, you listen to me. Fuck you. Fuck the CIA. Fuck Ike. You go ahead and write about your car and I'll write the Guatemala story myself. I already got enough material for a book. And when I get through writing it, Walter Carruthers is gonna sit down and tell me how Ike starved a million Germans to death back in '45. Have fun in Detroit. Adi-fuckin'-os, amigo." He slammed the receiver down and stormed back to his bar stool. Rudy had a fresh Gibson waiting for him.

"Did I hear you say you was writing a book, Pete?"

"Yeah, maybe you did." Pete downed the Gibson and had to hold on to the bar to keep from keeling over.

"Man, oh man," Rudy said, gazing at the gray afternoon drizzle, clucking his tongue, "the stories I hear in this place—*I* could write a book. Christ, could I write a book!"

"You're a fuckin' moron," Pete told him. "You couldn't write a postcard." He popped the onion in his mouth, then threw the empty glass against the wall on his way out.

*T*he thing Luther Fuller liked best about his job was giving tours of the assembly line. He loved to watch people's eyes widen, the way they flinched at the clanging of metal on metal, at the spark showers, at the sight of the men welding and hammering and riveting and cursing the cars together. There was always a little terror in those faces.

Luther also loved to sit around over beers after work and tell the younger workers how different things had been in the twenties and thirties, before the union. Even more than his brief glory days as a boxer, the Flint sitdown was the shining moment in Luther Fuller's life; it was when he became a man. He was working the second shift in the Buick foundry, which was where Negroes worked in those days because it was the closest thing to hell a car plant had to offer; and on Christmas Eve the men, frustrated by low wages and arbitrary dismissals and brutal working conditions, decided the time had come to shut down the line. It took about five minutes. They just pulled the switches and told the women in Cut-and-Sew to go home, then told the foremen to go to hell.

While GM and the union negotiated, the men inside the plant let their whiskers grow and got ready for trouble. When police and sheriff's deputies stormed the plant with tear gas, the strikers counterattacked with swinging wrenches and a barrage of nuts and bolts. During the pitched battle, Luther caught a Flint cop square in the middle of the forehead with a sockful of ball bearings. The cop went down and stayed down; and in that instant Luther Fuller became a man because he had finally found something he was willing to kill for, and that meant he had also found something he was willing to die for.

After forty-four days the strike was settled. GM reluctantly recognized the UAW-CIO, and the men marched out of the plant sporting beards, waving makeshift flags and singing. Luther had worn a beard ever since. He watched, with huge satisfaction, as the example he'd helped set in Flint swept across Detroit. Aluminum workers, iron workers, druggists, grocery clerks, shoemakers, cigar rollers, even Ford workers—they all sat down.

But nowadays few of the guys on the line wanted to hear about the bad old days. They took the union for granted. All the progress of the past twenty years—the improvements in working conditions and pay and job security, Luther's promotion to foreman, the opportunity for his son to work with his head instead of his hands—it was all necessary and good, but it saddened Luther that the line had been robbed of its fire, had been turned into just another job. Even the union, which had been a religion in the thirties, had become just another big, powerful, impersonal bureaucracy. Luther didn't even know the president of his own local anymore. Maybe it all had to happen that way, he told himself. Maybe that's always what happens when the powerless become suddenly powerful.

So when Ted Mackey's PR man called to say he was on his way out with a writer and photographer to follow number five hundred thousand down the line, Luther lit up. Once again he would get to see some terror on the faces of total strangers.

$\mathcal{T}$he real horror of the assembly line, Morey Caan decided, was not the obvious stuff—the roar, the rats, the icy drafts, the sparks, the barking foremen. As he walked along the line and watched the amazingly swift transformation of a bunch of stray metal into a chassis, then a chassis with an engine and a transmission and a drive train and a rear axle, then springs and seats and carpets and pink-and-black sheet metal and doors, windshields and chrome trim, tires and bumpers and hubcaps —it occurred to Morey that the true horror of the place was the monotony.

He studied the workers. He'd never seen such weariness. They all moved like demoralized robots. . . . *Zoop!* . . . a coil spring was popped into place. It wasn't that these men had to move all that fast or that the work was so physically demanding. But they were always in motion—*Bap!* . . . *Bap!* . . . *Bap!*—a piece of chrome trim went on, and they kept repeating the motions dozens, hundreds, thousands of times, because they all understood that the bright jelly-bean bodies kept coming through the ceiling from the paint room and landing on the finish line and moving toward them steadily, constantly, relentlessly, no end in sight. That was it: monotony magnified by relentless pressure. No wonder these men worshipped the lunch pail and the shift-change whistle; no wonder this was such a hard-drinking town.

Morey and Will Lomax and Spencer Wingo, a fat freelance photographer from New York who wore a red kerchief around his neck, followed Luther Fuller the entire length of the line. Dressed in blue overalls and a yellow hard hat, Luther shouted at them over the din, explaining the stages of the assembly process. Morey was too busy studying the workers to take many notes. The only thing he wrote down was: "Smells like burnt metal, sounds like a hurricane."

It took exactly forty-six minutes to make Bob and Sally Brunswick's Buick Century. Once it was washed and inspected, a man in white overalls and white gloves hopped in and drove it out into the cold yellow sunshine. He parked it on the lot with thousands of other new Buicks, then hopped out and sprinted back into the plant. A new car emerged every fifteen seconds.

Morey had to admire this historic, dripping chunk of steel and chrome and rubber and vinyl and glass. It was painted just like the Buick he drove to Memphis last summer: boiled shrimp and anthracite. It was the final product of monotony operating under relentless pressure, something terrible yet undeniably beautiful, a horrible miracle. With the plant there in the background, all pitted brick and barbed wire and chugging smokestacks, the springy new gumball cars made quite a picture. Spencer Wingo got down on one knee and snapped away.

"Now what happens?" Morey asked Luther.

"Well, now we ship it. Normally that'd be simple, we'd just wait for a truck to pull up and away she'd go. But today we got a small problem."

"What kind of a problem?" Will said.

"Too many cars, not enough trucks. Today we don't got *no* trucks."

"No trucks?" Will said. "That's news to me."

"Well, it's been going on three months now, at least twice a week," Luther said, scratching his beard. "Ain't exactly what I call news."

Morey loved this. The huge Negro foreman, who looked like he could pick up one of these Buicks by the front bumper, was getting his digs in on the bluesuit from corporate headquarters. Welcome to the Motor City, Morey thought, not so much a city as a two-fisted state of mind.

"So how do you plan to ship it?" Will said.

"We been hiring drivers. Anybody with a license who ain't drunk. Then we"—he looked at Morey—"maybe you better not put this in your article, but then we disconnect the odometer, the driver drives it to the dealership, they reconnect everything, wash it up, and it's delivered."

"Do you have a driver for this car yet?"

"Got a roomful right over there."

"Hold on a second, Luther." Will steered Morey over to where the pink-and-black Buick was dripping in the sunshine. "Wipe that shitty grin off your face."

"Come on, Will, you gotta admit this is rich."

"This is not rich. This is my worst nightmare."

"Will, we had a deal, remember? Complete access to the car from the sketch pad to the buyer's driveway, right?"

"Yeah."

"And you gotta admit that this is as much a part of the story as the wraparound windshield." Morey was thinking of the night he'd sat in the Oak Room at the Plaza Hotel eavesdropping on the argumentative Buick dealers. Hadn't they griped that Detroit was making too many cars and accused one another of boot-legging cars to meet quotas? Now Morey was seeing the car glut firsthand, was seeing GM disconnect odometers, hire drivers off the street, do whatever was necessary to get rid of the cars that kept popping off the line every fifteen seconds. He had a hunch this was just the beginning, and there was no way anyone, not even his best friend, could stop him from telling this story. "What's the matter, Will?"

"Aw, shit. So you caught me with my pants down around my ankles. It's my own fucking fault."

"What do you mean?"

"Think about it. I cooked up this campaign. I got you and *Life* interested. And now I've let you in on a whole world of shit—some of which is news even to me."

"So what?"

"So what? I'll tell you so what. They don't like surprises at GM. As a matter of fact they detest surprises. And if I know you, they're in for the worst kind of surprise—thanks to me."

"Will, we had a deal."

"Yeah, we had a deal. We *have* a deal. It's just that . . ." He looked off at the smokestacks, at the cloudless blue sky. "It's almost funny in a way. You know how much I used to hate guys like Lyndon Johnson and Joe McCarthy when I lived in Washington and how easy it was for me to learn to hate guys like Charlie Wilson and Ted Mackey when I moved here. Remember Engine Charlie's confirmation hearing last year?"

"Sure. I thought you were the one who kept forgetting."

"Those fucking guys—their whole lives are about power, how to get it, how to use it, how to keep it. They don't object to the money that tends to come with it—who would?—but what really matters is power. And you know something else?"

"What."

"The more power you get, the more you want. And it never fails to fuck you up. Never. You're looking at Exhibit A."

"So why's that almost funny?"

"Because—I get hold of a thimble of the stuff and I get so drunk I promptly shoot myself in the foot. That, my friend, is funny."

"So that means you'll go through with the trip—driver and all?"

"Yeah, sure." Will was smiling now, and he threw an arm around Morey's shoulder. "What do you say we go meet the lucky guy who gets to drive me right out of a job?"

Eight

*7*wo days later, Buick set an all-time sales record, and everyone who had anything to do with the design of the 1954 line was invited to a party at Ted Mackey's house. Every last one of them—except Norm Slenski, of course—showed up.

Claire Hathaway, Amos Fuller and Rory Gallagher were out on the glassed-in porch, inhaling cocktails. They'd started out discussing the decision to shelve the Wildcat, but that was too depressing, so now they were listening to Amos talk about the record company his boyhood hero Berry Gordy was trying to get off the ground.

"He needs people like us," Amos said, "people to design record covers, posters, stage sets, even costumes for the acts. Think how hip it would be!"

"Um . . . Amos," Rory said, "I hate to rain on your parade, but we design cars for a living."

"You mean we *used* to," Amos said.

"He's got a point," Claire said. "They've got me working on a gearshift lever for the '57 Roadmaster."

"And I'm doing instrument dials," Rory said.

"And I been hiding out in the men's room," Amos said. They all laughed and drank. Then they drank some more.

Suddenly Harvey Pearl, who hadn't been seen at the Tech Center in weeks, popped onto the porch, carrying a fresh drink. He was wearing an emerald-green suit. "Well," he said, pulling up a chair, "looks like everyone found the bar without too much trouble." They nodded. "I guess you're all down in the dumps because of the Wildcat." They nodded again. "Now listen to me. You can't let something like this get you down. It's the nature of the business. The Wildcat's not dead yet, but if it does get killed I'll see to it that each of you gets involved in something exciting. In fact, I'm already working on it."

Suddenly Claire stood up, excused herself and hurried down the hall toward the foyer. Just as she reached the bathroom door she heard Ted's wife call out behind her, "Harvey, there you are! Come here, darling, I've got something to tell you."

Claire stepped into the bathroom and left the light off and the door ajar. She heard Milmary's high heels clacking toward her on the marble floor of the foyer. The clacking stopped just a few feet from the bathroom door. Claire held her breath.

"Harvey," Milmary said, "where on earth have you been hiding?"

"Oh, just down at the house mostly."

"How's Taka?"

Claire fought off a wave of nausea and steadied herself against the wall.

"She's fine. Her bandages come off tomorrow."

"I've got some wonderful news." Her tone of voice made Claire lean closer to the door. She heard Milmary whisper, "I'm pregnant!"

"That's . . . that's wonderful, dear. Congratulations! But I thought you'd decided two was enough."

"I changed my mind. Can you keep a little secret?"

"Of course."

"Ted doesn't even know yet. You know how it happened?"

"Yes, my dear. I may be a bachelor, but I know all about the birds and the bees."

"No, silly. I used a hat pin."

"A hat pin?"

"I used it to poke holes in Ted's condoms—right through the foil. He had no idea."

"Why would you do a sneaky thing like that?"

"Because I made up my mind I wanted a baby and I knew Ted would try to talk me out of it."

"What's he going to say?"

"What *can* he say? I'm not going to tell him about the hat pin, of course. He'll have to be delighted. He won't have any choice. We *are* Catholics, you know."

Their footsteps receded down the marble tiles, then melted into the buzz in the living room. Claire heard Ted's booming laugh. She locked the door and turned on the light and in one smooth motion leaned over the black marble sink and vomited three times.

*T*aka Matsuda couldn't wait any longer to learn if she was destined to spend the rest of her life in purgatory. When Harvey stumbled in from the Mackeys' party, she took him by the hand. "Don't take off your coat," she said. "Come."

The night was cold and windy. The trees had been stripped of their last leaves, and the moon was almost full. She led the way down the path, still holding Harvey's hand. She unlocked the door to the bomb shelter with her key, stepped inside and turned on the gas lamp. It hissed and cast a harsh white light. Harvey noticed a new painting, a watercolor of Mirror Lake seen through the doorway of the bomb shelter: a cube of the dangerous outside world viewed from the last refuge. The leaves across the lake were a vivid red.

"Are you ready?" she said.

He nodded. Suddenly he was glad he'd let Milmary talk him into having one for the road. Taka took a step back. In the light her forehead looked yellow, like a bruise. She stared at Harvey's eyes as she slowly unwrapped the bandages from the lower half of her face. As soon as she finished, she shut off the lamp. "There is no hope," she sobbed. "I can see it in your eyes."

He hugged her there in the darkened bomb shelter and kissed the top of her head. "There's always hope," he said. "Always. I've already talked to the doctors in New York. They'll see us as soon as you like."

He held her until she stopped sobbing. Then he took her by the hand and, after locking the bomb shelter, led her up the moonlit path to the house. That night, for the first time, they slept in the same bed and woke up at dawn, bathed in sunshine, in each other's arms.

Nine

*W*hen she got the result of the pregnancy test, Claire bought a fifth of the most expensive scotch she could find and spent two days in bed drinking it. She left the color TV on with the sound off. When the scotch was gone, she turned the TV off and telephoned the man who had initiated her into the adult world. He would be able to tell her what to do about her first real crisis.

"Hello?" Professor Nabokov sounded groggy.

"Volodya, it's Claire calling from Detroit. Did I wake you?"

"Goodness no! What a delicious coincidence. Not fifteen minutes ago I finally laid Lo to rest."

"You finished the book! Congratulations!" When he didn't respond, she said, "What's the matter? Aren't you happy with the way it turned out?"

"Oh, I'm quite delighted. But I can't imagine that my beloved nymphet has a snowball's chance of seeing the light of day in America."

"Laid to rest," "a snowball's chance"—he really was a piece of work. "Volodya, I'm calling because I'm in trouble."

Without hesitating he said, "Do you know who the father is?"

Somehow she wasn't surprised. "It's my boss. He's married and has two kids. He doesn't even know yet." She started crying. "Volodya, I'm so scared. . . ."

"Well—please don't cry—unless they've come up with something new while I wasn't paying attention, it seems to me you've three options. You could marry the man; you could have the baby and raise it yourself; or you could call a boyhood friend of mine who had the good sense to flee Mother Russia and is now practicing medicine in New York. His sub-specialty is cleaning up messes such as this."

"I can't marry him."

"And why not?"

"He'd never break up his family . . . he's got to protect his career. Besides, he's an asshole."

"An excellent reason for rejecting a potential partner in Holy Matrimony. Could you go home to Iowa, have the baby there, raise it in the heartland?"

She'd already imagined walking up onto her mother's broad front porch and hearing those four killing words: "I told you so." "No, I couldn't go back home. Besides, I want to keep working—I don't want to give that bastard the satisfaction of getting rid of me."

"Well, then, I suggest you give my friend a call. He had quite a loyal following in Russia. I haven't decided if that's because Russians are less careful, more accident prone or less squeamish than Americans. Perhaps all three. At any rate, he has an excellent reputation."

He made it all seem so simple and sensible and inevitable. She called the number immediately and made an appointment to see Dr. Alexander Vasilevsky the following Tuesday in his office on Park Avenue.

Ten

*I*t had been bad enough for Will Lomax when Luther Fuller stood beside the Buick of the Year and announced that anyone with a driver's license who wasn't drunk would be hired to drive the car to Levittown, New York. It had been worse when Morey insisted on going through with the trip and his magazine article. And now this duo.

Neal Cassady, the driver, looked like an escapee from a psycho ward. At the very least he had a hot appendix. The whites of his eyes were yellow and his face was shiny with sweat and he held the steering wheel with the index finger of his left hand, which sported a filthy bandage on the thumb, and he talked nonstop from Flint all the way to Toledo: "Now gentlemen the loss of speedometer and odometer must be taken for exactly what it is namely something of utterly zero consequence because Jackoleo here and I *know time* as no one else knows time and in addition to being able to gauge the exact r.p.m.'s of this fine two-hundred-horse engine with four-barrel carburetion and Dynaflow transmission and thus our precise speed simply by the sound and the vibration coming through my right foot I am also able with the help of mileage signs posted by the Highway Department along this fine stretch of divided four-lane asphalt to calculate our speed in relation to time and vice-versa which is to say we've covered seventy-three point five miles which means further that at this precise instant the time is 11:43 a.m. Eastern Standard Time—"

"Close," Morey said from the back seat. "It's 11:45."

"Ahem, yass, well, praps I failed to account for that detour just before we crossed the Ohio state line at which the crew was laying down precisely three and one-half inches of hot blacktop over old pavements by way of preparing for winter with its inevitable frost heaves and busted shocks and other dilapidations of the physical plant. . . ."

Jack Kerouac, the quiet, dark-haired guy in the front passenger seat, had switched on a tape recorder and didn't even try to get a word in. He'd been sipping a jug of Tokay wine ever since they left Flint. Even Morey, one of the most relentless interviewers Will had ever known, failed to pry much out of him. Jack did say he wanted to get back to his mother's apartment in Queens to finish his novel, his chronicle of these ricocheting trips back and forth across the continent with Neal. He said he wanted to sleep between clean sheets. Will almost added that a bath might not be a bad idea. When Morey asked how he felt, Jack craned his neck and breathed Tokay into the back seat. "I'll tell you how I feel. I feel like a traveling salesman, a sad hipster Willy Loman, beans in my bag, nobody buying. I need a rest." Then he resumed his study of the scenery and Neal went on talking. An hour later he was still talking, and Jack said over his shoulder, "You fellas want some tea?"

"No thanks," Morey said.

"I could use a cup of coffee," Will said. "Maybe stretch my legs."

"No, I mean *tea*." Jack held up a fat cigarette with twisted tips. "Mexican. Guaranteed to make a Buddhist out of you."

Will felt like a spectator at his own funeral. Somehow this joyride wasn't happening, he kept telling himself. But there he sat in the back seat of the PR coup of the year, listening to a maniac with a busted thumb foam at the mouth while a magazine writer scribbled in a notebook and a brooding stranger slugged cheap wine and tape-recorded the moment for posterity. Wrong movie, Will kept telling himself. But the Buick just kept whistling merrily toward New York, its speedometer and odometer frozen on zero. What the hell, Will thought, a little Mexican Buddhism couldn't possibly make matters any worse. He took the lit cigarette from Jack and inhaled until it hurt. Then he handed it to Morey and sat back and began to enjoy the ride.

*T*hough he wouldn't have admitted it to anyone, least of all to himself, Ted Mackey was a desperate man when he arrived at La Guardia Airport. If he could just revive the Wildcat project, he would regain the momentum he'd been losing steadily for months, like a battery draining of juice. And if he could regain his momentum, all of his problems—the design leaks, Plymouth's recent sales surge, the rumblings that he wasn't in control of the ship—would be forgotten.

After checking into his suite at the Plaza, Ted headed straight for Broadway. He wanted to catch Marilyn Monroe on location, before DiMaggio had a chance to get in the way. Ted had learned from Marilyn's manager that she was playing a seductive television model in *The Seven Year Itch*, and he'd read in a recent Hedda Hopper column that DiMaggio, good Sicilian that he was, nearly blacked out with jealousy whenever his wife played such a role. He'd stopped visiting sets and locations where she was working because he couldn't stand to see her, half-dressed and purring, in another man's arms.

Since Ted tended to believe what he read in the tabloids, he was surprised to see DiMaggio on the edge of the mob that had gathered on Broadway. Ted was transfixed by DiMaggio. The Yankee Clipper was taller than Ted had imagined, bulkier through the upper body. He was wearing an expensive camel-hair coat over his dark blue suit, and his silvering hair was perfectly watered and combed. He was beyond glossy, Ted thought. He was radiant. He would have had no trouble fitting in on the fourteenth floor at General Motors headquarters. A dapper little man with a pen and a notebook was standing next to him. DiMaggio was staring straight ahead. Ted noticed his eyes never blinked, and he was constantly clenching and un-clenching his jaw.

Then Ted saw why. There Marilyn Monroe was, a pure plat-inum bombshell, standing over a subway grate on this chilly evening wearing nothing but a white dress and white shoes and a dazzling smile. Her nipples were hard. Every time a train rumbled beneath the grate, her skirt floated up around her waist and she smiled and flashbulbs popped and the crowd roared. She was wearing white panties. She had this crowd on a string, and she loved it. Such power was almost obscene, Ted thought; yet he, like everyone else, was frozen with fascination, physically unable to turn away.

When the bright white lights were shut off and Marilyn stepped off the subway grate, Ted turned toward DiMaggio. He was still staring straight ahead, still working his jaw. Ted moved toward him, but just as he was about to introduce himself he heard DiMaggio mutter to the dapper little man with the note-book, "I've had it, Walter. Let's get the fuck outta here."

Ted watched the two men hurry down Broadway toward Times Square and, no doubt, Toots Shor's. He was delighted to be rid of the jealous husband, but by the time he fought his way through the crowd he was horrified to see Marilyn slipping into a white limousine. He called out to her, but his voice was lost in the roar as the door closed. The driver honked the horn, the crowd slowly parted and the limousine raced into the night.

Ted was furious. He stormed to Toots Shor's and sat alone at the giant circular bar and inhaled two martinis. The only celebrity in the place was Frank Sinatra, who was sitting with his entourage and the proprietor at table 1. Toots kept calling him "Sinat" in a loud, braying voice. Ted left before Toots had a chance to slap him on the back and call him "Theodore."

From a pay phone at Columbus Circle he called the St. Regis. But the operator told him she was under instructions to hold all of the DiMaggios' calls. On his way to the hotel, Ted stopped twice more for martinis. The gin helped burn away his rage but did little to bolster his confidence. What had started out as a simple, clear-cut mission had suddenly become a minefield. When he finally made it into the lobby, he realized he was weaving. He squinted under the bright lights. The receptionist gave him a frosty look.

"Could you ring the DiMaggios for me, please?" he said. "Suite seven-eighteen."

"I'm sorry, sir, they've asked me to hold all calls. Would you like to leave a message?"

"No. I need to speak with them right now. Tell them Ted Mackey—M-a-c-k-e-y—is here from General Motors. They're expecting me."

"Sir, I'm sorry. Those were strict orders from Mr. DiMaggio."

"'S'okay. I'll wait."

He sat on one of the sofas by the fireplace. A fire was burning heartily, and it cheered him, chased the chill from his bones. But after an hour of pretending to read a magazine he began to feel foolish, like some groveling fan hoping for a glimpse of his idol. He realized there were half a dozen other people in the lobby pretending to read magazines, including the dapper little man who'd been with DiMaggio on Broadway.

How, Ted asked himself, had the general manager of the Buick Division been reduced to lurking in a hotel lobby hoping desperately for a word with a movie actress? As he stood up to leave, he noticed the elevator attendant and a bellhop looking at him, whispering to one another. Spinning through the revolving door, he thought he heard them laughing.

*A*s the pink-and-black Buick shot across the George Washington Bridge, a disc jockey bellowed from the dashboard: "Now here's a young man from Memphis who can flat light it up! You'll be hearing plenty from him, believe-a you me. The name's Elvis Presley, and the song's already number eleven on the charts, 'Good Rockin' Tonight.' "

"Elvis Presley!" Morey shouted. "Turn it up! I sat in on this guy's first radio interview in Memphis this summer! I can't believe it! Turn it up!"

"*Well, I heard the news, there's a-good a-rockin to-night . . .*"

"Oh yes oh yes oh yes!" Neal moaned, turning up the radio's golf-ball volume knob and smacking the black dashboard in rhythm with the slapping of the bass. "Morey knows time!"

They were all sweating, and even Will had stopped worrying. Why fight it? Of course he'd been helped to this point by Neal's hypnotic monologue and Morey's laughter and the sweet wine and Jack's bag of Mexican Buddhism.

"*. . . I'm gonna hold my baby as tight as I can. / Tonight she'll know I'm a mighty mighty man . . .*"

Either Will was primed by road fatigue or this was some brain-crippling marijuana, because the music roaring out of the dashboard was more electric and alive than any music he'd ever heard—including Ornette Coleman and Sonny Rollins that night in Hollywood—and the lights of Manhattan down below the bridge looked like a bed of coals and walking across them barefoot seemed like the perfect thing to do.

> *. . . I say meet in a hurry behind the barn,*
> *Doncha be afraid I'll do ya no harm*
> *I want you to bring along my rockin' shoes*
> *Cuz tonight I'm gonna rock away all my blues . . .*

Will looked down at his own shoes: black shiny standard-issue wingtips. He'd taken his jacket off in New Jersey, and now he loosened his necktie, unbuttoned his shirt, rolled up his shirt-sleeves. Something told him that he wouldn't be needing his

corporate uniform tonight. It was then, as Neal guided the Buick
down off the bridge and into the Manhattan night, that the title
for his book came to Will, bright and clear and true. *Of Mice
and PR Men* would tell all—the life and hard times of David
Dunbar Buick, the story of the postwar car boom, the birth of
this PR campaign, the sleazy things from bootlegging to over-
production that Morey would soon dig up for his magazine
article. Will's book would be a portrait of an orgy gone completely haywire. Of course it would cost him his job, but he
didn't care. What mattered now was his book and, even more,
the realization that he'd caught himself in time and now he knew
what he must do to make himself free.

*I*t was dark when Claire left Dr. Alexander Vasilevsky's office. As she walked south on Park Avenue toward Grand
Central Station, her only point of reference in this part of town,
a question occurred to her: do they perform these operations at
night to keep from getting arrested, or to protect your secret
when you leave the office?

The air tasted sharp and surprisingly clean. She gulped it and
said out loud, "How do you feel, Claire Hathaway?"

Not guilty. Not ashamed. But light. And empty, physically
empty. Humbled, purified, free. So many words came to her.
Alone but not at all lonely. Adrift but not lost. Grown up, brave,
wide awake, airy, hungry. Yes, she was very hungry. And she
was still in control of her life.

She wanted to be around people so she walked west toward
Times Square. It would be bright and crowded there, the sidewalks full of hustlers and theater-goers and tourists and whores,
the whole human gallery, people like herself, the confused, the
hungry, the alone, the adrift, the purified, the free. The very
people her mother had warned her to avoid. She quickened her
pace.

*7*he first stop of the night was some sort of ritual for Neal and Jack: Birdland. They commandeered a corner table and ordered beers and were instantly consumed by the heat and pulse of the place, the band at full gallop, the trumpeter bathed in blue light and blowing so hard his eyes looked like they were about to pop out of his skull. The vein in his neck was a blue rope, Will thought, a blue rope full of the juice of life. When the trumpeter finished his solo, the place erupted with applause, whistles, shouts; a bottle exploded against the wall. The trumpeter just shuffled off the bandstand and sat on the first empty bar stool and stared into space.

"Isn't he *wild*?" Morey said.

"He sure as hell is," Will said. "Who is he?"

"Shit, man, that's Miles Davis."

When the band took a break, Neal sprang to his feet. "Arrgh. Fap. Gotta call Ed Hinkle this instant!" Though Neal had driven from Flint to New York without shutting off the engine or getting out of the car, he actually seemed to be gaining velocity.

While he went to the phone, Will fetched fresh beers. Using his General Motors expense account was the least he could do to grease this joyride. At the bar, Miles Davis was talking to a Negro woman with the pulpiest, glossiest, reddest lips Will had ever seen. Her hair was the color of brass. "It just sorta happened," Davis was saying. "I just finally made up my mind to get off dope."

"Why?" the woman said.

"'Cause I got fed up with it. You know, you can get fed up with most anything. I just laid down and stared at the wall for two weeks. It was like having the flu real bad, only worse. I sweated, I shivered, my nose ran, I threw everything up, my pores opened and I smelled like spoiled meat."

Will took the beers back to the table and told Jack and Morey what he'd just heard. Jack took a crumpled notebook out of his pocket and started writing. "Real bad case of flu, you say? Two weeks staring at the wall? Smelled like spoiled meat?"

Suddenly Neal was jumping up and down, clapping his hands. "Bottoms up, gentlemen, it is without question the only thing to do now that we have made telephonic contact with Ed Hinkle and are expected instantaneously downtown at his studio where a jam session of major proportions is in full swing including cute little New Jersey chicks with their very own bongos, yes!"

And so they went racing downtown in the Buick, past a crowd watching a crew film a movie on Broadway, through Times Square dazzle and theater traffic, Neal threading through cars and buses and pedestrians as though they didn't exist, slowing for nothing and nearly flattening a staggering wino, who shook his fist and yelled.

"Whooooo," Jack said. "Sacred ghost of Forty-second Street."

*A*t the corner of Forty-second and Broadway, Claire watched a four-door Century run a yellow light and almost hit a stumbling wino. He raised his fist and cursed the car. Attaboy, Claire thought, don't let the bastards push you around. The wino promptly fell on his face in the middle of Broadway. Claire and a man in a yellow velour jacket dragged him out of the street and propped him up on a bench.

"Next time, sweetheart," said the man in the yellow jacket, "look before crossing."

Claire leaned against the bench to catch her breath. The wino smelled like a sewer grate, and she was exhausted and dizzy from the exertion. The doctor had told her to get some rest, but she didn't want to go back to her hotel room, didn't want to be alone with her thoughts. She wanted to hear a familiar voice. She'd filled her purse with coins for just such an emergency, but as she considered who she might try to reach she was surprised by how limited her choices were. She could call her mother and pretend to be checking up on her, but that seemed like a bad idea. She could call Rory Gallagher or Norm Slenski or Emily Buhner, but she couldn't imagine what she would say to any of them. The sound of Professor Nabokov's voice would probably make her go to pieces. There was only one voice she wanted to hear right now. Though she would not divulge her secret or her sorrow even to him, she wanted to hear his voice, his laughter. She found a pay phone in a theater lobby and called Detroit.

*H*arvey Pearl arranged a private corner room for Taka Matsuda at Mount Sinai Hospital. She loved the view of Central Park across Fifth Avenue, the leafless trees, the people walking their dogs, the young lovers holding hands, the re- minders that life was going on, would always go on, regardless of what happened to her.

While Taka met with her doctors, Harvey wandered through the park. He sat by the ice rink watching the skaters and realized, with deep and quiet satisfaction, that cars no longer mattered to him; they were the concern of strangers he would never see again. Sitting there watching the skaters carve their counter- clockwise circles, he decided how he would finalize the break with his past and begin his new life.

He walked the East Side streets until he found a Japanese restaurant, where he ordered a feast, more food than five people could eat, as well as two bottles of sake. He even bought cups and plates and chopsticks and had the waiter pack it all in a box. On the way back to the hospital he stopped for a dozen yellow roses.

When he entered the room Taka was asleep, so he quietly laid out the food and flowers on the table by the window. A nurse had found some candles for him, and he was lighting them when he heard Taka's groggy voice: "Harvey, is that you?"

"Yes. Come and eat and tell me about the doctors."

She was thrilled by the feast, and as she ate, carefully inserting the food through the slit in her bandages, she told him that these doctors were much more reassuring, much more confident they could make a difference. They had already treated one of the Hiroshima Maidens and were encouraged by the results. They showed her pictures. They told Taka she would never be exactly as she had been, but she would be close.

After dinner she allowed Harvey to talk her into having a cup of sake even though it was against the doctors' orders. It warmed her insides. Harvey drank a second cup, then a third and a fourth. They didn't speak for a long time. They simply sat there looking out the window as darkness fell and the lights winked on in the fortresses across the park. Taka loved the light at this time of day, the sun gone but the sky still blue.

When it was dark, Harvey blew out the candles and led her to the bed, stretching out beside her and taking her hands in his. "Are you scared?" he said.

"No, I am beyond being scared. I am trying to prepare myself to accept whatever happens—and to be grateful for all you have done."

"Would you like to make me very happy?"

"Yes, of course, Harvey. How?"

"First you must promise you'll do it."

"What is it?"

"Not until you promise."

"But what if I cannot do it?"

"Oh, you can do it."

"You are sure?"

"Yes, I'm sure."

"Please tell me first!"

"Not until you promise."

"Okay, I promise."

"Marry me."

She gasped. "But Harvey! I—"

"We could move back to California if you like. Or Japan. Or stay in Detroit. Anything you want. We could even make babies."

"I am too old to make babies. Besides, there is the atomic disease. And what about your work?"

"It doesn't matter."

"What if the surgery fails?"

"None of it matters. The only thing I want to do is spend the rest of my life making you happy."

They lay there in each other's arms without speaking until the sky turned black. Never in his life had Harvey Pearl felt such peace.

When the nurse came in with Taka's medicine, she was startled to see, in the light from the hall, that a man was lying on the bed, fully clothed, resting his head on the bandaged woman's shoulder. They were both asleep. They didn't stir, and the nurse backed quietly out of the room.

*A*mos Fuller was knotting his best silk necktie when the telephone rang. "O-rooni!" he said, continuing to fuss with the knot.

"Is that any way to answer the phone, young man? This is Claire."

"Claire! Where were you today? You missed the big news."

"What big news?"

"Well, for starters you and me and Rory are working for Cadillac after the first of the year. Got to redesign the Eldorado from the street up."

"Cadillac?"

"Ain't lyin', girl. John Nickles said ain't nobody can put fins on a car like the three of us. Funny thing is, I almost turned him down. Berry Gordy just offered me a job as artistic director—

dig it—but he couldn't touch the bread Cadillac's offering, so I'm staying put. 'Sides, my daddy told me if I quit GM he'd personally tear my head off."

Claire was speechless.

"Come on over. Rory's already on his way. We're going to the Paradise Club to hear Ornette Coleman, gonest sax man since Bird. I'm buyin' the drinks."

"I can't, Amos. I'm in New York. There was a little personal business I had to take care of."

"New York? Well, watch out for Mackey and the Pearl."

"What are they doing here?"

"Damn if I know, but some wild-assed rumors are flying. Harvey's lookin' for a new job, or he and Mackey's fixin' to jump to Ford together—maybe they're both about to get fired."

"Amos, I'm not believing any of this."

"Well, believe it, girl. Only thing you need to know is that you and me is over the top."

*N*eal squeezed the Buick into an impossibly tight parking spot on Perry Street and they all piled out. Will was out of breath halfway up the four flights of stairs. He was beginning to hallucinate.

Neal ripped the door open and plunged in first. The party was at a high roar, a crowd unlike anything Will had ever seen, everyone shouting and sweating and skidding around on the wet floor, dancing on chairs and tables. Someone was playing a saxophone in the kitchen, and people were banging spoons on bottles and pots and oatmeal boxes, a sort of urban jungle rhythm section, as a girl with chopped blond bangs pounded bongos.

Will and Jack retreated to the shadows in the main room, a high-ceilinged studio with nothing but a few mattresses and empty wine bottles on the floor and dozens of abstract spatter paintings on the walls. The air was thick with sweet smoke and sweat.

"I don't know about you, Jack," Will said, "but I could sure use some sleep."

"Do you know anything about Buddhism?"

"Beg your pardon?"

"Buddhism. Do you know anything about it?"

"Only the Mexican variety. Pretty potent stuff."

"Like I was just reading in the *Tao Te Ching*—'The further one goes, the less one knows.' "

"The *Tao Te Ching*, eh?"

"Neal needs to read that. Do you think much about power, Will?"

"All the time. I'm writing a book about it."

"You probably don't even know what power is."

"What is it, Jack?"

"Power is standing on a street corner waiting for no one."

"I see."

"Power is sitting at the Automat watching the old ladies eat beans." A pair of bongo drums on the floor caught his eye. "Do you know anything about tightening bongo skins?"

"Can't say as I do, Jack."

"Watch this." Jack picked up the bongos and held them over a candle. His eyes were red-rimmed and wild, his black hair scrambled all over his head, matted with sweat. "See, if you warm the skin it gets tighter. Makes a better sound. Like raindrops on a tin roof, a true tattoo."

"I see." Will was beginning to think he wasn't the only one who needed some sleep.

"Oh, shit!" Jack cried. A small, black-fringed hole bloomed in one of the skins. "I've ruined them!" He put the drums on the floor, covered them with old magazines and looked around to make sure no one had noticed. "Please," he whispered, "don't tell anybody." He looked like he was going to cry.

"Sure thing, Jack."

"No, I mean it! Promise me you won't tell!"

"Okay, Jack, I promise. Cross my heart."

He seemed relieved. "You know something, Will? For a PR guy you're all right."

And you, Will thought, have the social grace of an anteater. You drink like a fish, chain-smoke reefer, burn bongo drums, get paranoid, lurk in the shadows at parties and dream of sleeping between clean sheets in your mother's apartment. I hope, for your sake, you can write. "Thanks, Jack. You're not too bad yourself—for a writer. So where are you guys headed next?"

"I think Neal's leaving for Mexico City in the morning. Or maybe just Denver."

"Aren't you going along?"

"Hell no. I'm going to sit down and spit it all out."

"Spit what out?"

"This." He waved at the mob, the writhing, raucous mob in their toreador pants and chinos and berets, their beards and their chopped blond bangs, what Will had already come to think of as the uniform of nonconformity. Suddenly he felt silly, older than he'd ever felt, way out of step. He belonged at this party about as much as he belonged at General Motors. Rather than depressing him, this realization made him feel strong and calm. For once in his life he knew exactly what came next.

He went looking for Morey. He found him in a jammed bedroom taking slugs from a jug of wine and listening to a bearded guy with thick glasses and a radish nose shouting a poem from memory.

Will passed another bedroom where several people were wrestling on a mattress on the floor, giggling hysterically. The odd thing was that everyone was fully clothed. Will crossed the main room, gaining momentum. He had a life to rearrange, a book to write. At the door he passed Jack, who was rocking back and forth, staring at a candle, long gone. Will walked out the door, down the four flights of stairs. A cool breeze rustled the last leaves in the sycamore trees along Perry Street. He crawled onto the Buick's big back seat and fell into a black and dreamless sleep.

Eleven

*O*n the flight back to Detroit the next morning, Ted Mackey read Louella Parsons's account of the "sparks" that had flown on the movie set between Marilyn Monroe and Joe DiMaggio. "The combat continued in their suite at the St. Regis," Parsons wrote, "but the hotel staff refused to give a damage estimate. Perhaps the best way to tally the damage is simply to report that DiMaggio left late last night for California, and it's no longer a secret that America's favorite fairy-tale marriage is on the rocks."

Ted spent the rest of the flight drinking scotch and getting used to the fact that the Wildcat was a goner. A brutal closing sales push was now his top priority. He would start phoning every zone sales rep in the country as soon as he got back to the office. He managed a smile when he thought of how good it would feel to hold a gun to those bastards' heads one last time.

*D*ing! Ding! Ding! Wake up, old man! We have arrived!"

Will Lomax opened his eyes, and sunshine stabbed his brain.

He covered his face with his arm. "Where are we?" All he knew for sure was that he was stretched out on the back seat of the Buick.

"Rise and shine!" It was Morey. He was jumping around outside the car and shouting. "We're at Tucker Buick! Spencer Wingo just drove up to photograph the big moment! Hit the deck, Will!"

When he opened the door, an empty Tokay bottle fell out of the back seat. Mercifully, it didn't shatter on the pavement. Will climbed out, stretched, yawned, squinted at the sky, patted his hair. He was in the middle of an acre of shiny new Buicks. Hayes Tucker, Jr., was trotting toward him, wearing an electric-blue suit and a worried expression.

"Will! Glad you fellas made it!" Hayes shook Will's hand, glanced at the empty wine bottle, then at the car. "You're twelve hours late. Everything okay?"

Will could see gulls swirling in the cobalt sky beyond the roof of the dealership. The air was surprisingly warm for December, and it smelled of salt water. "Everything's fine, Hayes," Will said, freeing his hand. "We had to drive nonstop from Detroit."

"You *drove* it here?" Hayes scrambled into the driver's seat to check the odometer. He looked relieved to see all those zeros. "Boy, nonstop from Detroit. No wonder you fellas look so bushed. You wanna freshen up inside?"

Judging by Neal and Morey's hot-pink eyeballs, grizzly whiskers and crumpled clothing, Will supposed sprucing up wasn't a bad idea. But it occurred to him that their advanced state of disarray was the perfect way to illustrate what happens to the best-laid plans of mice and PR men.

"Freshening up," Neal said, "is a conceptual goof noodle that would scramble our collective brain pans into—"

"Where's Jack?" Will snapped. He couldn't stand to hear another word out of Neal. His T-shirt was gray, and the bandage on his thumb had completely unraveled.

"We dropped him off at his mother's apartment in Queens," Morey said.

"Don't be fooled by hipster externals," Neal said. "Jackoleo's actually quite a mama's boy in his—"

"Where's Spencer?" Will snapped.

"At your service."

Beaming, rotund Spencer Wingo was standing there in the sunshine munching on a bagel with three cameras dangling from his neck. He was still wearing the red kerchief. "Guess you boys had a pretty rough trip?"

"Rough," Neal said, "does not begin to describe the—"

"Neal, shut the fuck up," Will said. "Spencer, before we take the car over to the Brunswicks', I'd like you to get some color and black-and-white shots of us right here with the car."

"Your wish is my command."

"How soon can you get prints to me at the Plaza?"

"Couple hours."

"Great. Neal, Morey, Hayes—come on."

And so the beatnik, the journalist, the car dealer and the PR man lined up beside the greatest brainstorm of Will's career, its odometer frozen on zero, its front bumper and panorama windshield spattered with bugs, its floorboards littered with gum wrappers and empty bottles and reefer butts. They all shouted "Cheese!" and "Fuck you!" again and again as Spencer Wingo snapped away.

When the photo session was over, Hayes ordered a mechanic to take the Buick into the shop and clean it up for delivery. "And don't forget the odometer," he said. Then he went into his office to call Bob and Sally Brunswick and tell them to get ready for the biggest thrill of their lives.

*M*orey Caan stood alone at the Metropole bar drinking coffee and watching dusk descend on the great human scrum

of Times Square. He could have slept forever in that big, soft
bed at the Plaza, but Will had called an hour ago and ordered
him to be here at five o'clock sharp.

So there he stood, the dutiful friend, groggily drinking coffee
and listening to the Salvation Army bell ringer and hoping Will
would fail to show. Morey dreaded this farewell. What if Will
got down on his knees and begged Morey not to go through
with the article? All Morey wanted to do was catch the six
o'clock train to Washington, sleep in his own bed, then wake
up early and get to work on the article that was sure to ruin the
career of his best friend. Since the coffee wasn't doing any good,
Morey ordered a bourbon on the rocks and decided to wait until
five-thirty.

As soon as he finished his drink, paid the bartender and
stooped to pick up his suitcase, he heard Will's voice. "Going
somewhere?"

"Penn Station. There's a train at six."

"There's one at seven, too. Stick around. I'm buying."

Morey dropped his suitcase. Will had shaved, combed his hair,
gotten a shoeshine. In his dark suit and tie and overcoat, he was
the Will of old, Mr. Control. He was carrying a manila envelope.
He ordered two double bourbons, their traditional farewell
drink, a newspaperman's drink. "Guess where I've been?"

"Out having a nice quiet lunch with your buddy Neal?"

Will laughed, a single quick bark. "He really was a blowtorch,
wasn't he? Actually, I just paid a visit to Todd Loomis. Remember him?"

"Sure. He was the book editor when we were at the *Post*."

"Now he's an editor at Viking. I just pitched my book idea
to him."

"And?"

"Look at these first." Will opened the envelope and took out
a stack of photographs: color pictures of Bob and Sally Brunswick and their three towheaded children and their yappy terrier

standing out on their Levittown driveway beside their new pink-and-black Buick Century. Spencer Wingo had climbed up on a step ladder to get the shots, and the Brunswicks looked like they were facing a firing squad instead of a camera. Visible in the background were six more Centurys, one in each driveway on that side of Lindbergh Street. The lawns were all brown, but the cars were a riot of color: pink, aqua, canary yellow, sea-foam green, blood red, silver, peach.

"It's a pity *Life* doesn't run color," Morey said.

"That was my first thought, too." Will reached into the envelope for the pictures Wingo had taken at the Tucker Buick lot. When Morey saw the first one, he started howling. If it weren't for crew-cut, buck-toothed, blue-suited Hayes Tucker, Jr., the picture could've passed for a portrait of a ring of Benzedrine-gobbling car thieves. There was even a green wine bottle in the bottom right corner of the picture.

When Morey stopped laughing, Will said, "Believe it or not, this picture clinched it."

"Clinched what?"

"Todd liked the idea for the book well enough, but he was lukewarm about the title."

"You've already got the title?"

"Yeah, I'm calling it *Of Mice and PR Men.*"

Morey howled again. "Oh, that's fucking rich!"

"When I showed Todd the picture of us at the Tucker Buick lot, it all came together for him. Suddenly he loved the title."

Morey dried his eyes with his necktie. "Will, there's something I've got to tell you. Remember that salesman I was talking to while they were cleaning up the car at the dealership?"

"The guy who looks like a blackjack dealer?"

"Yeah, his name's Bill Voisin. Seems he got screwed out of some commissions and he's a little upset with Hayes. Anyway, he said disconnecting odometers is child's play compared to some of the shit that's been going on."

"Such as?"

"He told me GM's so determined for Chevy to beat Ford and for Buick to beat Plymouth that they've been making more cars than their dealers can possibly sell. So the dealers have been buying them from the factory, then dumping them on used-car dealers for a small profit. The factory looks the other way. Everybody wins. He also told me about ways the factory's been jimmying sales figures—registering cars in two and three different states, some wild stuff."

"So what are you waiting for?"

"You mean you aren't—you *knew* about this shit?"

"Some of it, sure. Bootlegging's an old trick."

"Then why didn't you tell me?"

Will looked out the window. Snowflakes had begun to fall, perfectly vertical, lovely and slow. "You know, boy, for such a smart little fucker, you sure can be thick sometimes. If I'd told you about it, I would've gotten shit-canned and you would've gotten shut off from the story—and we both walk away with nothing to show for our trouble. Now that it's all over, though, we're back on the same side of the street."

"So you're going to quit your job?"

"After your piece comes out I doubt I'll have much choice."

"And you're not going to try to talk me out of writing it?"

"Look, you used me and now I'm going to use you. I need your magazine article for my book—the messier, the merrier. And Loomis said that if your article's half as juicy as I promised, he'll offer me a contract the day it comes out. Now that you've talked to Bill Voisin, I feel sure Todd won't be disappointed."

"So I guess I better get my ass home and get to work."

"That would be nice." He clinked Morey's glass with his. "Here's to our writing projects."

"To our writing projects."

Then they drank in silence, listening to the bell ringer and admiring the soft and lovely snow.

Twelve

*O*n the day after Christmas, Milmary Mackey decided she couldn't hold out much longer. Walking down to pick up the mail, with snow flurries fluttering down on her, she considered how she'd broken the news about her first two pregnancies, always choosing a special moment—New Year's Day for Tommy, Ted's birthday for John. Yes, she would announce this one on New Year's Day, their twelfth anniversary. After Betsy finished cleaning up from the party, Milmary would get Ted alone by the crackling fire, fill two glasses with champagne, and say, "Darling, I have some wonderful news. . . ."

When she reached the mailbox, she noticed a moving van in Harvey's driveway. Men were carrying boxes from the house to the van.

She opened the mailbox. The envelope from the *Atlantic Monthly* was mixed innocently with the routine bills and tardy Christmas cards. It was too small to contain her manuscript. She tore it open and read out loud, into the falling snow:

Dear Milmary Mackey,
  We are delighted to be able to accept your short story, "The Enola Gay," for publication in our May 1955 issue. Please accept our standard fee and our sincerest thanks.

                                            Yours,
                                            The Editors

There was a check for five hundred dollars.

She whooped so loudly she startled herself, and the whoop came booming back across the frozen lake half a dozen diminishing times. Then she started running down the hill. She wanted Harvey and Taka to be the first to know. She felt like a little girl, like this was the very first snowstorm of her life, and she opened her mouth as she ran and let the snowflakes burn her tongue.

But when she knocked on Harvey's front door, one of the movers answered. "I'm sorry, ma'am," he told her, "but the Pearls left this morning for California."

Thirteen

When Morey Caan got back to Washington, the first thing he did was go looking for Pete Hoover. After a week of fruitless searching he finally found him in the most obvious place of all—in front of a half-finished Gibson at Bill's Grille.

"Where the hell you been hiding?" Morey said.

Pete jumped. He was so busy studying the onion in his glass he hadn't seen Morey coming. His eyes were glassy, and he needed a shave. "Been right here holding down the fort."

"So how's your Guatemala book coming?"

Pete coughed into his fist and lit a cigarette. "I learned one damn thing. I may be a hell of a spook, but I'm no writer."

"What happened?"

"Nothing happened. I got all my notes and tapes out, bought a big stack of typing paper, made a pot of coffee. Then I made another pot. And another pot. I didn't have a fucking clue where to begin."

"You still want to talk about it?"

Pete shrugged. "Might as well. Beats hanging around this dump. Let me buy you a drink first."

Rudy was behind the bar, still wearing that burgundy vest.

Morey ordered a bourbon on the rocks. In the mirror he could see the perpetual poker game at the back of the room; a retired Navy guy with muddy blue tattoos on his arms was dealing the cards, flicking them onto the green felt table.

"So," Pete said, "I guess you heard about Walter Carruthers."

"No. I've been out of town, remember?"

"That's right. Well, he quit State last week. Told me Roy Cohn has a four-inch file on that socialist group at Columbia. Cohn told him he was going to cut his balls off."

"So he quit?"

"Figured that was the only way Cohn would call off the dogs."

"Where's Walter now?"

"Sitting at home looking for a job. He told me he's dying to tell somebody about those German POWs. Naturally I mentioned your name."

"But why does he want to talk now? It's been almost ten years."

"It's funny, but Walter's more pissed off at Eisenhower than he is at McCarthy and Cohn put together. He thinks Ike could've squashed them a long time ago, and now he blames him for allowing this witch-hunt bullshit to get so far out of hand."

"He's got a point."

"Yeah, and he's got a hell of a story, too. He lives right down by the river. We can stop there on the way to my place, if you want."

"Let's go."

*W*ill Lomax had just dialed the city desk at the *Washington Post*. As the phone rang, he watched the blizzard and wondered if he was over-reacting. Once the familiar rhythms of his Detroit life had reasserted themselves, the whole New York trip began to seem like a long-ago dream. Maybe if he sat tight and saw what Morey came up with, the whole thing would blow over.

But no, after yesterday there was no turning back. When he heard that Norm Slenski was in the hospital, he went to visit him. He walked into the room and was shocked to see Norm's legs swaddled in plaster, from the thighs right down to the toes, and suspended from pulleys. His left eye was a slit in a lump of purple flesh. His lips were cracked and swollen.

"Will!" Norm said. The greeting was meant to be hearty, but it was barely a croak.

Will pulled a chair close to the bed. "What the hell happened, Norm?"

"Fell off the roof." He tried to laugh but winced in pain. "I keep forgetting about these broken ribs."

"So what really happened?"

"Coupla guys jumped me in the parking lot behind the Kosciuszko Club. Mean fuckers, too. Said they were friends of Jimmy Kowalski and Shep, two guys I owe a lot of gambling money to."

"What'd they look like?"

"Hard to say. It was dark. They both had hats on—gray hats, dark overcoats. They had baseball bats, too, and while they worked me over they kept saying they were Ty Cobb and Hank Greenberg. They laughed the whole fuckin' time."

Will didn't know what to say. Surely these were Ted Mackey's boyhood buddies. He waited until he saw tears trickling down Norm's cheeks; then he patted his hand and wished him luck and hurried away.

No, there was no turning back now. Will wanted to have nothing more to do with these people.

When the newsroom receptionist answered, Will asked for Phineas Spalding. After a few more minutes of watching the snow, he heard the familiar voice: "City desk. Spalding."

334 / MOTOR CITY

Will could almost see him—red galluses straining against the beer-keg stomach, wet yellow hair combed straight back, cigarette held between stubby orange fingers. He had about half a truckload of gravel in his voice. This man would never make it at General Motors, God bless him.

"Phineas, it's Will Lomax calling from Detroit. Merry Christmas and all that shit."

"Lord ha' mercy. What's new in Siberia?"

"The usual. It's snowing its ass off. Hasn't stopped in three days."

"So when are you going to come back to the civilized world and make an honest living?"

"Funny you should ask. How does next month sound?"

"Not bad. Next week sounds even better."

Will had to hand it to Phineas; he took everything in stride. "You aren't bullshittin' me, are you, William?"

"I'm afraid not."

"What happened? I thought you were their fair-haired boy?"

"It's a long story. The short of it is that I made my own noose, strung myself up—then kicked the horse for good measure."

"Aw, what the hell. I said all along you weren't cut out for that PR shit. You want the Senate beat back?"

"Actually, I was thinking of a desk job. Editing, maybe rewrite."

"A desk job? You're a writer, boy."

"Thanks, Phineas, but no more chasing senators all over town to cocktail parties. I'm tired of coming home so late I feel like I don't even know my own wife and kids."

"You mind giving me some clue what this is all about?"

"Look at the January twenty-sixth issue of *Life* magazine. Your old prize pupil, Morey Caan, is writing the cover story. That'll explain it. There is one more thing, though. I'm writing a book."

"You too? I swear to Christ everybody in this town's writing a fucking book. I even hear Mamie's writing one." There was a burst of gravelly laughter. "So what's yours about?"

"The best-laid plans of mice and PR men."

"Well, come on back home and get to work on it. I should be able to shake a little extra money out of these tight-asses and find you something on the desk with regular hours. Let me know when you're ready."

"Thanks, Phineas."

"Always a pleasure," he said, mimicking ads for his beverage of choice, I. W. Harper bourbon whisky.

Will hung up the phone and saw that the snow was coming down harder. For the first time since he followed that Buick down the Flint assembly line, he felt he was in control of his life. Phineas had made it seem so natural, so right. No, Will thought, I wasn't cut out for that PR shit. He turned off the light and went downstairs to give Margaret the news she'd been wanting to hear for the past four years.

Fourteen

*A*t ten o'clock in the morning on the last day of 1954, the General Motors board of directors met to clear up some routine year-end business. The atmosphere in the oak-paneled boardroom on the fourteenth floor was upbeat, almost jovial. After a week of relentless storms, the skies had cleared overnight, and now buttery shafts of sunlight poured through the windows. Even the chairman of the board, seventy-nine-year-old Alfred Sloan, Jr., usually so sour and humorless, looked tanned and spry. He'd just returned from two weeks in Palm Beach, Florida, where he passed his days reading stock quotations and weather reports in northern newspapers, then gazing with satisfaction at the warm green sea. One day, after seeing a dozen dolphins pass by, he even went for a swim.

There were other reasons for the high spirits in the boardroom that morning. Preliminary figures indicated that Chevrolet had outsold Ford to remain the most popular car in America, and Buick had edged Plymouth to finish number three. Nineteen fifty-four would surely be the most profitable year in the history of the corporation, with fat bonuses for executives and handsome dividends for stockholders. Despite the early hour, several members of the board lit cigars.

The first order of business was to name a new vice-president for styling. The board accepted the surprise resignation of Harvey Pearl without a murmur of debate because these men understood that while Harvey had created the Styling Section and had run it for more than a quarter of a century, he had also tutored a whole flock of worthy successors; filling his position was a simple matter of choosing the best one. When President Harlowe Kurtz submitted the name of Buick styling chief John Nickles, the board quietly and unanimously approved.

The board also gave its undivided blessing to Kurtz's realignment of several top management positions. Ted Mackey, who had guided Buick to its best year ever, was being put in charge of the new Market Research Division. Though this was a lateral move at best, Mackey would receive a 10 percent salary increase. Walter Chrisman, Oldsmobile's general manager, would take over at Buick and be succeeded at Olds by his top lieutenant, Hugh Marple. Again, there was no debate. The board members had already been briefed individually by Kurtz, and they understood that the decision to go with such a young, aggressive division manager at Buick had been a mixed success. He had outsold Plymouth, but he had also spent a lot of time and money trying to plug design leaks, had been forced to shelve a promising new car, and now rumors were swirling that one of his PR stunts was about to backfire and produce a damaging magazine article.

Clearly, the division needed a steadying influence at the helm, and plodding, predictable Walter Chrisman was the perfect man for the job.

Ted Mackey was not yet aware of any of this. He had no inkling that his career had suddenly stalled, or that tomorrow his wife would announce that she was pregnant with their third child, or that she had sold her short story and had begun writing a novel. As the board of directors meeting droned on into the afternoon, Ted was at home giving orders to the caterers who were getting the big white house ready for his annual New Year's Eve bash. The guest list was longer and more prestigious than ever this year. Harvey Pearl wouldn't be bringing Claire Hathaway, of course, but the party had already been written up on the society page of the *Detroit Free Press*.

Beyond that, all Ted Mackey knew for sure, all that really mattered, was that Buick had outsold Plymouth in 1954 and he had the warmest feeling in the world, the feeling that after all the years of struggle and striving he had, at long last, arrived.

A NOTE ON THE TYPE

The text of this book was set in Sabon, a typeface designed by Jan
Tschichold (1902–1974), the well-
known German typographer. Because
it was designed in Frankfurt, Sabon
was named for the famous Frankfurt
type founder Jacques Sabon, who died
in 1580 while manager of the Egenolff
foundry.

Based loosely on the original designs of Claude Garamond (c. 1480–
1561), Sabon is unique in that it was
explicitly designed for hot-metal composition on both the Monotype and
Linotype machines as well as for film
composition.

Composed by PennSet, Inc.,
Bloomsburg, Pennsylvania

Printed and bound by The Haddon
Craftsmen, Scranton, Pennsylvania

Designed by Mia Vander Els